NO KITTEN AROUND

A Magical Romantic Comedy (with a body count)

RJ BLAIN

No Kitten Around
A Magical Romantic Comedy (with a body count)
RJ Blain

Warning: This novel contains excessive humor, action, excitement, adventure, magic, romance, and bodies. Proceed with caution.

The last thing Reed Matthews needs in his life is a kitten, but when an orphaned tabby suckers him into becoming her caretaker, he's in for the ride of his life. Add in an angel determined to meddle in his affairs, a devil with an agenda, and a bucketful of bad omens, and he'll count himself fortunate if he survives the clash between heaven, hell, and his ex.

In this anything goes romp, there's no kitten around: if Reed wants to survive and regain control of his life, his only hope lies in the hands of an elf and his ex, a woman he's sworn to never see again.

ONE

Had I been a wiser man, I would've
just gone home.

HAD I BEEN A WISER MAN, I would've just gone home after work instead of greeting the weekend in a bar. Had I been a better man, I wouldn't have played the game, looking women in the eyes until I found one shallower than the average mud puddle. Had I been someone worth taking home, I wouldn't have introduced myself to the blonde, a woman who'd never be pretty in the conventional sense. I had what she wanted, however. Her heart desired pleasure without permanency.

That I could do.

A twenty bought us drinks and her an opportunity to take me home with her. A few hours in her bed offered me what most couldn't, a chance to look another person in the eyes without their heart's deepest desire coming between us. Her contentment made it worth my while—almost.

I didn't know the woman's name, nor did I care to learn it. In the light of a false dawn, as soon as I was certain she slept, I crept out of her bed. As I always did when I stole away like a thief in the night, albeit an invited one, I tucked her in, kissed her cheek, and hoped she'd one day find something to give her heart more life, more spark, and the happiness she'd never find flitting from man to man because she feared the pain of failed commitment.

That, too, I had glimpsed when I'd first looked into her eyes. It rarely came across so clear; desires showed through the strongest for me. Locked deep in her heart, hidden behind a shield of pleasure, her fears festered. I wondered if she'd find someone who could heal that wound.

I wasn't that someone. I had too many wounds of my own eating away at me from the inside and always would.

It took me almost an hour to walk back to the bar where I'd left my car, my hands shoved in my pockets, the image of a businessman who'd escaped the hardships of an office job like so many others. I'd left my hair disheveled on purpose to feed the impression I'd spent all my time drinking rather than pretending I enjoyed my night with a woman I could never love.

Everything went right to plan, up until I reached my car to discover a tiny tabby kitten had taken up residence on the hood. I supposed it had jumped from the low wall onto my vehicle, an old family car I'd bought from a destitute single mother because her heart had desired some way to provide for the children who'd never know their father.

I had paid twice as much as I should have for the piece of shit because she needed the money, spent a small fortune repairing it, giving it a paint job, and pretending I liked the damned thing.

The kitten stared me in the eyes and challenged me with a pleading meow.

Crossing my fingers, I took a defensive stance against the evils such a thing would bring into my life. I could barely take care of myself, the emotional equivalent of a train wreck.

A kitten was out of the question.

The kitten hadn't gotten the memo I wasn't interested in or prepared to take it home with me. It mewed at me again, its cry more insistent. I didn't need my sight, cursed magic that it was, to tell me what the little beast wanted. It wanted milk.

Then it wanted to destroy the world, for

that was what cats did when they weren't sleeping. They plotted to take over the world before they destroyed it, crushing it in their little paws.

My cursed eyes didn't tell me that was the kitten's heart's desire; animals didn't trigger my magic, for which I was grateful. Making assumptions about the tiny animal's intentions put me firmly in the 'monster' category, but I didn't care. Something that small and fluffy had to be the purest of evils, plotting the demise of anyone who crossed its path.

It'd probably settle for enslaving me and forcing me to do its bidding if I gave it even half a chance.

The kitten rolled onto its back and stretched out its paws, its little eyes wide open, staring at me, imploring me, ignoring my ward, and mewling all the while. The evil little shit saw my weakness and latched on, securing its victory with its pleading cries. I scooped it up, and it barely fit in my hand, which proved the fatal blow.

I couldn't just leave the damned thing to starve.

Cursing myself, I unlocked my car and slid behind the wheel, wondering what *I* would do with a kitten. As though sensing it had subdued me and made me its bitch, it quieted, further entrenching itself by nuzzling my hand, mouthing at me in search of the milk I couldn't give it—not yet, at least.

Where the hell was I going to find milk suitable for a kitten? Setting the hell spawn on the passenger seat, I dug my phone out of my jacket and searched for a local vet. I found the number of an emergency clinic, sighing before giving them a call.

"ACC, Felicia speaking. How may I help you?"

"I found a young kitten. Any chance I can bring it in for an exam? It was alone."

"The mother is probably nearby," Felicia replied. "Have you checked for her or any other kittens?"

I took a long, careful look around. The bar skirted an industrial zone, and given an hour, the street would become a death trap for the tiny animal. "I found it in the parking lot near a bunch of warehouses and factories near a busy street. Haven't seen any sign of a mother cat. It's crying and seems hungry."

"Any parks?"

"Only the concrete variety," I muttered. "Can I bring it in or not?"

"It's a hundred and fifty dollars for the vet to see the animal."

Great. Not only was my newfound kitten out to destroy the world, it was out to murder my wallet, too. I could afford a hundred and fifty for the exam, but I wouldn't like paying for a kitten I didn't want to keep in the first place. "All right. That's not a problem."

The woman gave me directions to the clinic, which would add an extra thirty minutes to my drive home. I glared at the animal. Once certain I'd disconnected the call, I waggled my finger at the feline. "You are an asshole."

The kitten slept, everything right in its furry little world.

I WAS the only person in the emergency vet clinic, a mercy all things considered. Felicia proved to be the receptionist, and she regarded the kitten cradled in the crook of my arm with an arched brow while I was careful to avoid meeting her gaze. The little shit had started trying to eat my suit the instant I'd picked it up. It had ignored my efforts to convince it suckling on my jacket would do it no good.

"That is a rather young kitten," the woman conceded, reaching over to a stack of papers to grab a few sheets. "I will need to make a file for you, sir. What is the kitten's name?"

All naming it would do was make it harder to let the damned thing go, and judging from the woman's smirk, she knew it. Maybe if I gave it an awful name, it'd rethink its decision to force me into adopting it until I could find a better home for it. "Kitten, Destroyer of Worlds." There. No one could be mistaken about what I thought about felines and their innate desire to rule—or wreck—the world. "Give it the last name of Overlord, if this is that sort of place. I'm pretty sure it's going to stage a takeover very soon."

She snorted her laughter. "You're not a cat person, are you, sir?"

"It had somehow gotten onto the hood of my car." I set the kitten on the desk. "I couldn't just leave it there."

The kitten tried to suckle from one of my knuckles. I upgraded its lethality rating to a prime evil, possibly on par with the devil himself. Kitten, Destroyer of Worlds had sharp, pointy teeth, and I smiled so I wouldn't grimace.

"Your name, sir?"

"Reed Matthews."

"Address?"

I gave her the PO Box I used in lieu of my residence, since no one believed I lived in an abandoned town an hour outside of civilization. The rare times someone insisted on me giving them the address to an actual building, I directed them to a mobile home I'd picked up a lot like my car, although I didn't live in it.

A formerly homeless couple did.

I paid for what they couldn't afford. They pretended I lived with them.

It worked well for all three of us.

I didn't miss the five hundred a month it cost me to pay the property taxes, their utilities, and the little things they couldn't afford even if they wanted to. In exchange, I maintained the privacy I craved, hiding where no one could find me, not without a lot of work. They had a place to stay, since neither ever managed to make more than minimum wage. Instead of rent, they paid for school.

They couldn't do both.

Damn it, I truly was a sucker. I really needed to stop looking people in the eyes. It was always the ones who wanted something so simple and sincere that got to me. The heart didn't lie. I'd learned that bitter lesson long ago.

The Olivers wanted to make a life for themselves, to be independent, and break out of the vicious cycle of poverty that haunted them. They tried so hard and got nowhere fast, and that sort of strain left marks on their hearts, marks I could see and feel whenever I made the mistake of meeting their gaze.

Week by week, they healed as they got closer to their hearts' desire.

It took Felicity ten minutes to open the file while Kitten, Destroyer of Worlds played on her desk, hunting a pen cap on wobbly paws.

"Dr. Elmond will be with you soon, sir. Please take a seat."

The kitten took advantage of the fifteen minute wait to play with my fingers and hook her claws deeper into my soul. What was I supposed to do with a kitten? I was mulling over that all-important question when the vet showed up. The older man offered a smile in greeting, his hands tucked into the pockets of his doctor's coat. "Good morning, Mr. Matthews. If you'd please come with me, I'll give your kitten a checkup and examination. I've been told you found it abandoned in the industrial quarter?"

For a city of less than fifty thousand people, Greenwood, Indiana did have a thriving industrial market, part of what made it the ideal place for me to spend my weekends. "Yes. I think it fell from one of the half walls onto my car. I found it on the hood."

Taking the kitten from me, Dr. Elmond held it up, making thoughtful noises in his throat while the animal cried its complaints for the world to hear. "All right. Come with me, please."

The examination took about thirty minutes, during which I learned I had a six to eight week old kitten weighing in at a big bad two pounds. Despite having named Kitten, Destroyer of Worlds an overlord, I had an overlady, and she was not happy with Dr. Elmond for inflicting several needles on her. She *really* did not like when he shoved a thermometer up her ass, either, not that I blamed her.

The vet thought her green eyes were odd, as at her age, they should have been blue, but when he claimed it wouldn't affect her health, I decided I didn't care as long as she could see and do whatever it was healthy kittens did.

With a declaration of good health in hand, I also inherited a bill for three hundred to go with my new kitten, a tiny harness with leash, a stick with feathers attached to a string, a case of wet food, several containers of milk, and a small bag of kibble. That the supplies doubled my bill didn't surprise me much. I was pretty sure the vet and his receptionist laughed at me the instant I hauled Kitten, Destroyer of Worlds and the foundations of her kingdom to my car.

To make matters worse, I needed to go to a pet store for even more things, including a proper cat carrier, a litter box, and all the other things a kitten needed to be happy and healthy. They'd given me a long list to point me in the right direction—towards bankruptcy.

In reality, I wouldn't really notice the lost money. Most of what I earned ended up stuffed in a savings account, and the rest went to my efforts to convince myself and society I wasn't nearly as awful of a person as I believed.

The weight of another man's death did things like that to a soul, and the two years I'd spent in solitary confinement as punishment hadn't done a whole lot to rid me of the guilt. If anything, being left alone in silence for so long only made it worse.

My sight couldn't hurt anyone, but I'd been treated just like a gorgon or some other monster capable of harming someone with their gaze. Had I been given another chance to redo my life, I would've never told anyone what I saw whenever I had the misfortune of looking someone in the eyes.

Still, my victim had deserved to die, although his death had been accidental enough. If he hadn't tried to rape a girl, I wouldn't have gotten involved, and if I hadn't gotten involved, I wouldn't have introduced his head to a brick wall getting him off of her. The blow had killed him. I'd meant to stun him long enough his victim could get away.

After, I couldn't bring myself to confess the full truth, so I'd lost two years of my life. It should have been five years, but someone had pulled some strings and forced an evaluation of my situation, declaring the punishment hadn't fit the crime. I'd never learned who. It hadn't mattered then, and I tried not to think too hard on it now.

I'd been too busy avoiding people, flinching from their touch, and otherwise doing my best to escape a different sort of prison—one of my own making. I'd lost another six to eight months in an odd sort of rehabilitation, the kind meant to give me a chance at having a life. The instant the judiciary system had let me go, I'd run halfway across the country, put on a suit, and dove headlong into the business world.

At least there, my cursed eyes were actually good for something. My sight came in handy when my job was to figure out what made people tick so my boss could get the upper hand in negotiations.

As always, despite my best efforts to turn my thoughts away, my memories fixated on the man I'd killed—and his victims. They had been burdened enough with his crimes and didn't need to be judged and socially crucified by a jury of their peers. I'd seen it too many times before. Man and woman alike brought the same tired, disgusting arguments to the table. The young women and girls had suffered enough.

When I'd looked him in the eyes, I'd seen the desire of his heart, and he loved it best when they screamed beneath him.

I rested my forehead against my steering wheel while Kitten, Destroyer of Worlds played with her leash, tugging at it in an attempt to free herself from her harness. Several deep breaths later, I forced my thoughts away from the past to my more immediate concerns.

For the first time in my life, I had a second mouth to feed, one entirely reliant on me, incapable of taking care of herself. That much Dr. Elmond had told me. She needed someone who'd feed her, give her a place to sleep, and take care of her, and while she'd probably be adopted fast enough, she'd spend at least a few days in a cage waiting for a home.

I'd lost the war at the word cage; I'd been in one for too long myself.

Kitten, Destroyer of Worlds would not sit in a cage and wait for a chance at a new life. Just like that, I ended up going home with an overlady who would inevitably rule over my life with an iron paw, for that was the nature of cats and the unfortunate men who served them.

TWO

My two pound kitten cost me almost
five hundred dollars.

BY THE TIME it was all said and done, my two
pound kitten cost me almost five hundred
dollars. I regretted bringing the fluffy,
purring little beast into my life about twenty
minutes after I brought her home and fed her
lunch. At the vet's recommendation, I'd first
fed her before starting the hour and a half
long drive home, and she'd done her business
outside while on her leash, while I had stood
safely upwind of her activities.

Had I known Kitten, Destroyer of Worlds
meant to bring ruin through biological warfare, I would have dumped her evil ass on the
wall and left without looking back. She used
her litter box willingly enough, but it didn't
spare me from the horrors she excreted. The
stench burned my eyes, peeled the paint off
the walls, and filled the air with fumes so

toxic I gagged—and fled to my bedroom on the far end of my small house.

It didn't help.

Breathing out of my mouth only made it worse. To escape, I ultimately cracked open the window, stuck my head outside, and questioned every decision I'd ever made in my life. When my stomach settled enough to face the horrors my kitten had wrought in her litter box, I'd discovered the second truth of cats.

Cats were assholes.

In her effort to erase the evidence of her misdeed, she had managed to fling litter everywhere, leaving a ditch in her box, as though she too had feared what she'd produced. Pinching my nose closed, I grabbed the little scoop I'd purchased with the box and did the work for her.

The mastermind behind the bio-terrorism attack waited by the bag of toys I'd purchased for her, standing on her hind paws and stretching in her desperation to reach the feathers dangling down. I retrieved the toy and shook it for her, somehow losing an entire hour to her and her wicked ways.

She picked my shoes as a place to nap, ignoring the fifty dollar bed I'd purchased for her. Taking advantage of the peace and quiet, I valiantly attempted to resume my routine, which involved a top to bottom cleaning of my five-room home, a cheap purchase I'd made when there'd been a few residents still left in Gypsum Creek, a played out mine that'd never produced much of anything.

I'd spent less than ten thousand dollars on the five acre property, which included a water mill, an abandoned barn, and the tiny farmhouse I'd restored enough to classify as habitable. If any of my co-workers discovered I'd become a carpenter, electrician, mason, and general handyman outside of office hours, I'd probably be laughed out of the building.

Contract negotiators were supposed to be above manual labor.

My first order of business was to check the water wheel, which generated the little electricity I used. Installing the solar panels on the mill's roof had been a last-ditch effort to fill up a lot of hours, although to keep from frying myself to a crisp, I'd gotten a real electrician to link it into the grid so the utility company had to pay me for supplying them with power.

Once satisfied everything was in working order, I went to work chopping wood. Without any neighbors to care if I pillaged their deadfall, I wasted time stashing logs in the decaying barn. Some I'd carve into misshapen blobs I'd pretend were supposed to look like something while the rest would heat my house in the winter months. At a rough estimate, I had enough wood to last me at least twenty years.

Night fell by the time I returned, my suit filthy and my feet sore from wandering around the woods without my shoes. One day, I'd get around to buying clothes meant for working outdoors. One day.

Kitten, Destroyer of Worlds howled at me the instant I opened the door, scampering across the floor to collide with my legs. She pawed at my pants and howled some more until I stooped and picked her up. In the time I'd been out, she'd left another present in her litter box, scattered more litter across my floor, and had somehow relocated one of my shoes halfway across the living room.

"You are an asshole," I informed her, carrying her to her dishes and doing my sacred duty as her slave to feed her and offer a bowl of milk for her enjoyment.

This time, I was prepared for her bio-terrorism attack, breathing through my sleeve while she finished her business. I made a show of burying it so she would hopefully learn. I doubted she would. I wouldn't put it past the two pound source of evil to know exactly what she did, doing it to spite me for some sin or another.

She probably blamed me for being stranded on my car's hood.

That night, instead of venturing out to some bar for a random hookup, I slept in my own bed and woke to a mouthful of kitten fur. Once again questioning my decision to welcome a murderous kitten into my home, I did the last thing a sane man would under the circumstances.

I texted my boss and asked if I could bring my rescue to work. If I had to suffer, so did my co-workers, and I suspected she was truly too cute to kill, which made her the ultimate vessel for some office revenge. When he replied with his approval, I smiled.

AS THOUGH SOMEHOW SENSING SHE was about to expand her kingdom, Kitten, Destroyer of Worlds cooperated with my efforts to get her and her things packed into my car for the Monday morning commute. I regretted the hour and a half long drive, a choice I'd inflicted on myself for the sake of privacy. When I told people I lived near Cataract, they thought I was crazy for living so far away from work.

It kept them from trying to get too close, since most people limited their adventures to a convenient twenty minutes.

Gypsum Creek *was* near Cataract, if one drove out to the middle of nowhere where a

pair of ruts as often as not served as roads.
With an official residency of one, two if I
counted my kitten, no one bothered with the
place. As far as ghost towns went, it wasn't
even an interesting one, as it lacked a single
rumor of ghosts to lure the curious.

It had rocks, but not the good ones collec-
tors favored.

Ten minutes ahead of schedule, I lugged
my kitten to the elevator along with her food,
milk, a fresh bag of litter, and a new litter box
tucked under one arm. I drew the attention of
everyone in the lobby, which I ignored as
always.

"Reed?" I recognized the voice of one of
my co-workers, a woman who wanted wealth
above all else in her life. Dani disliked me because I refused to show favoritism and cherry
pick the best of my new contracts for her, but
she couldn't get enough dirt on me to knock
me from my boss's good graces.

"Morning, Dani." I kept staring at the
closed elevator door, glancing every now and
then at the light marking its progress.

"Is that a cat?"

Did it make me evil if I contemplated
giving my kitten to Dani for the morning so
she might enjoy the tiny tabby at her worst?
Probably. I'd initially thought of my boss as
the best target, as he loved cats, but Dani
would do—her office was close enough to his.

"It is a cat of diminutive size, which I have been informed is traditionally called a kitten. This one is six to eight weeks old. I found her Saturday morning. Somehow, it seems I have ended up with this cat of diminutive size on a permanent basis."

"And why did you bring it to work?"

"Because Mr. Palandry said I could." If my boss's approval didn't pass muster with her, she could take it up with him.

"What's its name?"

"Her name is Kitten, Destroyer of Worlds —or that's what I told the vet, swearing I wouldn't be taking a kitten home with me. It seems I was wrong."

Laughter broke out around me, and I was grateful when the elevator doors swished open, allowing me to escape their mirth for a grand total of ten seconds until everyone joined me. I managed to stab the button for the sixteenth floor before I ended up shunted in the corner, my kitten's carrier resting between my feet.

"You don't seem like the kitten kind," Dani said, wiggling her way through the crowd to stand beside me. "Can I hold her?"

I chuckled. "I'll even let you take her back to your office if you keep her out of trouble and make sure she's fed."

If Dani wanted to play with the tiny tabby terror, she'd learn soon enough to fear the fluffy beast. Since Dani worked in an office with four other people as vindictive as her, I figured they could all suffer for a while.

"Really? Thanks, Reed. We'll take good care of her, promise."

"Just make sure she doesn't get out of your office. Stack a couple of filing boxes in front of the door if you want to keep it open. That should keep her in—and make sure she doesn't chew on any cables."

When we finally reached the sixteenth floor, I detoured to Dani's workspace, setting my kitten on her desk. I gave instructions on how to feed her and left Dani with a few toys I expected would see a lot of use during long, dull phone conversations. Before the woman could question my willingness and generosity, I beat a hasty retreat to my office, left the door open, and watched the clock.

Twenty minutes later, I heard the sweet sound of dismayed, horrified cries from down the hall—and I couldn't smell a thing.

When my phone rang, I smothered my smile and answered, "Reed Matthews."

"Reed," my boss murmured in my ear, and I detected the faint hint of his laughter. "I think I need to give you a raise. I haven't seen such a well-executed office revenge tactic in years, and that's saying a lot. You even followed every rule. That said, that is the vilest thing I've ever smelled in my life."

"That's funny, sir. I don't smell anything at all."

"Well played, Reed. Well played." My boss hung up on me.

I returned the phone to its hook, allowing myself a soft chuckle. The knock at my door promised trouble, but instead of Dani, I got an angel. Three of them visited the office often, much to my dismay, and at least once a week, they popped in to visit me, checking in on me as part of my long-term rehabilitation from solitary confinement.

Not only could angels see the secrets and desires of the heart, they could tell truth from lies, making them the vessels of justice—justice that only worked if the entire truth was told, something I had failed to do so long ago.

My entire body tensed, and I identified the angel by the blue and gold striping on her wings. She called herself Luna, although it wasn't her real name. Angels had biblical names, and Luna wasn't one of them. When I had realized I wouldn't be ditching my unwanted angelic visitors anytime soon, I'd made a point of reading up on them.

"Luna," I greeted, determined to be polite when I really wanted to ask her to leave me alone. Whenever I looked at her, I remembered, and I hated the memories almost as much as her presence in my life.

She stepped into my office and closed the

door behind her, a silent signal she meant to stay a while. And without fail, my schedule would be mysterious cleared for however long she needed. Without invitation, she sat down on one of the two chairs on the other side of my desk and made herself comfortable.

At least I didn't have to worry about seeing into *her* heart; beings without heads lacked eyes, which was the only silver lining in the storm cloud of her presence in my office.

"You threw out your mail again."

Why did an angel always come to see me whenever I tossed out mail originating from Mississippi? If I wanted to make myself miserable dwelling on the past, I'd go buy a bottle of vodka and earn a hangover at the same time. "As I have at a minimum of once a month for the past three years of my life. Surprise, surprise."

"What if I told you that letter could change your life?"

I paused long enough to do the math. "What if I told you we've had this conversation fifty-six times already? Having it again isn't going to change the outcome."

"Yet here we are, having the conversation yet again. You would make this much easier on yourself if you would open the letter instead of throwing it away."

"If you're gambling on human curiosity to get me to look at it, you're going to be waiting a long time. The answer was no twice last month, three the month before. The answer is no this month. I have made my home here. I even adopted a kitten. She's currently in Dani's office making her life miserable."

"I have seen your... kitten."

"The vet assured me Kitten, Destroyer of Worlds is indeed a kitten. So she's a little nasty when she uses the litter box, but that's hardly her fault."

"A little?"

I held my hands up in a gesture of surrender. "Did you really come all the way to the sixteenth floor to bother me about that letter? Is there something else you wanted to discuss?"

"Your progress following your imprisonment, of course. Pesky things, those ethic laws dedicated to the protection of humans—even humans with angelic and demonic blood, such as yourself."

I clenched my teeth. Maybe if I hadn't been estranged from my parents, I'd criticize them for having had me in the first place. If I hadn't been born, well, I wouldn't have had any worries over the Mississippi judiciary system's reluctance to lose track of me. "I have a job. I go to work every day, except when I get sick, which is rare enough my boss suggests I should at least fake it so the other employees feel better about themselves. I get along with my co-workers. Despite popular belief, I have not snapped and gone on a murderous rampage. I'm a functional member of society."

I knew better to ask the question Luna expected. If I gave her a single opportunity, she'd spend the next two hours lecturing me about the differences between living and survival, and I'd done a whole lot of surviving without really living in her opinion.

Fucking angels.

"You make good money you hardly spend, you have no real friends in or outside of the office, and you spend your weekends whoring yourself out to the first woman looking for someone who can make her feel good for just a night. You have a surprising list of charity cases, including the nice couple who lives in the home you bought for them but refuse to visit unless necessary. I hardly consider that functional."

Damn it. I pinched the bridge of my nose and closed my eyes. "What do you want from me, Luna?"

"Answers."

"If I give you answers, will you leave me the hell alone?"

If angels had heads or faces, I suspected

Luna would have glared at me for that one. "Negotiable."

Since we'd already left safe, civil waters, I flipped my middle finger at the angel. "This is my opinion of your answer."

The first time I'd heard an angel laugh, the sound had worked its way into my bones, easing the tension plaguing me from the day I'd been incarcerated for murder and had lost everything good in my life. Luna's laughter still touched that deep, broken place within, but it didn't soothe me for long. I remembered too much.

Luna's laughter sounded a lot like my mother's. My mother had never liked me much to begin with, and my crimes had given her the excuse she needed to take a hike, and because my father's heart longed only for her, he'd gone with her. My mother's heart desired life with my father before I'd been born.

I really didn't want to remember the rest, although I had no doubt Luna saw right through my silence.

While imperfect, my sight was a lot like theirs, courtesy of having two parents who were the children of angels and the humans they had loved. Neither were burdened with an angel's gifts—if I could call my cursed sight a gift. Swallowing, I released my resentment on a sighed breath. "Ask your questions, but I make no promises I will answer."

I blamed my kitten. Instead of a flat-out no, as our conversations had gone so many times before, I'd said something a little closer to a yes.

"Why did you lie to the judge, Reed? You could have avoided those years alone in the dark and quiet if you had simply told the truth."

I leaned back in my chair, shaking my head. Of course the angel would want to know that. "Why do you think?"

"What I think is not the same as what you know. I could look." Luna hesitated. "I've been asked to, but I won't. Why did you stay silent? Why didn't you tell the police the man you'd killed was raping a girl? Why didn't you tell them his death was an accident? You would have walked out of court that day with little more than a slap on the wrist had you only spoken the truth."

Our conversation had changed again. Never before had the angel spoken of what had actually transpired. Before, she had only asked why I killed a man, implying she believed his death an accident. Someone had told my secret, a secret she'd probably already known by looking into my heart and seeing its dark scars forever staining my soul.

I'd looked for the blight in the mirror, but my sight never worked on my own eyes.

"Who told you?"

I heard Luna rise, although I didn't move, not even when she came up behind my chair and stretched around me so she could reach my keyboard. "Here. Look. This was from this morning. There are several dismayed judges and cops in Mississippi right now. They asked for me to speak with you. Upon seeing this, I agreed."

Since the angel wouldn't leave me alone until I looked, I grunted, leaned forward, and opened my eyes. Luna had pulled up a news article, and I recognized the photograph of the woman in the picture, although she'd been much younger five years ago. In silence, I read her testimony, telling the world everything I hadn't, including how I'd pulled her rapist off her and into the wall.

Others had stepped forward, too, and the women formed a wall of solidarity breaking the years of silence, two of which I'd spent in prison for the man's death.

I clenched my teeth, inhaling through my nose and exhaling in a slow, steady rhythm. It didn't help.

I remembered waiting for the days to go by, the lights turned out whenever the guards came to my cell so I couldn't influence them with my talent, with my cursed, hated sight. I remembered the footsteps, straining to hear even a single whisper to convince me I wasn't actually alone in the dark.

"Every last one of them gave their testimonies before a jury with an angel and a succubus in attendance, making truth of their words known. Why did you lie?"

"I didn't lie."

"But you didn't speak the truth."

I shook my head. "Every word was true, confirmed by an angel. Every word, Luna. Written, recorded, and confirmed by an angel."

"If you had simply said you had killed in defense of another, you would have not suffered."

"And if I had, she would have suffered," I spat. "There. Does that make you happy?"

"Of course it does not make me happy, for it does not make you happy."

That startled me into silence, and my flaring anger died away. "I don't understand."

"Is it so difficult to believe someone might actually care for you, Reed? I may be an angel, but I assure you I'm quite capable of such human emotions."

"I killed a man. That's pretty against what you angels like."

Luna snorted, fisted her hand, and bonked the top of my head. "Intent matters."

"I wanted to kill him."

"Reason also matters."

I scowled. "He wasn't a very nice man."

Luna thumped the top of my head again

and circled my desk to return to her seat. "Tell me what you saw."

"He liked making them scream."

"It's not an easy burden to bear, seeing the truth of someone's heart. No one ever taught you how to close your inner eyes."

Close my inner eyes? If I listed the ways I'd tried, the stupid little magic rituals I'd attempted over the years without success, I'd be a long time writing them all down. "I tried every method in every book I've ever found. I've painted practitioner circles in blood, I even talked a gorgon into petrifying me, just to see if his gaze would blind mine."

"But an angel has never taught you?"

I threw back my head and laughed. "Which one? My mother's father or my dad's mother? They can't stand the sight of me. Every time they'd visit, the instant I showed up, they'd book it right out of town. Don't think I didn't notice the way you flinched the first time you met me."

"That was not why I flinched."

"Then why?" I crossed my arms over my chest, and not caring who saw me through my office window, planted my shoes on my desk.

"I know what your heart desires."

How many times had I grimaced over what I'd seen in someone's eyes? I couldn't count them. "That's fair."

"It's amazing. You can be a reasonable human being. I despaired this day would never come."

I suspected cats had learned to be assholes from angels. "I'm still not opening my mail."

I got the feeling Luna smiled. "Then you only have yourself to blame for what you do not know."

"Can we go back to our old conversation? I think I liked it better."

"How about not? We can talk more next week, after you've had some time to think over what you now know. Instead, why don't you tell me about your kitten."

"I think Shakespeare said it best, Luna: Hell is empty and the devils are here. It's entirely possible I adopted Satan."

If angels had foreheads, I was certain Luna would have been rubbing hers. "You try my patience."

I managed a smile for her sake. "I know."

THREE

I need to hide under your desk until
the woman with red hair leaves.

THE LAST TIME I had seen Kennedy Isabella
Young, it'd been at my sentencing, and she'd
looked me in the eye long enough to throw
the ring I'd given her in the trash. Then, I'd
seen all I'd ever need to know about what had
been left of us—nothing. Love and hate were
the opposites of the same coin, and the red-
haired woman I would've laid down my life
for without hesitation had turned face.

I wouldn't have just given her my life. I
would have offered her forever if she had
stuck around, but she'd been like everyone
else in my life that day. With blood staining
my hands, whatever had been between us had
shriveled to dust.

I had lost my place in her heart.

The instant I caught a glimpse of her
strolling across the office floor heading in the
vague direction of my office, I beelined for

the only sanctuary I could think of, one no
one would dare bother: my boss's office. Fortunately for me, he wasn't on the phone, and
when I tapped on his door, he waved me in. I
slipped inside. "I need a favor."

"You look like you've seen a ghost. What's
wrong?"

"I need to hide under your desk until the
woman with red hair leaves."

"Miss Young? She's one of the IRS auditors. What's going on?" My boss leaned to the
side for a better look out his office's window
wall. "She does seem to be headed for your
office, probably for a copy of your contract
files. That is part of what auditors do. I know
you dislike tax auditing, but hiding under my
desk is a bit much."

"She's one of the auditors?" Hell must have
frozen over, giving my Shakespeare quip a bit
more credence than I liked. Since when had
Kennedy liked anything to do with math?
Numbers had been my thing, something she'd
only bothered with because I enjoyed toying
with them and making them do fun things,
like make my boss money.

"There are at least fifteen of them running
around the office this week. You're going to
have to get used to them eventually. I know
you have trouble with government employees, but this is a little over the top. The auditors aren't going to bite you."

"I knew her." It hurt admitting even that little. The shaking started in my hands, as it always did whenever I thought about her. Given five minutes, it'd reach my chest, and then the worst would set in, the kind of breath-stealing anxiety that had landed me in the ER five times in the past year alone.

My boss groaned and ran his hand through his hair. "You just have to go out of your way to vex me sometimes, don't you?"

"Sorry, sir," I squeaked.

Not good. Squeaking was never good. Squeaking meant I wasn't doing the breathing thing like I was supposed to. If I didn't do the breathing thing, then I got to take a nice ride in an ambulance. Inevitably, I'd get a visit from a cranky angel the next day I was back in work, often a Monday, since I usually ended up having my attacks in a bar somewhere thanks to spotting someone who looked a little too much like Kennedy for my good.

Propping his elbow on his desk, my boss rested his chin in the palm of his hand and watched me with an arched brow. With his other hand, he picked up his phone and pressed several buttons. "Elise, please redirect the auditing team to the tenth floor for the rest of the day. Offer them my apologies, but we are going to be having a few unexpected and sensitive meetings on the sixteenth floor."

Once he hung up, he sighed, backed his chair away from his desk, and shook his head. "Just this once, Reed. You will never live it down, and so help me, if you faint under there, I will make certain Miss Young is the one to discover you."

To my credit, I didn't vault over his desk although I was sorely tempted to. I scrambled beneath, grateful my boss had picked an oak monstrosity with a veneer panel blocking sight of his legs. The psychologists I'd seen over the years about my incarceration-induced PTSD found it odd how well I tolerated dark, confined spaces.

I thought it was obvious, personally. When I went into enclosed spaces of my own volition, I had no issues. It was only when people started pushing me into spaces I didn't want to go I started having problems, like my first time outside of the prison and the security guard had pushed down on my head so I wouldn't crack my skull getting into the car. It'd been a habit for him when dealing with prisoners. I hadn't even been handcuffed leaving, but it'd been enough to trigger my first attack.

The doctor had claimed I'd faced too much stimulation after solitary confinement. The doctor hadn't appreciated my opinion regarding his statements. I should have been a bit nicer about it, but could anyone really blame me? When I said stupid shit, someone inevitably called me out on it. In my case, it was usually someone like Luna who couldn't mind her own fucking business.

Closing my eyes helped as long as I ignored the sounds of my boss getting up and heading for his door. Without him hovering, it was a lot easier to remember how to breathe.

I heard the office door open, and a moment later, my boss peeked under his desk, thrusting Kitten, Destroyer of Worlds into my hands. "You needed a therapy animal years ago. She'd do a lot better in your office rather than stinking up mine."

A laugh wheezed out of me, and I ducked my head and breathed through my kitten's soft fur. "Dani's office."

"There will be revenge, Mr. Matthews. Mark my words. When I come for you, the floor will be discussing it for years to come." My boss chuckled, and while he sat and scooted his chair forward, he gave me plenty of space beneath his desk. "Elise is getting rid of the auditors now, although I expect it will be a few minutes. They'd like to review your files today. I intercepted one of them and told them to just pillage your office for what they needed, but if anything was missing, I'd be taking it up with the IRS. They promised to have the files back to us at the end of the day."

"Remember how you said I should contract some sort of illness? I think I have a terrible case of the Black Death, thus I will be unable to come in for at least a week."

"Ring around the rosy, pockets full of posy? There are treatments for that."

"Rabies."

"Also treatments for that. You'd be out a day max for that."

"Well shit, sir. What the hell do I need to catch to get out of work for a week?"

"Use your vacation days. You have about four weeks of them banked up. You could also work from home." My boss nudged me with his shoe. "Since our floor is the victim of the surprise audits this week, I see no reason why you can't just take the week off. Keep your phone handy if I need you. No one is going to be pushing major contracts with them nosing around everywhere."

My boss's phone rang. "Yes, Elise? Ah, excellent. Thank you." He hung up. "It's clear. Elise convinced them we'd ferry the files for them down to the conference room. Miss Young has left the floor."

I heaved a relieved sigh.

The slight hiss of air heralded the worst stench I'd ever had the misfortune of smelling, and I wasn't the only one who gagged. Kitten, Destroyer of Worlds mewed her satisfaction and wiggled against my chest.

I was so, so tempted to toss my kitten across the room to escape the smell, but I couldn't do it. She was just too cute. I coughed, lifting my sleeve to my nose in the futile effort of breathing without wanting to die. My eyes watered, and blinking didn't help alleviate the sting at all.

"Go home and take your kitten with you, Reed." my boss begged in a strained voice. "Please."

I REALLY NEEDED to stop finding things on my hood. Instead of another kitten, I had an angel, and Luna fluttered her wings when I ignored her, opened the back door of my car, and set my kitten's things inside. Reaching between the seats, I situated Kitten, Destroyer of Worlds in the front. "Why are you denting my car?"

"To give you an excuse to replace it, of course. It would cost you an extra five twenty to fix, which you'll refuse. Then again, in twenty-five minutes, you're going to be involved in a rather nasty car accident, so the little dent on your hood will be the least of your concerns. As such, you're going to give me custody of your kitten so she isn't involved, thus sparing you a great deal of anguish. Don't worry, you'll live. You won't like it, but you'll live."

"Since when did angels start predicting the future?"

"I would call it less of a prediction and more of a very meticulous plan I happened to overhear by being a nosy angel who can't mind her own business."

I blinked. "Excuse me?"

"Was that too much for you so soon after your panic attack?"

"If you had a neck, Luna, I would probably be strangling you right now."

"It's like we were made this way on purpose." Luna laughed, and the tension cramping my muscles eased. "I speak truth. You have my solemn vow and oath on it. It's important your kitten isn't in the car with you when you are in the accident. It is also important her carrier remains in the car. I will keep her safe."

"So if I stay here for twenty-six minutes, I won't get into a car accident?"

"No, you'd just be in an even worse accident. I recommend driving home as normal. That will mitigate the accident to survivable levels. I'd be rather disappointed if you died today. I can't fix death."

I opened my mouth, closed it, and got out of my car, closing the back door. Sliding behind the wheel, I considered if I reversed really fast if I'd dislodge the angel from my hood.

"No, you wouldn't," she answered. "I'd be rather cross with you for trying, too. I could help you along a bit. I could suggest to a certain woman upstairs there's something interesting in the parking garage. I'm sure it wouldn't take much to convince her to cooperate."

Sucking in a breath, I gaped at Luna with wide eyes. The trembling feeling started in my hands again. "You brought her here."

"You could have just read the letter, but no. You had to be stubborn about it. If you hadn't insisted on being stubborn, I wouldn't have suggested your company be audited by the IRS. If I hadn't done that, then they wouldn't have slipped Federal investigators into the auditing crew. You only have yourself to blame. All I did was make a single suggestion. Of course, my other vic—tar—ah, patient, yes, patient—hadn't been expecting to see a certain name on the employee roster." Luna pressed her palms together as though she prayed. "Such a miraculous coincidence."

I groaned and slumped in my seat, bowing my head. "Why do you hate me so much?"

"If I hated you, I wouldn't have told you about the accident. I would have just stolen your kitten. I thought I was being generous."

I took several moments to beat my steering wheel. "You're completely missing the point!"

"I am?"

Praying for patience never worked, but I did it anyway. "Luna. What makes you think I want to be in a car accident?"

"Oh! You don't, of course. That would be silly. It'll be in twenty-two minutes. You wouldn't want to be late. It's rather important you're not late."

"Humor me, then. What happens if I'm *not* in the car accident?"

"Oh, it's very messy. Bullets to the brain always are. Your third option is drowning in the creek after you get shot in the chest, but I thought you wouldn't be a fan of that one. I really disliked the one where you're shoved through a sixteenth story window. For the record, you don't actually learn to fly before you hit the ground. You do splatter rather spectacularly and leave a rather startling large hole in the sidewalk, though. Shoddy work-manship over a storm drain. It's traumatizing for all parties involved. As far as deaths go, rather painless, since for you it's over fairly quick. I could tell you how many seconds it would take you to fall if you'd like."

"Pass," I choked out.

"What have we learned here?"

Closing my eyes, I hugged the steering

wheel and rested my forehead on my wrist. "Don't ask angels about the future."

"You were always a smart one. Now, what are you going to do now?"

"I'm going to go home and hope you're just fucking with me, Luna." Since I'd never heard an instance of an angel lying, I'd hope the future held something harmless like a fender bender, though I had to give her credit where credit was due. I wouldn't want my kitten involved in any sort of accident. "I'm not the cause of it, am I?"

"Oh, no. Not at all. That honor belongs to someone else entirely. You'll find out soon enough. Oh. When you get a chance, do pick up a weapon. I recommend a sword. You're really not very good with a gun. Angels typically aren't. It's the whole fair fight issue. When we go to battle, we prefer to kill our opponents up close and very personal. You take after us in that regard." Luna slid off my roof, circled my door, and tapped me on the shoulder. "Your kitten should come with me. Don't worry. You'll see her soon enough. It's just not a good time for her quite yet."

"I thought it was against the rules for you angels to interfere with mortal affairs."

Luna dismissed me with a wave of her hand. "It's been at least a hundred years since I've gotten in any trouble with Dad. Worth the risk. He should've known better than to let me out unsupervised for so long. I preferred it to the other options. Who else am I going to bother at least once a month if you get yourself killed today?"

"Anything else I should know?"

"Oh, yes. When you're 'helped' at the accident, just go along with it. I'm sure you'll figure out how to rescue yourself in short order. This is the only scenario where anyone wants you alive, so do try not to waste the opportunity, all right? Look on the bright side. Your value skyrockets if you live to see tomorrow." Luna patted my shoulder. "Now, why don't you hand over your kitten? You need to get on the road or you'll be late for a very important appointment."

I tried not to think too hard about what she'd told me, deciding to err on the side of caution, pushing away from my steering wheel so I could take Kitten, Destroyer of Worlds out of her carrier. Trusting my kitten to an angel couldn't do any more harm than an accident and a kidnapping. "Wait. They're going to kidnap me?"

"That's the idea, dear. It's really a stupid thing to do, when I stop to think about it. Oh, well. What can I say? Humans. They do such unnecessary things sometimes."

"What did I possibly do to deserve this?"

"Maybe if you had just read one of the letters instead of throwing them out, you wouldn't be in this situation right now. But no, you just had to go be stubborn. It's time to pay the piper. Try to have fun, dear." Luna plucked my kitten out of my hands, and my tiny tabby terror hissed and scratched at the angel without landing a single hit. "You'll have to work on that, little kitty. Completely ineffective. How are you going to live up to your name if you can't touch me?"

Maybe I hadn't actually made it out of my boss's office. Passing out during panic attacks happened often enough with me. I could believe I was having a really bad dream where an angel stole my kitten and warned me I was about to be in an accident. Traditionally, I called them nightmares.

Yeah, I'd just go with a particularly vivid nightmare. What else could I do?

"Die," the angel helpfully answered.

Angels really were assholes.

FOUR

I took the slow, painful route.

ANGELS DIDN'T LIE, but the wretched things could twist the truth through omission. I supposed she was probably right on the nature of the accident; to everyone else, the wreck probably did look accidental. I supposed it was nasty enough, although I wasn't sure.

I hadn't been awake to find out.

No matter how many times I sifted through my memories, I couldn't remember how I'd gone from conscious and driving to unconscious. I'd learn to recognize when I was at risk of dropping during a panic attack; my vision turned brown, red, and gray at the edges and funneled down to a pin-point of light while my body numbed. I jerked awake more often than not, the panic attack resuming right where it'd left off, although I always had an easier time calming after a collapse.

The doctors even had some fancy word

for it. Most of them thought time would help, but I didn't believe them. I thought one of them—only one—had the right idea.

It wasn't the two years I'd spent in solitary confinement that'd gotten to me. Abandonment changed people, but few lost everyone and everything at one time, and fewer still spent years waiting alone for those who wouldn't come. By nature, humans were social creatures, pack animals of sorts, requiring contact with others to remain healthy and sane.

Maybe my progress to becoming a functional member of society was more impressive than I liked to think.

Just like during bad moments, when I thought I'd shake my way out of my own skin, focusing my thoughts on something else helped. Something positive creeping in was new for me and distracting enough I could circle back to my more immediate concerns.

What had knocked me out?

It hadn't been a panic attack. I'd learned to pull over and wait them out, recognizing the first signs of trouble so I wouldn't end up getting myself—or someone else—killed. I even thought of myself as a good driver. I mostly obeyed the traffic laws, I was probably one of two people in the state who understood how turn signals worked, and I minded my own business. I didn't even honk at the assholes, although they tempted me from time to time.

No, a panic attack hadn't knocked me out. I was too careful about when I needed to stop driving and wait out the storm.

So what had?

I tried to open my eyes, but they refused to cooperate, my eyelids weighed down by some invisible force, the same one that kept my arms and legs immobile. The rest of my body was numb, too, although not in the way I usually thought of it. It took a lot of thought and concentration to recognize the sensation for what it was.

Someone had drugged me.

If I had been in an accident, a nasty one according to an angel, drugs made sense. Drugs would also explain how I'd gone from conscious and driving to my current state. I dodged narcotics of any sort, even the prescription ones designed to make handling my life a lot easier.

Drugs could mitigate the damage of old traumas, but I hadn't wanted them. The first few times I'd been prescribed medication, they'd left me floating in a haze, so disconnected the cost of functionality was my basic ability to perform anything beyond the simplest of tasks. One round had been enough for me. I'd clawed my way to functional without them, a daily battle I fought of my own free will. I could have made things easier on myself if I'd consent to the use of magic, magic capable of smothering the memories of my incarceration.

How the hell was I supposed to fight the influence of drugs? At least I recognized the fog in my head enough to realize someone had done *something* to me.

Whether dosed with sedatives or painkillers didn't really matter in the long run; either one would make a mess of anything I tried to do until they wore off.

Drugs also explained why Luna would suggest I cooperate. Until I could think clearly, I'd be more of a danger to myself than anything. I wondered what the angel had meant by the rest of her warning—and her odd belief I'd somehow be worth more assuming I survived. To who?

Why?

I couldn't think of any substantial reason I'd be of more value tomorrow compared to today. The longer I thought about it, the less value I could assign to myself. I was good at numbers and negotiation, which made me somewhat valuable to my boss and the company we worked for. Beyond that, I could disappear and no one had any reason to care.

I had no idea how long I hung in the void, conscious without truly being awake. A cramp in my calf jolted me to a more immediate awareness, one where every muscle in my body filed a complaint all at the same time. Pressure against my chest kept me from curling, and my entire body jerked. My attempt to suck in a breath through my mouth failed, and panic slammed through me as my lungs demanded air I couldn't provide.

It took a lot more effort than I liked to force myself to breathe through my nose.

With a little experimentation, I determined some nice, helpful person had decided duct tape belonged over my mouth. I'd had duct tape over my mouth once before, a test to see what it was like after watching a movie. As a teenager, I hadn't been the brightest, and I'd made my lips bleed when I'd finally ripped the tape off since peeling it carefully hurt too damned much.

The stunt had been one of many during my childhood.

I prepared for the worst and cracked open an eye. Apparently, my kidnappers feared my mouth far more than my sight, as they hadn't even given me a token blindfold. Somewhere behind me, a dim light illuminated a room filled with books. They were piled all over the floor, spilled off the shelves, and otherwise occupied every bit of available space as though they'd somehow bred right along with the dust layering everything, including me.

In the movies, kidnappers did a better job

of holding their hostages victim. My hands were bound with duct tape in front of me, my wrists pressed together, leaving the edge where I could easily get at it with my teeth— or use gravity to help rip through it. The silvery tape was strong, but it tore readily enough. The two or three layers wrapped around my forearms wouldn't hold me for long. Better still, my fingers were free, which made it easy to reach for the strip covering my mouth.

To avoid drawing attention to myself, I took the slow, painful route, scratching at the tape and easing it away, cringing at every pulled hair. Judging from the state of my new beard, I'd been taken at least a day ago. A fringe benefit was the fact with a few pulls, the tape separated from my skin, leaving it stuck all over the short hairs.

On the bright side, I wouldn't have as much work to do next time I shaved—and I could yank it off in one fell swoop without the sound of it pulling from my skin betraying me. Clenching my teeth and bracing for the pain, I secured a grip on the edge and ripped.

There was a special place in hell for people who put duct tape sensitive places, including on my face.

With tears blurring my eyes, I went to work on the next challenge, the tape wrapped around my wrists. With the seam marking the end in easy reach of my teeth, I opted for the quieter, slower method of loosening the end and peeling it off. The more violent method worked faster, but it involved lifting my arms over my head and jerking down while straining at the tape. My shoulders already ached, and I hadn't even moved my arms much yet.

I'd save the fast, noisy way for desperate measures.

By the time I'd gotten enough of the tape loosened I could get a good hold on it with my teeth, my lips bled. It took several tries to peel away enough so I could squirm, get my hands near my feet, and pin the end with my shoe. It didn't take long after to unwind the tape from my arms, although I squeezed my eyes shut and clenched my teeth at the final stage, which ripped all the hairs off my arms.

To make matters worse, beneath the tape were a few scabs, which pulled free with the final tear, resulting in streaks of blood smeared all over my skin. With soft curses muttered under my breath, I freed my legs, although I was spared additional torture thanks to my slacks, which would never be quite the same again. A closer inspection revealed cuts in the black fabric and a few bloody gashes on my legs beneath. One of the nastier ones had even been stitched, and I bet it'd make walking a living nightmare.

After a full pat down, I determined I was one big bruise, sported several gashes someone had bothered stitching in their effort to keep me alive, and had no broken bones. I considered Luna's phrasing and determined if shed blood served as the qualifier for nasty, I had been in a rather nasty accident, and I would not like the process of separating my clothes from the cuts that hadn't been treated.

Throughout the entire process of freeing myself and checking how badly I'd been injured, the library remained quiet. My nose itched from the dust I'd stirred up moving around, and if anyone did come to check on me, there'd be no way of hiding my activities, not without effort. Bracing for the inevitable pain, I staggered to my feet, my breath hissing through my teeth.

One problem down, too many to count left to go.

SOMEONE HAD, in their infinite wisdom, decided to dump me at an old, abandoned farmhouse in the middle of nowhere. Footsteps through the dust marked where people had come and gone. In the drying mud outside, I identified at least three distinct set of prints, although there could have been more. The one set almost made me laugh.

What sort of woman wore high heels in the mud during a kidnapping? I gave my ox-fords a rueful look; the leather would take a whipping, and if they were like any of the other pairs I'd destroyed over the years, they wouldn't keep on ticking. They'd fall apart and inflict blisters and misery on my feet be-fore giving up the ghost.

Then again, maybe the woman had the right idea. At least she'd only get her toes wet, where my socks would be soaked the instant I stepped out of the building. I took a long look around, scowling at the open, rolling fields and distant trees. Until I reached the shelter of the woods, anyone would be able to spot me. Maybe I'd gotten free from the duct tape, but I wouldn't be running anywhere anytime soon. Just standing made my stitched calf throb, and the hike wouldn't do me any good.

Sitting tight wouldn't do me any good, ei-ther. Unless I developed a taste for mud-con-taminated water, I'd dehydrate long before I starved, and I'd rather take my chances with a stream than stagnant puddle water. While I had the skills necessary to maintain my rickety little house in the middle of the woods, I didn't look forward to the idea of

hiking through the woods in a torn suit, recently tenderized in a car accident.

The average raccoon could kill me and eat
me for dinner, and I would give a mouse
equal odds.

The only smart thing my kidnappers had
done was take my cell phone. I appreciated
having my wallet and keys, since I'd be able to
take care of myself the instant I found civilization. It puzzled me they'd taken the keys
from the ignition, but I wouldn't look the gift
horse in the mouth quite yet. Just to make
certain my keys and wallet were intact, I
pulled them out and checked. Someone had
gone through my wallet, moving the cards
around, but everything was still present, even
my cash. My keys were a mess, caked with
blood and mud.

Later, once I hid away in somewhere I
considered even remotely safe, I'd have to
think long and hard over why my kidnappers
would retrieve my keys and put them in my
pocket and leave me with my wallet. If they
wanted me alive, it made some sort of sense,
but it would have been better for them to take
everything and leave me incapable of staging
an escape at all.

Then again, maybe they'd believed I
wouldn't be able to break free. Since that possibility made some sense to me, I ran with it.
There were many other possibilities, and I

fear I'd lose points off my IQ score if I thought about them too much.

The only thing I could think of worse than being kidnapped was being kidnapped by idiots.

My first step into the mud squished, and cold water oozed through the laces and into my shoe. Grimacing at the slimy chill, I walked in the footprints of one of the men who'd come before me to help hide my tracks, following their path until I reached the weed-infested gravel road leading away from the house. A decade ago, the fence might have deterred me from heading for the field, but the posts had decayed down to stumps while the crossbars lay broken between.

Had the fence still stood, I would've been stuck on the road. As it was, I adopted a limp to keep from pulling the stitches too much, and my entire leg throbbed from the effort. I re-evaluated the stupidity of my kidnappers. The real idiot was me, testing my luck on a busted leg.

If I didn't find civilization, I'd contract a serious case of death, although if Luna had spoken the unadulterated truth, I'd be choosing the way I went out rather than having my brains shot out, shot in the chest before drowning, or shoved from a sixteenth story window. Death by raccoon made for a better headline, and if I was going to go out, I wanted it to be memorable.

Knowing why someone wanted me dead or captured would've helped, too, but I could only handle one problem at a time. At least raccoons were easy enough to find. The damned things infested the woods in Indiana. All I had to do was walk for a while and one would show up.

I laughed a soft, hoarse laugh all the way to the woods.

FIVE

So much for a memorable headline
detailing my death.

WHILE I FOUND A RACCOON, it didn't seem interested in murdering me and feasting on my body.

So much for a memorable headline detailing my death.

To add insult to injury, the raccoon bolted for a thicket, running as though hell chased it. I supposed that was accurate enough. In order for angels to have children with humans, as my two angelic grandparents had done, they did have to consort with demons in a rather intimate fashion. I'd gotten the biology lesson when I'd been little, although it never really made sense to me how someone who was a sixth incubus, sixth succubus, one-third angel, and not quite a third human equaled a human. Worse, there was a few percentages of 'other' from my father's side of the family.

He had promised to tell me one day what else I was, but I doubted he would. I'd only found out because my mother had lobbed it at my father when she'd been pissed at him over something. Thinking back on it, I doubted she'd known exactly what the 'other' was, either.

I took a breather, gritted my teeth, and resumed my hike, determined to forget about the past and worry about more important things, like finding a phone—or possibly a hospital. A hospital would be a good bet, as the sort of throbbing my leg insisted inflicting on me suggested I should take care of it, stat.

I hated hospitals. Worse, I hated the thought of having to explain to the police I had no recollection of being in a car accident and had woken up bound in duct tape. My pride had taken enough of a beating along with my bruised and battered body. Muttering complaints and curses under my breath, I forced myself to keep marching.

If I stopped to rest, it'd only be harder to move later. After two years of confinement, I'd done enough physical therapy to respect how painful stiff muscles could get.

Fortunately for me, the abandoned farmhouse wasn't far from civilization. I emerged from the trees along a paved road, which headed straight for three buildings. The post office didn't surprise me, especially if the town was large enough to justify a gas station *and* a police station.

If it was a place like Gypsum Creek, the post office would be the last to go, clinging to life until the bitter end. Technically, Gypsum Creek's post office still operated, but since the only occupied residence—mine—had mail delivered twice a year in the form of tax notices, the carrier cheated and stuck to the neighboring town.

Over the years, I had learned delaying made my anxiety worse, so I marched resolutely towards the police station to get the humiliation over with. I'd be safe enough from a panic attack, unless one of the cops happened to be a pretty girl with auburn or red hair. Then I'd have problems, but I wouldn't have to say a word to get the point across anyway.

I'd be making acquaintances with their floor unless I remembered breathing was mandatory.

With trembling hands, I pushed my way through the station's front door and headed for the front desk. Unlike the others I'd been to, there were no bulletproof glass walls separating me from the cop. The lobby felt more like a doctor's office than a police station, all hard, white lines, metal chairs painted white, and sterilized tiles.

The cop's mouth dropped open when he saw me.

Waiting only made things worse, so I blurted, "I was in a car accident, kidnapped, and dumped in some farmhouse not far from here."

When I said it, it sounded even more embarrassing than I had initially anticipated, and heat spread over my cheeks. The station lobby offered no places to hide or pretend I didn't exist. I swallowed, my entire body so tense my trembling graduated to shaking. I shoved my hands in my jacket pockets to hide them.

The man blinked, reached across his desk, and picked up a form, which he set on the desk in front of him. Picking up a pen, he gave it a click. "Your name, son?"

"Reed Matthews."

"The location and time of the accident?"

I shook my head. "I don't remember. I was driving between Indianapolis, Indiana to Cataract, where I live."

The cop dropped the pen. "Did you just say Indiana?"

I thanked my lucky stars my kidnappers hadn't taken my wallet. Digging it out of my pants kept my hands busy, and while I couldn't hide my shaking, having something productive to do helped. I pulled out my driver's license and offered it to him.

"This says Gypsum Creek. Where's that?"

"Town next door to Cataract, sir. It's not on most maps." I gave it a few years before it vanished off the face of the Earth altogether, my residency the only reason it still had a zip code. "It's a pretty small place."

"You're a long way from home, son. Why don't you go on and have yourself a seat? You look plum tuckered out."

Plum tuckered? I took the single sidestep required and sank down onto the plastic and metal chair. My leg approved, and I stretched it out to take pressure off the stitched gash. "I'm afraid to ask."

I was, too. How far could I have been taken following a car accident?

"This here's Arkansas, son, spittin' distance from Mississippi. If you're talking about the Millers' old place, that there be on the Mississippi side of the line, and if you take a hike a few hours north of here and dodge the river, you'll hit Tennessee if you're not careful."

Terror took many forms, sometimes robbing me of breath, sometimes making me shake, and sometimes, it wrapped cold, deathly hands around my throat and squeezed. I knew the line dividing Arkansas and Mississippi; it followed the heart of the river most of the time, leaving odd holes where nature had run its course and rerouted the riverbed. There was only one such place near Tennessee where the river had once curved into Mississippi, leaving a little oasis of Arkansas on the wrong side of the river. "Old River Lake?"

"You've been here before?"

"Close by," I choked out. A stone toss to the east and north put me right around where I'd grown up, although I hadn't known Old River Lake had warranted even a gas station. "Lake Cormorant."

It wasn't too far from Horn Lake, where I'd killed a man and ruined my life.

"I know it. How long you've been up in Indiana? Like it?"

"A few years now. It's fine, I guess. Different."

That had been why I'd picked the state.

"All right. What can you tell me about this accident, son?"

"Absolutely nothing. I was driving home, next thing I know, I was in that farmhouse."

"With duct tape right over your mouth, from the looks of it."

I lifted my hands and touched my face, grimacing at the patch of smooth skin and my raw mouth. "Yes."

"Tell me what you can, son, and start with your car. Make, model, year, and who it's registered to if it isn't yours."

Since I doubted a backwater cop would

believe me if I told him an angel had warned me I'd be in the accident, I told him some of the circumstances leading up to my leaving work early, informing him I had occasional issues with anxiety and my boss had suggested I take some vacation time. The rest I told him straight up, detailing how I'd escaped.

Talking about it helped a lot more than I expected, especially when the cop didn't seem like he was ready to mock me for my situation. If anything, he accepted my story readily enough, piquing my curiosity. "You're not surprised by this."

"You ain't the first one, son, and you ain't gonna be the last. We've gotten into the habit of checking that place three times a week now, makin' sure there ain't anyone abandoned there. We had two last week alone, one the week before. They're usually left in the front room and not in the back, and most ain't clever enough to get free, though you're the first sayin' you done got grabbed out of a car accident. First one out of state, too—them folks have all been from Mississippi so far."

My mouth dropped open, and I stammered something.

The cop must have interpreted my stammering as some form of a question, as he chuckled and shrugged. "Should've been here first time it happened. Guess they were right worried no one would check the farmhouse, since we done got a call about it from the Mississippi side of things. We're closer despite bein' on the wrong side of the line, so they done gave us jurisdiction to trot on over and have a look-see. Got tired of makin' the hike themselves. Bagged us a gas station at least to go along with our post office. We're gonna end up a regular town at the rate we're goin'."

"Why the hell would anyone hike all the way up to Indiana to bring me *here*?"

"Who the hell knows, son. We ain't got hide nor hair on these people or why they grab folks and dump 'em there. We've got this down to an art, so you just sit easy. It'll take the ambulance a while to get here, but that's how it goes. Everyone gets a ride to the hospital for a check, I'll file the report, and you'll go on your merry way after the Mississippi folks look you over."

"All right."

The cop grabbed his phone and stabbed his pen against the buttons. "Hey, Charlie Dean, I got us another one over here at Old River Lake, and this son ain't local; driver's license puts him from Indiana, and looks like they roughed him up a bit more than the others. Son done claims they pulled him out of an accident, and he don't remember nary a thing about the crash, either. Looks the part, though, and a bit unsteady on his feet, so you better be sendin' over a good white coat to have a look at him." The conversation didn't last long, with the man relaying my name, driver's license number, my car's plates, and general description of it before the crash, although I expected there wasn't much left if Luna was to be believed.

I wasn't sure what I believed anymore, but there was definitely something fishy going on.

IT TURNED out my kidnappers had had me longer than I thought; the ER doctor estimated I'd been injured at least four or five days ago, and blood tests revealed I'd been pumped full of a cocktail of antibiotics, painkillers, and a sedative. I'd pulled a few of the stitches on my hike through the woods, although all in all, I hadn't done much damage. The process took six hours, most of which I spent in a sterile room thumbing through magazines a nurse had brought to keep me amused—or at least contained where she wanted me. The only one of any interest was a financial rag I'd read twice already, but read a third time so I wouldn't end up reading about the mating rituals of animals.

When the test results came in, I endured

an hour-long scolding by Dr. Laski, who had spoken with my physician in Indiana. She must have given him a lecture over my stubbornness and general refusal to take medications for my anxiety, judging from the man's inability to drop the subject. "Medications are there to help you. Is there any reason you insist on refusing helpful medications?"

How many times would I need to have this conversation? I sighed, contemplating if rolling up one of the magazines and beating myself in the head with it would put me out of my misery.

"He's more stubborn than the average rock and equally dense," a sickeningly familiar voice announced, her tone as cold and hard as the last time we'd spoken five years ago. "He's hard-headed, rather stupid for someone with his IQ, and prone to giving misleading yet truthful information. If you'd like a rock to discuss his issues with, I can get you one from the parking lot. If my information is accurate, which I believe it is, you'd have better luck with the rock."

If I closed my eyes and breathed in deep, maybe I could convince myself I was actually trapped in a nightmare, one occupied by one Kennedy Young, who my primary doctor likely blamed for the majority of my issues, of which there were many. The years hadn't dulled her edge.

She wielded the truth like a sword and had no problems cutting people with it. Fool that I had been—fool that I still was—had loved her for that. She took shit from no one, especially me. Had I sacrificed a too young girl to the judgment of her peers, I supposed Kennedy wouldn't have left as she had, although I doubted she would have stuck around, either.

Everything would have been different. The doctors in Indiana would have been thrilled with my acknowledgment of that fact, something I'd spent the past three years avoiding with steadfast determination.

In some ways, Kennedy was far more of an angel than I was despite her mostly human heritage. Like most folks, she had her fair share of 'other.' What that 'other' was I hadn't learned; it made no difference to me—just like I hadn't quite gotten around to confessing I was far more angel and demon than human despite what my driver's license proclaimed.

Pedigree hadn't been important to either one of us back then.

"This is a private area," Dr. Laski snapped.

"Kennedy Young, CDC and FBI liaison," my ex declared, and I heard the crack-snap of a leather wallet being flicked open with a little too much force. "Investigations."

Way back when, she'd been in school

hunting a business degree in advertising while I'd been playing with numbers, and the memories of meeting her haunted me like everything else. I'd been a semester from my degree when I'd landed in prison, an education I hadn't finished despite my doctors—all of them—suggesting I should.

If I ignored her, if I pretended she didn't exist, I might be able to get through the next few minutes without succumbing to my growing unease. It hadn't quite blossomed to full-fledged anxiety yet, but it would.

It always did.

"When I am done discussing matters with my patient, you may have your turn questioning him. The waiting room is that way, Agent Young."

"I'm under orders to remain with Mr. Matthews to ensure there are no other incidents. I won't get in the way, but I'm not leaving."

"Very well. Don't get in the way over there, preferably in the hallway. Don't get in the way of nurses and people who actually belong here. This is a hospital. If you need to question my patient, you may do so outside of my hospital."

I cracked open an eye and checked the walls, disappointed to discover I was in a room without windows. I didn't care which floor I was on; had a window been available, I would have quietly let myself out, and I wouldn't even care if I left a dent in the sidewalk. Since my routes of escape were blocked, I began running through my list of techniques that sometimes helped keep me from making close friends with the floor. First, I counted my breaths, fighting the urge to hyperventilate. Once I started floundering like a fish out of water, I lost.

"Now, Mr. Matthews. As this influences the prescriptions I'll be writing out for you, please elaborate on your refusal to take certain medications."

I appreciated how Dr. Laski avoided revealing anything unnecessarily to Kennedy.

I kept breathing. When my doctors in Indiana found out, they'd probably give me a gold sticker for good progress. Not only had I avoided fainting, while the subject of my worst nightmares lurked somewhere behind me, I hadn't made a run for it yet—or found a piece of furniture to hide beneath.

"If I had a chemical imbalance or other medical issue requiring medication, I would take it, Dr. Laski." A better man, a wiser man, would have waited until the source of his problems left, but if Kennedy insisted on staying, I wouldn't accept the blame for what she heard. That ship had sailed long ago, right along with my peace of mind. "All those medications do is mask the symptoms. They do not cure it, for there isn't a cure short of a complete rewriting of my memories. I refuse. I am the product of my circumstances and choices, and I refuse to be rewritten or erased because I'm not a desirable member of society."

I refused to claim I hurt nobody being as I was, but I had—I did. Despite what my doctors believed, I listened to them even when I didn't agree with them. They viewed my endless fountain of guilt and remorse as something positive, a symptom of a killer who hadn't meant to kill, someone who could be rehabilitated and released back into society.

They liked cases like mine. They believed I could one day live the sort of life they envisioned for me. Sometimes, when I lowered my guard, I wondered if I could. All they knew came from my file, which proclaimed me a victim of the courts, someone who had faced a punishment beyond what the crime deserved.

The sound of silence hung in the room, thick and smothering.

I breathed, and I counted each one. Ten breaths went by, then twenty, before Dr. Laski blew out a gusty sigh. "The painkiller I wish to prescribe has low risk of addiction, but it also functions as a low grade sedative, which puts it in the same class of medications you typically refuse to take. While you are taking it, it will help mitigate some of your general anxiety symptoms. It works well with the antibiotic you'll be taking. You would be expected to take it for approximately two weeks. The other options have significant impairment."

"Define impairment."

"Dizziness, nausea, lethargy, and other inconveniences my preferred painkiller lacks."

"All right."

Dr. Laski frowned and leveled a glare at me. "You're not going to argue or refuse to take them?"

"I'll take them as prescribed."

"I had been informed you were unreasonable over this issue."

Why wasn't I surprised? Why couldn't any of my doctors comprehend I only wanted to take medications when necessary? "You're prescribing the medication for the right reasons. If I'd been in a car accident at home and they were prescribed to address injury or infection, I'd take them."

"Then I will expect these to be taken exactly as prescribed." Dr. Laski's gaze shifted to the doorway behind me. "Perhaps you can make yourself useful and make certain that happens since you're his assigned babysitter."

While the implication I needed a babysitter stung, I had to admit the man had lobbed a well-aimed verbal bomb in Kennedy's direction.

Her slow clap almost made me smile. "I wasn't aware I was attending kindergarten classes today. It seems I overdressed. If you're quite done, I'd like a chance to question Mr. Matthews sometime today. I would request you hurry, but I'd rather the pharmacy not lose precious hours attempting to translate scribble. Perhaps you should have Mr. Matthews do the majority of the handwriting, unless this kindergarten class happens to have discovered the existence of computers?"

Within five minutes of them bickering and hurling childish insults at each other, I wondered when I had become an example of sanity in a world gone mad. After ten, I contemplated routes of escapes.

After twenty, I had had enough. "If you two are done fighting like an old married couple, I'd like to at least start the paperwork so I can go home sometime this year."

I should have known better than to draw attention to myself.

SIX

Clicking the pen kept me from
stabbing it through the forms.

DR. LASKI CALLED in my prescriptions, repeated his instructions for taking them
enough times I was ready to lose my temper
along with Kennedy, and sent for a nurse,
who brought a big stack of papers for my discharge along with an invoice. My insurance
had declined coverage due to the hospital's
location, leaving me with two thousand reasons to find a new provider the instant I got
home, one that acknowledged hospitals and
doctors existed outside of the state of
Indiana.

I scowled at the papers and tried to pretend Kennedy wasn't near the door watching
me. Clicking the pen kept me from stabbing
it through the forms. Once I reclaimed some
semblance of control over my temper, I went
to work, the act of keeping my handwriting

legible helping to distract me from my mountain of other problems.

"You're going to have to acknowledge me at some point."

Since ignoring the problem wasn't going to make her go away, I finished the page I was working on and focused on my breathing again, counting until I could resume writing without my shaking hands betraying me. Maybe there was something to the theory exposure helped. The jolt of hearing her voice didn't seem as bad as when she'd first come into the room, taking fewer breaths to work through until I could function without my vision fading around the edges.

"Reed?"

Hiding wasn't an option anymore; when I was honest with myself, it never had been. All I'd done at the office was delay the inevitable, especially considering she'd made the hike from Indiana to Mississippi to hunt me down. If I were more stubborn than the average rock, she was a diamond ready to grind me to powder. "Just ask your questions so you can leave and go back to doing whatever it is CDC and FBI liaison investigators do. Better yet, go ask the cop from Old River Lake. There's nothing for me to tell you I haven't already told him."

"It doesn't work that way."

I clenched my teeth and concentrated on

filling out the forms, pulling out my wallet to get out my insurance card, not that the damned thing was worth the amount I spent on it each month. I copied the identification number and contemplated throwing it in the trash. With a single flick of my wrist, I could express my opinions on what I felt about our last meeting.

Instead of the fear I'd feared so much, I ended up with a deep-seated rage, the kind that boiled beneath my skin and threatened to burst out in an inferno. I firmed my grip on the card, focused on the trashcan, and sent the card sailing across the room. It hit the wall, ricocheted against the corner, and toppled inside, the plastic bag rustling. "Pity."

"Is there any reason you just tossed your insurance card in the trash?"

"Not much point in keeping what does me zero good." I signed the last sheet, got to my feet, and careful to keep my eyes focused anywhere other than her, I headed for the door. "I'll be getting a new insurer once I'm back in Indiana—one that's actually useful out of state."

I hunted down the nurse, gave her the papers, and waited for the next phase of the discharge process, which involved my credit card and a payment terminal since the hospital didn't want to do a delayed billing. I probably could have talked them into it if I'd been inclined to put in the effort, but I had more pressing concerns, including ditching one Kennedy Young.

Kennedy missed the memo and followed along. The click of her shoes indicated she wore heels, something she'd avoided before I'd gone to prison. I'd always thought it interesting about her. Given five minutes, access to a closet, and a pair of stilettos, she could have taken the modeling world by storm if she wanted. Instead, she had gone a different route, wanting to make other model-pretty people rise to stardom from the background.

Once upon a time, she'd tried to get me to pose for a camera. I'd done it exactly once and hated the whole process of sweating under hot lights, pretending to be someone I wasn't so some company could use my image to make a pretty penny. In that case, I'd been modeling underwear, something I found almost as distasteful as Kennedy's unabashed enjoyment of me showing off my chest for the photographer.

They'd even used baby oil so I'd look all glossy for the camera.

I'd lost all the muscle and tone, refusing to do the work to gain it back, leaving me thin and lacking the six pack many women desired, which worked well enough for me. My Friday and Saturday night outings didn't fea-

ture models anyway. Their appearances
meant little to me.

It took an extra thirty minutes to finalize
the paperwork, which Kennedy observed in
silence. I made it all the way to the elevator
before she cleared her throat.

"What?" I snapped.

"I'm parked in the secondary visitors' lot."

"Of all of the whatever-you-ares, how is it
I got stuck with you?" I hit the button for the
ground floor with a little more force than
necessary, and instead of breathing to keep
my anxiety from getting the better of me, I
struggled with the anger I'd never
anticipated.

In every nightmare where I met her again,
it'd always been fear—the fear of rejection,
the fear of her loathing, the fear of the unknown. I'd never imagined I had enough life
left in me for anything like resentment or
anger.

She'd been right enough to hate me, although I hadn't told her or anyone the full
truth. I didn't want her to know it, either.

All it would do was confirm how much of
a coward I was, and that pissed me off even
more.

"To make a long story short, my boss
said so."

"How wonderful. Look. I want something
clear. I want to go to a store, get clothes that

aren't bloodied, muddied, and ripped, take these fucking medications, and go home so I can sleep for a week. I'll compromise on the going home part. If sleeping in a ditch gets rid of you faster, I'm okay with that. Ideally, you will stay here, I will go back to Indiana, and we never see each other ever again. I moved to Indiana so I wouldn't have to run into people like you. Ask whatever questions you need to ask. Then do a take two and get the fuck out of my life."

"Since when did you get so snappy?"

"Since you threw your engagement ring in a trashcan." The elevator dinged and opened, and it took me a moment to locate the signs directing me to the taxi stand, ignoring the ones for the visitors' parking lot. "You could have at least had the decency to throw it in my face, but that would have been asking you to get too close to me, wouldn't it? Heaven forbid I ruin your reputation even more. Couldn't have let anyone know you'd been dumb enough to agree to marry me at that point, right?"

"All right. I may have deserved that."

I strolled through the hospital until I reached the waiting area nearest the doors, locating a clock mounted on the wall. "I'm giving you exactly ten minutes. Ask your questions. But in ten minutes, I'm leaving, and I won't be leaving with you."

When twenty seconds went by and Kennedy said nothing, I took the offensive and told her everything from the moment I'd seen her in my office to waking up in the abandoned farmhouse. I even told her about Luna, her warning, and my kitten. I left nothing out, including the suffocating, paralyzing anxiety and PTSD that sent me to several doctors too many times a month.

I gave her the ten minutes I had promised, shut my mouth the second they were up, and left without another word.

WHILE I DIDN'T VIEW myself as a control freak, I felt a lot better the instant I bought new clothes, got changed, and made plans to haul my ass from Mississippi to Indiana. The taxi driver waited for me to do the minimum shopping required to be able to take the first flight out of the hell hole I had once called home. To escape, I'd have to make the hike north through Horn Lake to Memphis International Airport, and the thought was enough to leave me shaking.

My primary goal was to make it home, detouring long enough to hunt Luna down and retrieve my kitten. Despite being a weapon of biological destruction, I looked forward to taking Kitten, Destroyer of Worlds home with me. An hour with her favorite feathers on a stick would do me even more good than a full assault on the wood pile—and hurt a lot less, too.

I should have known Kennedy wouldn't give up so easily, her bright hair betraying her presence in the domestic departure terminal. Tightening my hold on my new bag, I considered the best option to get rid of her again. "I have nothing else to say to you."

"Part of my job is to make certain you make it home safely, so here I am."

"You followed the taxi."

"Wasn't exactly hard, nor was it difficult to figure out you'd be coming here, which made it easy enough to get ahead of you when you stopped at the pharmacy to fill your prescriptions." Her tone implied Kennedy was smiling her smug smile, but I refused to look in her direction at all.

I didn't want to risk even a glimpse into her eyes. I'd seen too much already. Instead of answering her, I headed for the ticket counter.

The slender envelope Kennedy shoved in my face startled me into dropping my bag. "I took the liberty of acquiring tickets. The flight leaves in an hour, so I thought you'd appreciate not missing it."

I would not lose my cool *or* drop from a panic attack. Repeating my decision to myself, as though it might somehow prevent either from happening, didn't help much. When I didn't move, Kennedy shoved the envelope into my hand before bending over and grabbing the strap of my bag. "The flight leaves in an hour," she repeated.

The ticket, in its flimsy paper envelope, rustled in my shaking hand. I swallowed and nodded, careful to keep my gaze averted. How could two words be so damned difficult? The last thing I wanted to do was thank her for anything, but I forced one out to at least pretend I could be civil.

Several deep breaths later, I recovered enough to take my bag from her, shrugging the strap over my shoulder.

"If the cops had done their job right, you would have been checked for evidence at the hospital and your clothing confiscated. That's the suit in the bag?"

Not trusting myself to speak, I nodded.

"I'll be confiscating it when we land, and I'll make sure no one in security gets any bright ideas about sifting through it. Maybe the labs can get something useful out of it, although I doubt it."

It didn't matter to me either way, so I shrugged.

"This will go a lot smoother and faster if you cooperate."

"I told you everything I know." I took a

closer look at the boarding pass to get the gate number and headed towards security, aware of my ex falling into step with me. "What else could you possibly want?"

"A chance to talk with you."

"You had your chance. You had two years' worth of chances. Whenever you wanted, you could have requested a visitation. You knew that because you were at the sentencing. You knew the only way I'd see anything out of that cell was if someone requested visitation. You decided to toss your ring and walk. Why should I talk to you now?"

"I was wrong."

Maybe a year ago, maybe two years ago, maybe even three, I would have felt something other than disgust at those three words. Maybe any other day, I would have gotten something out of it other than chest-tightening pain. I shook my head. The truth always won out, no matter how much I hated it, and I both cursed and hated myself for admitting it. "You weren't wrong. I did kill him."

"Accidentally, something you neglected to tell anyone, even me," Kennedy hissed.

"Especially you."

The reason for it hurt, too, just like everything else. I blamed the angelic blood in me for my inability to remain silent—or my doctors, who'd been battling me for three years trying to get me to admit the full truth.

Kennedy sighed. "Why?"

"Because you would have started digging. You wouldn't have let it go." The Kennedy I had once known wouldn't, either. She would have chased down every scrap of information until she'd discovered the full truth. The longer I thought about it, the more I realized she belonged in the field she'd changed to following my incarceration, no matter how much I resented her presence.

"Because you didn't want anyone to point fingers at the girl you helped."

I assumed Kennedy had seen the interview Luna had showed me, and I echoed her sigh. "I made my choice, you made yours. It's over. Ask whatever questions you need so you can go back to doing whatever it is CDC and FBI liaisons do when they aren't masquerading as IRS auditors."

In the security line, Kennedy kept quiet, and I followed her lead readily enough, limiting my talking to answering the guard's questions. Kennedy took my bag, flashed her badge, and declared it as evidence, thus preventing it from being searched although it was run through the x-ray machine. Within twenty minutes, we were at the boarding gate with too much time to spare.

I picked a seat overlooking the airport, watching the planes taxi to and from their gates.

Since Kennedy couldn't leave well enough alone, she sat beside me. "You've changed."

"What were you expecting?"

"A little bit more willingness to talk to me."

"You had your chance. Just let it go. Go back to your life and let me go back to mine."

"I've seen your file, Reed. You never finished your degree. You've stalled out in your career. You're stalled out everywhere. No friends, either, at least not the kind you meet up with after work. None of your co-workers even know where you live. You gave them a PO Box in the wrong town, and while there are several property deeds with your name on them, we're not even sure exactly where you live. The one address we tried had a nice couple living there who couldn't tell us where you lived after we made it clear we knew you weren't actually living with them. They made rather valiant efforts to hide that, too. Last check, we hadn't been able to figure out how to access your second property, as there are no roads that go there."

"And thank you for listing all of my short-comings. Is there anything you'd like to add to the list?"

"You did rescue a kitten, although she's rather odiferous."

I scowled. "Don't say mean things about Kitten, Destroyer of Worlds."

"Reed, she made an *angel* gag. Your co-workers are horrified something so damned cute can smell so damned bad. Your boss has threatened to invite your kitten to work if people kept goofing off. She should be registered as a weapon."

I suspected Kennedy had learned the hard way my kitten produced toxic waste. "It serves Luna right for taking custody of my kitten. If you want answers, she's the one to talk to. She knows more about what's going on than I do."

"Luna, as you name her, refuses to answer our questions. She won't tell us anything except she visited you before you left the office building and took your kitten so she wouldn't be hurt, implying she knew you were going to be in an accident and had taken action despite angels typically refusing to interfere with human affairs."

I'd have to thank Luna later, if only for the satisfaction of hearing the frustration in Kennedy's voice. It made me petty, but I didn't care. If Kennedy insisted on poking her nose in my business, she could suffer, too.

I was in no hurry to welcome her in any sense of the word.

"I had no idea it was going to be anywhere near as bad as it was for you, Reed. I'm sorry. If I'd known…"

"I'm pretty sure the judge told you exactly

what would happen. There was no secret made about solitary confinement. Everything was laid out by the court, rather accurately." I had to give the court system that much credit; they left out few details of what I faced, although I'd gotten out three years early.

I tried not to think too hard of what sort of man I'd have become if I'd stayed the full five years in that cell. Maybe there was something to the medications making it easier.

I wasn't shaking nearly as much as I expected, all things considered.

"You were guaranteed visitations."

I shrugged.

"How many people visited you? It wasn't listed in your file."

Staying silent took too much effort and hurt too much. In a way, I preferred the panic attacks. With them, I knew what to expect even when it seemed like the world broke apart around me. "No one visited me, so there was nothing to list in my file," I replied, my tone devoid of emotion.

The call for boarding spared me from continuing the discussion.

SEVEN

*Landing was a generous word, one
that wasn't entirely appropriate for
the situation.*

HAD I taken the ten seconds to think it
through, I never would have taken a nap on a
plane with my ex sitting next to me, pinning
me in the window seat in a clever way to prevent my escape.

Once upon a time, the one thing that annoyed Kennedy the most about me was my
innate ability to sleep through anything other
than my alarm clock. She'd been convinced a
bomb could go off without waking me.

Turns out she was right, mostly. Instead of
a bomb, bad weather flipped the plane over
its knee and spanked it, but I dozed right
through the landing. Landing was a generous
word, one that wasn't entirely appropriate for
the situation. Most people used crashed.

When I thought of crashes, fiery doom
and destruction came to mind rather than
panicked, screaming passengers beelining for

the exits. While I yawned and stretched, others flailed. The ringtone Kennedy had used to wake me still went off in her hand, and I suspected she glared at me. Come hell or high water, I would not look my ex in the eyes.

"Well, this is fun," she announced, crossing her arms over her chest and sulking in her seat. "We crashed. You slept right through the plane crash. How the fuck does someone sleep through that? Did you not feel that turbulence? The turbulence that knocked the plane right out of the sky? That turbulence."

I'd fallen prey to panic attacks often enough to recognize the precursor babbling. "Deep breaths, slow, and count them," I suggested while I angled in my seat to work the kinks out of my knee. Rotating my ankles came next, and I grimaced at the tingling in my toes, promising I'd hate the instant I got up and tried to walk.

Kennedy sucked in air between her teeth.

"It helps if you use your nose. All panting will do is making you hyperventilate faster. In and out, through your nose, and count—and don't rush it." I showed her by breathing in deep five times. It gave me a chance to smell the air, which was clear of smoke. No smoke meant no fire, which suited me just fine. A glance out the window revealed dark skies and sheets of rain hammering the ground and streaming off over the glass. Were airplane windows made of glass? I tapped it with a knuckle but couldn't tell from the sound.

As far as I could tell, the pilot had ditched the plane in a field.

"How the hell can you be so calm about this?" she hissed at me through clenched teeth.

Which answer did she want? Probably not the one where I confessed I had enjoyed my nap, rather pleased over how much better I felt. Careful to avoid eye contact, I observed the noisy, frightened people flutter their way to the exits with the coordination of a blind three-legged dog. Not even Kitten, Destroyer of Worlds cleared a room so fast, although I needed to do a few extra experiments on the unsuspecting to be certain of that.

Kennedy gave my shoulder a shake. "You better not still be asleep, Reed!"

I'd probably regret laughing at her later. "There's no smoke."

"What?"

"There's no smoke. No smoke means no fire, and even if there was a fire, it's pissing worse than a cow on a flat rock out there." Lightning illuminated the sky, and I craned my neck for a better look at the clouds, whistling at the churning clouds. "I guess the plane exploding would ruin my evening." I pondered that for a few minutes while waiting for the rest of the passengers to escape. Kennedy remained seated, and while she breathed through her nose, she also rubbed her forehead, probably questioning all of the decisions she'd ever made in her life.

I waited until most of the other passengers cleared out. "Now would be a good time to do the leave the plane thing. That is customary following the plane crashing."

"How the hell can you be so damned calm about this?"

"Are you injured?"

"Well, no."

"Then you're not dying. Just get out of the damned plane, Kennedy." I fished my bag out from beneath the seat, shouldered the strap, and got to my feet. In case she hadn't put two and two together to get four, I pointed at the nearest exit. "That way."

The stewardess at the exit glared at me and my bag, and Kennedy hesitated at the threshold. "Necessary medications are in there."

While it wasn't quite a lie, I still raised my brows at her deliberate twisting of the truth.

"Oh." The woman went to help my ex scramble down the inflatable slide, but Kennedy had already taken the leap on her own, and I followed after her, soaked within a breath of leaving the cabin. Thunder rumbled, and the driving wind and rain flattened the wheat field. At the bottom, I regretted the lack of stairs, my leg informing me it had had quite enough of my bullshit.

Lightning split the sky and the crack of thunder deafened me. Shaking my head and rubbing my ears, I followed after Kennedy, who kept her distance from the huddled passengers gaping at the downed plane. I looked it over nose to tail and couldn't spot any damage. "What happened to the plane?"

"Don't know. Hit turbulence, engines cut out. Got lucky; nothing but fields and farmland here, so the pilot brought it down and coasted to a rather bumpy halt. Which you slept through. How could you sleep through that? I had to play a damned alarm on my phone to wake you up."

"Is this one of those things I should just apologize for because no matter what I say, I'm screwed?"

"Yes."

I threw my hands up in the air. "Fine. I'm sorry I slept through the crash."

"Please tell me you didn't fall asleep while driving, thus crashing your car."

"I'm pretty sure I didn't fall asleep while driving. I pull over if I'm having an attack, thank you very much."

"And how do you know to pull over?"

"It's pretty obvious. If the shaking hands

isn't enough of a clue, the constriction in the chest, difficulty breathing, or the tunneling of vision tend to get the point across. So I pull over and wait it out, assuming I don't pass out. And even if I *do* pass out, it's a lot easier to manage after."

"And you refuse to take medication."

"Short of having two entire years of my life erased, medication isn't going to do jack shit," I snapped. "Happy?"

"No. Of course I'm not happy."

"Could have fooled me."

"Is this where we have a spectacular fight?" my ex asked in a mild tone.

"Will one make you go away and leave me alone?"

"Probably not. I was stupid, I was hurt, and I knew everything would be different in five years. I shouldn't have quit you the way I did. That was wrong. You deserved better than that."

"But you still would have quit."

"What was I supposed to do? Wait five years? For what? At that point, you'd become someone who'd never be accepted back into society. Horn Lake isn't that big of a place, and news like that spreads fast. If you had told the truth, everything would have been different."

I could only see one way out of the discussion I didn't want, and I faced it down despite the growing tightness in my chest. "Do you think I haven't already thought of that? Two years, Kennedy. That's how long I was completely isolated from the world, all because someone—probably my mother—made certain it was recorded I wasn't fully human and had a sight talent."

"I had wondered about that. You never told me you had a sight talent. I had no idea until the sentencing."

"Well, now you know."

"Not specifically, just that it's hereditary according to your file."

"Fine. You want to know the truth? I was glad I killed that asshole. He loved nothing more than listening to women scream when he raped them. That's what I saw. Maybe I hadn't meant to kill him like that, but after I saw what I had, he wasn't leaving that alley alive. So I'm just as bad as you thought I was then."

"The testimonies made it rather clear he liked when his victims fought. It's becoming quite the sensation. A convicted murderer, released after a two-year sentence was deemed cruel and unusual punishment, is exonerated following the testimony of a single witness who reported, with an audience of two angels, that you had taken action in defense of another. Then other victims stepped forward and backed the first woman. The

man you killed used to have a good reputation—not anymore. And thus a local villain
becomes a hero overnight as the true circumstances of the case are revealed, proving the
court system is not, as many like to think,
without flaw. The new villains, the ones not
being reported in any of the papers, are then
left stewing in their own guilt—as they had in
silence following the initial release, which
had made the local papers, as the cruel and
unusual punishment verdict was verified by
angels. Why is it there are so many of angelic
blood interested in you, Reed?"

With my leg protesting standing on it, I
sank to the ground, not caring how muddy I
got. I suspected the downed plane would
serve as a rain break as soon as someone verified the whole thing wouldn't go up in a big
ball of flame. "What's this? My file didn't reveal the secrets of the universe?"

Kennedy sat beside me and hugged her
knees to her chest. "You're human, so it's considered classified information. I have authorization to look, but I'd rather hear it from
you."

"I'm not quite a third human." The
thunder boomed while the lightning crashed,
shaking the ground with its fury, illuminating
the field and the plane in its blue-white glow.
I blinked the spots from my eyes and muttered a curse at its intensity. Then I chuckled

a bit at the absurdity of the situation, right down to having been in a plane crash the third time in my life I'd ever taken a flight anywhere. "If we were wise, we'd go find a ditch to chill out in until the storm passes."

"In the eyes of the law, you're still human." She hesitated a moment, reached over, and gave my sleeve a tug. "Why would you want to go hide in ditch?"

I pointed at the plane. "Tallest object. Lightning likes striking big objects made of metal. Science 101."

Cursing, Kennedy scrambled to her feet. "Reed, you asshole!"

"What? It's the truth."

"Does it look like there's a ditch anywhere near here?" she hissed.

I glanced in the direction of the other passengers, grateful the storm hid their eyes from mine—and that they couldn't hear us arguing over the storm. "I was mostly joking. You want to go hide in a ditch now, don't you?"

"In a word, yes. Getting hit by lightning or exploding plane shrapnel is not my idea of a good time."

"You've been watching disaster films, haven't you?"

"Reed."

Pleased at having nettled her, I took a good look around, sighed, and shook my head. "All right. Fine. There's probably a ditch edging the field somewhere; often is, but it's not my problem if it's flooding."

"I'd rather drown than be struck by lightning or sucked up in a tornado, spit out, and pulverized."

I thought of the churning clouds overhead and decided it probably wasn't a wise idea to tell her those kind of clouds could, at nature's whim, produce twisters. "What about the others?"

"They can find their own ditch if they want one."

I frowned, risking a glance in her direction. Facing the plane, her expression had turned sour, not from anger but likely fear. In the time I'd known her, I hadn't thought she feared anything. Then again, we'd both been born and bred in Mississippi, and when storms blew in from the sea, she was among the first to evacuate when the going got rough.

Now I knew why, and it amused a smile at me. Kennedy Young wasn't as invincible as I'd once thought, and that somehow made the whole absurd idea of being stuck with her a little easier to bear.

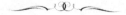

INSTEAD OF A DITCH, I found a gully, one

deep enough we'd have trouble getting out of it once we got in. I found a few trees, too, and I gave them a wide berth in case the sky took offense to their existence and blasted them apart with lightning.

"Maybe this was a dumb idea," Kennedy confessed, creeping a little closer to my side. No matter how many times I'd put a few feet of distance between us, she closed the distance as though afraid I'd get blown away in the next stiff breeze. The wind was more likely to knock me over than blow me away, but without any idea of where we were—or if we were in tornado country—I decided there was a bit of wisdom to sticking close together, especially with night falling.

Indiana wasn't a hotbed of tornado activity, although we saw a few days a year where nature had a hissy fit and decided the state needed a few to keep things lively. So instead of scooting away from her as I'd done the rest of our walk, I kept an eye on her.

Next time, I'd remember to keep my eyes on the ground, especially when near a gully. My foot slipped, I hit the mud hard, and slid down the slope to splash into stream below, yelping at the intimate introduction to every last rock on the way down. At half a foot deep, I wasn't at any real risk of drowning, which was a good thing. My duffel bag went down with me, and since I hadn't tenderized myself enough for its satisfaction, it hit me in the face.

"Reed!" My ex slid her way down on her heels, stumbling the last few steps before splashing to her knees beside me. "You all right?"

"How the hell can you do that in those shoes?" I demanded, pointing at the offensive heels, which by some miracle hadn't broke and were still on her feet. "What happened to wearing practical sneakers, anyway?"

"I was at a meeting when we got the call you'd been found. Didn't have time to change before I got on my flight. I've been told sneakers aren't acceptable business appropriate apparel." She shook her head. "Be serious. You all right?"

"I've had better days." I got my elbows beneath me and shoved upright, groaning as my back protested the motion. "I'm pretty sure this isn't what the doctor ordered."

"Plane crashes and subsequent falls into ditches typically aren't."

"I'd call this more of a gully or a ravine."

"Same difference."

Instead of arguing with her, I got to my feet, dripping rain and mud. I retrieved my bag, glad all of my medications had come in sealed bottles; unless my luck turned really sour, they wouldn't be ruined. "Let's find a place to wait this out. Ideally, we'll find a spot with some coverage about halfway up."

I pointed at the slope. I'd fallen at least twenty feet, although I considered myself fortunate. The flashes of lightning exposed other sections of the ravine with a lot more rocks. If the area was anything like Gypsum Creek, the looser soil would be at risk of crashing down in a mudslide.

"Flash floods," Kennedy muttered. "We've landed in hell."

"I always thought hell would be a lot dryer, truth be told." I held my hand out and cast a doubtful look at the stormy sky. "Leaving the crash site was probably stupid."

"Probably?" Grumbling curses, Kennedy trudged out of the water and followed the shore, examining the slope. "I should have thought that through better. What am I looking for?"

"Rock outcropping should do, with a bit of space beneath it. Enough to keep the rain off—and hail."

"Hail?" Kennedy squeaked, whirling to face me.

I focused on her chest, which was a mistake. The rain plastered her blouse to her, and in glow of the frequent lightning strikes, I got a good look right through the white material at the lacy bra beneath. I shifted my gaze to her shoulder, which was still covered by her blazer jacket. "Happens during bad storms sometimes."

"You're serious."

Since I couldn't quite seem to stop sneaking peeks at her chest, I turned so I wouldn't look at her at all, limping out of the stream to help search for a suitable spot to camp out until the storm passed. "Yeah, I'm serious. Hail's nasty, and I'd rather not get hit in the head with it."

"Isn't hail just like hard snow? It's just ice pellets, right?"

I decided against telling her hail liked showing up right before a tornado spawned and made a circle with my thumb and finger. "Sure. In a bad blow, they can get this big—or bigger."

"Holy shit." Kennedy shook her head. "Nope. I refuse to believe in golf ball sized hail."

My laugh escaped before I stopped it. "You're really scared of storms, aren't you?"

In true Kennedy fashion, the woman stooped down, grabbed a handful of mud, and flung it at me.

EIGHT

Rain isn't supposed to plop.

THE OUTCROPPING KENNEDY found was a recipe for disaster. While it met all of my criteria, one problem stared me in the face. While it would offer a certain amount of shelter from the rain and wind, if we both wanted to benefit from it, we'd have to get close and personal to fit. After three years of whoring myself out to any woman who wanted a fling, I didn't think too much about naked women.

Kennedy in her soaked business attire reminded me just how beautiful a woman she was, something I had worked hard to forget. Huddling with her in such close quarters meant trouble for me—a lot of it. A panic attack I could deal with—I didn't like them, but I knew what to expect.

The shelter, such as it was, represented a lot of uncharted waters.

I glared at the sky and its roiling, spinning

clouds before trudging my way up the slope. Large rocks offered handholds and better footing than I expected.

Kennedy ducked into the opening, making a pleased sound. "It's pretty dry under here. Will this do?"

I cursed under my breath and took a closer look at the spot, which was a bit larger than I had initially thought. While we'd have to get a bit cozier with each other than I liked, we wouldn't be crawling all over each other to fit. "It'll do," I confirmed, sliding inside. With a little work, we could even stretch out while waiting for the storm to go by. The angle of the stone kept most of the wind and rain out, too.

Settling into my half of the niche, I closed my eyes and practiced breathing. Pretending Kennedy wasn't there wouldn't help for long. She would open her mouth soon enough and remind me of her presence. All I had to do was avoid looking at her until her blouse dried off.

Remembering how attractive I found her hadn't factored into any of my plans and did a disgustingly good job of short circuiting my anger. I had more reasons than I could readily count to be angry and hurt. Yet one little thunderstorm, a little rain, and a white top undermined me in far too many ways.

"Reed?"

Under no circumstances would I indulge in any form of temptation with my ex. I kept telling myself that until I almost believed it. I couldn't even blame the plane crash, adrenaline, and the excuse that such things often happened in life or death situations. "What?"

"Rain isn't supposed to plop," she whispered.

I listened, and sure enough, instead of the patter and splashes of heavy rainfall, in the lulls between the thunder, something hard smacked into wet, thick mud. I cracked open an eye, leaned forward, and peered down. Sure enough, chunks of hail hammered the ground. "And that would be the hail."

Hail hurt, and I grimaced at the thought of anyone caught out under it. At least the other passengers, if wise, would take shelter beneath the plane. The plops intensified to a drumming so intense the ground shook from the barrage.

Kennedy pressed close to me, and when she leaned forward for a better look, I slapped my arm against her shoulders and shoved her back. "Not a good idea."

"Okay. Why not?'

"Don't stick your head out from the cover of the rock if you're going to watch." I showed her, leaning forward as much as I dared without being at risk of being clunked in the head with a hail ball. "One of the larger ones can punch a hole through a windshield."

"Holy shit." Kennedy scrambled back. "Curiosity is sated. Why is it hailing?"

"I'm not sure I should answer that question."

"Reed, why is it hailing?"

"Do you still watch those disaster films you like so much?"

"Maybe."

I interpreted that to mean yes. "Do the math."

She was silent for a long moment, then she cursed me, starting tame and working her way through every profanity in English, and when she started rambling nonsense, I rubbed my temples. A headache brewed from a blend of the storm's incessant thunder and her foul mouth, although I cracked a smile at her suggestion of where she'd shove a unicorn's horn if given half a chance.

All grinning did was encourage her.

"Forget the horn, I'll shove the whole damned thing up your smug ass, Reed Hampton Matthews!"

Game over—or on, depending how I looked at it. An entirely unwilling laugh burst out of me. "You're really scared of thunderstorms."

"This is not a thunderstorm. It's a natural

disaster. One where we get sucked up into a tornado, spit out, ground to paste, and killed."

"Tenderized by hail first."

"Your file lied to me. It claims you have no sense of humor, avoid other humans, and otherwise lay low, with a notation you might spend the weekends away from home. I'm not sure about that, since no one can figure out where your home is. That was something your co-workers said, that you sometimes mentioned you spent the weekends out. No one knows much, though."

I was starting to dislike the frequent mentions of my file, in part because there never seemed to be anything positive about me in it. "I have a sense of humor."

"Really, Reed?" Kennedy snorted. "You used to find things amusing, you used to laugh regularly enough, but you've never really had a defined sense of humor."

"I deliberately gave someone I didn't like my kitten along with instructions on how to feed her. I planned this so the kitten would grace the other end of the office with her rather potent stench. I think that's evidence I have a sense of humor."

"What *did* that poor woman ever do to you anyway? When I saw her, she was puking into a trash can. And yes, I met your kitten, and yes, she truly smells *that* awful."

"She was pissy I wasn't cherry picking the

good contracts for her." I shrugged. "Office politics. She wants to look good for my boss's boss's boss, who is the CEO. That means performing well in her cell group, which I manage. Since office pranks are frowned upon, I had to get creative. When I discovered my kitten truly wanted to destroy the world through her litter box use, I thought my kitten-loving boss would like meeting her. Then opportunity knocked because Dani liked my kitten. She looked so interested in my kitten. I was just giving her what she wanted."

"I never thought you'd end up in management in any form. I always thought you'd be crunching numbers in analytics."

"My doctors thought it'd be good for me to work in negotiations, as it forced me to interact with people."

"They said solitary confinement had been hard on you."

I closed my eyes, leaned back against the rock, and sighed. I assumed she meant my doctors, but I wasn't certain. "Who, exactly, is they?"

"The CDC; their file on you is a bit more complete than the FBI's, which essentially informed us you were an angel with a bad case of misfortune. Some of your information is sealed, mostly relating to your specific genetics. The CDC's file is related to your release and the corrections to your criminal record—

which has been overturned and classified as a case of accidental death, in case you were curious."

Kennedy watched me, and I was careful to avoid meeting her gaze. "Perhaps a better question is why the CDC gave you, my ex, that information."

"I was specifically requested because of our relationship. Since you were refusing to acknowledge any communications, official or otherwise, stamped from Mississippi, the CDC requested individuals who had known you prior to your incarceration. Long story short, I was called in and asked to review your file. I was actually in Indiana investigating a different matter in the same company, but since you aren't entirely human, you fell under my jurisdiction." She sighed. "Did you really hide under your boss's desk to avoid me?"

Damn it. I should have known she had found out about that. "It was either that or have a panic attack and pass out on his floor."

My doctors would have been proud of me for how readily I acknowledged the truth. Maybe my limited success with therapy had actually been a lot less limited than I believed.

"I had assumed it would be awkward, not that you'd be terrified of me."

"I got over that part pretty quick and graduated to pissed, so don't worry about it."

"I noticed you were cranky for a while there, especially in the hospital." Kennedy crept closer to the edge of our hiding spot. "Reed?"

"What?"

"What's that noise?"

Noise? I joined her, careful to keep my head beneath the safety of the protruding rock. I'd ignored the hail pummeling the ground, but when I stopped to listen again, I realized it had tapered off. The thunder rumbled, softened, and even the rain eased.

The clouds growled, deceptive in its low tone—not thunder. Thunder rolled, rumbled, crashed, and cracked, comforting in its irregularities. The constant tone grew stronger with every passing moment. I sucked in a breath, retreated, and grabbed Kennedy's arm, pulling her with me. "That's not a good sound."

"Reed? Don't tell me that's what I think it is."

Oh good. I wouldn't have to tell her. I could just go straight to a brand new sort of panic attack, the type where I potentially looked right down death's throat. "What sounds like a train and really sucks?"

"Your ability to tell bad jokes at the worst time possible."

"I was more going for tornado, but I suppose that works, too."

"I don't believe in huge chunks of hail, and I don't believe in tornadoes, either." Kennedy crammed herself as far back as she could, rubbing her arms. "You're really cursed, aren't you? First you're in a car wreck, then you're kidnapped, dragged halfway across the country, and then on the way home, the plane crashes—which you sleep through!—and here we are, about to get mulched by a tornado."

Reaching out of the safety of the rock, I snatched a piece of hail, which was closer in size to a baseball than a golf ball. "This is hail. Allow me to present this as evidence. It is hard, it is really cold, and it is made of ice. It also fell from the sky."

To make sure she got the point, I touched it to her ankle. She kicked, and her shoe went flying, bouncing off the stone to fall into the water below. "Damn it, Reed!"

"I'm not fetching your shoe." Just to make sure she really knew it was ice, I touched her with it again. "Hail is ice. See? Cold." I tapped the hail to her ankle several more times. "It's hail, Kennedy. Claiming you don't believe in it doesn't change scientific fact. Hail is real. Large hail, like this piece, is also real." Since I had taken leave of my senses anyway, I slid the piece of ice up her slacks, running it along the curve of her calf.

Kennedy kicked the shit out of me with her bare foot while I laughed.

SOMETIMES I TOOK the whole serenity in the face of things I couldn't change thing a little too far. I couldn't change tornados, but I sure as hell could pretend I wasn't listening to one outside, the wind screaming and drowning out even the thunder. Using Kennedy as an outlet made me the villain of the hour, but she held part of the blame, too.

Most people took the gloves off to fight, but she kicked her second shoe off, launching it out to join the first, and pummeled me with her feet while I wielded a chunk of wet ice. She squealed loudest whenever I got near her toes.

I'd forgotten how ticklish her feet were, and ice seemed to make her reaction so much worse.

"The instant I get my hands on you, you're a dead man, Reed!"

Unfortunately for her, I remembered her feet weren't half as ticklish as her ribs, and it took a single swipe of my fingers along her side to earn a scream. When she did get her hands on me, she probably would try her best to kill me, and I'd deserve it. With grim determination, I freed my hand by doing the worst thing I could think of.

I dropped the piece of hail down her blouse, aiming for where an opened button exposed hint of her cleavage. While she shrieked, flailed, and went fishing for the piece of ice, I stroked my hands down her sides until she laughed so hard she could only writhe, squirming to evade me.

It would have been a lot easier to secure my victory if I'd stop laughing. Laughing made it hard to catch my breath, which turned holding her down a challenge—a challenge she wasn't going to lose without putting up a fight. An uncontrolled kick of her leg and a knee to my gut turned the tables.

She hadn't forgotten I had a ticklish spot, too, and she clawed the back of my knee.

I banged the back of my head into the rock and yelped.

"Shit. Reed?"

At least I hadn't smacked my nose. Broken noses hurt like hell. "I'm fine."

Digging the hail out of her shirt, she flung it at me. "You asshole!"

Even at short range on a soft toss, ice to the face hurt. I yelped again, clapping my hands to my nose. It hurt, but I doubted she'd broken it—broken noses tended to drop me to the floor almost as often as panic attacks did. I needed to do something about that, although I could argue I was by going to my therapy appointments as scheduled. "For something that doesn't exist because you don't believe in it, hail to the face hurts."

"I meant to hit your shoulder."

"Point bank range and you miss? Your aim sucks. Please tell me you don't carry a gun."

"Normally yes, but I don't have a carry permit for Indiana, so I'm unarmed."

The wind's screaming settled to the roar of a train, continuous and drawing closer, close enough I was about ready to jump out of my skin—or be tempted into taking a look out and up. I'd never been outside during a tornado before. The rare times one came close to Gypsum Creek, I waited in my worn little house and hoped the thing wouldn't blow down around my ears.

She was wrong about my sense of humor. I had one, it was just depressingly morbid and liked to show up at the worst times.

If I kept distracting her, maybe she wouldn't really appreciate the sound wasn't thunder despite sharing certain similarities. Thunder couldn't chew up houses and spit them out as late-night snacks. "They don't need to give you a gun. All they need to do is hand you some ice. You'll be the most dangerous woman in the state."

"Reed!"

I made a show of rubbing my nose. "At least you didn't break it. I hate breaking my nose."

"Because you faint worse than a girl."

The woman had the mind of a steel trap, and once something went in, it didn't leave. I grunted, acknowledged defeat with a nod, and retreated to my side of the niche. "It's a bit of an inconvenience."

"A bit? I could flick your nose and…"

I really didn't like the way her voice trailed off. It meant she was thinking, and once she started thinking, she started making trouble for someone. I tensed, jerked in her direction, and almost forgot to avoid looking her in the eyes. I lowered my gaze to her chin, which drew my attention to her mouth.

In the flashes of lightning, I saw her smile.

"Reed." She breathed my name, and not even the storm could drown out the sound. "I'm really bad at this."

Huh? "Bad at what?"

Her waved hand took in me, our hiding place, and the storm all in one smooth motion. "This. All of this. I was supposed to start off with apologizing, then I was supposed to do some groveling. On my knees. I almost wore a skirt, too. Then after I was done groveling, I was supposed to do something else, but I got stuck on the first part and forgot. I had a list, but I left it in Indiana."

Once again, I recognized the precursor rambling of an anxiety attack taking root, especially considering someone with as good a memory as hers started forgetting things like one of her lists. "Deep breaths through your nose and count them."

Even I could be useful for something sometimes—and despite what my doctors thought, I *did* pay attention during the sessions, even though it was a lot easier to think about taking action than actually doing it.

I was my own worst enemy.

Kennedy hiccupped. "There's a tornado about to suck us up and spit us out and you're telling me to breathe through my nose."

"I'm sure any tornados in the area will—"

A bang and flash of light caught my eye, and from the other side of the ravine, a blossoming ball of fire illuminated the night and shook the ground. The screaming wind stilled, and in the lull, metal rained down, thumping and splashing into the mud below. My mouth dropped open, and I crawled to the ledge.

Kennedy joined me, and she covered her mouth with her hands. "Was that the plane?"

I couldn't imagine what else could be so large it shook the ground and exploded in a fiery ball of death, doom, and destruction. "Hey, Kennedy?"

"What?"

"That whole thing about hiding in a ditch?"

"What about it?"

"Good idea." I followed my own advice and breathed through my nose. "I think that was the plane."

"I'm pretty sure we left the plane at least a quarter mile away, Reed."

"That's one way to put it."

"I'm never watching a disaster movie ever again," she whispered.

I laughed, shaking my head. Her, stop watching those flicks? Hell truly would freeze over first. "Don't make promises you can't keep. Next time you watch one, you'll just modify your running commentary on the fallacies of the film to account for new information. It seems tornados can, in fact, pick up 747s and fling them a quarter mile."

"And that hiding in a ditch actually works."

The stream below reflected the smoldering wreckage and lightning. "I think if we'd been in the ditch without cover, we'd be dead right now, Kennedy." I pointed at the wreckage littering the ground. "See?"

"Ditch with cover," she amended.

Kennedy's phone rang, and she spat a curse, digging it out of her pocket. "What the hell? I have reception?" She swiped her hand across the screen. "Young."

To give her the illusion of privacy, I slid closer to the ledge, keeping an eye on the sky in case it decided to fling more hail in our direction. Its plane-tossing hissy fit seemed to have calmed the storm, settling it to the occasional thunder, lightning, and light drizzle. I was aware of her talking on the phone, but I ignored the conversation.

A slender hand snagged my collar and yanked me back. "Here, talk to Mr. Matthews. He can explain."

The next instant, her phone was in my hands and she was shoving it in the general direction of my ear. "Uh, hello?"

"Mr. Matthews," a man greeted. "I'm Gordon Liehosen. Agent Young tells me you can explain what is going on?"

Kennedy pointed at the plane in a frantic motion.

"The plane crashed. When the weather worsened, I suggested we might go to lower ground, as an open field makes a very bad place to stand when there's a lot of lightning —especially by a downed plane full of jet fuel. We found a nice spot to take shelter in a ravine. Unfortunately, a tornado seems to have picked the plane up and relocated it rather violently."

Kennedy made a strangled noise in her throat.

"Agent Young seems to be having some issues accepting the violent relocation of our plane, Mr. Liehosen. I can recommend a good therapist or two in Indiana."

I deserved to be smacked, but I wished she hadn't hit the back of my head, which had already suffered a close introduction with a rock.

"Where are you?"

"Uncomfortably close to where the tornado relocated the plane, which is about a quarter mile or so from where we'd left it." I tried not to think too hard about the other passengers—and hoped they had either gotten away or never realized what had hit them.

"Please ask Agent Young to send your coordinates to arrange for search and rescue, Mr. Matthews."

"Can I make a request?"

"What?"

"No more planes." I offered the phone back to Kennedy. "He's asking about coordinates for search and rescue."

Kennedy took the phone, put it to her ear, and made an annoyed sound, turning the screen to show the call had ended. "Sorry about that. He wanted to make sure you were actually still alive."

"What, were you planning on killing me and leaving my body in a ditch?"

I really needed to learn not to provoke a woman. It was bad for my health.

NINE

Pointy death traps.

THE STORM BLEW itself out long before search and rescue arrived, and I regretted going along with Kennedy's idea to check out the wreckage for survivors. With the departure of the heavy rain, thunder, and lightning, she transformed into a cold, detached, and practical professional determined to do her job.

Since I wasn't really sure what her job actually was, I cooperated without comment. Her fetish with disaster films probably had something to do with her expectation of a lot of bodies. Nature cared nothing for humans. If anything, I suspected the planet we called home would've been happy if our entire species kicked the bucket, since we often did far more harm than good. It took over twenty minutes to find a way out of the ravine, a hike Kennedy made in her bare feet since she refused to look for her shoes.

"Death traps," she muttered when she thought I couldn't hear her. "Pointy death traps."

Reevaluating my initial verdict of cold, detached, and practical professional to cold, grumpy, and practical, I kept quiet and decided to admire the view, since she insisted on going up the slope first while cursing about men with more stitches than sense. Since I resembled her remark, I went with what she wanted.

The path of least resistance would keep me out of trouble for a while, or at least buy me enough time to figure out how my life had been turned completely upside down, rather like the jet. It took me several tries to reach the top, and I needed Kennedy's help to scramble over the ledge without sliding down to the bottom yet again.

Parts of the plane still burned, but the rain kept the flames from spreading while offering enough light to make out the destruction. The trees skirting the top of the ravine had been reduced to mulch, and the ground hadn't fared much better.

"Where's the rest of the plane?" Kennedy crossed her arms over her chest, shifting her weight from foot to foot.

"Would you like my shoes?"

"No. Unlike you, I'm healthy and unhurt. Cold feet won't kill me. They could kill you."

"I would like to point out they're soaked, mud got into them, and they squish when I walk. It's a bit late for worrying about cold feet."

"Reed, keep your damned shoes on."

I held up my hands in surrender. "I just don't want you to cut your feet."

"I'll get a tetanus shot after search and rescue gets here. No big deal. A few scratches are nothing compared to getting shot, and I've done that a few times. My recommendation: don't."

"You've been shot?" Maybe I had a bucketful of reasons to be angry at her, maybe I still wasn't sure what I thought about spending any length of time with her, but I didn't want her hurt. I'd done enough hurting for both of us, although very little of it physical. Then again, my panic attacks got physical enough.

"Several times. As a bit of free advice, never get shot in the ass."

Hold on. Ass? Someone had shot Kennedy in the ass? Given the choice between dealing with a tornado-tossed plane or coming to terms with someone shooting my ex in the ass, I went with the plane. I could understand planes. When they weren't tossed out of the sky, they flew rather reliably. Most didn't end up the chew toy of a twister, but that was hardly the plane's fault.

Instead of replying, I walked around the wreckage, coming to the conclusion she'd been right about only part of the plane having made it to us. Where *was* the rest of the plane? I shoved my hands into my pockets and glared at the ruins, which I determined to be everything behind the wings.

On my second walk around, I headed in the direction of the field, crested the small hill, and found the rest of the plane. It had dive bombed, sticking straight out of the ground, one wing broken off while the other was mostly intact. The cabin—what was left of it—smoldered like a burned-out torch.

"I suppose I should be grateful the storm waited until after we had landed before doing that to the plane." Kennedy stepped to my side, and she ran her hands through her hair. "I haven't found any bodies. Have you?"

I shivered. I'd seen exactly one body in my adult life, and I had killed him. My quota for bodies had been filled for the rest of my life. "No."

"Shit. I take that back." Kennedy pointed.

Stupid fool that I was, I looked.

Thanks to Kennedy's love affair with disaster films, I'd done more than my fair share of research verifying if the nonsense she spouted during her commentary of them had any truth to it whatsoever. During a bad blow, twisters flung anything in its path every

which way with no care of what—or who—it
damaged.

Under no natural circumstances would a
tornado leave the bodies of its victims piled
together, easy to find without being tangled
in any wreckage. Distracted by the plane, I
hadn't looked to the sides, and when lightning turned night to day, I struggled to believe there could be so many of them.

I spun, slipped in the mud, and landed on
my ass.

"Reed?"

"I think you were right about the bodies."
The breathlessness of my voice coupled with
the tightness in my chest warned me the
worst was still to come. I knew I needed to
breathe, but I floundered, stuck on my brief
glimpse of the dead. A twisted little part of
me suggested they could still be dying.

Every rare now and then, someone got
flung by a twister and ended up in a tree,
alive to tell the tale. Miracles happened in a
world angels and demons visited, where humans toyed with the laws of physics with
magic because they could without any real
care if they should.

Scalding hands cupped my face, and
Kennedy crouched in front of me. "Reed."

My name, her lips, her presence far too
close for my comfort, and too many bodies to
count spelled another utter disaster. I

promptly forgot everything anyone had ever tried to teach me about conquering panic attacks, all so I wouldn't do something embarrassing and potentially dangerous, which included faint in my ex's arms.

I was out long enough for search and rescue to arrive, although they hadn't quite managed to excavate me from Kennedy's grip. Blinking, I walked my way through how I'd gone from conscious to slumped against her, my head pillowed against a rather soft and pleasant place my head had no business being.

A helpful paramedic ruined my enjoyment of my situation, flashing a bright light in my eyes. Someone must have taught all doctor types the same post-collapse script, as the questions the guy shot at me seemed awfully similar to the ones in Indiana. I even managed to answer most of them, although I derailed at the questions regarding where I was.

'Kennedy's breasts' wasn't the answer the paramedic or my ex wanted. Somehow, I survived through the next few minutes of my life, although my right ear would never be the same again.

"I think he's fine," Kennedy grumbled, her fingers still locked on my earlobe. She leaned towards me and hissed, "If I find out you did that on purpose to get near my breasts, you will live to regret it. I will haunt your doorstep for years and ensure you suffer."

Was that a threat, a promise, or both? If it was a threat, I wondered how effective it would be. She hadn't even been able to find my house. With some careful planning, I could become a hermit, emerging only when I needed some groceries. If it was a promise, I couldn't imagine what the hell she thought she was doing.

Then again, I had a serious case of mixed signals. My head wanted to make an immediate escape to safety, preferably somewhere quiet, dark, and devoid of women for the rest of eternity. My body wanted somewhere private with a woman, a rather specific one I shouldn't have any involvement with whatsoever, and spend the rest of eternity discovering if physical therapy might do me a great deal of good.

I was even willing to bet it wouldn't take me long to remember what she liked.

"It wasn't on purpose," I mumbled, tilting my head to ease the pressure on my ear. "I'm sorry."

Kennedy sighed. "I'm the one who should be sorry. I didn't check the weather before the flight, then it was my stupid idea to have a look around. I didn't think we'd actually find any bodies."

"If you can walk, Mr. Matthews, the ambulance is over there." The paramedic pointed. "If you're otherwise uninjured, take yourself to it."

"I'm fine." I probably lied. I never was fine after a collapse. I wobbled, and I often wobbled my way right back to the floor unless I took a lot of care. At least I'd dodged a secondary attack—assuming I avoided another look at any bodies. To prove I wasn't a complete liar, I lurched to my feet. Kennedy helped, and I sighed my relief she stopped torturing my ear in the progress. "An ambulance—"

"Is necessary," Kennedy snapped.

"You've gotten bossy," I muttered. While she'd always been a bit prickly, especially when it came to certain things, the years had sharpened her edge.

Underneath the dread, the fear, and the resentment I'd harbored was a masochist, as I had no other explanation as to why I hadn't run for the hills, pleaded for mercy, or responded with the flight instinct sane men displayed when in the presence of a woman too much to handle.

"Shut up and walk, Reed. Watch your feet, and for fuck's sake, don't look to your left. I should have known that would be a problem. My stupid fault."

"To be fair, I had no idea that would happen either." If she couldn't handle my inability to handle certain things—including her presence—she'd have a lot more trouble in the future if she stuck around. "At least this time I didn't go straight into the next one. That's improvement."

Two years ago, it had been a guarantee. The realization gave me something most of my therapy appointments didn't: hope.

In a strange way, I had Kennedy to thank for that. If I could handle the onslaught of emotions being near her caused, from the highs of inappropriate desire to the lows of loathing and regret, I could recover from the rest, too. Just like my doctors wanted, I could be me again.

That thought alone consumed me all the way to the ambulance, Kennedy at my side every step of the way.

I PROTESTED the necessity of going back to yet another damned hospital my insurance company refused to pay for. Apparently, Kennedy had retrieved my card from the trash, which resulted in a brief but volatile argument. She won.

The card ended up back in my wallet, I lost three thousand dollars to the ambulance, another two to the ER, and ended up with a serious case of grumpy. Instead of taking out my irritation on the nearest trash can, I tested the effectiveness of breathing exercises on my rage. It didn't help all that much.

"You may have been correct on the usefulness of your card outside of Indiana," Kennedy conceded.

"I'm going home and becoming a hermit. No one is invited except for Kitten, Destroyer of Worlds."

"I still can't believe you named your kitten that."

"That's what cats do. They plan to take over the world, and once they have done so, they destroy it for it's no longer interesting for them."

"I'm concerned for your kitten's safety."

"You're joking, right? That little demon is going to cost me at least eighty bucks a month to feed. No one told me kittens cost a fortune when I rescued her off my car. By the end of the weekend, she made it perfectly clear who owned my house. Hint: it's not me." I sighed, shoved my wallet in my pocket, and gritted my teeth through the remainder of the paperwork. "An angel better be able to take care of a kitten."

"Or what?"

"I'm going to pluck Luna's feathers." I indulged in some serious pen clicking. "All right, Miss FBI or CDC Agent, or whatever the heck you are. Why the hell would someone grab me from a car accident, stitch me up, cart me to Mississippi, and dump me in an abandoned farmhouse plagued with such incidents? Although from my under-standing, the other 'guests' were at least from the same state. Until me. Aren't I lucky?"

"You're rather sarcastic when you're pissy."

I clicked the pen some more. It didn't help. "I have several thousand reasons to be pissy."

"I'll look over your policy in Indiana and see what loopholes are present. That's one benefit of working with the CDC. If you're lucky, you'll be able to get reimbursed for most if not all of it. Government mandated hospital visits are usually covered, they just try to worm their way out of it with a bogus clause. Give me ten minutes, a few forms, and your policy. I should be able to sort it out."

I risked a glance in her direction, but she was focused on her phone. "I'm going to take you up on that. I'm still not showing you where I live, though. If you want to know, you'll have to figure it out on your own."

"You're a person of interest now, Reed. You're going to end up with a babysitter until we figure out who wants you—and why."

"Luna knows something. Go demand an-swers from her."

"You try bossing an angel around. Let me know how that works for you."

"There's a trio of them who enjoy bothering me at work. It's very frustrating." I shrugged, signed the last of the papers, and stood so I could hunt down a nurse and finalize my escape. "I refuse to fly, so if you're booking something on that phone of yours, it better not involve a plane. I may not look like much, but I can still run a fast mile, and unlike you, I have shoes."

Kennedy stretched out her legs and wiggled her toes, which were still dirty. She'd made a point of wiping her soles so she wouldn't track foot prints all over the hospital, but she hadn't bothered with the rest of her feet, her ankles, or anywhere else for that matter, including her face.

I pointed at her. "You have mud streaked across your nose."

"That's nice. Is it a good color on me?"

"It's mud."

"Look into a mirror sometime soon before you talk too much about my face, Reed."

Heading for the door, I waved the clipboard in dismissal. "And here I thought you would have been happy to discover I don't need to preen in front of a mirror to know I'm pretty. Even when muddy." The crash must have rattled my brain in my skull, since my mouth decided it no longer cared to be restrained by common sense. If I was going to flirt with death, at least I'd earn my beating. "But you always did like your pretty men dirty."

"Damn it, Reed!"

I chuckled and hunted down a nurse.

TEN

I'd rather not have to drag you in
there by your ear.

TEN MINUTES after leaving the hospital, I discovered what Kennedy had been up to on her phone. I scowled at the posh hotel, the exact sort of place I never would have dreamed of visiting while covered in mud and blood. Crossing my arms over my chest, I regarded the glass-fronted building with marble lobby with narrowed eyes.

"The room has a super fancy jet tub with built in heaters and everything, so we can soak all we want without the water getting cold. It also has a really large shower. Don't be a wuss. I warned the hotel we were involved in a plane crash and there would be mud. My boss sent clothes for us, too. That's the nice thing about being a liaison. They take clothes seriously. It looks really bad for both organizations if I look like I just finished attending my own murder."

"Or mine," I muttered.

"March, Reed. I'd rather not have to drag you in there by your ear. If you delay me from taking a shower, I will."

"My wallet doesn't thank you for this."

"My boss is reimbursing me for the entire bill, including room service. Of course, that's on the condition you share a room with me, but I thought you'd prefer that to paying the nightly rate here." Without waiting to see if I followed, Kennedy headed for the doors.

Once upon a time, I had lived with Kennedy, upgrading from an on-campus dorm room to an apartment in our last year of school. Sharing a hotel room made sense. It kept costs down and coordination simple. Everything else about the situation, however, spelled trouble.

It took me until she reached the front doors to force my feet into motion. I'd survived a plane crash and a tornado with her. A hotel room was nothing compared to that. I'd take one bed, she'd take the other, and I would spend a sleepless night pretending beds didn't exist so I wouldn't splash in the gutter designated for perverts and think too hard about a lot of things better off forgotten.

There would be no fraternizing with my ex in a posh hotel room.

I kept on telling myself that while Kennedy handled checking in. The hotel em-

No Kitten Around   137

ployees didn't even flinch at our appearance, which impressed me a lot since I sure as hell grimaced when I caught my reflection in the polished marble. We both needed a shower. Within ten minutes, we were on our way up to the fourth floor, shedding dirt every step of the way.

In the elevator, I did my best to avoid touching anything to limit the amount of cleaning the staff would need to do. "Hey, Kennedy?"

"What?"

"If you need a model for domestic violence, I'm probably a good candidate right now. How's the camera on that phone of yours? You could make a decent dime to the right buyer."

She snorted. "No, Reed. While accurate, I'm not photographing you while you look like you were run through the wringer."

"But you wouldn't have to use makeup. You know how much I hate makeup."

"And the camera, lights, posturing, and everything else to do with someone taking your picture."

"Well, yes. The cameras are terrible to me. They add at least ten pounds, straight to my hips." I averted my gaze in time to avoid meeting her glare, although I caught a glimpse of her scowl in the elevator's mirrors. "What? Are women the only ones allowed to complain about the extra camera pounds?"

"Everyone I spoke to has pretty much agreed you completely lack an ego, are unaware you're model material, and do very little to draw attention to yourself. You get an attitude when someone screws up your perfect little work world, but otherwise, you're quiet and reclusive."

"A few people keep telling me things like that."

The elevator dinged and the door slid open. Kennedy stepped out, planted her hands on her hips, and frowned at me over her shoulder. "Those would be your therapists, of which you have several, not that they've been able to make much progress with you, as you're incredibly stubborn. We had a lovely discussion regarding your stubborn streak, Mr. Matthews."

I needed to find whomever had thought it a good idea to send my ex poking her nose into my personal business. Once I found them, I would begin with subjecting them to Kitten, Destroyer of Worlds. I'd make up the rest as I went, but I would get satisfaction somehow. "How lovely. The insights your presence must have given them will haunt me for years, I'm sure."

"They were intrigued to learn about some of the details you hadn't bothered telling them, yes. They're confident your sessions will be more productive in the future. One even asked if I would attend a few. I may have agreed dependent on your willingness and authorization from the CDC. Unfortunately for you, they already have authorization from the CDC. They'll discuss the matter with you soon, I'm sure."

The thought of Kennedy attending one of my therapy sessions stopped me dead in my tracks, halfway out the elevator. As though sensing I was either incapable or unwilling to take the next step, she turned, grabbed the front of my shirt, and pulled me forward. I squawked at the collar digging into my throat and strangling me. "Do your deer in the head-lights impression in our room. It's more con-venient to deal with if I can just drag your ass into the shower and blast you with cold water to get you to snap out of it."

Instead of waiting for an answer, she hauled me down the hall to our room, pausing long enough to unlock the door. To keep her from relocating me through force, I stepped inside, flicking the glowing switch to turn on the lights.

The spacious room contained a king-sized bed.

It was going to be very, very difficult for me to forget beds existed, especially if Kennedy still had the habit of stealing heat from those sharing sleeping space with her. Once she locked onto a living furnace, she fought to keep her heat source close at hand.

It was going to be a long night.

Kennedy squeezed by me, closing the door behind her. "I had the choice between two rooms, no jet tub, or a big bed and jet tub. I thought you'd be able to live with a big bed and a nice tub. Go shower. I have to take care of some work first."

A cold shower might save me from myself and my overactive imagination, one quite eager and willing to provide suggestions on the things I could do with a woman on a bed that nice. That the woman happened to be Kennedy threw me for a loop so intense I stood frozen, eyes wide while I held my breath.

Not only would I have a cold shower, I would take the time to remind myself why any interest in Kennedy in any fashion was a terrible idea. I closed the bathroom door behind me, exhaled, and stripped, tossing my wallet on the vanity and stuffing the rest in the garbage. With so much blood and tears, I wouldn't even make the attempt to salvage my clothes.

Clothes could be replaced. I'd just have to hope Kennedy had actually made arrangements like she'd said, else I'd be running around wearing a towel, which would make things even more awkward. Unless things had changed, I'd have to keep a close eye on her, as she'd help my towel have an accident so she could admire the scenery.

Unless something had changed, Kennedy enjoyed a good look at a pretty man as much as I liked admiring a beautiful woman, although I had never 'tripped' so I could pull off her towel. It'd become a game—me trying to keep my towel where it belonged while she did her best to steal it. When I lost I won, and when I won I lost, so it was always in my interest to lose whenever possible.

It took a lot more work than I liked to rid myself of the mud and dried blood, and the effort left me exhausted. I contemplated the tub, my aching muscles begging for relief. The rest of me just wanted to flop somewhere, close my eyes, and forget about life for a while.

Maybe I could manage both. The sloped side of the tub made a perfect spot to lounge and nap without drowning. With a little bit of soap, I wouldn't have anything to worry about if Kennedy decided to invade and take her shower. If I took too long, she would.

That she hadn't already impressed me.

Screw it. I'd take the risk. After everything that happened, I needed a chance to relax.

THE BLARE of an alarm ruined my nap, and once I got my hands on Kennedy's phone, I was seriously tempted to smash the damned thing. Cracking open an eye, I glared in the direction of the noise.

Kennedy sat on the edge of the tub, and she wasn't wearing a thing. "I had time to shower, confirm the tub is big enough for two, and that the water does stay heated. You slept through it. I could have done whatever I wanted to you, and you wouldn't have noticed a thing. Not that I would, but you get my point."

I did. She also reminded me that women were tricky. I wiped my hand over my face, mumbling a curse over how much she unsettled me.

She never failed to steal my breath, and not even the circumstances of our separation could undermine those memories.

"That alarm is awful," I grumbled, stretching out and letting the jets work their magic on me. "Please turn it off."

"Hasn't anyone told you it's not wise to sleep in a tub? You could've drowned." Kennedy shot a stern glance at me but turned the alarm off, rising and setting her phone on the vanity, safely out of the way. When her back was turned to me, I admired her.

Years ago, she'd been slender enough, but she had refined herself to the smooth curves of a fit woman combined with the hint of muscle warning me not to underestimate her. I'd stayed slim, but I'd abandoned traditional workouts, doing chores to stay somewhat fit.

"Sorry I delayed your shower."

"I knocked about five minutes after the tub stopped filling. You didn't answer, so I checked in. When I saw you were down and out for the count, I invited myself in and showered. Since you slept through my shower concerto, I decided to enjoy myself in the tub. Then you slept through that, so I got out and fetched my phone. The bed's more comfortable."

I draped my arm over my eyes. "Is there any reason you're naked?"

"Ex sex. I've been told it's spectacular, so I want to find out. We've had a bad day. Let's end it on a completely inappropriate but nice note. No one said we couldn't." Kennedy strutted to the door, hips swaying every step of the way. "No one said we could, either. Actually, I'm pretty sure one of those doctors, during a mandatory therapy session, said it'd probably be an exceptionally bad idea. Actually, without me even asking, he told me I shouldn't even think about it. Something about inducing a panic attack. Are you going to have a panic attack sleeping with me? That would be a bit problematic."

"Are you drunk?"

"No. I just haven't gotten any in a while, I've had a bad day, and the worst you can do is say no. I don't have a whole lot to lose."

"You really want ex sex. With me."

"I don't have any other exes, so yes. With you. We're not counting one-night stands as exes, are we?"

"I suppose not."

"Just don't get the sheets wet coming to bed, Reed."

I had no idea what was going on or why. I wasn't really sure I cared, either. "Let me get this straight. You want me to get out of this nice warm water, get dried off, and then join you in bed, where we won't actually get any sleep because we're going to take a complete leave of our senses and have ex sex all night long."

"That sounds about right. Are you coming?"

Why not? What was the worst that could happen?

I knew the answer; it'd been staring me in the face all day long and well into the evening, when I was a man enough to admit it. When I slipped and forgot about what had broken us apart in the first place, when I forgot I wasn't supposed to be in love with her anymore, I remembered.

Love and hate were the opposite sides of the same coin, and no matter how many times I flipped it, I never could get it to land on hate. Falling in lust with the woman was one lethal step away from falling in love with her all over again.

"Reed?"

My name on her lips did terrible yet wonderful things to me, and before the night was over, I meant to hear it again. I drained the tub and went to work drying off so I wouldn't get the sheets wet. "I'm just saying goodbye to my common sense, so why don't you make yourself comfortable. I'll be out in a minute."

Kennedy giggled.

When I finally emerged from the bathroom, she had snuggled under the comforter, her red hair fanned out on the pillow. She had her hands over her head, a tie wrapped around one wrist while the rest of it dangled. A second tie covered her eyes, and my brows rose. "Well, well, well."

"Ex sex with a twist."

"And a Windsor knot, apparently."

"I read somewhere ex sex was better blindfolded."

"And your little bracelet?"

"I got bored while waiting." She wiggled under the blanket. "I saved one for you to wear tomorrow."

"You're assuming you're going to be in any condition to go anywhere at all tomorrow. When I'm finished with you, you're going to

be having a difficult time walking in a
straight line," I promised. That, at least, I
could do well. She'd enjoy it, I'd make certain
of that. Best of all, I wouldn't have to worry
about my cursed sight, either.

I just hoped I wouldn't regret it when
morning came.

ELEVEN

He kept staring at your breasts.

AT ELEVEN SHARP with less than two hours of actual sleep, Kennedy checked us out of the hotel room, herded me to a black SUV, and slid behind the wheel with no evidence of having stayed up most the night. She talked to a pair of FBI agents who'd delivered the vehicle while I grumbled complaints and buckled into the passenger seat.

How the hell could she be so awake? My pride stung; despite being tired and bruised, I'd pulled out all the stops, even going as far as getting creative with every tie in the hotel room. I'd managed to even ruin two of them, but I'd salvaged the third with a little help from the iron and ten minutes.

Somehow, her contacts had procured a suit for me that almost fit. Someone with a sharp eye would notice the slacks were a tad too short or that my cuffs didn't align just right with my sleeves, but I'd pass muster with most. I adjusted my tie again while waiting for Kennedy to finish exchanging pleasantries with the pair of agents.

The older one, a man who could've been her father, kept staring at her chest. I wanted to gouge his eyes out for his inability to keep his gaze from wandering. The extra ten minutes lost to the man's inability to shut up while drooling all over my ex tested my patience so much I had to bite my tongue to keep from flinging a few curses in his direction.

Kennedy rolled up her window, started the engine, and snickered. "You're so grumpy. Do you need some coffee?"

"He kept staring at your breasts. Of course I'm grumpy."

"Territorial, too."

I scowled, plunked my elbow on the arm rest, and stared out the window. "He could've at least tried to hide that he was looking at your breasts. I have nothing against men looking at breasts, but couldn't he at least attempt to be dignified while doing it? That made all men look like we're incapable of restraint."

"If I wasted my time punching every man who couldn't keep their eyes above my shoulders, I'd never have time to get anything else done. I do have an advantage over them. When they're busy drooling over my chest, they often forget how to think, so it's easier to get the information I want out of them." With a soft chuckle, Kennedy hit the road, and I appreciated the quiet. Unlike a lot of people, who instantly turned on the radio or music, she just drove.

I lasted all of ten minutes before a mixture of curiosity and annoyance got the better of me. "How the hell are you so damned awake?"

"Magic."

I blinked. Was she being serious or brushing me off? If I asked, would I make things worse? Could they get worse? I wanted to offer her a second chance at ex sex to redeem myself—or at least restore some of my bruised dignity. Curiosity won over annoyance and frustration, and I sighed. "Magic?"

"I'm a shocker, a low grade but rather useful talent. In short, I stole some electricity from the hotel and gave myself a boost."

I groaned and watched her through the window's reflection. "That was awful."

"Awful? What are you talking about?" She shot me a glance before returning her attention to the road.

"In short? A boost?"

The silence lasted well over a minute. "I didn't mean it!"

"Shocking."

Kennedy flipped her middle finger at me.

"You're saying you needed to use magic to

recover." Relief and satisfaction led to a rather inappropriate smirk.

"How the hell else was I supposed to get out of bed and drive anywhere today? I didn't think you'd actually mean it when you said the entire night. Warn a woman next time!"

"I did!"

"Warn a woman that you actually mean it. Wait. That's not right, either. Every man I've ever been with has made the same stupid claim. All night long, they promise. All the time. What do I get?"

I could make a few guesses. Some of the feistier women I'd gone home with hadn't been shy about the expectations and usual disappointments, which made it a lot easier to give them exactly what they wanted. "Ten minutes and some frustration?"

"You're being generous."

"How awfully rude of them." I clucked my tongue. "I'm pretty sure I told you I was only about a third human."

"You look like a man, walk like a man, and talk like a man, therefore you are a man. And your file very clearly says you're a man." Laughing, she shook her head. "All right, Reed. I'll stroke your ego a bit, as you deserve it. That's the first time I've ever had to give myself a boost after staying up too late on a work night having a fling."

"So, I don't have to beg for a redo?"

"I had to use magic to restore base functionality this morning. Actual magic. You reduced me to needing magic to crawl out of bed—and I mean *crawl*. I had to shower because I couldn't get my leg over the tub's ledge."

Unable to resist smirking, I stretched out my legs, careful to avoid pulling my stitches any more than I already had. "Coffee would be good, and I need to see what I have to do to take my prescriptions."

"Probably breakfast. We're about a five hour drive from Indianapolis, so I'll get us there, take you home, and start the real investigative work tomorrow after some sleep. The FBI is working with local law enforcement in Indiana and Mississippi to try to gather enough information to work with, but we'll need to do an extensive questioning session to get your part of the story—and see if we can put together any solid leads."

"I need to pick up my kitten. Luna has her."

"We're aware. Your kitten's fine. We can pick her up on the way to your house."

"You're arranging this so you find out where I live, aren't you?"

"In part. Until we find out why someone wanted you bad enough to crash your car and take you all the way to Mississippi just to dump you somewhere you'd be found, you'll probably have some form of guard. For the moment, that guard is me."

"You're a bodyguard, too?"

"My talent makes me the equivalent of a living stun gun. Useful, especially if I want my target alive for questioning."

"That's a low grade talent? Seems useful to me."

"The high grade talents can manifest lightning. I max out as a good stun gun. Perfect for my line of work, but not exactly packing the mystical punch the high grade talents can." Kennedy sighed. "It's definitely useful, and since it's not classified as danger-ous, it does open doors. It's part of why I'm effective as a liaison between the FBI and the CDC. My talent works on most sentients."

"I don't remember you ever zapping anything."

"Late bloomer."

With a five year gap since I'd last spoken to her, I wondered what else had changed, al-though I couldn't force myself to ask. Settling with a wild night of ex sex and going home— hopefully to get on with the rest of my life— seemed like a good way to close the book to me.

Digging into the past wasn't much dif-ferent than digging my own grave. "I just have the sight talent."

"And it's not one you like all that much,

is it?"

"Not particularly."

"It's also why you haven't looked me in the eyes once yet, is it? Or anyone, actually. You look at noses or mouths, not at eyes. If you think you're at any risk of looking someone in the eyes, you flinch. You're most comfortable in the dark, so your sight relies on at least some lighting, but not during thunder storms, so I suspect it only takes a moment for your sight to activate."

Underestimating Kennedy and her powers of observation was a mistake I wouldn't make again. "I should have known you were paying attention."

"Investigator," she reminded me. "It's my job to pay attention, and I do my job best when no one thinks I'm paying attention."

"And thus you undermine yourself by telling me that."

"Hardly. First, I'm not investigating *you*. I'm investigating those who crashed your car, kidnapped you, and dumped you in Mississippi. If I really wanted to question you, you would have been the one blindfolded, but I wouldn't have taken any chances and just tied you to the bed. I'm sure I could have gotten enough material to make some rope from your ruined suit."

I took my time thinking that through. "I'm pretty sure I have some rope at my house."

"I see you found the concept of ex sex enjoyable."

I smothered my smile. "I may have been selfish. If I were a real gentleman, I would give you a fair chance to do whatever you want. I'm trying to be considerate. I'm not sure we've had a sufficient exploration of the theory ex sex is actually spectacular. That is what you pitched me. *Spectacular.*"

"I'm thinking I may have underestimated your willingness to indulge in things we really shouldn't be doing. I'm also thinking your doctors have no idea you're motivated by good sex."

"No, no. Not good sex. *Spectacular* sex."

She laughed. "Point to you. I'd say your doctors would be really interested in learning about this, but let's just keep this dirty little secret to ourselves."

I arched a brow. "Oh? Why?"

"You're joking, right? There'd be a line to get to you first, and you know full well how I feel about lines."

"Avoid them whenever possible, and may some god have pity on the souls of any who make you wait more than five minutes," I muttered.

"I see you remember."

I'd always been told honesty was the best policy, but it never failed to leave a sour taste in my mouth whenever I thought about everything I had—and hadn't—done. So much would have been different if I had been willing to throw a victim under the bus to save myself. I blamed the angel in me for that.

I blamed the demon in me for everything else.

Maybe if I were a bit more human, a lot would have been different. I'd seen it with my sight so many times, the twisted desires of the human heart. I guessed I understood my father a lot more than I liked.

For so long, Kennedy had been everything I had ever wanted. No matter how hard I'd tried, forgetting her just hadn't been in the cards. Me, forget her?

Never.

No wonder I had more problems than my therapists could shake a stick at. Falling in lust really was one fatal step from falling in love, and for me, my coin just didn't have a second side. How could I hate her?

I just couldn't.

"Reed?"

"I'm supposed to be mad at you, you know."

"Supposed to be? You're not?" Kennedy made a thoughtful noise in her throat. "You should be. What I did to you was unforgivable."

"Unforgivable? Hardly. The first piece of advice I'd give to someone on a sinking ship was to get off to avoid going down with it. That's not unforgivable. That's smart."

"No, it's unforgivable. I should have stayed. I should have visited. I should have done something more than—" Kennedy clacked her teeth together.

I didn't need to be an investigator to figure out she'd slipped about something important. Letting the silence fall, I thought it through. Her slip implied she'd done something. The what of it eluded me. Her tone made me think she'd felt it had been important, but not enough to make up for leaving as she had.

In the years since my release, I'd learned all emotions carried weight, capable of shackling me, binding me, and crushing me beneath them if I let them. The good, the bad, it didn't matter. Even good emotions could smother me. It wasn't just the isolation that had gotten to me.

Alone, I felt too much.

Hating Kennedy would have been the easier thing. I'd definitely resented how she'd walked out of my life, but I couldn't deny she'd made the right choice. Resenting her would have been easier, too. Her one act, how she'd walked away, was only one piece in a huge puzzle. How could I hate the entire picture because of one piece of it? I couldn't.

Falling in lust had been too easy, and I was

beginning to understand why.

I'd never fallen out of love with her despite everything.

That realization made the rest a lot easier to handle. Mistakes happened, be it for the right or wrong reason. I'd made them, and so had she. Maybe we'd move forward in different directions, but with a few words, I could ensure we'd have a chance to move forward without unnecessary burdens.

I couldn't forgive myself for everything I had done, but I could forgive her. I could discard those shackles. The weight of those unspoken words wouldn't have to burden either one of us, no matter how difficult they were to speak.

"It's forgivable because I've already forgiven you, Kennedy. You were upset. You had every right to be upset, too. We had so many plans, and instead of preserving them, I'd thrown them away. If anything, you're the one who is supposed to be forgiving me. I was the one who didn't tell the full truth."

It turned out I wasn't the only one susceptible of having a panic attack, but at least Kennedy's instinct was to slam a pedal put her foot on the brake instead of the gas. It didn't save the SUV from a quick trip into the ditch. I hit the shifter and put the vehicle in park.

I wasn't even sure what I'd said that'd hit

her hard enough to induce a panic attack, but I understood. Sometimes, the littlest thing could trigger one for me, and no one else understood why. If she wanted to tell me, she would—when she was ready.

Then I laughed long and hard at the irony of it all while trying my best to convince my hyperventilating ex breathing was necessary and it worked a lot better when she didn't flounder like a fish out of water.

BETWEEN HER SLAMMING THE BRAKES, steering us into a ditch, and my haphazard shifting of gears, we had dropped the SUV's transmission on the ground. While Kennedy remained in the vehicle trying to come to terms with the fact she'd pulled one of my stunts, I examined the damage. I crouched, drumming my fingers on my knees.

Short of a lot of tools and a lot of parts, the SUV wouldn't be going anywhere in a hurry. I turned, regarding the road with a scowl. One lane each way without much of a shoulder to speak of, the road was the worst sort of place for mechanical problems of any sort.

Parts littered the asphalt, and I shook my head at the metal pieces, which indicated *something* had broken when she'd slammed the brakes. The ditch had just finished the job.

I rose to my feet, climbed the bank, and went to get a closer look at the pieces still on the ground.

Sudden deceleration shouldn't have left parts of the car on the ground, especially not the calipers—two of them. I stared at the primary part of the brake assembly, a chill sweeping through me. One caliper failing meant bad news and could happen in an older vehicle—or if the bolts got loosened. Two falling out at once meant trouble.

"Uh, Kennedy?"

"What, Reed?" she whispered.

There was no nice way to say it, so I drew a deep breath and dove in head first. "You better call your FBI friends, because I think someone might have tried to kill us."

"What?" Her howled curses made my ears hurt, and my ex scrambled out of the car and up the bank to join me. "What are you talking about?"

At least she wasn't completely down and out for the count still. I could work with gasping but functional. "Deep breaths and count them," I advised. Once she obeyed, I pointed at the pair of calipers on the ground. "That's part of your brakes. You hit them, they fell off. Then we went in the ditch and dropped the transmission. I'm pretty sure that sort of catastrophic mechanical failure shouldn't happen on a newer car. Any one of those things happening could be a fluke."

"All three of them happening is by design," she muttered.

"Right."

"Okay. This isn't good."

I reached out, slipped my hand into her pocket, and retrieved her phone, offering it to her. "Perhaps you should call your boss and tell him."

Her hands shook, but she nodded. Instead of calling, she took pictures of the calipers, slid into the ditch, stopped, and snapped pictures of the undercarriage and the dangling transmission. I followed, looking over her shoulder.

She texted the images, and the contact label informed me her boss was about to get some very unpleasant news.

Within twenty seconds, her phone rang. With her expression grim, she answered, "Young."

It didn't take long for the conversation to sour and join us in the ditch, although Kennedy wisely amended her statement to avoid mentioning why she'd hit the brakes in the first place. When she finally hung up, she turned to me but said nothing.

"If I had known you'd react that—"

She shut me up with a kiss.

TWELVE

You didn't break the car so we had to
go to a hotel room tonight, did you?

I KISSED MY SANITY, common sense, and
peace of mind goodbye. In the grand scheme
of things, who needed sanity, common sense,
or a peace of mind when I could have
Kennedy? Maybe in a ditch after a car accident wasn't the brightest idea, and to my
complete disappointment, Kennedy came to
the same conclusion. She broke away from
me, covering my eyes with her hands, which
made it difficult to keep kissing her.

A pity, that.

"I have one question for you, Reed."

"What?"

"You didn't break the car so we had to go
to a hotel room tonight, did you?"

"I solemnly swear I didn't intentionally
break the car. I may have contributed to the
transmission dropping by shunting it into
park like I did, though. I definitely had

nothing to do with the calipers ending up on the asphalt."

"Good."

"I wouldn't even think of it. Sabotaging the brakes could get someone killed—and not just us." I frowned. "Is there a reason you're covering my eyes?"

"It seemed like a good idea at the time."

Since I was following the honesty policy, I said, "I'm very confused. And maybe it's a good thing you're covering my eyes, because I want to find out if ex sex in a ditch is as spectacular as it is in a hotel room."

"Not in a ditch we aren't, especially not a ditch that's now a crime scene."

How disappointing. "That's a pity."

"It seems I've made more than one miscalculation."

"I'm sorry I made you crash the car."

"You surprised me is all."

"You slammed on the brakes and jerked the wheel."

"I slammed the brakes, but the wheel did the turning all on its own."

"Maybe that happened when the brakes broke." I frowned, casting a doubtful look at the car. "Or the steering was sabotaged, too."

"I lied. I have another question for you."

"Go for it."

"When did you become Mr. Popular?" Kennedy lowered her hands from my eyes, turned, and kicked the SUV's tire. "At least this was an FBI vehicle and not a damned rental. They're going to love having their SUV returned to them in pieces."

"I'm no expert in investigations, but I'm pretty sure you're not supposed to be kicking the evidence."

"The evidence can kiss my ass!" She kicked the tire again, spun around, and crossed her arms over her chest. "So help me, if some dumb fuck shows up trying to get you, I'm going to shock the shit out of them— literally. I will literally shock the shit out of them, and the forensics team can kiss my ass, too."

All right. I held my hands up in the universal sign of surrender. "I have no idea what I did to make people want to either kill me or kidnap me and dump me in Mississippi. My life is boring, I make other people money, and I try to make as few ripples as possible. I have no idea what I did, I swear."

"You rescued a kitten that should be filed as a weapon of biological warfare. That's hardly boring."

"Point to you," I conceded.

"And getting kidnapped and dragged to Mississippi isn't boring, either."

I indulged in crossing my arms, leaning against the SUV, and scowling at the ground. "Then there was the plane crash, a tornado, and then because the plane crashing once wasn't enough, the tornado crashed it again."

"Also not boring. Last night was anything but boring, too."

"And yet another point to you."

"Under other circumstances, I would claim you then made me crash the car, but considering the number of parts left on the road, I'm pretty convinced the first time I hit the brakes hard, there was going to be a crash."

"I'm going to just claim something startled you into slamming the brakes without specifying what. That's totally honest."

"I'm going to second that motion."

"I'm pretty sure there was some sort of rattle at the end there, too."

"Definitely."

"I meant every word I said."

"I know you did. You just surprised me is all." Kennedy dug her toe into the torn-up grass and weeds, kicking a rock up the bank onto the road above. "I ended up going dumpster diving to get it back."

I tried to imagine her in a dumpster, and the idea was so foreign to me I couldn't. "You went dumpster diving."

"If I'd been smart, I would have just got it back right away, but no. I waited until they tossed the trash and went dumpster diving."

"I'm afraid to ask if you found it."

"Considering there was no fucking way I was leaving that dumpster until I did, of course I found it."

I still couldn't imagine her digging around in a dumpster for any reason, let alone to retrieve the ring she'd thrown out—and rightfully so. Worse, I wasn't sure how—or if—the knowledge she'd gone dumpster diving changed things.

Considering she'd never been the type to dig through a trash can for any reason, often begging me to do it for her when she'd accidentally thrown out something she needed, it changed things. It changed a lot of things.

Old doubts, doubts I thought I'd abandoned years ago, resurfaced and reared their ugly heads. My eyes never lied. I'd lived the entirety of my life with that certainty. My eyes never lied, and Kennedy had hated me in the courthouse. I'd been so certain of that.

Yet she'd gone climbing into a dumpster to fetch the ring I'd given her, a ring I'd saved pennies and nickels to buy, one that didn't even have diamonds. I hadn't been able to afford the one with the diamonds, so I'd gotten her a ring with an opal instead. Diamonds were supposed to last forever, but the opal had more fire, reminding me of her far more than any clear stone ever could.

I couldn't bring myself to ask what she'd

done with it after digging it out of the dumpster.

"It turns out opals are really delicate and shouldn't be carried around in wallets," she mumbled.

All right. I struggled to process the fact she had carried the ring around in her wallet to begin with, assuming the stone had somehow broken as a result. "Well, any time I'm told a rock should take a bath in olive oil, I wonder about its durability."

"To be fair, my wallet didn't survive the incident, either."

I went from hesitant to confused, joining her in digging up rocks and kicking them around whenever I found one. "This is doing more damage to the crime scene, isn't it?"

"If you're not going to let me kick tires, I'm kicking rocks."

"I never said you couldn't kick the tires, I just pointed out you were kicking evidence." I scooped a rock up onto my toe, tossed it in the air, and caught it, focusing all of my attention on the game to see how many times I could bounce it off my shoe. "You really carried the ring in your wallet."

"I stopped carrying my wallet in my back pocket after getting shot in the ass. Also, opals and wallets? Definitely not bulletproof."

I blinked and the stone bounced off my foot and fell to the ground. "Let me see if I have this straight. You were carrying your wallet in your back pocket, and someone shot you through your wallet."

"Right through the ring, too. I had opal shards in my ass, Reed. The surgeon wanted to know why I was carrying a ring in my wallet. Apparently, he didn't appreciate picking out opal shards from my ass. It wasn't a good day."

No matter how long I thought about it, I doubted I'd be able to wrap my head around our conversation—or accept she had actually retrieved the ring and carried it around with her until its ultimate demise in her wallet after being shot in the ass. "I would think being shot would automatically make it a bad day."

"Well, I don't recommend getting shot for starters."

"I'll keep that in mind."

"Do."

"I don't recommend getting into car accidents you can't remember. Waking up in Mississippi wasn't my idea of a good time."

"At least this is an upgrade, you remember this one."

"Technically, I caused it."

"I'm going with whoever sabotaged the car as being the one responsible for causing the crash. Otherwise, we never would have ended up in the ditch."

"That's fair." I rubbed my temple, the start of a headache brewing behind my eyes. Instead of the trembling anxiety I should have endured, I got a mix of confusion, annoyance, and something far more dangerous: the hope things could get better, no matter what direction Kennedy and I took with our lives.

We could walk away with clean slates, unburdened by bad circumstances. We could spin wheels and go nowhere fast, too. Other options lurked on a distant horizon, ones I hesitated to even consider. I'd gone from unable to think of anything else to accepting what I couldn't change and all the way back to the precipice. I'd spent years trying to move on for a few minutes to send me circling right back to the beginning.

"Well, isn't this awkward?"

The distant sound of an approaching vehicle drew a sigh out of me. "No, awkward would have been if I had gone with my first plan, which involved having ex sex in a ditch. We would've gotten caught. Good luck explaining *that* away."

"I really wish I had my gun right now."

"I hope you're saying that because of the car."

"Yes, Reed. I'm not going to shoot you because you're a pervert and want to have sex in a ditch. Who am I to judge? I blindfolded myself and used a lure of ties to get your attention."

"Good to know."

THE CAR PROVED to be a police cruiser, which made Kennedy far happier than it did me. It took counting my breaths to control my growing anxiety.

The older cop, a man with more gray hairs than black ones, didn't pay me much attention, focusing on talking with Kennedy about the circumstances of the crash. His partner, a woman who couldn't have finished police academy long ago, wouldn't stop staring at me, and she insisted on getting in my face.

Some cops believed the truth could only be discovered by staring someone in the eyes. My nervousness grew the longer she hovered, and I expected she would begin her interrogation the instant she thought she had unnerved me enough to catch me in the act. Of what, I had no idea.

I hadn't done anything wrong.

Since I couldn't ask the woman to stop staring at me, I dug out a rock with my toe and bounced it on my foot while I waited for Kennedy to finish dealing with the cops. When the cop stayed silent, I bounced the stone from foot to foot, aware the oxfords would be scuffed beyond redemption given twenty minutes.

Instead of breaths, I counted how many times I could bounce the rock without losing it.

I made it to thirty, then Kennedy swept in and punted it up and over the road. "You should think about joining a soccer team with that sort of footwork."

"You stole my rock." I kept my gaze lowered, searching the churned soil for a new one.

"Officer Hank wanted to know if you noticed anything unusual when the brakes busted."

"I definitely noticed when they hit the asphalt and we ended up in the ditch. Beyond that, nothing mechanical. You hit the brakes, the calipers dropped, then you lost control of the vehicle. It happened pretty quickly."

"You a mechanic, Mr. Matthews?"

"I know just enough to get myself in trouble with my actual mechanic. I can do the basics and identify some parts, but that's it. I'm better at the at-home stuff, but I try to do my own work on my car whenever possible." I shrugged. "Calipers are pretty distinctive."

"Transmissions, too." The cop crouched beside me, peeking under the SUV and pointing underneath towards the engine. "I'm no mechanic, either, but I'd bet my badge your axel dropped along with your brakes. You're damned lucky your car didn't flip right over its own nose."

I got on a knee and leaned over for a better look at the SUV's undercarriage. "Can that even happen?"

"It happens time to time, usually at highway speed."

I grimaced. "That sounds painful."

"Not for long." The cop turned to Kennedy. "How long have you had the vehicle?"

Kennedy nudged my foot with hers in what I interpreted as a warning to keep quiet. "It was dropped off by the FBI this morning a little before eleven. We were in the hotel lobby when they brought it in, and no one messed with the car. The other driver got out, gave me the keys, and we talked for a few minutes before we left."

"Did you drive straight here?"

Getting to my feet, I dusted my slacks off the best I could, although I left a spot of mud on my knee to go with the muck covering my shoes. The woman frowned in my direction.

"No. We had a quick stop for breakfast, but Mr. Matthews stayed in the car while I went inside."

"No one came near the car while she was inside," I added.

"And neither of you noticed anything odd?"

I shook my head. "It sounded fine until she hit the brakes, then we were in the ditch."

Officer Hank shook his head and pointed down the road. "You're lucky you weren't a half mile farther along the way. The ditch is a lot deeper there."

"How much deeper?" Kennedy shoved her hands in her pockets and shot the SUV a sour look.

"About a hundred feet. Someone goes through the rail every year without fail and gets themselves killed. The river's about twenty feet deep at the bottom there. Locals call it Devil's Bend, especially during a cold snap. What brought you this way, anyway?"

Kennedy hopped to the driver's door, opened it, and pointed at the SUV's navigation panel. "GPS. Route was already programmed in."

"Who did it?"

"I don't know. Not uncommon for someone to plug in the best routes for visiting agents. I assume someone from the FBI did it when prepping the car for my use." Kennedy planted her fists on her hips, and I suspected only the presence of the cops kept her from aiming another kick at the wrecked vehicle. "I do the same when my vehicle gets designated as a loaner to a visiting agent.

More efficient for those who know where they're going to handle the navigation. It isn't a secret we're headed to Indianapolis."

"Would've saved you some time through rush hour, but without traffic, taking this road would have added an extra half hour to your trip—and a lot of gas."

I wondered which one of us was the target, as I hadn't had any trouble at all until Kennedy Young had stormed her way back into my life. Then again, I hadn't any trouble at all until I'd adopted Kitten, Destroyer of Worlds, either.

Either way I looked at it, I was screwed, and I couldn't tell which one of them was the most dangerous of all. Both of them had managed to worm their ways places they didn't belong, like it or not. I was just along for the ride, for better or worse.

I really needed to stop accepting the things I couldn't change. One day, it would probably get me killed.

THIRTEEN

You will, of course, view this as a miracle.

IT TOOK a lot longer than I thought for the FBI to arrive, people to go over the crime scene, and Kennedy to finish answering questions so we could escape and finish our trip to Indianapolis. What should have taken five hours ended up taking twelve, an hour of which involved a CDC representative checking over the new SUV from bumper to bumper, giving the all clear before allowing us to hit the road.

I ended up driving the final hour of the trip to avoid another accident. While Kennedy cursed complaints, she pulled over and swapped seats with me readily enough. It took her less than five minutes to fall asleep, which suited my purposes perfectly. The first thing I did was tap into her phone with the SUV's sound system, calling a number that eventually put me in touch with Luna, who promised to bring Kitten, Destroyer of Worlds to a gas station on the outskirts of the city.

In the week I'd been gone, my kitten had grown. She seemed happy enough to see me, rewarding me with a purr, although I suspected she just wanted to escape the angel's clutches. Kennedy slept through the acquisition of my feline, and I buckled her carrier into the back seat in case something happened.

"You'll make it home without incident," Luna promised, and she gave a soft, airy laugh. "You will, of course, view this as a miracle."

The angel vanished in a flash of golden light, and I waved my fist where she'd been standing. Kitten, Destroyer of Worlds cried in her carrier. I couldn't blame her. Wailing over the injustice of it all seemed like a good way to release stress. Then again, I could think of a lot of other things I could do, too.

Sighing, I got back on the road and headed for home, taking advantage of Kennedy's exhaustion to keep its location a secret for a little while longer. The FBI's SUV would have a few new scratches from plowing it through the brush my car fit through without issue, but a few minutes and a paint pen would get rid of them—if I cared enough.

After having trashed one vehicle, I thought a few minor scratches wouldn't draw much attention. At least they'd get the SUV back intact. I hoped.

True to Luna's promise, I did make it home without incident, and my house seemed the same as I left it. I parked, killed the engine, and stretched. Kitten, Destroyer of Worlds continued singing the sad song of her people in the back. Reaching over, I poked Kennedy's arm. "Rise and shine. We're here."

She snorted, jerking upright. "I didn't do it!"

Laughing, I shook my head, unbuckled my seatbelt, and slid out of the SUV. "If you're expecting luxury, run away now. We have arrived, and I even managed to retrieve my kitten without issue."

My furry bundle of biological warfare howled for release. Instead of obeying her demands, I retrieved her in her carrier, grabbed the oversized plastic bag with her things, and headed for my front door, leaving Kennedy to either follow or not as she saw fit.

If my ramshackle home bothered her, it didn't slow her down at all. I let myself in, grateful my keys had managed to make the trip all the way from Indiana to Mississippi and back. While I could have hiked to the waterwheel to dig out the hidden spare, I thought I'd limit how many times I shocked Kennedy to once per hour or so.

"I'm not sure I want to let you live here," she muttered, poking the ragtag veneer with her toe. "What if I huff and puff?"

"You won't blow my house down, but I'll enjoy watching you try." Stepping inside, I set Kitten, Destroyer of Worlds by the door and attended to the most important part of her care, her litter box. "Last I checked, she has not quite mastered the art of using her litter box effectively. The litter does a good job, but she enjoys making the world suffer. My advice? Bury it fast."

"Oh god, she's one of those? It's even worse than I thought."

"It seems I've invited Satan home with me, and she's rather cute and fluffy." I waited for Kennedy to close the door before releasing my feline demoness from her carrier.

She beelined straight for her freshly prepared box. I sighed.

Within half a minute, Kennedy gagged, turned heel, and fled my house.

"Thanks, cat," I muttered. The subject of my displeasure kicked litter all over the floor, created her usual pit, and high-tailed it for my bedroom. Something thunked down the hall, and before I had a chance to take a single step, Kitten, Destroyer of Worlds zoomed back into the living room and pounced my leg, digging her tiny claws into my slacks and holding on for dear life. With my kitten firmly attached to my leg, I hobbled across my living room to vanquish my eye-watering foe.

"You're terrible."

The subject of my complaint dug razor-sharp claws into my leg, and grimacing, I bent over to peel her off. The front door creaked open, and Kennedy peeked inside. "Is it safe yet?"

"As safe as it gets with this beast." Setting my kitten on the floor, I headed to the couch and flopped on it. I should have saved myself the effort of removing my furry friend, as she climbed my leg and took up residence on my lap. "Do you think she missed me, or is she planning some form of revenge?"

"She's a cat. Always assume revenge."

I laughed and petted my kitten. The little ball of terror purred, which I interpreted as reward for doing my job as her human slave correctly. "Don't tell Kitten, Destroyer of Worlds this, but you get used to it pretty quick, although I may be buying stock in air freshener in the near future."

Whether too tired to keep lurking outside or she accepted her fate, Kennedy came inside and closed the door behind her. "It's a lot nicer on the inside."

"I'll get around to fixing the exterior eventually—it's all cosmetic issues. You should have seen it when I bought it. Most of the town was already on its way out the door."

"What town is this?"

I shot her a salute. "Gypsum Creek."

"Okay. There was a property with that town on the deed, but we couldn't actually find the town."

"Population of one, just the way I like it. I'm pretty sure I scratched that SUV to hell getting it back here, too. Technically, there's still a post office, but it runs out of Cataract next door. Mailman gives me a ring if I have anything, and I pick it up to save him the effort of trying to get back here. If you were looking for a road, well, I'm afraid I can't help you there. I have a lovely set of tire ruts I maintain."

Kennedy strode across my living room and plopped onto the couch beside me. "You literally became a hermit. I was unaware businessmen could become hermits. Yet here we are." She sucked in a breath. "Wait. You've lured me into the woods, haven't you?"

It didn't take me long to figure out where she was going with her train of thought, and despite myself, I laughed. "You're safe. I don't have a basement. I do have a creepy mill in the back, though. I use the waterwheel to generate electricity. Actually, this would be a pretty good place to hide out during the apocalypse."

"Now that's a selling point. Should the world as we know it come to an end, I may come hang out with you and your cat."

"I have my own source of electricity, enough firewood to last well over a decade, and a lot of untouched forest filled with wild animals. The creek also has fish. Even got my own well, but should that fail, I catch rainwater, too. What can I say? I'm resourceful."

"You probably got bored."

"There might be a bit of truth to that."

"So what else do you do around here besides practice survival techniques?"

"Sleep. I have picked up a new hobby of serving my feline overlady."

The kitten in question stretched out over my lap and yawned.

"You've been suckered. I just thought you should know this."

"Yeah, I figured that out when I ended up paying several hundred dollars at the emergency vet and couldn't force myself to get mad over it."

"All right, I'll give credit where credit is due. She's too cute to kill, which explains why you subject yourself to that godawful smell."

I laughed, stroking my hand along my kitten's soft back. "My man card is in my wallet. You should take it. I'm this kitten's bitch, and that probably loses me my right to carry a man card."

"Your man card is safe this time. I can't say I would have been able to resist her, either. I'm pretty sure it's in the cat handbook on how to take over Earth. Humanity has only been spared because cats are too lazy to carry out their evil plans."

"I'm pretty sure you're right. How am I supposed to prevent the cataclysm? Feed her on time and make sure she doesn't stink me out of house and home?"

Kennedy jabbed me in the ribs. "No kitten around, you. This is serious business."

It took every scrap of my will to avoid groaning. "You don't have to get so catty about it."

"Oh, stop your caterwauling already."

I sniffed and lifted my chin, turning away from her so she wouldn't see me if I cracked a grin. "I prefer to think of it as having a hissy fit."

Kennedy groaned. "Now you're just yanking my tail."

"Now, now. You know I wouldn't do that. Just paws, take a deep breath, and smooth your fur a bit. There's no need for us to get into a catfight over this."

With a strangled scream, Kennedy grabbed one of my throw pillows and smacked me in the face with it. "You son of a bitch!"

Kitten, Destroyer of Worlds darted off my lap with an indignant hiss. Laughing, I shielded my head with an arm. "I'm in the doghouse now, aren't I?"

Drawing a deep breath, Kennedy got to her feet and hoisted the pillow. "See Reed? See Reed run."

Lurching off the couch with a laugh, I ran for the door. "Purrfect. I guess I better stop pussyfooting around, then."

I almost made it before the pillow connected with the back of my head. I scooped it up, launched it back, and took the chase outside, slowing long enough to make sure Kennedy closed the door behind her to keep Kitten, Destroyer of Worlds contained inside, thus sparing the Earth from her evil.

KENNEDY CAUGHT me near the creek, relieved me of my wallet, tossed it to the safety of the rocky shore, and shoved me into the water. Laughing hysterically made it difficult to fend her off, but at least she gave me a chance to catch my breath before dunking me. When she finally let me up for air, I classified as half-drowned.

"Worth it," I gasped, wiping my hand over my face.

"That was cruel and unusual punishment, you bastard!" She shoved me into the deeper water again, and I fell in with a splash and a laugh. "You need more exercise, Reed. I shouldn't have been able to catch you that easily."

"Hey, I did pretty well for someone with stitches." Anyway, I didn't want to get away. Being caught was half the fun, although I wouldn't tell *her* that. I'd just enjoy the consequences of my capture. "Maybe I took that a little too far, but I'm not sorry."

"Of course you're not sorry." Kennedy waded deeper into the creek and splashed me. "I suppose I should be happy you still have a sense of humor left. I'd wondered after what your co-workers said when you were taken."

"It's very subtle."

"There's nothing subtle about your kitten."

"The best payback happens when no one expects it."

"I don't even need five minutes to poke holes in that excuse."

"I sieve."

"Reed Hampton Matthews!" She lunged for me, flopping into the water in front of me, and I darted out of her way, laughing when she emerged with a spluttered squawk.

Waiting until she surfaced, I smiled, set my hand on the back of her head, and dunked her. "Oops."

Payback came in many forms, and Kennedy used the water's natural abilities to conduct electricity to zap me. I yelped and went under. Before I could do something stupid like drown, she snagged me by my collar and hauled me to shore, where she began phase two of her punishment.

From head to toe, she attacked every single one of my ticklish spots until I writhed on the shore and pled for mercy. I could've fought back or launched an offensive of my own, but I accepted my fair share of the punishment with as much grace as I could, which wasn't very much.

A man with a tendency to squeal when tickled too much often lacked grace. When she finally relented, I rolled onto my stomach, groaned, and fought to catch my breath. "You win."

"I should have visited you. I should have stayed. I should have done a lot differently."

The shift in subject blindsided me, and I used my prone position to keep my face hidden. She didn't need to see my confusion or uncertainty any more than I needed to look into her eyes. "I already forgave you, Kennedy."

"But why?"

It'd take a lifetime of therapy before I would be ready to confess the truth I'd barely figured out for myself, which eliminated telling her I still loved her. The truth was a funny thing; it could be twisted, it could be hidden, and it could be many things, too. Right down to making my eyes water, it was too much like an onion, and I had a long way to go to reach its heart. "Because I do. Just ask any one of my therapists how infuriating I can be. I'm sure they can tell you all about it."

While strained, Kennedy laughed. "I didn't have to ask. The instant they realized we had a warrant to get your personal information due to your kidnapping, they were happy to treat us like we were the therapists instead of them. Still. What I did to you was unforgivable."

"Already forgave you," I reminded her. "That automatically proves you wrong. I win."

"Reed."

"You're just going to have to get around to accepting I forgave you. Ask any one of my therapists. They'll agree with me. I'll even tell them to tell you. I'll go in with you, and I'll order them to do so."

"Maybe playing in the creek wasn't a good idea. Are your stitches all right?"

I laughed, marveling at her ability to change subjects without warning. While my awareness of my stitches had crossed my mind for a split second, I'd discarded the potential of risk in favor of fooling around and playing in the water, something I hadn't done in years. "I'm sure I'm fine. If I'm not, I'm sure a doctor here will be happy to tell me how stupid I've been. I should check the waterwheel before I go back inside anyway."

"At least I think I can eliminate your personal property as a motive. I'm not sure you have anything a kidnapper could possibly want."

At the rate she was jumping around, I was going to get whiplash trying to follow the conversation. "I don't have a whole lot, no. Unless they want a suit collection fitted for me. I own more suits than I probably should. I would have gone off the grid completely, except I like getting paid for providing electricity. I've got solar panels up at the waterwheel, too. If you wanted to find my house, all you needed to do was ask the electric company. They have an access road they clear four times a year to check their meter by the mill."

"I'm going to remember that next time I have to track down a hermit. I'm hoping that's never. I was starting to think you were some incredibly detailed hallucination, as you existed on paper and people were positive you were real. Outside of your work and appointments, you're incredibly hard to track down. There should be limits to how secretive you are."

"You want to know, don't you?"

"I'm a bit curious."

I got to my feet, stretched, and strolled in the direction of the water wheel, water sloshing in my shoes every step of the way. "I'd call myself a whore, but whores get paid. I don't. I'd spend my weekends at the bar, and since I don't drink a whole lot, I'd end up hooking up with someone." I shrugged. "I guess I'm a bit of a slut."

"Are there any women you've been with who might want to kidnap you?"

"I doubt it? At most, I'd give them my first name—if that. Hell, I don't know the names of most of the women I've slept with. I'm pretty careful. I don't go home with the same person twice. I can't think of a reason why."

"I can. A ready supply of great sex might motivate women."

I wasn't sure how to take that, so I went with the obvious one. "Ex sex in a creek?"

"Too cold. Now, ex sex in your bed? I'm all in. You don't have to ask me twice. I present this as evidence of my point."

"If someone wanted me for sex, why would they get me into a car accident bad enough to require stitches and leave me in Mississippi without the sex? That makes zero sense. Now, that said, there *was* a set of high heel prints at the house, so I can't completely eliminate sex as a motivator."

"I've been with my fair share of men, Reed. You make them all look like inexperienced virgins. I just figured you'd gotten a new girlfriend."

"No new girlfriends. Just a very long list of one-night stands."

"Practice makes perfect."

"That sounds like a good explanation. Better than the other one I have." I chuckled, shook my head over the casualness in which Kennedy delved into my sex life, and guided her to the waterwheel, stopping to watch it do its work and enjoy the sound of falling water. "The mill was here when I bought the property, but I fixed it up. At first I thought it had something to do with the failed mining operations here, but I think it was meant for grain. I never quite figured that out. I took out a lot of the old equipment, got the power company to install an electric generator, and connected it to the grid and my house. Cost me more than the property, but it's pretty reliable and I can do most of the maintenance on my own. I added the solar panels recently. The lines to my house are buried, so unless the wheel fails, I don't have to worry about losing power during a storm."

"All right. I'm definitely coming here in

case of apocalypse. Do I want to know your other excuse?"

While she already knew I wasn't fully human, I shrugged it off. "It's not important. Tomorrow will be questioning, right?"

"Correct. My boss wanted tonight, but after the accident, he decided tomorrow would be soon enough. We have a ten o'clock appointment in downtown Indianapolis."

"Then we should probably head back to the house, get something to eat, and get some sleep."

"You're probably right."

FOURTEEN

Kitten, Destroyer of Worlds was
dubbed an official therapy cat.

IT TOOK three days of questioning for the FBI
and local police to determine I truly knew
nothing at all, a claim I ultimately needed
Luna to confirm as the truth. Luna refused to
elaborate on the things she had said, which
turned the investigation from me to her, for
which I was grateful. I should've used my
rights to have an angel verify the truth
sooner, but it'd taken me the three days to
work up the nerve to do it. After the first day
with no leads, no idea why anyone would
want to bother with someone like me, and no
need to waste someone of Kennedy's skills on
an investigation deemed low-priority, she left
my life once more.

They needed her in California, and I
didn't ask her why nor did she share the circumstances.

Before she left, she kept her promise and

helped me with my insurance company, and
they promised to reimburse me for everything. I wasn't happy with them, they weren't
happy with me, but for an extra ten dollars a
month, they'd open my coverage to all fifty
states and abroad.

I figured Kennedy's contacts in the CDC
had something to do with that.

Either by plan or a twist of fate, I was
being questioned by her co-workers when
she left town. Pruning trees kept them
healthy, and there wasn't enough left of us to
save, so cutting it away in as painless a
fashion as possible worked out for the best.

In a way, I wanted to thank my kidnappers. Only because of them, whoever they
were, I thought I could actually move on and
maybe do all those little things my therapists
insisted would let me live life again rather
than just surviving through each day. I even
managed to walk my way through the realization without having a panic attack.

A week later, I returned to work, but
things had changed. Kitten, Destroyer of
Worlds was dubbed an official therapy cat by
one of my doctors, who loved the idea of a
grown man carrying around a tiny terror of a
tabby. My kitten approved, as she loved
riding on my shoulder so she could better see
the planet she ruled and would one day destroy. Of my coats, the wool one with a hood

proved her favorite, as she'd make herself at home in the hood when she wasn't reigning supreme on my shoulder and shedding on me.

As my official therapy kitten, Kitten, Destroyer of Worlds claimed my office as her grand audience chamber. The hallway became the prime gathering spot for impromptu meetings, meetings I ignored while doing my work. I added a sign to my door counting the number of days since the last vicious kitten attack, although it usually remained at zero.

My kitten liked trying to trip people by attacking their feet.

I went three blissful weeks without a visit from an angel. I almost made it four before Luna made an appearance, materializing in front of my desk rather than bothering with mundane things like knocking on my door. Kitten, Destroyer of Worlds hissed and dove under my desk, spitting feline curses at the angel.

While tempted to join my kitten in hiding, I pretended Luna didn't exist, reading over one of the latest contracts for an expanded financial portfolio my boss wanted to bag.

Luna sighed. "Knock, knock."

"I haven't gotten any letters from Mississippi, but if I did, I would still throw it out just to piss you off." I scrolled down the document, jotting down a note on something I needed to review later. "Is there any reason you skipped walking across the floor and knocking like a polite sentient?"

"You aren't happy to see me."

"The last time I saw you, you were getting me into shit with the FBI because you wouldn't give them any details on why I had been kidnapped, why you took my kitten so she wouldn't be involved in the accident, and why you hadn't just notified anyone you knew exactly what was going on. Furthermore, since you knew and warned me about the accident, my insurance isn't covering it, as they view the accident as willful endangerment. The only reason my premium isn't going up is because I have an otherwise perfect record and it was verified I had no blame in the creation of the accident. They wanted to claim your warning about the accident counted as willful endangerment. Thanks for that. I didn't already have enough trouble without that adding to it."

I had gotten a barely running junker to get me to and from work until I could figure out what sort of vehicle I actually wanted. Sighing, I saved my work and gave the angel my attention.

Luna presented the dreaded envelope stamped from Mississippi. "I thought I'd save you the hassle of throwing it out and just bring it to you this time. I snagged it out of sorting room at the post office. Wasn't that considerate of me?"

"And here I thought they'd stop coming after last month." I scowled but snatched the envelope out of the angel's hand. With a flick of my wrist, I pointed at her with it. "Give me a reason why I shouldn't just toss this and maintain a perfectly good tradition. I have a lot of work to do, so I don't have the three hours to satisfy you on whatever discussion you might actually want to have."

"Now, now. There's no need to get snide, Reed."

I rolled my chair back, thumped my foot on my desk, and pulled my slacks up to my knee, twisting my leg to show off the red scar. "The stitches came out three days ago, Luna. I might even be off the painkillers and other medications next week if it keeps healing as well as it has been. Let me remind you humans can't just snap their fingers and have all of life's little problems disappear. You have an agenda, and I'm pretty sure it doesn't actually involve you being helpful to me. Helpful would have been dishing out some of those secrets of yours rather than making me look like an idiot in front of the FBI."

"You didn't look like an idiot in front of the FBI."

"Oh? What part of this makes me look intelligent? I told investigators an angel told me I could either get into a car accident, get tossed from a sixteenth story window, or be shot in one of several gruesome ways. The one just flat-out laughed, right up until you confirmed I was telling the truth. Thanks for that, by the way. If you had just told them you had given me those options from the start, I would have been spared a great deal of questioning. My auto insurance company laughed at me. If you angels actually believed in the finer points of life, including money, I'd be asking you to pay up for my new car since they aren't going to be paying a cent. Thanks for that, too."

Luna sat on the edge of my desk, making a sound suspiciously like a chastising tongue-clicking.

"Beings without heads should not mock mortals making noises like that. That's awful, Luna. Stop it."

"Just because you can't see my head doesn't mean I lack one. Despite what you believe, I do have a head. It's just so magnificent you would be wiped out of existence should you see it. Mortals tend to fall over dead when looking into the glory of the heavens for some reason. So inconvenient."

I sighed and dropped the envelope onto my keyboard, glaring at the letter. "What happens this time if I don't read the damned letter?"

"Nothing, not for a while."

"So something will happen."

"Something always happens. Even taking your next breath has a consequence. You never asked me if something good or bad happened."

I hated angels. "You're a very frustrating individual, Luna."

"I've invested many centuries of practice to become so. Thank you for noticing my hard work."

"If I open the damned letter, will you leave me alone about it?"

"But you'll surely want to talk about it."

"If you're all-seeing, looking into the future and all that, is there any reason you're so insistent on bothering me?"

"You need a nudge in the right direction."

"Right according to you or to me?" I snatched the envelope up, slapping it against the edge of my desk a few times. "Because the way I see it, the only one actually benefiting from your machinations here is you."

"Would I do that?"

"Yes, you would."

"Do you truly think so little of me?"

I didn't think about it for very long. "Yes. To you, I'm probably the equivalent of a bug. An interesting bug, for the five or ten seconds of your lifespan I entertain you. In a blink of an eye to you, I'll get old and die. In a few hundred years, you won't even remember I existed. That's the thing about angels. They don't care about this little moment in time. It's all about the future, and not necessarily *my* future. So, what's in it for you, Luna?"

The angel laughed. "What is in it for any angel?"

"How the hell should I know?"

"Language."

I tossed the letter onto my desk and considered how many times I would need to smack my forehead onto the edge to put myself out of my misery. "You invited yourself into my office without knocking. I'm pretty sure if you wanted nice language, you'd just go back to heaven where you belong."

"You're in a mood today. A rather vocal one, far more so than during any of our other meetings." Luna sighed and sat. "Mortals. You simply must insist on exercising your free will. Do you have any idea how much trouble that causes?"

"I'm in a mood today because I have work to do, work that doesn't involve pandering to you and your condescending ego. If you actually want me to look at this envelope, then give your solemn vow you'll stop meddling in my affairs. No more popping up and telling me the future, taking off with my kitten because you want things to go a certain way. And no getting others to meddle in my affairs, either. And no, I really don't care how much trouble it causes. You can chalk that one up to my terrible case of mortality."

Luna grunted.

To test her claim she had a head I just couldn't see, I snatched the envelope, got my feet off my desk so I could reach over and swipe the paper in the space her head should have been. If she had a head, it was nothing but air. "Illusionary head, then?"

"Or perhaps I left it at home."

"That's a bit awkward. Are you telling me all you angels just leave your heads lying around?"

"You'll never know."

"Such tragedy. Choose, Luna. Into the trash it goes, or you give your solemn vow to stop meddling in my affairs. Either way, I'm happy with the situation."

"What ever happened to your sense of mortal curiosity? This would be so much easier if you were curious about what was inside," she complained.

"I'm going to raise my opening fee if you whine." I hovered my hand over my trashcan to discover Kitten, Destroyer of Worlds had an interest in the letter, too. I waved it for her, and she jumped in her effort to claim it as yet another one of her conquests. "I could just give it to my kitten as a toy. Might be a more effective way to get rid of it than the trashcan."

Luna crossed her arms over her chest and spat, "Mortals."

"That's going to cost you your solemn vow to stop meddling in my affairs and something that costs you a disgusting amount of money but might be useful to me, like a new car."

"How about a sword?"

"Only if you're paying the sword maker of my choice, plus you're paying for the lessons to learn how to swing it around. I don't want any swords *you* pick."

"Since when did you become so suspicious?"

"Do you really want me to start listing the reasons why I don't trust you?"

"I could find out if I truly desired."

I lowered the letter closer to the floor so Kitten, Destroyer of Worlds could get a better grip on it with her claws and teeth. "Let me help you figure it out. We'll start with the car accident you manipulated me into participating in. Rather than, you know, preventing it in the first place. If you hadn't said anything, I would have been in the car accident anyway."

"But then your kitten would have been involved, too."

"That's life, Luna. You should try it some-time—life without being immortal. But you should know this already. People die. So do kittens. Sometimes, people and their kittens die in car accidents. It happens. While I can't really blame you for caring more about my kitten than you do about me, just another one of those pesky mortals with free will, it's still rather annoying. Since you've managed to make me look like an idiot *and* have done your fair share of manipulations, I've had enough. Pay up, or the kitten shreds—and possibly eats—the letter. I promise I won't be reading it."

"When did you get a spine?" she hissed.

"I'm going to guess around the time a tornado tossed a jet at me. It missed, as you can tell. I can raise my price again if you'd like. I don't mind."

"Sarcastic, too."

"Well, you're the one who popped in and interrupted my work." Since she hadn't declined my offer, I kept Kitten, Destroyer of Worlds from doing more than leaving a few holes in the envelope before showing the angel the damage. "I'm sure my kitten would like to keep playing with it. I think she thinks it's food."

"Fine. Pick your smith, but I will pick the instructor. If you're going to play with sharp objects, at least you should learn from the best. Maybe you'll live. I'll be back in a week to pay for your blade."

I smiled and waved the envelope. "Then I'll read this. Your vow, Luna."

"Very well. I solemnly swear I will cease meddling in your affairs, purchase the sword of your choice from the smith of your choice, and pay for your lessons, effective as soon as you read the letter."

I grabbed my letter opener, sliced through the envelope, and pulled out two sheets of paper. The first was the statement of my release and pardon, complete with a wax seal stamp certifying it to be an official copy. Wrinkling my nose, I checked it over, but it matched my copy of it. Setting it aside, I checked over the second letter.

I had no idea who or what Lucavier Buioni was, but I recognized a pretentious invitation when I saw one, inviting me to visit Mississippi to discuss the circumstances of my incarceration and eventual exoneration. He favored haughty language, so I pegged him as an older species of the supernatural bent. If Lucavier was a spin off Lucifer, I suspected a demon or devil, and not one of the nicer ones.

Incubi and succubi ranked at the forefront of known demons, but many more types lurked in the dark places of the world, and

they weren't interested in pleasurable de-
bauchery.

"I'm not sure if I should be flattered or
not, although I do have one question for you
—and answering it won't classify as meddling. Consider this a single exemption, Luna.
But you have to answer honestly if you answer at all."

"I'm an angel. I'm always honest."

"Don't forget who you're talking to, Luna."
I folded both sheets of paper and set them on
the edge of my desk. "I may not be a match
for you at the lying without lying game, but
I've done my fair share of it." I clacked my
teeth together. "I lost everything playing that
game, so don't play it with me right now."

"Humans are interesting creatures. Just
when I think they're no longer capable of
surprising me, they do. Very well. Ask your
question."

"Why do you want me to meet this Lucavier fellow? And don't even ask me to try to
pronounce his last name."

"I believe it's perhaps Italian in origin. I
could have been wanting you to see the official copy of your innocence."

"As an angel capable of seeing into the
past and future, I'm sure you already knew I
had a copy. Nice try. Why do you want me to
meet this fellow?"

"Aren't you more interested to know why he's so interested in meeting you?"

"If I was more interested, I would have asked. No, I want to know why *you* want me to meet him."

"I choose not to answer at all."

"And that's an even more interesting answer than if you'd just told me the truth. Next week, Luna. Do try to make an appointment so you don't interrupt my work unnecessarily."

When she vanished in a flash of golden light, I laughed. I dropped the envelope on the floor for Kitten, Destroyer of Worlds to play with and went back to work.

FIFTEEN

I aimed for functionality.

WHILE I WOULD HAVE THOUGHT the art of forging swords would have gone the way of the dodo hundreds of years ago, Indianapolis had over fifty blacksmiths specialized in bladed weapons. Under the guise of wrapping up a little extra work, I stayed late, spreading my time between actual tasks I needed to do and finding a heinously expensive, good quality weapon capable of making even an angel cry.

If Luna had been wise, she would have given me a spending cap. I suspected she forgot the nuances of mortal life, including the value of money, but she was an angel. I had faith she could figure out how to pay for a sword I was going to pick based on a lot of factors, none of which included my skill with a blade of any sort. The blacksmith I hired would likely hate me for it, too.

I aimed for functionality and work of art,

and if I could have a weapon that had a certain amount of wow factor to it, even better.

I narrowed my search to five blacksmiths in the area, and I hoped one of them would be able to give me some insights on who might be the best person to forge a weapon perfect for getting a solid jab in at an angel. Once I finished the work I used to keep me in the office after hours, I picked up my phone and dialed the first on my list, a centaur who went by Hamhock.

According to the little research I had done, Hamhock held a good reputation as a knowledgeable blacksmith specialized in weapons of all types, mastering none but known a great deal about them all, which made her ideal for my situation. With luck, she could point me in the right direction.

"Hamhock's Forge," a woman barked after the third ring.

"My name is Reed Matthews, and I'm looking for some information about having a sword commissioned."

"Sec. Lemme get da boss."

The phone clattered on something hard, and I ended up listening to a series of grimace-inducing thuds, grunts, and a couple of yelps. Shod hooves on stone warned me of a centaur's approach to the phone.

"Hamhock speaking," the airy soprano of another woman said.

"Reed Matthews. I'm looking for information on having a sword commissioned. Any chance you can help me?"

"I forge swords. What type are you looking for?"

"My goal is to have a weapon so nice it makes an angel weep with jealousy, especially after she pays for it and it sinks in it belongs to me and not her. I might actually need two, one I can learn with, and then the actual sword once I won't utterly disgrace it." I allowed myself a single chuckle. "Price is no issue, as I have the solemn vow of an angel she will purchase the weapon of my choice. I figured I'd let someone who knows swords better than I do tell me what sort of blade is best for me."

"That's an interesting request. I'm not skilled enough to make that sort of weapon."

Perfect. I liked her honesty, which supported my thought she would be just the right person to talk to. While I wasn't surprised, I faked a disappointed sigh. "All right. Maybe you can start me off figuring out what sort of sword is suitable for me, and I'll buy one to learn while I look for someone who might be able to make one for me?"

"Now that I can do. Are you busy tonight?"

"I'm free. I was about to leave work."

"Do you have the address of my forge?"

I relayed the address I had found on the internet. "That the place?"

"It is. How long will it take for you to get here?"

"Probably thirty minutes if traffic isn't bad. Call it forty to be on the safe side."

"I'll be waiting, Mr. Matthews."

"Reed, please. Thanks for your help." I hung up. Maybe Hamhock couldn't forge the sword I wanted, but I wasn't against spending some money to better my plan of getting a sword that would make Luna think twice about future meddling. I trusted she wouldn't break her vow to me, but I wasn't stupid enough to believe she wouldn't meddle elsewhere.

It took five minutes to catch my kitten, who insisted on zipping between my feet, climbing places she shouldn't, and otherwise doing her best to drive me insane. When I got my hands on her, she mewed, nuzzled me, and purred, thus dodging the scolding she rightfully deserved.

Damned cat.

Once I had her harnessed, I shrugged into her favorite coat and dumped her on my shoulder, her leash secured around my wrist in case she decided to attempt an escape. She'd tried it once but hadn't gotten far before I'd stepped on the line and brought her to a rather sudden stop.

"You're supposed to be a therapy kitten, not the reason I finally take a dive off the deep end," I muttered, scratching her chin on my way down to the garage to my junker. "This Hamhock lady is going to laugh in my face when I bring you over. I'd lock you in your carrier, but I expect you'd try to wreck it and cost me even more money, you evil little beast."

The evil little beast in question pounced my hand and mouthed at my knuckles.

At least Kitten, Destroyer of Worlds didn't mind being leashed so she couldn't bother me while I was driving. Once certain she had adopted her habit of looking out the passenger window, I headed for Hamhock's Forge to learn if the centaur would laugh in my face or at least have the common courtesy to wait until I left.

Thirty-six minutes later, in the battered heart of Indianapolis's industrial sector, I parked in the only free spot in front of a former warehouse. The building had seen better days, but instead of more traditional repairs, Hamhock had patched the worn siding with broken weapons of all shapes and sizes, creating what might count as art to someone with an interest in the aftermaths of battle.

Kitten, Destroyer of Worlds hissed and hid in my hood.

The front door, decorated with a fan of swords, opened. When I thought of centaurs, I thought of horses, felines, or wolves with the heads and torsos of humans; it varied between species. Most centaurs avoided the places I went.

The woman who trotted out barely came up to my shoulders, was coal black from head to hoof, and she held her chin high so she could look me in the eyes. "You Reed?"

Too late to flinch away, the jolt of connection slammed through me, and the chest-tightening I associated with yearning tore at me. In most cases, my sight manifested as a mixture of images and feelings. With Hamhock, it came as a rush of emotion, the longing for the thrill of battle, one she believed outside of her reach.

That was new. Normally, I only saw the desire and not the obstruction.

Hamhock believed herself too small and too weak to battle alongside the others of her kind, a weakness rather than an asset. She fought in the only way she knew how, with the weapons she forged for her kin. No matter the size, no matter the shape, she would provide. She lived through the work of her hands without ever satisfying her weary heart.

To mask my discomfort, I held out my hand while diverting my gaze to the relative safety of her forehead. "I'm Reed. You're Hamhock?"

She gripped my hand so hard my knuckles turned white. The pigheaded man in me wanted me to accept her challenge, but I settled with a firm squeeze. "That's me. Are you aware there is a cat in your coat?"

"I've been informed she's my therapy kitten and should go everywhere with me. Mostly, she gets into trouble and makes me question my sanity, but she's too cute to kill. Her name is Kitten, Destroyer of Worlds. I picked her up as a rescue, but I've been told it would do me some good to take care of another living thing for some reason. She's grown on me. I can put her in her carrier in the car if she'll be a problem."

"Interesting. She's no problem. Come on in, then. You won't be running into battle with a two-hander, but I think I might be able to work with you. What sort of tricks are you packing?"

Since I doubted she'd be happy if I told her what I'd seen, I settled with a half-truth. "Nothing of use. I've been told I should avoid guns."

"Why?"

With my luck, Luna would spill my secrets anyway, and since I was putting my weapon selection in Hamhock's hooves, I figured being upfront would serve me better than secrecy "I'm only about a third human, and the rest of my genetics seem to favor getting up close and personal with people."

"Angel spawn?"

"No, but both of my parents are."

Hamhock looked me over head to toe, and she flashed me a predatory smile. "Now *that's* interesting. Come on in, watch your step, and point at the first weapon to catch your eye. We'll start there."

I wasn't sure what I was expecting, but a minefield of blades scattered over the floor wasn't it. Small paths, barely enough for Hamhock to navigate, meandered through the selection. Hundreds of weapons of all shapes and sizes waited, from daggers no longer than my finger to swords taller than I was.

"Holy shit," I spluttered, freezing in the doorway to gawk.

"I may have gone slightly overboard laying everything out. I'm not the best smith on the block, but I'm versatile. If it's a weapon, I can forge it. And if I can forge it, I know someone who can make one beautiful and lethal enough to make even angels cry." Easing her way through the room, which was easily fifty feet across, Hamhock stood by a set of battered steel doors, scarred by what I suspected were hoof scuffs. "So, have a look. Tell me what you like."

It only took one look around the room to realize I knew nothing at all about swords. When I thought I recognized a katana, there were four other blades similar to it of varying lengths. Picking my way through the weapons, I wondered how anyone could learn to forge so many different types.

The first one to make me stop and stare wasn't a sword at all, not exactly, but a staff with a curved blade on its end. I pointed at it. "What is that thing?"

"That is a naginata, a Japanese weapon similar to the European glaive. It's used in several forms of martial arts and is good on both the offense and defense. It's traditionally used by women, but you're no Hercules, Reed Matthews. I'd go so far to say you're rather scrawny. While there are heavier naginata better suited for warrior men, perhaps one meant for a woman's hand might better service you. You are not too tall, you are not broad in the shoulder. You are not manly like the men they give the monsters of swords to."

"Ask the trees in my back yard. I'm mean with an axe."

The centaur chuckled and picked her way across to the naginata, which she grabbed and swished through the air. "Now this would prove a challenge for a master to craft a piece worthy of making an angel cry. This weapon fell out of favor before the Edo period in

Japan. Firearms and the subsequent shift in warfare spelled the weapon's demise—of sorts. Its purpose changed. It became a woman's weapon. Later, it became a symbol and a part of a woman's spiritual growth. Now, it is a hobby, changed far from its roots on the battlefield. It has been a long time since anyone has used a naginata in the old way. To bring someone into a lost art so old? Yes, I know the perfect woman to inflict you upon. It will be an honor watching her weep."

"I'm sensing a theme, and it involves tears."

"Of which you will contribute many."

"Delightful."

Hamhock smirked and thumped the butt of the naginata on the ground. "Tell me why you pointed this weapon out to me over all the others."

I turned to the weapons similar to a katana, gesturing towards them. "I thought I recognized a katana, but saw there were several weapons similar to it. At that point, I figured I really had no idea what I was looking at. So, I looked around." Shrugging, I pivoted to face the centaur.

The naginata's blade brushed against my throat, and had its edge been sharpened, I would have bled. "What do you see now?"

Kitten, Destroyer of Worlds scrambled onto my shoulder, hissed, and smacked her paw against the weapon. She paddled it, her tail lashing as her strikes proved rather ineffective. "My decapitation if I'm not really careful."

"A good answer. Let me ask you a new question." Hamhock eased the naginata away from my throat and tapped its butt against the floor. "Why do you want a sword?"

"I have an angel who keeps meddling in my affairs, so I think I'm going to need it along with a crash course in not dying." I grimaced. My pride wouldn't like my next words, but if I was going to trust Hamhock to help me pick a weapon, then she needed to know my suspicions. "While I have limited faith said angel will stop directly meddling, I think she gave up too easily. Considering she was willing to make an agreement with me about buying a fiendishly expensive sword and provide the training to use it, something tells me I'm going to need it."

"Self-defense, then."

I nodded. "It's just me and my cat. There's no one else in my life."

It seemed strange without the past haunting me quite so much, leaving me more alone than I'd been before the day Kennedy Young had crashed back into my life. Our paths had led different places, and I hoped she found whatever it was her heart desired, grateful I'd dodged finding out. I'd done so well avoiding eye contact with people until Hamhock.

The centaur's desire would bother me for a long time. It always did, when I slipped and caught a glimpse without being prepared. When I went hopping through bars, I readied myself for the inevitable, then I basked in the glow of their contentment.

I doubted their satisfaction would last long, but I'd savored the respite.

"Might I recommend a Carolingian sword?" After returning the naginata to its place leaning against the wall, Hamhock crossed the room, stretched out her front legs, and picked up a sword with a blade a little over two feet in length and a short hilt with a rounded pommel. "It's versatile enough, and I think it could send an interesting message."

"Message? What message?"

"'Don't fuck with Vikings' comes to mind."

"Vikings?" I narrowed my eyes and regarded the blade with a healthy mix of doubt and caution. "That's a Viking sword?"

"It sure is. Best of all, it's meant to be used with a shield, and nothing is quite as much fun as bashing someone's face in with a shield. Not only do you get to protect yourself, but you'll look stylish while doing so."

My brows took a hike. "Vikings were stylish?"

Hamhock shot a glare at me. "I'll have you know the Carolingian is the forefather of many a great sword, including the arming sword."

"Arming sword?"

With a long-suffering sigh, the centaur bowed her head. "Think Excalibur."

"Wasn't Excalibur supposedly fairly plain as far as mystical lost swords went?"

"It was. But Excalibur came from an era of knights and chivalry and twisted ethics. No, for you, I think a beautiful but brutal weapon is best. Your foes will look at you and see a pretty man, a modern-day elf without the pointy ears. All willowy and lovely. Then they'll underestimate you. It'll be too late for them, for by then, you'll have whipped out your sword and taught them a thing or two before lopping off their head and using it as a weapon, too. It's always important to use both hands in battle."

It took gargantuan effort, but I somehow managed not to laugh. "So basically, my mantra should be something along the lines of 'pretty as elf, vicious as Viking?' The actual Vikings are probably rolling in their graves. I don't even want to ask about the elves." While I'd heard of elves, I'd never met one, nor did I have any interest in meeting one.

"I think you misunderstand," the centaur replied in a grave tone. "There is nothing more vicious than an elf, and fewer still more beautiful than one. My father always warned me to steer clear of the elves on the battle-field. They sometimes forget they're sup-posed to kill their dinner before they eat it."

That startled me enough I gaped at the centaur, so surprised I hardly noticed when I met her gaze and held it. "Say what?"

"Never underestimate an elf. It would be the last thing you do. Yes, a Carolingian blade is perfect for you. But can it be done? Now that's the real question."

"Can what be done?" I asked, although I feared the answer.

"Transforming you into a modern-day elf, of course. How else can we mere mortals make an angel weep?" Hamhock pranced in place. "Yes, this is perfect, and I know just the woman to make your sword."

"Luna is supposed to pick the instructor. She said she only wanted the best to teach me."

"There is no better teacher, and should she tell you otherwise, it is a lie." The cen-taur's smile chilled me. "Do you know what happens should an angel lie?"

"No, I don't."

"Now *that* would be interesting. I do hope we get to find out."

I worried but kept my misgivings to my-self. A sword was only part of the puzzle. The real trick was learning to use it, and I got the feeling my life would be turned upside down in a new and unusual way—one that would keep me busy outside of work for the first time since leaving Mississippi three years ago.

SIXTEEN

The only mysteries I enjoyed were the ones I wasn't involved with.

HAMHOCK PROMISED to call me in the next day or two with more information on how much my swords would cost along with an introduction to the woman who would forge them and teach me how to use them. I spent the drive home that night wondering how so much could change so fast.

Bargaining with an angel meant trouble, especially when the angel was unhappy with her end of the deal. I'd either done something right or wrong by challenging her, but I had no idea which. Until I had a chance to speak with Lucavier, I would be blind to the full reality of my situation. In that, Luna had been right.

Every action I made would have a consequence. Inaction also had consequences, if Luna was to be believed.

However, I doubted. I doubted everything

the angel said from the moment she'd warned me of the accident and subsequent kidnapping. None of it made sense. Why kidnap me and dump me in Mississippi? The why was almost as confusing as the how; a mystery to everyone, including me.

The only mysteries I enjoyed were the ones I wasn't involved with.

Despite it being a work night, my anxiety and curiosity got the better of me. Why would anyone kidnap me? Was my inaction regarding the letter—an invitation of all things—the reason for it? If so, was Lucavier somehow involved?

The more I thought about it, the more my suspicions turned in one direction: Luna's.

Immortals surpassed any magic humans could ever hope to possess, even the odder ones like myself. Then there were the truly magical races, like Hamhock and her centaur kin. In a lot of ways, humans were the ants of the sentient world, hiding in every nook and cranny, thriving despite adversity, stronger than their size would imply. I found it odd I still classified as a human. Then again, I couldn't classify as an angel or demon, either.

Even vanilla humans could tap into more practical magics than mine, although I had dabbled as a practitioner enough that I could cause problems if I put my mind to it. Then again, maybe magic held the solution to my problems.

It'd been months since I'd last dabbled, giving up the hope of blinding my angelic sight. If I turned my attentions to other forms of magic, a different sort of solution could be found. Angels weren't the only beings capable of discerning the truth, and in my efforts to blind my cursed sight, I'd found ways to augment my hearing so I could tell if someone lied, too.

Once I figured out what the spell did, I'd buried it, hiding it among my research. Seeing things was bad enough, but hearing the truths of someone's words unnerved me almost as much as seeing the desires of their heart. However, unlike my sight, I could make it work no matter the distance.

When I called Lucavier, I'd know the truth of his words, and I'd be able to learn a bit more about what was so important three angels would harass me about his invitation to speak with him. As far as spells went, the truth one was simple enough.

It only took a little bit of water, a drop of my blood, and a rune drawn on paper to cast, although it came at a price. Until I burned the sheet, I couldn't lie. Until the page ignited, destroying my blood, even omissions would prove difficult to contain.

I would need to watch every word and choose them with care.

Fortunately for me, it was a skill I'd mastered long ago, starting with the day I had willfully incarcerated myself for a young woman's sake. With a grim smile, I went inside my home, released Kitten, Destroyer of Worlds, and headed for my bedroom.

While I had told Kennedy my home lacked a basement, I hadn't been entirely honest. Technically, the crawl space didn't count as a basement, although it served the same purpose. It hid what I didn't want the rest of the world to find.

Most accepted practitioners as a part of society, a way to tap into magic the untalented couldn't. Some excelled at it, capable of doing anything with enough research, practice, and supplies. I fell somewhere in between. Some things came as naturally as breathing, including the truth spell. Others, such as the art of breathing flame or dousing it, eluded me.

Instead of a rectangle, I had shaped the trap door so it matched the irregularities of the hardwood planks. It made the space awkward to access, but if I needed to get to anything in an emergency, it was probably already too late.

My sort of practitioner magic took time to cast, making it less than ideal for anything

I needed in a hurry. I fetched the jar of calligraphy ink, my feather quills, and the heavy paper I liked best for my experiments, hiding the space when I finished. Through the whole process, Kitten, Destroyer of Worlds watched me, the tip of her tail twitching.

"It's nothing that interesting," I informed her, setting everything on the counter and spreading them out. Given a few seconds, I was willing to bet my kitten would knock over the ink and track little black paw prints all over my house, so I took care to work my foot under her tiny belly and shunt her aside whenever she started eyeing my pants as a method of getting a closer look at what I was doing.

Ten minutes later, with a faint discomfort in both ears indicating I'd accomplished something with my rune, blood, and a drop of water, I dug out my phone and Lucavier's invitation. Calling someone at a little before eleven at night counted as rude, but if the man was determined enough to mail me at least once a month, he could cope with some inconveniences.

With only the element of surprise in my favor, I'd use whatever cheap tricks I could to get a handle on what Luna—and Lucavier—wanted with me. I expected nothing good.

The phone rang, and on the fifth tone, I

was about ready to give up when the line clicked.

"Lucavier," a man barked with a hint of a growl in his voice.

Truth.

Magic manifested in different ways, even when using the same spell, but I'd never heard a ghostly rendition of my own voice in my ears whispering to me before. I eyed the circular rune, wondering if I'd somehow done something to one of the sketched knots ringing the inner portion of the drawing.

"Reed Matthews. An angel annoyed me into opening your letter."

"Mr. Matthews." The man's growl turned to something eerily similar to Kitten, Destroyer of World's best purr. "I've been waiting a long time for your call."

False.

I narrowed my eyes, wondering how someone could tell a lie in so few words. I could believe he had been waiting for my call; he'd been sending the letters for years. I decided it had to do with the duration of his wait, implying he belonged to a long-lived species. To Luna, three years wasn't long to wait, so I could assume the same applied to Lucavier. "Is three years truly a long time for you, though?" I asked, forcing myself to sound amused.

"Not at all."

Truth.

Just what I needed in my life, another immortal—or someone so long lived I barely counted as a blip on his radar. "Then let me get straight to the chase, then. I have a couple of questions for you, and in exchange, I'll listen to whatever you have to say to me on the phone."

"In person would be better."

"Then answer a few of my questions in exchange for considering making a trip to see you." Bargaining with Lucavier from the gate would either help or hinder me, but I'd rather annoy him than end up his walking mat, which I'd probably end up anyway despite my efforts.

"That seems like a fair trade."

Truth.

"I have two or three questions to start with."

"Ask."

"Did you have anything to do with my impromptu trip to Mississippi recently?"

The silence bothered me, although I couldn't put my finger on why. Then Lucavier made a soft noise, a blend of a growl and huff. "Had I known you were in Mississippi recently, I would have paid you a visit and spared us both this verbal dance."

Truth.

The trick to asking questions was to get as

much information as possible without revealing anything. With my next question, I'd
hit two birds with one stone—and find out if
he had anything to do with the SUV's crash at
the same time. "So you know nothing of the
car accident?"

"I have no idea what you're talking about,
Mr. Matthews."

Truth.

While I wanted to ask if Lucavier had a
connection with Luna, the memory of the
angel putting blame directly on the letter and
my refusal to read it bothered me even more.
"All right. Besides you, who else knows about
what was inside the letters you sent to me?"

"You ask odd questions, Mr. Matthews."

Truth.

I choked back a laugh. "I won't argue with
that."

"The postman knows I send letters to
your address, although he doesn't know
what's inside—or she, when the alternative
carrier is working. The local courthouse
knows, as I put in frequent requests for certi-
fied copies of your exoneration. I do rather
appreciate not having to do that anymore, so
thank you for that. The courthouse employees do not know why I requested the
records. I suppose the stationary company
wonders why I keep buying the paper stock
in packets of five rather than just buying in

bulk. I would have saved myself some money had I not underestimated your stubbornness and aversion to my inquiries. As for the contents itself and my invitation, the gentleman in charge of maintaining my household is aware, in case he needs to make preparations for your visit. One of my maids is also aware, as she is in charge of ensuring all guests to my home have everything they require. I have told no one else, and those in my household would not share my business with anyone else."

Truth.

Well, well, well. I found his honesty refreshing—and startling. Few said so much without even the hint of a lie in their words "Thank you for being so candid with me, Lucavier. Please, call me Reed."

"Excellent. I have been following your case since your initial court trial and found your rather deliberate withholding of the truth to be of great interest to me, especially considering the circumstances. Manipulating an angel into verifying the partial truth of your statement was an interesting choice. I wish to discuss this with you in person."

Truth.

"I'm not sure that's worth me making a trip all the way to Mississippi to talk about in person. It's quite simple."

"Not as simple as you might think."

Truth.

As long as the paper remained with the rune, I couldn't tell a lie, not even by accident. I thought through Luna and her angelic companions. All three of them had spoken to me of the letter, although Luna's interest in it surpassed the others. "You might be right. Were you aware that there are potentially three angels who seems rather keen on me making your acquaintance?"

There was another long silence. Kitten, Destroyer of Worlds pawed at my leg and mewed.

"Is that a cat I hear?"

With a soft laugh, I bent over and scooped up my kitten, cradling her in my arm. "Yes, I have a kitten. She's not quite four months old. She's a rescue but has been dubbed a therapy kitten. If I do decide to accept your invitation, she'll need to accompany me."

"You have a therapy kitten."

"Kitten, Destroyer of Worlds prefers to think of herself as a queen, probably of the universe. I'm merely her loyal, dedicated servant."

"You seem like a far more jovial individual than I was expecting, Mr. Matthews."

Truth.

"Therapy seems to be working." I set my kitten back on the floor before planting my elbows on the counter and staring down at the rune I'd drawn and stained with my blood. "One of the three angels in particular seems most keen on me making your acquaintance."

"I have no idea why any angel would want us to meet."

False.

"Can you think of a reason why someone might go through a great deal of effort to try to kill me to prevent us from meeting?"

"No, not that I can think of."

False.

"That's interesting." I traced my finger along the paper's edge, wondering how to deal with the man who wanted to meet me and had reason to believe someone might want me killed to prevent it. "True to our bargain, I'll consider meeting with you. I will need time to think about it, however."

"Of course. That's fair."

False.

I wondered about that. Did he not feel the matter deserved thought? "Unless there's something time sensitive about our meeting?"

"Possibly."

"If it's that important to you, perhaps you could come to Indianapolis. I've only recently had my stitches out, and I'm still taking medications, so I'd rather not travel right now." The truth was a funny thing. I spoke it, yet I toed the line; I felt the pressure in my ears increase, as though the magic warned me I strayed too far from honesty. "I also have some commitments here in town I'm uncomfortable abandoning."

The pressure eased.

"I hadn't considered coming to see you in Indianapolis."

Truth.

"I'm afraid I'm not a very good host and don't really have a home suitable for an esteemed guest, but there are some lovely hotels in the city serving all manners of individuals. I'll have to go over my schedule at work tomorrow, but if you can come to me, perhaps a meeting can be arranged."

"I'll admit, that does change quite a few of my plans."

Truth.

Change worked well for me. If the plans of others changed, I stood a better chance of avoiding any traps. "I understand. How does this work as a compromise? I'll give you my number, and should you decide to come visit Indianapolis, perhaps we can have a meeting. I'll be blunt with you. I have reason to believe there's more to this than meets the eye, and if associating with you will continue to elevate my risks of contracting a serious case of dead, I'd like to know about it. Your letter has already caused me numerous problems. I may be a mere mortal, but that doesn't make me the doormat for angels and whatever you might be, Lucavier."

"I find it interesting you didn't address yourself as a human."

Truth.

"The law views me as human, but I barely qualify as far as I'm concerned."

"The man you killed deserved his fate, Mr. Matthews. His death doesn't make you a monster."

Truth.

The unexpected validation from a stranger meant far more to me than I had thought possible. "No, his death isn't what makes me a monster."

"Then what does?"

Lucavier asked a good question. I thought about it, and he waited in expectant, patient silence. "Genetics."

The truth truly was a funny thing, as even the magic believed my reply was nothing but the truth. When combined, I suspected angels, demons, and mortals had great potential to become a monster. To humans, the demon in me already classified. To angels, the demon in me definitely classified, although I found it ironic and hypocritical the angels would willingly consort with demons to have a child with a mortal in the first place.

Monster was a good word for what I was, a blending of three things belonging to three different worlds. The dash of 'other' didn't help my case at all, although I wondered what else I was.

For some reason, I doubted it was something nice like an innocent faery.

"How curious. You are an interesting man, Reed Matthews. I look forward to meeting you. Give me a call in a few days. You have my number."

Truth.

Lucavier hung up on me, leaving me no closer to the truth although a bit better equipped to learn it. I burned the rune and my blood in my fireplace and spent a long time staring at the ashes, left with far more questions than answers. I walked away with one suspicion: I had a devil problem on my hand to go with my angel problem, and I didn't like it.

THE NEXT MORNING on my way to work, I bought myself a laptop. I had a company machine meant for working from home, tethering to my cell phone, but I'd been so reclusive I'd never wanted or needed one of my own. My first plan would be to research the possibilities, and I'd accomplish it staying late, squeezing in a few extra hours under the guise of playing catch up.

Once Hamhock got back to me, I expected a precarious balancing of my schedule. I wasn't even sure what was involved with learning how to use a sword or any form of martial art, but I expected a lot of bruises. As long as I could keep them limited to the shoulders down, I'd be all right. My co-workers were used to me having scuffed hands, something no one bothered me about after coming up with some excuse about liking the outdoors.

I waited until everyone else had left to set up my new laptop and get to work exploring parts of my life I'd otherwise ignored. At least I didn't have to think hard about what my first step would be.

Ever since the expansion of the Center for Disease Control and Prevention to oversee all things magical, one of its missions was to teach the general public what was out there, the type of sentients lurking in the world, and otherwise prepare humanity for its probable extinction. Only a paradox kept humanity even partially human, and I was living proof it worked —for now.

If magic obeyed the science of genetics, my parents would have either become angels, demons, or a conflicted mix of both. Instead, they were human, and not even very good ones. They weren't purebred—few were—but my parents were the closest humanity got despite their flawed heritage.

I had no idea what I actually classified as. While the CDC's public databases included many combinations of parentage to give expecting parents an idea of what was in store for them down the road, few had angelic blood at all. According to the CDC's files, angels reproducing with humans only happened once every five to ten years. I counted as a rarity among rarities, and I wasn't even an interesting one.

While my sight came from my angelic heritage, I had none of the classic symptoms of a demon on the rise. Women didn't throw themselves at me, although I usually had no trouble finding the ones who would be interested in taking me home with them. Had I showed any signs of being an active incubus, the CDC would have partnered me with an actual incubus until I learned to control my abilities.

I didn't have any of the classic symptoms of being a succubus, either, which involved a heightened empathic connection with just about everyone—and an ability to sense when someone was fertile. I'd heard incubi shared that trait with succubi, but I hadn't done much research into it. I counted my blessings with that one.

My emotions gave me enough trouble

without having to cope with the emotions of others, too.

Thanks to some magical law, instead of two powerful beings getting together and giving birth to a god, they got a human. Unfortunately, that same law didn't give a shit what happened a few generations down the line, resulting in some humans of questionable heritage with magic ratings far surpassing sane levels. In true human fashion, society celebrated them when they appeared, gave them the best jobs, and put them on pedestals for the world to admire.

Magic brought with it money, prestige, and power beyond their abilities. The CDC kept a close eye on them, too. Everything had a price, and the CDC made it clear that those with great power also had great responsibility —and a one-way trip to the grave if they screwed it up too much. When I thought of it that way, I didn't really mind my low magic rating.

It beat having a death sentence hanging over me all the time.

In the end, everything circled back to Luna and her interest in me. My angelic grandparents avoided me, as did my demonic ones, something I never really understood. They visited my parents often enough when I wasn't home, leaving me to catch glimpses of them on their way out the door.

I guess it actually made sense I had more issues than three therapists could readily address. On a high note, at least I hadn't snapped completely. If my ancestry was any indication, I could've ended up going on a rampage. I wasn't actually sure how demons fought, but they surely had a bad reputation for a *reason*. In a way, I viewed demons as more of a threat than angels.

Angels were a known, comfortable threat to humanity. People knew about demons, but beyond the sexual drives and urges of the incubi and succubi, few knew much about what they could actually do. Luna had dropped hints about my sharing certain things with angels, such as a lack of skill with firearms and a preference for swords.

I had an angel's sight. Luna implied I'd find I possessed an angel's affinity with blades.

What did my demon ancestry bring to the table? It wasn't an addiction to sex; I went without readily enough, and I didn't exactly miss my weekend forays seeking a partner. I couldn't even blame Kennedy for that, although she'd done a hell of a lot to remind me there was more to sex than just physical pleasure.

I liked that part well enough, but the entire game had changed with her, again. When I thought about it, I didn't even mind it all that much. As long as I kept avoiding looking people in the eyes, I could cope. The temporary relief of looking without *seeing* wasn't worth the hassle, not any more. I could find something else to occupy myself, like playing with my kitten and preventing her from destroying the world after she finished taking it over one unsuspecting mortal at a time.

The realization sank in I'd crested some peak, one that made it a lot easier to look on the bright side of things. My therapists would find that interesting. I even considered giving one of them a call—or, even better, making an appointment to meet a new one and start from scratch.

If I could take it from the top and work my way through every mistake of my life without cracking, I'd consider myself a functional adult. I chuckled, shook my head at my folly, and forced my attention back to my research.

Assuming Luna had told me the truth, I had at least two traits in common with angels. What could demons do? I had a decent enough grasp on their sexual abilities; while demons weren't exactly common, they weren't uncommon either, and I remembered my basic sex education courses, which included a section on succubi, incubi, and their presence within society.

Approximately a quarter of the population

had a trace amount of demon in them, although usually from an incubus. While succubi would offer their services to an angel, it was far less often.

For whatever reason, human women attracted angels more often than human men. I had my suspicions after seeing the desires of men and women alike. Women were more likely to desire a child as their deepest wish. Women were more likely to desire permanency, too.

Few men were like my father, who longed for only one thing: my mother. I'd seen enough of the world to understand just how unusual an unwavering, undying love for someone was.

In that, I was my father's son, but that was where our similarities ended.

Unlike him, I'd let Kennedy go. My father would never let my mother go. He would chase her to the ends of the Earth to stay with her, and he would give his final breath for her sake. I longed for what he had, but I was different in one critical way.

I wanted the same in return.

Kitten, Destroyer of Worlds clawed her way onto my lap, and I yelped at the unexpected feline assault. She paid no heed to her dagger-like talons attached to her cute, tiny paws, turning in circles several times before curling up and flicking her tail over her nose.

"Have I been neglecting you?" I muttered, unable to stop myself from smiling while I stroked her back. "I don't suppose you hold the secrets of the universe, do you?"

Obviously, my kitten had better things to do than humor me, as she went to sleep and ignored my questions. With a soft laugh, I returned to my research, hunting answers to questions I'd ignored for far too long.

SEVENTEEN

What happened to an angel who
lied?

IF I WANTED to learn the truth about my situation and pinpoint the nature of Lucavier's
interest in me, I needed to identify the unknown elements of my genes, which meant a
date with the CDC. The tests were expensive
unless there was just cause for them, but I
thought I'd be able to get them to rule in my
favor.

Change began with a phone call to my
doctor with the request for a genetic test, and
I cited my desire for a better understanding
of my family history as the just cause. As
progress was progress, no matter how
strange the progress seemed, my doctor
promised to refer me to a CDC specialist.

I left work at ten in the evening, pleased
with the progress I'd made finding out more
about my heritage so I might be able to understand how I'd become embroiled in a situ-

ation involving a devil and an angel. I
wondered if it had something to do with my
parents and their contribution of genes. I'd
never asked which angels or demons made up
my genetic makeup.

Everything I'd read indicated the children
of angels didn't receive the same scrutiny or
experience the same prejudices I did, although Luna implied I wasn't avoided for the
reasons I thought. I wasn't sure if I believed
her.

Hamhock had planted a seed of doubt I
couldn't forget.

What happened to an angel who lied?

My thoughts amused me the entire drive
home, and I eased my car down the trail
leading to my property to discover a vehicle
waiting for me with a red-haired woman
perched on the trunk.

Instead of a panic attack, I got a hefty dose
of general confusion. Not that long ago, she'd
gone to California, and I'd believed I would
finally be able to continue on with my life, at
ease with where we'd left off.

Somewhere along the way, I'd gotten lost
—or she had. No, she had. Gypsum Creek
was nowhere near California, and I'd just
gone to work and met a woman about
forging a sword.

The only way I'd find out what Kennedy
was doing at my home was to ask her, so I

killed the engine and prepared to face her again, torn between excitement and worry.

Kennedy arched a brow as I got out of my car. "I was starting to think you'd be gone all night. That would've ruined my plans."

Maybe Kennedy hadn't gotten lost after all, which added to my sense of excitement. "I thought you were needed in California."

"I went to California, finished my business in California, and after about five minutes of thought, decided I'd wander my way back here and impose on you. My boss was delightfully confused by my insistence I'd be coming back here. He regretted asking why but approved my time off while he pursues a transfer closer to the area."

"You're transferring?"

"I am. Mississippi's too fucking hot and muggy for my blood, and I have a few good reasons to stick around."

Her presence at my home implied I was one of those reasons.

Had anyone told me my life would completely change within a few weeks, I would've laughed at them and recommended my doctors. I'd have to thank Luna for ensuring I hadn't missed my date with a car accident, too. Of all the disasters to happen in my life, that one had given me what I needed most and had done some serious work on giving me back what I wanted most in life.

I wondered what my heart would tell an angel; I couldn't think of anything I actually wanted. Another chance at life topped my list, and I could grab it in both hands if I wanted. Making the decision to take the chance to see what would happen with Kennedy didn't take me long.

As she wouldn't understand my smile, I did my best to hide it. "You're going to be disappointed to learn Indiana has issues of its own in the weather department."

"Perhaps so, but the company is superior here. I'm concerned you'll get into trouble if left unattended."

I couldn't blame her for her correct assumption, especially as I had a mess of angels and devils on my hands. As soon as I got her inside, I'd get her opinion on the situation. It hadn't occurred to me to ask someone from the CDC directly for intel on my current set of problems. "How long are you going to be in town?"

"That depends on a lot of things. Let's talk about it inside. Your kitten probably needs to perform her acts of biological warfare after such a long drive from work."

"Would you believe I sometimes delay going inside a while knowing what's going to happen?"

"Without hesitation. And how is your therapy kitten doing?"

"She feels neglected if I leave her for even ten minutes without paying her dues."

"Well, that's a cat for you." Kennedy slid off her car and strode towards me. "Your therapists are going to either hate or love me."

"There comes a point where repeated instances of ex sex results in the ex part being stricken from the record, right? And I'm pretty sure if you're living with me, even temporarily, the claims of ex status aren't valid." I wasn't sure if I wanted her to confirm we might be able to build from the rubble or if I hoped she'd get angry, put me in my place, and set expectations at something far shallower.

As always, she got under my skin.

It occurred to me I never needed my cursed sight to recognize what my heart had desired all along, which made me far more similar to my father than I liked to think. Even buried beneath the anger and resentment, it'd always been her.

"We can discuss that inside. I'm expecting you'll require a trial period, a full disclosure on my work so you'll know my likely travel schedule, when you might be allowed to travel with me, and so on. And the issue of your therapy kitten."

"My therapy kitten stays, non-negotiable. She might be plotting to destroy the world, but she's my menace to life on Earth. I'm a jealous cat parent, apparently."

"I was more thinking you might need a therapy puppy to go with your therapy kitten."

In college, we'd both wanted a dog, something our apartment hadn't allowed. "I'm willing to negotiate on a therapy puppy if we can find one that the therapy kitten likes."

"I brought a candidate with me."

My brows rose. "You brought a puppy with you?"

"I found it on the side of the road aban-doned. I couldn't just leave it!"

Having heard that story before, I wouldn't blame her. "Kitten, Destroyer of Worlds, I fear Kennedy has been suckered as I have been suckered. Please accept your new canine friend with minimal fuss. So, Kennedy. What did you name it?"

"I figured I'd take a page out of your book, so I named him Puppy, Savior of Worlds."

I clamped my mouth closed so I wouldn't laugh. I choked, coughed, and retrieved my kitten from the car. "We're possibly the worst pet owners ever to walk the face of the Earth."

"I'd say we're compassionate human be-ings who can't let helpless animals starve, and he's done nothing but drink milk and sleep since I found him. He's cost me a fortune, though."

"I know that story. How old is he?"

"He's two to three weeks old, and he gets special milk for at least another week. The vet called it a replacer milk, but I was able to find it at the grocery store. Right now, he's sleeping. Actually, I always think he's sleeping unless he's wiggling around. His eyes aren't fully open yet. The vet was a little worried about that, but his eyes don't seem to be bothering him. It could just be because he's malnourished. Puppy, Savior of Worlds has another appointment next week to see how he's doing."

"Sucker," I teased, bringing Kitten, Destroyer of Worlds to Kennedy's car. "Let's see if the myth of cats and dogs is true, shall we?"

"Inside, just in case the next world war breaks out. Not that it'd be much of one. He's really small and won't be able to put up a fight."

"What breed?"

"Corgi. The vet thinks he's a purebred, too. He'll be a nice dog for us."

I wondered how I'd gone from resentment to being intrigued at the idea of sharing space with Kennedy and two pets. Had I progressed farther than I thought, or was I clinging to what might have been? I didn't think it mattered much. Moving forward seemed to be a combination of taking step backs and ditching the baggage I didn't want to take with me into the future.

Of all the baggage I'd carried around with me, a second chance with Kennedy seemed a hell of a lot better than an endless stream of unhappy one-night stands. All it would take was a single look into Kennedy's eyes to know the truth of her heart.

I was afraid to look, but I wanted it more than I'd wanted anything else in years.

"I'll keep her leashed until we see how she gets along with him," I promised, hauling my cat and the rest of my junk to the front door. While Kennedy had warned me her puppy was small, he was even smaller than I antici-pated, and I worried I'd become a doting pet parent within the hour.

I performed the typical shuffle to unlock my door without losing my kitten or drop-ping anything, but I disrupted my habits to let Kennedy go in first so she could get settled with her puppy. "Did you remember how to get back here or did you call the power company?"

"I may have lost an hour or two poking my nose through town to find the entry, but I managed without having to rely on the power company, and I made sure my rental was small enough to get here without scratching it. You don't mind me imposing on you?"

"Not at all. And all things considered, that probably makes me a weirdo," I admitted.

"You've progressed from panic attacks to ready acceptance pretty quickly. Your doctors are going to be happy."

"Or horrified I'm inviting my ex to move in with me with her young puppy."

"That, too. Do you think flowers will work on a bunch of upset doctors?"

"Probably not. Since you've admitted you have some disclosures to make, I have a few disclosures to make, too."

"Sounds good. Where should I put the puppy?"

"Set him on the floor, and let's see what happens."

As though aware something new and interesting was about to happen, Kitten purred and wiggled in my hold until I set her on the floor. Kennedy knelt and released her puppy, and he wiggled on the carpet, wagging his tailless rump.

"What happened to his tail?"

"He's a Pembroke Welsh corgi. They don't have tails. I was worried, too. There's another breed of corgi that has a tail, but he's not it."

"Okay, I have to admit, he's cute. I can't blame you for being suckered in." Uncertain of what my kitten would do, I kept a firm hold on her leash before letting her loose to investigate the pale wriggling ball of fur on the carpet.

As with everything else new and exciting in Kitten, Destroyer of World's life, she locked onto the puppy and wasted no time investigating, her tail twitching as she approached.

The puppy's high-pitched whining noises cinched the deal. Even if the next world war broke out in my living room, I'd have to find a way to make it work somehow. That the puppy came bundled with Kennedy didn't matter.

The puppy stayed, and there were no if, ands, or buts about it.

"I know that look," Kennedy said, her tone light with laughter. "He's *my* puppy. I found him."

"I'm pretty sure you said something about introducing me to a therapy puppy, so he's mine, but you can live here too and visit as often as you want."

"As that falls in line with my plans, I can work around that, but I'm going to require equal visitation rights to the kitten, too."

"Only if you help scoop the litter box."

"Harsh."

I grinned. "Maybe a little. We could just say we're both in need of therapy and we've decided to share our therapy pets."

"Think a cat and a dog will be enough therapy for the pair of us?"

"I hope so. I like to think I've been getting somewhere lately."

"You didn't panic when you found me at your house tonight, so I'm going to go out on a limb and say you have."

Oblivious to our conversation, my kitten crept closer to Kennedy's puppy, stretching out her nose to sniff. When the puppy kept whining, she reached with a paw and nudged the squirming ball of tan fur.

I bet the puppy wanted milk, and he was willing to try his luck on my kitten's paw. Kitten, Destroyer of Worlds turned her head towards me as though asking what I'd brought into her house. As fur hadn't started flying immediately, I unharnessed her and let them figure things out. "Where's the puppy's milk? I think he's hungry. I'll get Kitten fed so we can deal with round one of her biological warfare for the night."

"It's in the car with my bag."

"Go get your things and make yourself comfortable. I'll keep an eye on the beasts."

The beasts seemed indifferent to their situation, and after determining Puppy, Savior of Worlds wasn't a threat to her domain, Kitten, Destroyer of Worlds bounced to her food dish for her evening offerings. The puppy's whine intensified the instant my kitten abandoned him for her supper.

Of everything I'd heard about cats and dogs, we'd dodged a bullet or ten, and I wondered when the shootout between the pair would happen. I could see Kitten, Destroyer of Worlds waiting until her foe could put up more of a fight.

In an act of blatant bribery, I gave her more wet food than normal hoping to convince my cat I wasn't abandoning her for a ruthlessly cute puppy.

It didn't take long for Kennedy to return with a duffel and a suitcase. She dumped the load by the door, huffed, and returned to her car.

"I think she brought more than just a bag," I informed to my therapy kitten. "It's an invasion, and I think I've already surrendered. Obviously, I have a weakness for baby animals. I wonder what my therapists will say about that the next time I see them."

"That's a good question. I accept the terms of your surrender."

"There were terms?"

"No, there wasn't," she replied with a smug smile. "I brought a puppy to make your surrender easier to bear."

While Kitten, Destroyer of Worlds had sunk her claws into my soul through obviously demonic means, the puppy's helplessness had an innocent edge, and I worried the forces of heaven and hell would take over my home. "For the record, the puppy wasn't necessary to successfully stage your invasion, but I find myself utterly incapable of rejecting him."

"I swear, I was just coming from the airport when I saw something on the side of the road. I stopped and found the puppy. I would've been here several hours earlier, but I had to find a vet and buy supplies for him. The vet offered to try to find him a home, but I didn't want to leave him alone in a cage."

"That's how Kitten, Destroyer of Worlds secured her place as my feline overlady. Your canine overlord has taken advantage of you. I just thought you'd appreciate knowing the truth."

"Yeah, I figured that out around the same time I was giving a pet store seventy dollars for a dog bed."

"And here I thought fifty for the cat bed my cat usually refuses to use was expensive."

"We're suckers."

"Definitely. In good news, I can take him to work with me if you have to work and can't take him with you. My boss won't mind, especially when I tell him he still needs to be bottle fed."

"I have at least a week off, but when I have

to travel, I'd appreciate if you could care for him."

"I'm pretty sure that's what people who share living space do for each other by default. I'm afraid to ask how much stuff you've abandoned in Mississippina."

"Not as much as you'd think. I've done a lot of traveling for work. You're not the only one who needs a good therapist," she admitted. "You're just better at admitting it and going to sessions. Your therapists would have a field day with me."

Certain they would, I fetched my cell, thumbed through my contacts to retrieve Dr. Dentannin's number, the poor bastard saddled with any late-night questions, confessions, or urges to communicate I might have. In the years since moving to Indiana, I'd called him a handful of times, each one following a hospitalization due to a panic attack.

He'd love me waking him up to ask if he wanted to tackle Kennedy's issues along with mine.

I connected the call and listened to the ringtone.

"Did you have a panic attack, Reed?" my therapist asked.

"For the first time in our relationship, I'm pleased to inform you that I'm not calling you due to a panic attack. I have a question or two for you."

"Are you all right?"

While I understood why he asked, I fought the urge to roll my eyes. "I have a two or three week old puppy in my house. I'm pretty sure 'all right' has my picture next to it in the dictionary right now. I seem to have developed a bad habit involving the adoption of young animals. Should I be concerned?"

"Not at all. It's a good development. May I inquire where you got a puppy? I've been considering suggesting you volunteer at an animal rescue since you rescued your kitten. That was a pleasant surprise. How is Kitten, Destroyer of Worlds doing?"

I loved that I could coerce a professional into addressing my ridiculous feline by her complete name without any sign of shame. "She's doing well. She's curious about her new roommate, but she's deemed he isn't a threat, so she's having her dinner."

"Do you need an authorization to classify the puppy as a therapy animal? I can get the paperwork done."

"Actually, I need you to evaluate someone. She probably needs therapy as much as I do, and she brought this angelically cute puppy into my home. I'm incapable of evicting the puppy *or* the woman. I can't tell if I'm the hostage or if they're the hostage, but I've determined it's a mutually beneficial arrangement."

"Your ex brought a puppy to your house, didn't she?"

"She found it abandoned on the side of the road on her way here from the airport and got suckered, Dr. Dentannin. I can't judge her. I got suckered by a kitten. She says he's a Pembroke Welsh corgi. He's pretty adorable."

"Puppies usually are. While I was considering exposure therapy as a viable option, you didn't have to go to extremes, Reed."

"I wouldn't say *I* went to any extremes. I just drove home from work. Oh, I'm picking up a hobby."

"You? A hobby?"

"Well, I guess it's more like a sport. Is fencing a hobby or a sport?"

"Fencing can be both. Something physical would do you good. If you're going to pursue the extreme exposure therapy route, perhaps insist Ms. Young join you for lessons."

"Hey, Kennedy? Want to play with swords with me as a hobby?"

Her brows went up. "I'm not sure if I should be concerned, but I'm game."

"She's game. Now, about the actual reason I called."

"Go on, Reed."

"Kennedy probably needs therapy as much as I do and she made the mistake of saying so where I could hear her. Are you up for a challenge? I'm pretty sure both of us in a therapy session is going to be a challenge. I'm not even sure if we're in the denial phase yet or not."

"You blitzed through the denial phase around the same time you crawled under your boss's desk to avoid a panic attack. You went through the anger phase in Mississippi, and you're progressing nicely to the acceptance phase. I would like a joint therapy session to discuss the hazards of your approach with Ms. Young, but your ability to adapt to this situation has far surpassed our expectations. I have a theory, which is why I'm supporting her presence in your life at this stage."

When any one of my doctors came up with a theory, things usually became uncomfortable for me in a hurry. "What theory?"

"Your family history and base genetics indicates you probably share more traits with your angelic and demonic ancestors than your human ones. Your angelic ancestors are monogamous by nature, and they're known to develop bonds with humans until the human's death. Your demonic side allows you to recreationally wander as long as you're not engaged in an official relationship, something you've done to fill the void in your life. Ever since you've been in therapy with me, you've pursued relationships without substance. However, there's the issue of your demonic side. Demons, including succubi and incubi, *are* capable of forging bonds with humans after long-term exposure. Typically, these bonds dissolve after the birth of a child, but there are known cases of the bonds becoming permanent. This is typically the case when an angel is involved. While it usually takes two or three generations for magical abilities to pass down, it's feasible you've gotten a full dose of these inclinations from your parents, who are categorized as vanilla humans with diverse genetics. With your interplay of genetics, it's entirely possible you've bonded, on some level, with Ms. Young. It's also feasible this bond is a two-way street, which would help explain many of your difficulties *and* her inclination to show up at your home. Logically, you've been processing her return into your life remarkably well. If anything, I'd compare your reaction to an addict getting a hit in the worst phases of withdraw."

I looked Kennedy over, thought about it for a few moments, and realized he was likely right. As far as drugs went, Kennedy packed a far bigger punch than any medication a doctor had ever managed to make me swallow. Knowing my father, who lived and breathed for my mother, I could readily buy what my doctor was trying to sell me. "I'm not going to bother arguing with that assessment. You're basically saying this is my fault."

"Essentially, yes. I'll confer with the CDC

to see what the probability of this is. It *could* also be a matter of your unknown genetics. There are several species known to form bonds with others, including elves, various brands of divinity, shapeshifters of certain species, gorgons to a degree, harpies—"

"Harpies?"

"Harpies are rare, but they're intriguing if you want some disturbing evening reading. Harpies are masochistic sadists. They form bonds with human men for reproduction purposes before killing them. They then wallow in their grief before it's time for them to reproduce again. We've been doing some research into possible causes for your reactions to Ms. Young, even before your request for a check of your genetics."

"I see you've been a step ahead of me."

"It's our job. Genetic influences would explain a lot. If she's willing, a disclosure of Ms. Young's genetics might help with your case."

"Hey, Kennedy?"

"What?"

"Would you be willing to undergo a DNA test?"

"Why?"

"Dr. Dentannin seems to think there might be genetic reasons for you taking leave of your senses and bringing yourself and a puppy to my home for a probable permanent duration, but most of the blame is probably mine."

"My genetics are on file with the CDC, so it's a simple authorization form away. I'll consent, sure."

"Do you happen to know the results?"

"I do."

"Here's Kennedy," I informed my doctor before handing her the phone. "You talk, I'll do chores."

She chuckled, took my phone, and shook her head with a smile. "Good evening, Dr. Dentannin. It's nice to speak with you again."

I left her to discuss her genetics with my therapist while I tried to figure out how to transform a home meant for one and a cat to two, a cat, and a dog. If she held some of the blame for my leave of absence from my common sense, I'd find out about it soon enough.

ANY OTHER DAY of the week, I would've been concerned about Kennedy talking to my therapist for an hour while I struggled through making Kitten's and my home fit the addition of a puppy and a woman. My closet would be a problem; my suit collection took up most of it, and I'd have to do some serious culling to make space.

Kennedy found me with a suit in each hand trying to decide which one would get the ax.

"Is that an Armani?" she blurted.

I checked the label. Sure enough, I'd been on the brink of axing a suit that had dinged me at least three thousand. I frowned, put both back and decided to change my approach based on how much I'd spent on the damned things. That helped; within five minutes, I had a pile of ten candidates for donation on the bed while she watched with an arched brow.

"Reed, should I be concerned?"

"I have to put them somewhere so you have space in the closet. I should've checked the labels first. And yes, they're both Armani. Normal people buy jeans. I buy suits. I'm not even sure why I had two of them."

"The one cut was for formal events, the other was for business meetings with people with more money than sense. They're both good suits. If you put either one on the bed, I'm returning them to your closet. I don't need much space in the closet, by the way. Please tell me you own something other than suits."

"Not much," I admitted.

"You do your chores in a suit?"

"Not the expensive ones. I might be crazy, but I'm not that crazy."

"We need to go clothes shopping and get you casual clothes."

"This weekend," I agreed.

"So, what's this you were saying about fencing?"

"It's not technically fencing. Someone recommended I pick up some form of self-defense, and it was strongly suggested I should avoid firearms due to my heritage."

"Angels use swords when they use weapons at all."

"Exactly, and I have enough angelic blood Luna said I'd be wise to avoid firearms. Against my better judgment, I trust her on that part. I'm going to get lessons on how to handle a sword. I'm also having a nice weapon forged on Luna's dime. Cutting a deal with an angel wasn't one of my smarter moves, but it was the only way I could think of to get her to leave me alone. She's up to something. I just don't know what."

"It's concerning when angels meddle in the affairs of humans. They don't unless it's important, and their perspective on what's important tends to be a little different from ours. What else did she want?"

"She wants me to meet with a demon or devil of all things. He's from Mississippi, and he's been trying to contact me for years. I've been dodging his invitations, as I have a severe allergy to paperwork from Mississippi."

"Understandable. Have you found out anything about this gentlemen?"

"His name is Lucavier, and I'm inclined to think he's a devil rather than a demon. Everything I've read about demons leads me to believe he's not one. What I don't know is why I have an angel and a devil interested in me. Whatever the reason, it can't be good."

"That's an understatement. The last time devils and angels had interest in the same person, three cities were wiped off the map and a dragon took up residence in Florida."

While I'd heard about the destruction of three cities in Georgia, I hadn't dwelled on it, nor had I paid it more than minimal attention. However horrifying the loss of life, there hadn't been anything I could do about it. "I wasn't paying all that much attention to it, honestly."

"Few did. It's easier to cope that way. Georgia's a mess, but the cities will revive faster than anyone expects. A pair of archangels, the devil, and the devil's heir and her consort are involved in the rebuild."

"*The* devil?"

"Satan himself, yes. The CDC has been running around like a chicken with its head cut off about it. That the forces of good and evil are working together so openly is worrisome. The CDC is worried that's just the opening volley, but no one has any idea what could possibly happen next. The dragon's built himself a castle in Florida and seems content to stay out of sight unless he's hungry, and when he's hungry, he puts in an order for a couple of cows, paid for through some human associate. The CDC's decided to leave that mess alone for now, as honestly, we're not sure if we have the weaponry required to take out a dragon capable of razing and devouring three cities in as many days."

"Is that part of your job as an FBI-CDC liaison? You keep track of these incidents?"

"In part. Whenever there's a legal issue magic might be involved in, liaisons are called in to offer insights into the situation. I'm often a legal consultant, so my job is to help the various departments in the FBI and CDC get their ducks in a row. Sometimes, my job is to go to a site, look over the evidence, and assign it to the FBI or the CDC. I have authorization to do that in some cases. Other times, I help with evidence gathering and evaluation of dual-jurisdiction cases. In the case with your work, I was brought in because you have a special flag. That flag essentially marks you as someone to handle with care, so a liaison needs to be on hand if needed. It's also a step up from general law enforcement. If you're charged with anything, your case would immediately be bumped to the FBI due to the cruel and unusual punishment verdict."

"Sending you should've classified as cruel and unusual punishment." I arched a brow at her.

"I really hadn't expected you to hide under your boss's desk. I was more expecting a screaming match, but you didn't even give me much of a dose of that, either. Initially, I hadn't been told you suffered panic attacks at the mere mention of my name. They gave me better disclosure after your kidnapping. I probably would've asked someone else to come had I known."

"That's probably why you weren't told. I'm astonished my therapists didn't kill someone for even suggesting you be tossed into the same building with me."

"I have it on good authority they authorized it, and maybe that's why they hadn't initially told me. My boss told me after I went to California. The CDC really wanted you to make progress, so they bent a lot of rules."

I scowled. "They were probably pissed I'd stalled in therapy."

"That's what I gathered. Exposure and shock therapy might've been extreme, but I'm comfortable with saying it worked."

"Considering I'm trying to clean my closet so you have room to fill half of it, I think you're right."

"I'm still worried about your kidnapping. It makes no sense. Why would someone make you disappear for almost a week? They'd gone to a lot of effort to keep you alive but made it easy for you to escape on your own. It doesn't make sense."

I'd tried to avoid thinking about the accident and all the trouble it had caused. "I don't know. I have trouble imagining why one person would want me let alone several, and there were several distinct sets of footprints."

"I'm inclined to agree. Kidnapping an adult isn't easy, and considering they had to pull you out of wreckage, several people had to be involved. I've seen the pictures. You weren't getting out of that car without help. Frankly, I'm amazed you survived the crash at all. They crunched your vehicle like a tin can."

"It could have been trashed after the accident. I don't remember anything of it. One instant I was driving home, the next I was in the farmhouse. What bothers me most is Luna's insistence my kitten shouldn't be in the car during the accident. Luna isn't the type to give a shit what happens to anyone outside of her areas of interest. But why would an angel have any interest in a cat?"

"That's a very good question. As I said, what angels perceive as important is a little different from what we think is important."

I frowned, shrugged, and did another

sweep through my suits in search of a cheaper one I could donate. "I don't suppose you know what would happen to an angel if she lied, do you?"

"They fall."

"They fall? From grace?"

"It's only happened once that I know of since the CDC started recording all things magical. The angel fell out of favor and was unable to return to heaven. Without being able to replenish his spiritual energy, he started to degrade. The CDC isn't quite sure about the progression, but it's believed the angel needed energy and tried to get it from any source possible. He started targeting angelic children to siphon their divinity. Two people were seriously injured, and it's luck alone no one was killed. The angel eventually corroded."

"Corroded? How?"

"Fell apart. The pictures were pretty gruesome. It looked like a decapitation gone horribly wrong."

"Did the angel have a head?"

"Yes, but his was so corroded the CDC was unable to learn anything about it."

"Why do you know so much about angels?"

Kennedy sighed and sat on the edge of the bed. "When I found out you had a trio of angels monitoring you at the CDC's request,

I looked into them. I found the file about the fallen angel by accident. It was disturbing."

"What happened to the people he attacked?"

"They recovered, but it took the help of an archangel. Their divinity was stolen from them, and it seems only a direct conduit from God could fix it, and the archangels tend to be the only ones who can open that conduit unless *He* appears and handles it directly. That's something I don't have access to: the CDC locks down the movements of the divine pretty tightly, so while I can get access to the basics, appearances and similar records are sealed."

I wrinkled my nose at the thought of any divines paying Earth a visit. Earth had enough problems with magic without the heavy hitters joining the fray. "Were there any notes on how long it took for the angel to fall after he lied?"

"According to the file, witnesses claim it was immediate. The instant he spoke a falsehood, his wings darkened and patches of his skin decayed. He lasted several months before death. As far as I can tell, there's no hiding an angel's fall from grace, but we only have one known instance."

I shook my head, wondering what could drive an angel into suiciding through telling a falsehood. "Did the file mention what the lie was about?"

"Yes, it did."

When Kennedy didn't elaborate, I listened to her silence. I would wonder what had been so important to drive an angel into sacrificing his divinity and life, but some questions were best left unasked.

If Kennedy wanted to tell me, she would.

"Instead of worrying about emptying my closet, I should probably be more worried about finding a place closer to work. My commute is long."

"Three hours a day is more than just long."

"I didn't have anything else to do with the time." I couldn't turn back time, and while my angelic ancestors could peek into the past, they couldn't change it. "That's changing, it seems."

"Between the two of us, I think we could afford a second property. I'll sell my place in Mississippi, as I wouldn't ask you to move back there."

I doubted I'd ever be able to return to Mississippi for any length of time. I wasn't even sure if my parents still lived there or not, but I had no intention of going anywhere near where they might be. Running into them topped my list of people I wanted to avoid, and my angelic, demonic, and human grandparents took the next six spots. I still didn't know why my angelic grandparents avoided me so much, but I guessed it had something to do with the unknown percentages of my heritage courtesy of my father.

They didn't avoid my father, but I had a theory about that. What if my sliver of impurity had taken a dominant form? If my father was just a gene carrier, perhaps angels didn't mind being in his presence.

What if my mystery genetics were a little like my cursed eyes? Neither of my parents saw matters of the heart quite like I did.

"Hey, Kennedy?"

"What is it?"

"Outside of demons and devils, what types of beings would angels avoid?"

"That's a good question. I don't know. Why?"

"My grandparents have always avoided me. Now I'm wondering why."

"Who knows? I've given up trying to understand the motivations of angels and devils."

"Not demons?"

"Demons are born on Earth. That makes a difference. Perhaps you just have a bit more angel in you than they like to admit for someone born on Earth."

"That's pretty petty." The instant I said the words, I wondered if the truth was something as simple as ancient prejudices.

I had angelic sight, but I wasn't an angel.

"It's not like you'll have to worry about angels often. Just don't get the attention of a fallen angel. I think you'll be fine. You have a bigger problem to worry about first."

"I do?"

Kennedy pointed at the bed. "We have business to attend to, and your suits are in the way."

Some problems had simple solutions, and I wasted no time dumping them onto the floor. "As a new resident of Gypsum Creek, I'm afraid I'm going to have to charge you a welcome tax. I accept all forms of intimate payment."

"That must be the incubus in you talking."

Or the succubus, but I wasn't going to quibble about it. "I bet it'll be the first time in your life you'll actually enjoy paying taxes."

"Only an idiot would argue over this. Show me what you've got, Reed. We don't have all night."

EIGHTEEN

What sort of monster dumps twenty
new contracts on my desk on
Thursday morning?

THANKS TO ONE KITTEN, a puppy, and a
shared dog bed, I came within a hair of
calling in sick so I could stay home and ob-
serve the pair carefully. Ultimately, Kennedy
urged me out the door so I wouldn't disrupt
my habits more than I already had. Kitten,
Destroyer of Worlds seemed displeased to be
separated from her new companion,
protesting in howls until I got her into
the car.

Chaos waited for me at work in the form
of twenty new companies desiring contracts,
and in a complete leave of his common sense,
my boss assigned them all to me and my team
with one notable caveat: he wanted me to
handle them personally.

I hauled the stack of papers to my boss's
office, knocked, and waited for him to let me
in. When he did, I dumped the source of my

growing headache onto his desk with a thunk loud enough to silence the muted conversations in the hall and shared offices nearby.

With a nudge of my foot, I closed his door, and to make it clear he'd crossed every last one of my worker bee lines, I slapped the files hard enough my palm stung. "There is zero chance in hell I'm going to be able to finish this within a week."

Delivering the bad news so bluntly might get me fired, but if it did, I had enough money saved I could live for months before having to find another job. I had a few new things I could spend my time on, including making certain Kennedy needed a boost to get out of bed every morning.

"Well, I see you've determined you actually do have limits rather than doing your best to do the impossible. This is a new development. You were even thirty minutes later arriving to work than usual. I had three people in my office wondering if you'd gotten into another car accident."

"I have guests, and one of the guests is a puppy still being bottle fed. One minute, I'm getting ready for work. The next? I'm petting the puppy. The puppy has some form of magical power that alters the course of time. As such, I was late getting out the door."

"As far as excuses go, it's an amusing one." My boss glanced at Kitten, Destroyer of

Worlds. "I'm surprised that furry terrorist didn't try to kill the puppy."

"They were sleeping together this morning. I almost called in sick because they were sleeping together. I regret not having called in sick after seeing these files. What sort of monster dumps twenty new contracts on my desk on Thursday morning?"

My boss arched a brow. "One who had twenty contracts dumped on his desk Wednesday afternoon with direct orders to make you handle them because you're the best man I have on the team."

"Your boss might be a devil."

"I was thinking the same thing when I inherited the stack. You can dump some of the research work onto your team, but the bosses want you handling the actual negotiations. I would've distributed them better if I could, but the uppers were clear: *you* need to handle the negotiations."

To handle the negotiations, I needed to do the footwork, which meant I'd be working more overtime than I cared to think about. "Can the files come home with me?"

"Unless you're planning on living here until the end of next week, it's likely unavoidable. I'll let the bosses know you're game but need to take work home with you. I'll try to talk them into incentives for working on such a tight schedule."

"Which ones are the most important?"

"That's the problem. They're all important."

"If you're trying to make my Thursday a sad, miserable day, you're doing a good job of it," I complained, picking up the stack. "I'll try to rank these and send a prioritization list for your approval. It's going to take a literal miracle to push through twenty contracts next week. A literal miracle."

"Well, you are part angel. Go make miracles happen, Reed. If anyone in this hellhole can, it's you."

I left before I succumbed to the temptation of throttling my boss, his boss, and his boss's boss.

LUCAVIER BUIONI HAD it out for me, and he was responsible for eight of the twenty contracts. I suspected a few others were his doing, too. In some ways, his meddling simplified matters for me. Once I approached him and made it clear I knew he was behind all the contracts, I could unravel the tangled weave of lies, aliases, and corporate fronts, allowing me to kill multiple birds with one stone. I respected his tactic; if his goal was to meet with me face-to-face, blanket dumping potential contracts with my company was a good way to do it.

The amount of money on the table for business management would've caught the immediate attention of the company's CEO, ensuring that only the better negotiators would handle the contracts. Lucavier's assumption I was one of the better negotiators amused me.

I was, but I only had my heritage to thank for that. Kennedy had me pegged; I liked crunching the numbers far more than I liked arranging the contracts to make the number crunching happen. After I handled the issue with Lucavier, maybe I'd take the dive, finish the schooling I'd abandoned, and try my hand at the job I thought I'd wanted growing up.

Involving Kennedy might cost me, but I'd ask her for her opinions. With her background, she might have better ideas.

Leaving the ruts of my past completely and going into a new field might do me a world of good. My original plans of forgetting Kennedy had gone up in smoke. I suspected if my therapists realized how much change she'd brought into my life, my therapy animal privileges would be revoked. Eventually, I'd get Kitten, Destroyer of Worlds used to staying home alone with Puppy, Savior of Worlds, likely resulting in the utter destruction of my—no, our—home.

As I expected, my research into Lucavier's corporations and activities would make or break me. I threw myself into the work, pulling out comprehensive records of every single corporation he lobbed at my company, tracking down sister and parent companies with a ruthlessness I usually reserved for the trickier contracts to land on my desk.

In the financial ball game, Lucavier didn't bring *that* much to the table. I'd handled contracts worth twice as much.

Those contracts, however, didn't stink of treachery quite like a devil's dealings.

After lunch, I brought the files to my boss to make several odd requests, one of which I hoped would get me fired so I wouldn't have to deal with the damned mess.

When I entered his office, files in hand, my boss sighed. "It's barely ten after one, Reed. When you come into my office fresh off lunch, you're telling me something I'm not going to like."

"I'm going to need a good tablet to handle these contracts, sir. There's substantial overlap in these files, and I want to be able to take notes more efficiently. I'd also like to be able to take it home. I think I can condense these to a handful of meetings, but I need to verify the overlap over the next few days and draw up a proposal for the company owner in charge of the overlapping contracts."

"Overlap? What sort of overlap? I was told these were independent contracts."

I thumped the files onto my boss's desk, separating out Lucavier's corporations. "These companies are all companies branched from a firm owned by Lucavier Buioni. It wouldn't take much to suggest we ask Mr. Buioni to handle the negotiations of all these companies personally. He's listed as a primary shareholder on all of them. There are a few private companies I suspect are also under his general umbrella, but that's why I'd like the tablet, so I can look into it more efficiently."

"Risk level?"

"If all of these contracts were to pass, he might be accused of establishing a monopoly; the investment sectors are very close. It is feasible we might be dragged into the lawsuit if these proposals were to go through as is." I shrugged, flipping open the largest of the proposals, handing the financial page to my boss. "This one is the largest concern. With this proposed move, he could wipe out the family-operated businesses, do significant damage to the larger companies, and form a monopoly in the area. It would depend on if his activities have a monopoly elsewhere."

"Sector?"

"Home renovation and construction contracting."

My boss's brows went up. "You think it's possible for him to develop a monopoly in that field *here*?"

"With the amount of money he's willing to invest, the number of business takeovers he's proposed, and his base strategy, I certainly think it's a possibility we don't want to ignore."

"Some of those big businesses have been in operation here for over a hundred years. It'd take a miracle to unseat them. Hell, our building is maintained by them. Most of the bigger buildings here are."

"It'd be a nightmare for everyone here if this transition happened. It's bad enough when the maintenance is late a day. Imagine what would happen if a new company swept in all at once. Every business in the area would have troubles just because of problems with their building."

"Conspiracy theories are not your thing, Reed. Don't get into conspiracy theories, especially when they have enough viability to worry me. Please go back to your office, pet your cat, and rein those thoughts in. You're entering nightmare territory."

I chuckled. "But it's a possibility. Most of his corporations, that I can tell, are business centric. Advertising. Accounting firms. A law firm. One retail branch that's large enough for corporate presences in buildings. It'd be a brilliant way to disrupt productivity of other businesses. If he controls when and how maintenance is done in their buildings, he could plan renovations during a sensitive time and influence worker productivity."

"While I'd like to say employees can work through that, we both know it'd be difficult, and that logic is interesting—and terrifying. It's also logistically difficult or impossible to pull off, I think."

"Oh, I think it's logistically possible. If he knows a rival company is in crunch time, he can disrupt activities and lower quality of their work through renovations, and it's often not difficult to tell when a company is on the move. Is that the motivation? Who knows? I don't really care, honestly. I just think the building a monopoly aspect is worth looking into. I'd rather we not run afoul of the state's monopoly laws."

"All right. I'll have a tablet for you by the end of the day and the auth to take it out of the building along with digital copies of the contracts and everything we have on the corporations. You figure out what this Lucavier's goal is, and when you do, come to me so I can take it to the bosses. I definitely think you're onto something. If he was on the up-and-up, he wouldn't be trying to hide his connections to all of these contracts."

I gathered the files, claimed my victory

with a nod, and replied, "Will do. Do you want me to approach Mr. Buioni and acknowledge we know he's involved with multiple contracts?"

"For now, let him think he has the upper hand, but arrange to meet with him about the contract openly from him. We'll play it by ear. Keep me in the loop. I don't care what time it is, but if you find out anything about this guy, call me."

"Understood."

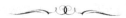

KITTEN, Destroyer of Worlds disliked Lucavier's files, and whenever I took my eye off her, she tried to eat the papers. I couldn't tell if she wanted to destroy my work due to boredom, being a cat, or if she knew something I didn't. My haphazard entry to cat ownership taught me to be careful around the fluffy entity.

She ruled over me with an iron paw, and something about my work annoyed her. I placed most of my bets on her wanting to play and thinking I was giving too much attention to the contracts. The rest went to her being some form of higher being, cunning in her ability to convince me she needed me to care for her. Damned cats.

I couldn't wait to get home and get a dose

of Kennedy and her wickedly cute puppy. One of them would cure me of the sense of dread plaguing me over Lucavier's interference with my work life. If our pets slept together again, I'd need therapy to recover.

I could live with therapy for an overdose of our pets being adorable. I'd sign myself up for multiple therapy sessions to avoid dealing with a damned devil determined to butt into my affairs. Short of going into hiding, I needed to haul ass on my plans to protect myself. When a devil came calling, *something* would happen.

Delaying the contract negotiations long enough to grasp the basics of swordplay and acquire a weapon would be my first step. If I could make the concerns about a monopoly stick, I could delay proceedings for several weeks—maybe even months—while my company's lawyers found a way to work around the current laws.

The legal department could limit my contact with Lucavier until I was better prepared to handle meeting with a devil.

Then again, devils played the long game. I likely had time. How much would be the question, but I'd have to haul ass. After being in the sights of an angel, a devil didn't surprise me. I needed to find out why.

As far as I knew, I'd only inherited an angel's sight, and it was more of a burden than anything else. Was my sight to blame for Lucavier's interest in me? Meddling with more practitioner magic would lead me straight into trouble, but I needed facts in a hurry.

My boss hadn't banned me from communicating with Lucavier. Playing my cards with care would win me the war, but how could I call him without betraying I knew eight of the contracts were his? Listening for the truth might give me an edge in negotiations—and reveal his plans.

If I asked the right questions.

The mystery bothered me through the rest of the day, punctuated by my kitten's attempts to destroy as much of the paperwork as possible. It took my boss two hours to get a tablet for me, and I wasted the rest of my day photographing the documents with it because the person with the digital copies had left work early due to illness.

I found that as fishy as the entire lot falling onto my desk, but I kept my thoughts to myself. There was only so much I could do without my boss worrying I'd lost my mind. After work officially ended, I called Hamhock.

"Hamhock's Forge," Hamhock's assistant answered.

"Is Hamhock around? It's Reed Matthews."

"Yes, she is. One sec."

One sec was closer to five minutes, but I

played with Kitten, Destroyer of Worlds while I waited.

"Evening, Reed," Hamhock said. "What can I do for you?"

"I wanted to find out if it would be possible to push up lessons and the practice sword any. I might have a bit of a devil problem in my near future."

"A devil, you say?"

"Yes. I'm pretty sure he's a devil. Might be a demon, but I don't think so."

"Looks like you were on the right track. I've got a sword I can loan you for lessons, and you'll start on wooden blades to limit injuries for the first few sessions. I'll put in a call. How soon can you work evenings on this?"

Considering my soured luck, I needed to protect Kennedy, too. I hoped she wouldn't take offense to me volunteering her for lessons. "Tomorrow. I might be bringing a friend, too. If this devil comes after me, he might go after her, too."

"I'll warn your instructor. Your friend good at firearms?"

"She's licensed, but not here."

"I'll let your instructor know, and I'll have a second weapon ready. Tell me about your friend so I can pick a blade."

"You know that Japanese death scythe?"

Hamhock laughed. "Naginata. Yes."

"That. I think she should use that. If the instructor can teach her."

"Your instructor was born with a weapon in her hand, Reed. She can teach any weapon. I'll have a naginata ready. I'll call you with the address tomorrow. Is around this time good?"

"Around this time is good. I'll warn my friend she has a date."

"Do yourself a favor, Reed. Don't call this a date. It would be a terrible date. Call it a self-defense class. Act worried. You do worried well."

I sighed. "I should be upset, but you're right. Worrying is something I'm good at."

"I'm sure that habit will be beaten out of you. Bring casual clothes. What you wear will be ruined. Bloodstains are a bitch to get out."

"Remember how I said worrying is something I'm good at? I'm worrying now."

Hamhock chuckled. "It'll put hair on your chest. Don't worry, Reed. You should survive."

With 'should' being the keyword, I'd need to prepare my will. Then again, an angel had meddled in my affairs, and after I'd driven her off, a devil had taken her place. I should've prepared my will the instant Luna and her angelic brethren had popped into my life. I considered running away, but I doubted I'd be able to run far enough to keep a devil from finding me. "That's something. Anything else I should know?"

"Bring a carrier for your pet. It's safer for her, and your instructor would feel guilty if she ate someone's pet."

"She eats cats?" I blurted.

"She's an elf. She eats whatever she wants. I've learned it's best to simply let the elves do what they want. You're less likely to end up on the menu that way. In good news, clients are excluded from her list of edibles. I wouldn't worry too much. It's been a few years since someone pissed her off that much. As far as elves go, she has a good control over her temper. Think about it this way. If you can stand up to an elf, no angel or devil prone to visiting Earth will have a chance against you."

"Elves can beat angels and devils in a sword fight?"

Hamhock laughed. "Angels and devils just wish they could match an elf. I'll see you tomorrow with your practice sword and your friend's naginata. Do try to keep your head attached to your shoulders. I'd like to see what you're made of."

She hung up, and I dreaded what tomorrow would bring.

NINETEEN

Love, hate, and everything between
were complicated.

KENNEDY POUNCED the instant I got home,
and I wasn't sure if boredom had done her in
or if she'd actually missed me while I'd been
at work. I decided it didn't matter, although
both Kitten and Puppy were not pleased with
the delay of their hard-earned supper.

Our therapy animals would have to accept
there were some forms of therapy they
couldn't participate in.

Being pounced the moment I walked
through the door did a good job of making
my common sense dribble out of my ears.
Some claimed love and lust were fickle
beasts, but a quiet truth lurked beneath the
surface.

Love, hate, and everything between were
complicated, and I couldn't place my feelings
for Kennedy or their evolution into a box,

pack it away, and forget about it. Heartache
added to the complications, but I couldn't
deny the one thing capable of patching everything that'd gone wrong in my life.

Despite everything, I'd never stopped
loving her.

I could guess what an angel saw in my
eyes, and her actions led me to believe we
both fought to pick up the shattered pieces
and glue them back together again. There'd
never be the clarity of an untested love for us
again. That had shattered with everything
else, but like a Japanese potter restoring a
broken jar, we could use gold to rebuild our
relationship into something new and
beautiful.

We didn't have to return to the past.

The long drive and stressful day did me in
even more than Kennedy's enthusiasm, which
made it difficult for me to crawl out of bed to
handle the basic necessities. If I wanted to
survive long enough to learn how to use a
sword, I needed to move closer to the city. I
loathed the idea of adding more to my list,
but I saw little choice.

I couldn't handle three hours of driving,
learning a sword, and Kennedy. I'd die of exhaustion within a few weeks.

With far more pep in her step than I could
readily handle, Kennedy flitted through the

house, fed my kitten in a blatant attempt to steal her affections, and watched me with a smug smile.

"I need your talent." I made it to the couch and sprawled. "Can you give me a boost?"

"Sorry, Reed. It doesn't work that way. You look absolutely ragged, though. Did something go wrong at work?"

"I need to move somewhere closer, and it seems I have to also move a woman, a dog, and a cat when I do so."

"I have a week before my boss will get me back on rotation in the area. I spoke to him while you are at work. I also spoke with your therapists. For hours. Why don't you let me worry about the housing situation? Even when I go back to work, my schedule flexes enough I can handle most of the details. You'll have to sign paperwork, but that'll save you a headache."

"You mean migraine. That's what paperwork gives me. It gives me migraines."

"Yet you're a contract negotiator for a major acquisitions firm. I've seen some of your work. It's pretty impressive. Of all the files and contracts we reviewed, yours were the cleanest. They're also the hardest to audit, as *everyone* is convinced you're up to no good yet we can't catch you at any of it."

I snickered and allowed myself a smug

smile. "That's because I'm never up to no good. I keep every single one of my contracts legal. I refuse to negotiate on a contract with anything illegal in it. That's why I'm a team lead. Every contract that goes through my team goes through me first, and if I think there's anything fishy about it, I bump it to legal. They dumped a set of twenty on my desk this morning, and it's bad news. I'm already bumping it to legal, and I've barely gotten started yet. But, that leads me to a very important problem I need to talk with you about."

"What's wrong?"

Discarding everything Hamhock had suggested about not calling our upcoming torture session a date, I replied, "We have a date tomorrow."

"A date? We do?"

"We're going to beat each other with sharp objects. There might even be blood involved."

"We're going to *what*?"

"I'm going to learn how to use a sword. You're going to learn how to use a Japanese battle scythe. I have decided this because a centaur almost beheaded me with a Japanese battle scythe, and I was appropriately intimidated. As such, I want you to learn how to use the Japanese battle scythe, too."

"A Japanese battle scythe? What the fuck is a Japanese battle scythe?"

"Come on a date with me tomorrow and find out."

"Why are we going to beat on each other with swords and Japanese battle scythes?"

"I've been told I'll be useless with a gun plus it's in my interest to learn self-defense. With a sword. I also coerced an angel out of a very expensive sword and the best trainer money can buy. I suggested you should join me. Well, I asked if a friend could join me, and my contact thought it would be feasible. Here we are. Come on a date with me. One involving us beating each other senseless."

Kennedy laughed so hard she cried. "I can't refuse an invitation like that. You look so hopeful. If you need someone to hold your hand through your self-defense lessons, just say so."

"I need someone to hold my hand through self-defense lessons. Please."

"I'll come hold your hand, and because you're trying so hard, I'll even let you call it a date. Do you have appropriate clothes for this?"

"I was going to sacrifice one of the junker suits until I run out of suits I can sacrifice, honestly."

"Actually, I like that idea. If you learn how to fight in what you usually wear, it'll be better for you. That's a good plan. When is your self-defense class?"

"Hamhock'll call me with the time and location, but it'll be after work. I've been told we'll need to put our pets in their carriers for this."

"Why?"

"Their safety," I replied, pleased it was utterly true. Not getting eaten by an elf was a definite safety concern. "Kittens and puppies might get hurt if they get underfoot while we're playing with swords and Japanese death scythes."

"That's fair enough. All right. I'll start doing the footwork on finding us a place closer to your work tomorrow. Do you want a house, an apartment, or a condo?"

"I prefer houses because I fiddle. There's no point in denying I fiddle. I'm okay with fixing up a run-down house if you can tolerate living in it while I'm fixing it up."

"If you tell me what to do, I can help with the fixing."

"That won't be an issue, but I'll warn you now: I can get bossy."

Kennedy laughed at me. "I'd pay good money to see that, Mr. Matthews. That said, I plan on buying you extra ties tomorrow while I'm out so you can get in sufficient practice being bossy."

"You're a very, very wicked woman, Kennedy."

"Someone has to be wicked in this relationship, and no matter how many times you try to claim you're part incubus and succubus, I'm onto you. You're an angel in disguise, and I refuse to entertain any argument on your part, sir."

I arched a brow. "Is that a challenge? I'm not sure it's a smart idea to challenge a man who's part incubus and succubus, Kennedy. I might be an angel by day, but after dark is a completely different story."

"Prove it," she murmured, aiming her most seductive smile at me.

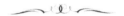

I SOMEHOW FORGOT to eat dinner, although the somehow part of the equation involved a former ex who'd popped back into my life and resumed her place—rightful, in my opinion—as my no-longer-ex girlfriend. I'd have to ask her if she agreed with her resumption of said status, but I struggled with my old habit of assuming the worse. The drive to work the next morning seemed longer than normal, especially as Kitten, Destroyer of Worlds insisted on attacking the window every time she spotted a bird. Her excited chirping reduced me into laughing so hard I pulled over so I wouldn't crash.

Pulling over in the middle of nowhere caught the attention of a cop, who pulled over to add a little spice to my crazy morning. The older woman tapped my window, and wiping tears of mirth from my eyes, I rolled down the window. "Good morning, Officer," I greeted.

Amazingly, the expected panic attack didn't come.

"Is there a problem, sir?"

I pointed at my therapy cat, who still stood at the window and chirped at a flock of birds swooping over the nearby fields. "There's no problem, ma'am. She's my therapy cat, and she's been making a fuss. It was funny enough I pulled over so I wouldn't be laughing while driving."

She blinked at me before staring at my cat. "Your therapy cat?"

I needed to thank my therapists for the official documentation claiming she was a support animal. I popped open the glove box, retrieved the papers, and handed them over. "Old trauma, ma'am. She helps when I have panic attacks."

"I've heard of therapy dogs, but therapy cats are a new one. Hey, whatever works. I won't ask how you got the authorizations for a support cat, but this looks in order. Were you aware this form allows you to get her an official support animal vest?"

It was my turn to blink, and I gaped at the cop. "It does?"

"Yeah. This is the higher tier form. I'll get you the number for the vest. I'm surprised the authorizer didn't provide one."

"Maybe he didn't think she needed it?"

"Give me a minute and I'll get you the number." The cop took my form and returned to her cruiser.

I arched a brow at Kitten, Destroyer of Worlds. "You're not just a therapy cat. You're an official support animal. Don't let that go to your head."

As expected, my cat ignored me.

Within five minutes, the cop returned with a business card, which had a handwritten phone number on it. "Here you go, Mr. Matthews. The vest should make things easier on you when you go shopping or into public spaces. Is your condition a problem with driving?"

"I pull over if I think there are going to be any problems, ma'am. I've had this for several years, and I have a good record. My cat mostly helps me at the office and home."

"Well, drive safe, Mr. Matthews." The cop gave me a nod and returned to her vehicle.

I hoped meeting with the police on the way to work wasn't an omen of the future. If it was, what sort of omen was it?

The birds flew away, and Kitten, Destroyer of Worlds turned to me with a sad, questioning mew.

"There'll be more birds on the way," I promised, easing my car back onto the road and turning off my hazard lights. "There's nothing to worry about."

A BLOCK AWAY FROM WORK, the heavens opened and a flock of dead pigeons rained down on my car. I slammed the brakes around the same time the thumps of impact triggered the airbags. My face throbbed, and in typical cat fashion, Kitten, Destroyer of Worlds protested the sudden deceleration with howls. Since her howls proved ineffective, she attacked my air bag, pulling at the end of her buckled-in leash.

I was grateful my replacement car was modern enough to register there wasn't a human occupant beside me, sparing her from being smacked, too.

Airbags to the face hurt like hell, and I wanted to stab the damned thing for punching me in the nose. To add insult to injury, I bled. I considered myself fortunate I hadn't broken anything. Shunting my car into park, I leaned back in my seat and listened to the mayhem of car alarms, honking, and screaming on the busy street.

At the rate I was going, my meeting with the cop would be the only pleasant part of my day. Grabbing my phone, I took a picture of the countless pigeon bodies decorating my busted windshield, the car in front of me, the sidewalk, and the road. Texting it to my boss, along with a note I'd be late due to unforeseen circumstances, would cap my rotten day and invite more questions than I wanted to answer.

Within a minute, my phone rang.

"Reed, what the hell is that picture you just sent me?"

"Look out the window," I suggested. "An entire flock of pigeons seems to have dropped out of the sky onto my car. I'm definitely going to be late."

"Are you all right?"

"Bloody nose and probable whiplash. I think I'll be all right. Kitten, Destroyer of Worlds seems okay, too. My car, however, doesn't appear to have emerged unscathed."

"Take the day. I'll bump your contracts over to legal for review on the monopoly clause; everything I've read so far says your gut instinct is right, so I can delay the negotiations for at least a week. I'll also get legal to do a full trace of all the corporations to see if that whole batch is connected. It'll have to be done by legal anyway. Can you send me a list of the companies that you've identified with connections?"

Sirens wailed, and I grimaced at the

thought of even more ER visit bills headed my way. "I can. I might be delayed a few minutes. Emergency responders are starting to arrive."

"That was fast."

"I bet dispatch lit up when people started calling in about a mass accident. Hell, I'm just glad I didn't hit anyone and no one hit me. That might be a miracle." Others hadn't been so lucky; the car in front of me had rammed into the car in front of it. Slamming my brakes had prevented me from joining the chain.

Paying attention while driving paid off in case of the unexpected mass die off of pigeons.

"You're probably right. You sure you're all right? No panic attacks? Do you want me to send someone down the street?"

"I'm all right. I have Kitten here, although she's mad as hell I hit the brakes."

"Buckled in?"

"She was. She seems fine. Her airbag didn't go off. Mine did when the birds hit the hood and I hit the brakes."

"You sure you don't want me to send Dani over to get your cat?"

"I'll keep her with me in case I need to take her to the vet. I probably will just to be safe."

"Good call. Seriously, give me a ring if you

need anything, Reed."

"A tow truck would help, honestly."

"I'll make the arrangements; pay me back later."

"You got it. Thanks."

My boss hung up, and I stared at my phone, wondering what I'd tell Kennedy. As the photograph and text tactic had worked on my boss, I tried it with her.

She called me even faster than my boss, which made me unreasonably happy. "Reed? What the hell happened?"

"I've heard of it raining cats and dogs, but birds just rained on my parade—and my car. Pigeons. I'm mostly fine; got a damned bloody nose from the airbag, but I didn't hit anything and no one hit me. Kitten's fine as far as I can tell, but I'm going to take her to the vet to be sure. My boss is calling for a tow, assuming it can get to me in this mess."

"I was about to leave to meet with a real estate agent. Do you want me to cancel?"

"No, it's all right. I just wanted to let you know. The boss told me to take off, so while this is a mess, we'll do as planned tonight, although I suspect I'll be getting a new car. Mine's seen better days."

My insurance company would laugh at me and point at their Act of God clause, so I wouldn't even bother with making a claim.

I'd just tow it, scrap the vehicle, and find something else.

I counted my lucky stars I hadn't bought something new, settling on a junker as a stand-in. I'd take Kennedy with me when I shopped for a new vehicle, and I'd factor her reactions into my final choice. I'd even consider something new. With my luck, if I tried to save a few bucks on a used, it'd face the same fate of its predecessors.

While I waited, I cleaned the blood off my face. My jacket wouldn't be the same, but its dark color hid most of the stains. By some miracle I refused to question, I hadn't dripped on my white shirt, which would make hiding my mishap easier. Within an hour, the cops made their way to me, and it took them less than ten minutes to give me the accident forms and come to the conclusion I had no idea what had happened or why. An hour later, the tow truck reached my car, and the driver shook his head at the carnage. "Where do you want me to take it?"

"The nearest scrap yard that'll give me something for the metal and parts. I have a cat with me, so I'll get a cab to meet you there."

"I was already warned about your cat. She's not a problem. Load her on in and make yourself comfortable while I get this hooked up."

Within twenty minutes, the tow truck driver escaped the chaos, heading for the outskirts of town to one of the many junkyards. Kitten, Destroyer of Worlds sat on my lap, her ears pinned back at the change of our routine. I expected her to flip, taking her sour temper out on me, but she kept her claws sheathed and limited her protests to the occasional hiss.

The junkyard operator took one look at my car, which still had a few pigeons on it, and laughed. "I've seen a lot come through here, but this is the first time I've gotten a wrecked car with birds still attached. What'd you do? Get tired of them damned city chickens and plow through a flock?"

"Air bombardment downtown," I replied, and unable to help myself, I laughed, took out my phone, and showed the man the picture I'd taken. "I've never seen anything like it."

"Damn, that's something else. You scrappin' and callin' it a day?"

"How much can you give me for it?"

"It still run?"

"Engine still worked after, the brakes were fine when it happened, and I didn't hit anything. Just damage to the body and windshield as far as I know. The airbag did deploy. I just don't think it's worth replacing the windshield and repairing the body. My insurance probably won't cover it."

"Let me check the book and see what I can give you. Put it there," he ordered, pointing at an open spot near the junkyard's office. "I'll call the boss and ask; don't get many vehicles through here just needing body work."

The tow driver dumped my car where instructed and bailed, leaving me alone at the junkyard with a cranky Kitten who seemed ready to literally destroy the world for the disruption to her routine. I sat on the crumbling curb, put her on my lap, and used the end of her leash as a toy to give her something to play with while we waited.

My phone rang, and with one hand occupied playing with my cat, I answered without checking the display. "Reed Matthews."

"Hello, Mr. Matthews. My name is Samantha. Hamhock asked me to teach you how to use a sword along with a friend, who I understand will be using a naginata."

"That's correct. Thank you for calling. Where do you want us and when?"

"Meet me at Hamhock's. I'll guide you to where we'll train and make your future training schedule. Am I correct in my understanding you're a raw beginner?"

"Yes, ma'am. I am."

"You're late to the sword, but I can make you passable. Maybe. If you're determined. I recommend you be determined. I dislike failure."

"That's fair. Did Hamhock tell you about our pets?"

"She did, yes. I've been told you'll have carriers for them?"

"Yes. The puppy is young enough he'd be hurt if he got under foot. Kitten is smart enough to stay out from under foot most of the time, but I'd rather be safe than sorry. Just need to have a place to put them, and we need to give the puppy his milk every few hours."

"A very young puppy, then."

"A rescue. Kennedy found him on the side of the road and brought him home. My doctors want Kitten going with me everywhere."

"What is this kitten's role?"

"She helps if I have a panic attack," I admitted.

"A feline therapy animal? Most humans rely on dogs. How interesting. I will accommodate these animals. Be aware neither will likely enjoy my company."

I had no idea what made Samantha so damned scary, but I'd find out soon enough. "What time do you want us at Hamhock's place?"

"Six. Don't be late."

"Understood. I'll see you at six then, Samantha."

She hung up, and before I had a chance to worry about Samantha, the junkyard employee emerged from the office and said,

"The boss wants to talk to you about your car."

With my cat and her things in tow, I headed inside the building to see what I could get for my car and rendezvous with Kennedy for our date with disaster.

TWENTY

Maybe the centaur could give me a
few pointers.

ALL THINGS CONSIDERED, I appreciated the
thousand dollars I got for my car; it would
cost me a lot more than a thousand to repair.
If a dent on the hood cost five hundred, I
didn't want to know how much replacing the
entire exterior of my vehicle would cost. Add
in the glass, and I could buy a whole new
used car for the same price of fixing the old
used car.

Between the accident, waiting for the tow,
and scrapping my car, I doubted I'd have time
to take Kitten, Destroyer of Worlds to the vet,
but she seemed to have emerged unscathed.
At a loss of where to go until I was supposed
to meet with Kennedy, I texted her to tell her
I'd finished dealing with my car and would
head to Hamhock's place early.

Maybe the centaur could give me a few

pointers before my first lesson—or some advice on how to survive the lessons.

My phone rang, and I checked the display. When Kennedy called, I answered, and I swiped my finger across the screen. "Hey."

"I'll come pick you up. I've gotten done everything on my list," she announced.

At least she'd had a productive day. "Any luck?"

"I had luck. Was it good luck or bad luck? That's for me to know and you to find out." She chuckled, and I wondered what sort of trouble she was going to get me into next. "Where are you? How's your car?"

"Since inviting you to self-defense torture probably isn't a good date, how does car shopping sound? I would've spent more repairing it than I spent on the damned thing, I think. The entire exterior was hosed."

"I never would have thought pigeons could do so much damage. You and your kitten are all right?"

"I think so. Kitten is acting like normal, and she didn't seem bothered when I'd hit the brakes. Her airbag didn't deploy."

"Kittens are tough. She's probably fine. We'll keep an eye on her, and if it looks like something is wrong, we'll take her to one of those emergency clinics. From past experience, we'd be waiting for hours for someone to see us, and honestly, I don't want to miss this self-defense torture date."

"I was specifically warned I shouldn't present this as a date. You might hate me."

"I think it'll be fine. I've been to plenty of self-defense classes. It's required as part of my work. I also go to the range several times a week to maintain my carry permit. I'll have to get a permit for Illinois, but it won't take long; I just need to get my papers in from Mississippi and do a qualifying shoot. That should happen next week." Kennedy huffed. "I think I can handle anything you throw at me."

"I'm going to remind you of this when I'm right," I warned her.

"It'll be a cold day in hell, Reed. Tell me where to pick you up. Since we have some time to blow, we'll get something to eat."

I gave her directions to the junkyard, listened to her confirm the address, and ordered her to drive safely, which earned me a low chuckle and a promise she'd try to avoid mass aerial assault by diseased pigeons. Dinner with Kennedy would make a nice start to the evening, which would inevitably sour once the beating portion of our doomed date began. I found odd comfort in one thing, however: if subjecting Kennedy to the mercies of an elf didn't cause us problems, little would.

Half an hour later, she arrived in her rental, grinning when she spotted me sitting on the curb with Kitten, Destroyer of Worlds and everything needed to keep my kitten somewhat content. "That cat has you whipped. I just thought I should let you know."

"I'd figured that out the instant I realized I was going to be taking a ball of fluff to the vet and keeping her without any actual say in the matter."

"It's always good to accept defeat early. It gives you more time to figure out how best to cope with the situation. While I feel sorry for the pigeons, I'm pleased with the results. You're now completely at my mercy."

"For the record, had you said that to me six months ago, I probably would have suffered an instant panic attack and fainted." Either exposure therapy had worked wonders or I'd finally accepted everything, but my heart rate didn't even spike admitting the truth, offering me some hope my future would be free of anxiety-induced hospitalization and blackouts.

"You're the first man I've met to readily admit he faints."

"After the first ten or twenty trips to a clinic or ER because of fainting, it's pointless to deny it. For the record, I blamed you for every incident."

"Rightfully." She joined me on the sidewalk, leaned over, and grabbed my kitten's bag, offering me a good look down her shirt. "You all right?"

"Never better," I replied, shamelessly enjoying the view.

"Enjoying yourself?"

Busted. "If you're expecting me to feel any shame for this, I'm going to remind you of my mixed heritage, two-thirds of which includes incubus and succubus. Has anyone told you today that shirt does wonderful things for your figure?"

"Not yet."

"That shirt does wonderful things for your figure."

"Thank you. Now, get your kitten and let's get something to eat. I'm starving. I've been to so many viewings today I want to scream."

"Find anything worthwhile?"

"I'm thinking about it. In the meantime, I secured an apartment big enough for two downtown through work; we have a month and a half to find someplace permanent, but that'll give us some time and cut out some of the drive. If you're all right with it, we'll stay at your place in the boondocks over the weekends."

"That sounds like a plan I can get behind." I expected it would take me time to get used to needing the extra time I'd once spent on the commute to and from work.

When I'd been stuck in a mire of depression, I'd avoided thinking about why so many preferred to live closer to work. To them, those minutes mattered. Instead of driving, they wanted it to spend it with people they loved. They hadn't understood me because I'd been hiding from even the chance of re-forging those connections.

"Good. Please tell me that's not one of your expensive suits. You got blood on your jacket."

"It's not. It's one of the sacrificial lambs; I wasn't sure if I'd have time to change before our self-defense lesson started."

"Smart move. You sure you're both okay?"

Kitten, Destroyer of Worlds took over her usual place on my shoulder and gave Kennedy a disapproving look. Stroking the kitten to soothe her earned me a nuzzle. "I think we're fine, but I expect I'll be sore in the morning with a new collection of bruises thanks to the airbag. I'll probably feign misery for positive attention."

"It's less effective when you warn me what you're doing."

I grinned at her. "I'm just being honest and hoping for positive attention."

"You're something else, Reed. Get your ass in the car."

Bossy attention worked, too, but I wouldn't tell her that. She'd figure it out on her own soon enough.

WHEN SHE'D SAID DINNER, I'd expected to eat at a restaurant, but Kennedy had other plans for us, and they involved a fully furnished apartment arranged by the FBI, minimal time for eating takeout, and a queen-sized bed. I'd need to figure out how to resist Kennedy sometime in the future, else I'd be too worn out to make use of anything I learned during my lessons with an elf.

Had I been wise, I would've taken a nap of the restful sort. As always, Kennedy made all sense escape, but I liked the sort of trouble she brought with her. I'd been right all along.

Love and hate were the opposite sides of the same coin, and we'd somehow made our coin do a complete flip, but along the way, I thought we'd one-upped ourselves. Before I'd killed a man, we'd never been tested, not truly.

We'd made mistakes, and Kennedy carried the brunt of their weight; it showed through the most when she thought I wasn't watching. I wondered what I'd see if I looked into her eyes. The temptation lurked just beneath the surface, but I resisted.

Fear played a part in that. It always did. One day, I hoped to have the confidence to meet her gaze without worry of what her heart desired. I wanted her to desire me as much as I needed her to fill in the spaces that'd been empty and broken for too long.

I needed to develop a serious case of courage and look her in the eyes, but at the same time, I liked not knowing.

I liked the anticipation of seeing what she'd do. I liked watching her help us mend the pieces without my sight adding any securities or insecurities.

For better or worse, I harbored the hope we'd be all right as long as we both worked at repairing the harm we'd done to ourselves and each other. What time couldn't fix Kennedy had, and I wanted it to be a two-way street.

Figuring out how to accomplish my goal would be the real challenge. I couldn't rely on time's supposed magic to fix things. I'd seen the years wear away at me without repairing any of the damage. I couldn't rely on the passage of days, months, or even years to change anything.

I'd need to have a long talk with one of my doctors about the sudden shift of perspectives. Was I wise to roll with it and readily embrace the change I longed for? Was I setting myself up for worse failure down the road?

Picking up where we'd left off tempted me. I had the money for a ring, although knowing she'd picked up a career requiring her to use firearms to protect herself would change my choice of band. I wanted to get her something she could wear, not something she'd have to pocket while on shift.

I'd think about it, and if the time seemed right, I'd act.

But first, I needed to survive training with an elf. Stretching so the stiffness from the accident wouldn't set in, I considered warning Kennedy about the nature of our instructor. Assuming the elf didn't run us both through the wringer, if we emerged unscathed and together, I figured our relationship would survive just about anything.

Kitten, Destroyer of Worlds protested leaving the creature comforts of the apartment with a hiss but settled as soon as I had her harnessed and riding on my shoulder. She'd have reason to hiss when I kept her in her carrier for a while. With luck, she'd limit her revenge to using her litter box and 'forgetting' to bury her biological warfare.

With my luck, she'd wage biological warfare on multiple fronts, opting to deposit hairballs in my shoes before sleeping on my

face to ensure I properly submitted to her evil
ways.

"That's one cranky cat," Kennedy observed, setting her puppy, who seemed content to keep sleeping, in his carrier. His
replacer milk and other supplies went into
Kitten's bag, earning a disapproving hiss from
my feline overlady.

Scratching under her chin soothed the
beast for a few moments, transforming her
hisses to purrs. "She might be jealous."

"There's a good reason for that. She's
your therapy cat. She probably gets jealous
whenever anyone holds your attention
over her. I've heard that's a tendency of
cats." Kennedy smirked and leaned towards Kitten, Destroyer of Worlds. "Don't
worry. I'm aware you're a package deal,
and I'm not going to take him away from
you."

I worried my kitten would rip Kennedy's
hand off, but she accepted the offered petting
with a purr.

"She's going to become your overlady, too,
if you're not careful."

"And my puppy will become your overlord. There's no point in fighting the inevitable. Give it up, Reed. We're owned."

If joint ownership by pets kept Kennedy
around, I was all in. "I for one am eager to
welcome my feline and canine masters."

"That's the spirit. Go get your ass in the car so we're not late for our date."

WE GOT to Hamhock's with twenty minutes to spare, but despite giving ourselves extra time so we wouldn't be late, our new instructor had arrived before us. At first glance, Samantha resembled a human with pointy ears, but when she caught sight of me emerging from Kennedy's rental, she smiled.

Sharks had nothing on her teeth, teeth meant for one purpose: tearing meat from bones.

Kitten, Destroyer of Worlds, perched on my shoulder with her fur sticking up on end. Then, as she had no sense of self-preservation, she hissed.

Samantha laughed. "What a brave little feline."

Kennedy got out of her car and smacked her hand on the hood. "Reed Hampton Matthews, you did *not* tell me the instructor was an elf. I swear, you're going to pay for this."

Samantha's smile broadened into a mischievous grin. "That is because Mr. Matthews is wiser than he looks. Did you miss me, Kennedy?"

"Wait. What? *Miss* you? You know each

other?"

What had Kennedy been doing with an *elf*? My exposure to elves had been limited to scholarly interest, but everything I'd gathered from my reading—and Hamhock's general warnings—implied what I'd read had more than a few grains of truth to it. The top rules for dealing with an elf involved not running and not pissing one off.

Or picking a fight with one. Picking a fight usually ended in becoming the elf's meal.

"Sammy's the bitch the FBI calls in when they need help whipping someone into shape in a hurry."

Resentment dripped out of Kennedy's tone, and I stared at her with wide eyes. "Kennedy, has she taught you before?"

"Taught is *not* the word I would use."

"What is?"

"Tortured. Legalized torture she was paid to participate in."

Samantha beamed. "I missed your special brand of terror, Kennedy. You look at me, you know you want to run, but you know if you run, I'll take my time catching you because I was hired to get you in shape in time for your basic training. Maybe if you hadn't been a depressed mess in need of extra work, I wouldn't have had to give you the special treatment."

"Maybe you need my therapists more than I do, Kennedy."

"Reed, you didn't tell me we were being trained by an *elf*."

"I thought you'd run away," I confessed. "I told you this would be a very bad date."

"You. Are. The. Worst."

"But I'm the worst who arranged for training with an elf so you can use a Japanese death scythe, Kennedy. Focus on what's important here. A Japanese death scythe."

"Why the hell aren't *you* running away screaming?" Kennedy wailed. "The first time I met her, I made it three miles before she took me out. She needs to go play football instead of torturing me."

"The football players just run away. We've discussed this before. Also, he's not running because he's negligibly human. I took the liberty of pulling your file, Mr. Matthews. And yes, I have special clearance to access the CDC's files, and I abuse it at my leisure. I take training seriously. Knowing about you is critical for me to train you properly. I needed to see what I had to work with. Kennedy, he's utterly incapable of being frightened of me. When I found out he had attachments to you, little missy, I couldn't reject Hamhock's invitation to train you. I'm being paid good money to be entertained. Of course, when I was originally contacted, it was only to work with Mr. Matthews, but I'd heard you were in the area, and as there are interesting notes about you two in his file, I was hoping it would be you accompanying him. I love when I'm not disappointed."

"You are a thief of joy," Kennedy muttered.

Her complaint only pleased the elf. Facing me, Samantha said, "Hamhock tells me you want her using a naginata. Why?"

"Hamhock could've taken my head off with that thing without putting in any effort. Even with a sword, I wouldn't have been able to get to her before I'd lost my head. I've been told guns won't work for me, so that caught my attention. If Kennedy's getting a sharp, pointy object to protect herself with, I want her able to decapitate people before they have a chance to hit her."

I astonished myself with my blunt brutality in what I wanted in the weapon, and I sucked in a breath, my eyes widening.

Even Kitten, Destroyer of Worlds seemed taken aback by my declaration.

"I think you vastly overestimate my ability to decapitate anyone, Reed. The sentiment is appreciated, though. I'm usually armed. With a gun. That has better range than a Japanese death scythe. If me swinging around a Japanese death scythe makes you feel better, I'll do it. You're also going to pay for this for eternity, Reed. E-ter-ni-ty."

I gulped. On one hand, an eternity of suffering at Kennedy's hands meant trouble. On the other, she'd have to stick around for an eternity to make it happened. It reminded me of her quest to relieve me of my towels. When I won, I lost, and when I lost, I won, so I'd focus on the benefits of her wrath, which kept her around for an eternity.

"I wouldn't sound so confident in your inability to decapitate someone with a naginata, Kennedy. The weapon is a good choice for that purpose. It's a woman's weapon, one meant for spiritual growth *and* prowess in battle. I'm sure his decision-making process didn't factor the spiritual elements of the naginata, but that's a forgivable crime. I will teach you both the naginata and the katana, albeit your focus will be on the naginata. The katana will be your weapon of choice in close quarters. I considered a shorter blade, but it would leave you defenseless in the longer ranges. I don't have time to teach you a third weapon."

"Two?" Kennedy wailed. "That's not fair. Why do I get two and he only gets one?"

"Simple. You will be competent. He will be a master. A master marries only one blade. You will be a versatile guard for his back capable of filling many shoes. You're a jack to his king."

"Thief. Of. Joy."

"Before I begin training you on weapons, you need to be physically conditioned for the work. Tonight, I will be generous. I have acquired videos for you to watch that will show you elves in battle. This is what you will learn. After you watch, you will enjoy your rest. Tomorrow, you will begin your training. I expect nothing but the best from both of you, and I will beat the conditioning into you if I must. I have prepared a list of exercises you will do every day to limber your bodies and prepare for your real schooling, which will begin in two weeks. If you do as you're told, in two weeks, you will be sore but limber. You'll also be fit enough to keep up with my teaching. But make no mistake. You will hurt. You will hurt so much you will wish you had the skill needed to kill me. You won't. I'm an elf." Samantha smiled. "You are not. Any questions?"

I raised my hand.

"Yes, Mr. Matthews?"

"Does death by elf count as an Act of God for insurance purposes? If I die from this, I'd like my burial expenses to be covered."

The elf tossed back her head and laughed. "Why are you worried about burial expenses? If I kill you, Mr. Matthews, there won't be enough left of you to bury."

TWENTY-ONE

Well, you're going to get your
money's worth.

THE MEETING with Samantha took less than
an hour, and she introduced us to the
wooden weapons we'd be training with in
two weeks. To make sure we remembered
what was in store for us, we were told to take
the practice weapons home and get used to
their presence along with a warning to not
play with them.

She even gave us a memory stick with a
video we were ordered to watch immediately
if not sooner. I wondered at that, but I figured Samantha didn't want to have to correct
any bad habits we might pick up trying to
figure out how to play with them on our own.

Once we escaped, I got into Kennedy's
rental and waited for her to explode.

"You're something else, Reed Hampton
Matthews."

"In my defense, while I knew she was an

elf, I had no idea you knew her. All I knew is that she's the best sword instructor money can buy."

"Well, you're going to get your money's worth. How the hell did you make arrangements for *her* to teach us? She's almost impossible to hire. I only got a round with her because of some damned, prissy angel incapable of minding his own business."

"Essentially, that's how I got her. An angel interfered."

"I fucking hate angels. Present company excluded. The other elements of your genetics make up for the angelic contamination."

I chuckled, checked on the animals locked in their carriers, and buckled in, earning the silent loathing of my cat. "Sorry, Kitten. It's not safe for me to put you on my lap, and it's not fair to poor Puppy to have to be locked in his carrier when you're free. Tell him to get bigger quicker so you two can ride leashed in the back together."

"You're something else."

"I had no idea you had a history with an elf!"

"She's an elf, Reed. Don't you know elves *will* eat people who piss them off?"

"Don't piss her off, then."

"It's literally impossible to breathe the

same air as elves without pissing them off. They hate humans."

"If she hated humans that much, wouldn't you have already been eaten?"

"I think the government paid her not to eat me." Kennedy gripped the steering wheel until her knuckles turned white, and I wondered how long it would take her to buckle in and start the car. "She was totally thinking about it. How the hell are you able to stand around with absolutely no care you might be eaten. I ran. For three fucking miles. That bitch chased me for three fucking miles!"

I frowned, watching Kennedy out of the corner of my eye. "Deep breaths and count them. You're going to work yourself right into a panic attack. She's not going to eat you. She's being paid a ridiculous amount of money by an angel to teach me how to use a sword. I'll pay her extra not to eat you. I'm okay with that. I'll leave you in the car until I've negotiated her 'don't eat Kennedy' fee."

"How can you be so damned relaxed about this?"

"I'm going to go with temporary insanity, foolish bravery, and general stupidity. Smart people are terrified of being killed and eaten by an elf. You know, if they've done any research on them. At all."

"Have you?"

"Enough to know if I were wise, I'd be scared, too. Honestly, I just want to live through whatever an angel and a devil might possibly want with me, and if that means being taught by an elf, well, if she kills and eats me, I'm just killed faster. I'm pretty sure people get killed when angels and devils get into arguments on mortal soil. With me in the middle. That's what's happened here. There's an angel, there's a devil, and I'm stuck in the middle. I basically need to hire the elf to keep me alive. But she might kill and eat me." I slumped in my seat. "When I put it that way, I sound like a lunatic."

"A desperate lunatic."

"A desperate lunatic who gets to go to a nice apartment with a pretty woman for the night?"

"Why is that a question?"

"I have to survive your wrath over a close encounter of the elf kind first."

"I can't believe your self-defense instructor is her. That's just wrong." Kennedy sighed, buckled in, and beat the steering wheel for a while before starting the engine. "She means every word, for the record. She will hang us both out to dry if we don't do every last thing on her list. Worse, it's a trap. If we just do every last thing on her list, she'll be disappointed. Do. Not. Disappoint. Her."

"I take it you have disappointed her."

"She added two extra miles to my daily

runs every time I disappointed her. And she doesn't understand the concept of resetting the disappointment clock. She'll run us both to death."

"Why do I have the feeling you're a very good runner now?"

"Because I didn't want to get eaten by an elf."

"At the rate you're going, you're going to need a therapy animal to help you cope even more than I do. Honestly, I'm expecting to have Kitten's therapy paperwork revoked with how much I've been progressing."

"They won't revoke a therapy animal without at least a year between panic attacks or other symptoms of trauma. You're safe for at least a year. And honestly, the goal is to get you to the point you don't need her around to keep you from having a panic attack. And anyway, she's worked miracles for you."

Kitten, Destroyer of Worlds had done a lot to help vanquish one of my beasts, but I recognized the truth despite Kennedy doing her best to hide it behind several pounds of tabby cat. My kitten had planted a few important seeds. Kennedy held responsibility for the rest of my improvement.

I could live with that.

"You played your part."

"Damn it, Reed. If I had done a lot of

things differently, you wouldn't have needed a therapy cat in the first place."

"Is this the phase in our relationship where we play the blame game to see who holds the most responsibility before we go to that apartment you got and continue the argument in bed? We could skip the whole first part of that and just go straight to bed."

"We can't go to bed until we watch this video or the elf will kill and eat us."

"Every scenario ends with being eaten by an elf, doesn't it?"

"Until we're done this? Yes. We're going to get eaten by an elf."

"I'd say I'd protect you, but honestly, you're better equipped with the advantage of being able to use a gun. I'd just stand there and look helpless. Currently, aren't you supposed to be protecting *me* from the elf?"

"You want to protect yourself from the elf? *Run really fast.*"

"But she doesn't like when people run from her. As such, isn't it safer to not run?"

"She doesn't like having to exercise to catch lunch."

"Well, think about it this way. If you survive the elf, you should be able to survive just about anything, right?"

Kennedy glared at me, snorted, and didn't say a word. I twisted in my seat and regarded Puppy, Savior of Worlds with a resigned sigh.

"Looks like it's you and me in the dog house tonight, pup."

"You only have yourself to blame. I mean, really, Reed. An elf?"

As I was already in trouble anyway, I asked, "Do all elves scare you or just Samantha?"

"Have I told you lately you can be an ass-hole, Reed?"

She hadn't, and I discovered I'd missed it. "Obviously, I haven't been working hard enough to earn such a reward."

"You're something else. Fine. I don't know if all elves scare me, but Sammy sure as hell does."

"I'm sure we'll be fine, Kennedy. How bad can she be? You survived her once. You can survive her again."

"You'll see," she promised. "You'll see."

THE INSTANT we arrived at the apartment, Kennedy dug out her laptop and set up the video we'd been ordered to watch. I released Kitten, Destroyer of Worlds, and she pounced my leg, batting at my slacks in a bid for attention. She went on my shoulder while I released the miniature hound of war from his carrier, scooped him up, and returned him to his bed. "Does Puppy need to be fed yet?"

"In an hour," Kennedy reported. "Come watch this so Sammy doesn't make an excuse to have us for breakfast."

Chuckling, I joined her on the couch, giving my kitten a few strokes before setting her on my lap. With a disgruntled flick of her tail, she abandoned me to join her new brother in his bed. "I'm almost disappointed we didn't get to experience World War Pet."

Kennedy glanced up from her work and smiled at the unlikely pair. "Maybe it's because he's so young? They're really cute together."

"I'm not sorry I picked an elf to teach us, but I am sorry I didn't warn you first."

"Your logic wasn't wrong. If you had told me, I probably would've run. Had I run, Sammy would've enjoyed hunting me and dragging me back by my hair. That woman simply doesn't know when to quit."

"Do you think an elf will be able to teach me how to defend myself against an angel and a devil?"

"If she can't, you're hopeless. I'm pretty sure the elf could eat them for breakfast and be hungry before lunch."

"Did you really run from her the first time you met her?"

"Like a bat out of hell. It's a documented response. Most humans will bolt when an elf comes calling. No one really knows why. Survival instinct, probably. It's more unusual you treated her like you would anyone else you're meeting for the first time. Fuck. She's probably disappointed she didn't have to chase you. She *loves* a good hunt more than life itself. We're so fucked."

"It'll be all right, Kennedy. Think about it this way, you get to learn how to use a Japanese death scythe *and* a katana. I get to wield a fake Excalibur and pretend I'm a knight when I'm more like a duck."

"You'd make a decent knight."

I chuckled and relaxed, stretching out my legs while waiting for Kennedy to subject us to Samantha's video. "I'm barely a page at this point."

"With Sammy teaching you, you'll be ready to storm the castle in no time. She'll beat competence into you."

Of that I had no doubt. "What do you think is on this video?"

"I don't know, which is almost as scary as going through another training course with that damned elf."

"Let's get this over with, then." I batted Kennedy's hands away from her screen and hit the play button.

The video began with warfare, the kind movies dramatized while dodging the horrors of the battlefield. I recognized some of the footage from World War I. The image of a massive flamethrower spouting a torrent of burning oil into enemy lines evoked a wince from both of us.

"I think she's going for the instill the horrors of combat route," Kennedy muttered. "It's working."

I agreed. Refusing to be unnerved by a video, I watched, crossing my arms over my chest and grunting.

It didn't take long for me to discover the World War I footage was a warm up for World War II, and the elf took her gloves off in her choice of clips to terrorize us with. Until I'd watched, I hadn't known it was possible to vaporize someone's head with a machine gun.

"Don't get in close range and eye level of a machine gun, Kennedy. It doesn't end well."

"Good advice. I'll make sure to follow it."

If Samantha's goal was to showcase examples of mass human brutality, she succeeded with flying colors, progressing from war to war, conflict to conflict until we toured an entire world of violence. On more than one occasion, I winced at the savagery. Death came in many forms, and I suspected Samantha meant for us both to be intimately familiar with every way possible for a human to die in combat.

After working her way through warfare,

she'd decided we needed a taste of accidental death and dismemberment.

After an hour and a half, I emerged feeling fragile and unfortunately mortal. Kennedy stared at me with wide eyes. "What the hell did we just watch?"

"A lesson in mortality?"

"A hundred and one ways a person can die," she countered.

"I'm pretty sure there were more than a hundred and one different types of death in there. Also, I think I've developed a permanent and lasting fear of steamrollers."

"Forget the steamroller. I'm never going near a window with an iron fence beneath it ever again."

"I'm not sure I want to get into a car again, either," I confessed.

"She seems to have an unhealthy interest in the numerous ways car accidents can kill somebody."

"Maybe she's trying to convince you you have better odds of survival if you stick with the elf?"

Kennedy wrinkled her nose, narrowed her eyes, and considered her laptop. "Or give us both a complex where everything, including her, is out to get us."

"I got attacked by an entire flock of dead pigeons today. I think I'm safer with the elf. Do you think a sword can stop a bullet?"

"I really doubt it."

"Think I can get a bulletproof vest? I feel like I need a bulletproof vest." I shook my head, laughed, and retrieved the manila envelope with our marching orders for the next two weeks. "Do you think she was maybe trying to convince us it could be worse when we look at what we're supposed to do before our first actual lesson?"

"Now *that* I can easily believe. All right. Hit me with it. What does Sammy want us to do before she decides we're worth teaching?"

I returned to my seat beside her and pulled out a stack of sheets. The top declared we both had to do the same tasks to physically condition us. A pair of keys slipped out.

"Keys?" I scooped them off my lap and held them up.

Kennedy stole the papers and flipped through them, and she sucked in a breath. "I think she's lost her mind, Reed."

"Why would you say that?"

"There's a property about ten miles outside of town. A lot. She claims she has leveled the lot, but we're to turn the downed trees into lumber or firewood. The keys are for a cabin she dumped on the edge of the property. According to her, we should be grateful she catered to our delicate sensibilities and installed indoor plumbing but the rest of the creature comforts are our problem. We're to report to the property when we aren't working. While we're there, we're to be cutting wood like we mean it, and may God save our souls if we leave any logs by the time two weeks have come to an end." Kennedy sighed. "She even included a picture of the lot."

I peeked. Hundreds of downed trees littered the image. "If she thinks we're cutting all that up in two weeks, she's mad."

"She's going to be so disappointed," Kennedy whispered.

"They're not huge trees," I pointed out, tapping the photograph. "Did she specify how much needed to be viable lumber?"

"No. She just said it had to be cleared and repurposed for something useful."

I allowed myself a smug grin. "From personal experience, it's a lot faster to deal with a fallen log if you're going to be using it to make a cabin. You just need to take all the straight ones, hack them to the right length, and remove the branches. We don't even have to strip the bark. She didn't say we had to turn them into planks. Everything too crooked or small to be used for logs we'll cut into firewood and sort by tree type. We'll save a lot of time that way."

"You sound too happy about this."

"Are you kidding? If there's one thing I'm good at, it's cutting wood. But there's method to her madness."

"There is?"

I showed Kennedy my calloused hands. "After two weeks of cutting wood, the blisters you'll inevitably get will be healing to callouses, and trust me when I say you want those callouses when you spend a lot of your time cutting wood. I have no doubt it applies to swords and Japanese death scythes."

Kennedy's eyes widened, and she took my hand in hers, running her fingers over the toughened skin. "I hadn't thought of that."

"What else is on the list?"

"A lot of running, and she says there are monitors for us to use in the lodge to track how far we've run."

"Define a lot of running."

"Tomorrow, we're to run a mile. The next day, we're supposed to run two miles. She's being generous and keeping us at two miles for a few days, after which we're supposed to run three miles. Our last day of the schedule, she wants us running eight miles."

"All at once?" I blurted.

"She didn't specify. I assume she just means throughout the day."

"I bet she wants it all at once to build our endurance. Maybe we can run as much as we can and hope for the best?"

"There's no way we're going to survive running eight miles and chopping up a bunch of wood."

"You're probably right, but we're just going to have to deal with it. Anything else?"

"She very specifically states we're not allowed to die, we're supposed to keep hydrated, and that she expects us to eat properly while training. As it's 'impossible for mere humans to cook, do all assigned training, and run' she will provide sufficient sustenance. We're expected to eat every bite, or we'll regret it."

"That sounds rather menacing."

"You only have yourself to blame for this. *You* hired an elf to teach you. What were you thinking?"

"Obviously, I wasn't."

"If you get us killed, I'm haunting your lanky ass for all of eternity, Reed."

"And if I don't get us killed, you'll be seeking out revenge for the rest of eternity for subjecting you to Sammy?"

"That sounds about right."

"So, no matter what happens, you're sticking around for all eternity?"

"As a single lifespan is insufficient to make you properly pay for this travesty, yes."

I could work with that. "As I don't want to know what will happen if we disappoint an elf, I think I'm going to see about using some vacation time and working at this cabin in the woods."

"Good lord, Reed. At least call it a cottage

in the forest. That way, I won't feel like we're accepting an invitation to our murder."

I laughed because it was true. "I'm sorry. I'll see if I can work at our lovely new cottage in the forest for the next two weeks."

"We're doomed," she predicted.

I could only hope she wasn't right.

TWENTY-TWO

I thought we'd done well.

TWO WEEKS of following an elf's every order went about as well as I could expect. The lot had more trees than I had anticipated, Lucavier demanded more of my time than I liked, and no matter what I did, someone found a way to interrupt me, resulting in a chaotic dive to finish everything I needed to do each day.

The only thing I managed to fully accomplish was the running, and I only got that in because Kennedy refused to further disappoint the elf. All in all, she handled the two weeks far better than I did.

For all Kennedy proclaimed she was terrified of the elf, the woman viewed the lot as a challenge to overcome, and she attacked the downed trees with a vengeance. Between the two of us, with her working most of the time while I helped whenever I had a free moment, we managed to clear a quarter of the property.

I thought we'd done well.

Samantha showed up on our last day, took a look at the lot, and shook her head. "Humans."

I recognized disgust when I heard it.

"For the record, this is mostly your fault, Reed."

"Better than completely my fault, which was where we were at last week. But if I hadn't tried to work *and* clear the lot, we could've gotten twice as much done. But I will say I do bear most of the burden of failure on this one. She did most of the chopping."

Samantha sighed and bowed her head. "Why did I agree to this?"

"I'm pretty sure I'm paying you a lot of money to train us without killing and eating us," I replied.

"I'd say you're correct, but in reality, an angel is footing the bill."

"But I made her, so it still counts. It's forced payment to make her leave me alone. I'm pretty sure if I'd let her pick the instructor, I wouldn't have gotten someone anywhere near as determined to see us succeed as you."

"Flattery will get you nowhere, Mr. Matthews."

"It's just the truth. The way I view it, I spared Luna from a lie by making sure I actually hired the best instructor money could buy, and that's you. I promised Kennedy I'd pay you extra to not eat her, so bill Luna extra for that."

"I always have enjoyed charging angels extra for my work. It's a joy in life. Very well. I will add extra charges to ensure you both survive my training without being killed and turned into dessert."

"See, Kennedy? It's not all bad. We're not breakfast, lunch, *or* dinner. We classify as dessert."

"She may not kill and eat us, but she's going to find some other way to punish us for failing to clear the lot," Kennedy muttered.

"I do enjoy when my students realize the truth without me having to go to extremes. It's so painful for my students when I have to go to extremes. Show me your hands," Samantha ordered.

I held out my hands for her inspection, as did Kennedy.

If I judged the elf by her hands, I'd believe her as delicate as a flower, but her slender fingers hid iron strength, and she traced her fingertips over my fingers, palm, and thumb. "These hands have seen a lot of work."

"I have about twenty years of firewood in my barn. I chopped wood to fill the time for the past two years," I admitted. "I figured this was an exercise to build callouses on the hands so when we started working with the swords we'd have fewer blisters to contend with. I'm guessing ax callouses aren't much different from sword callouses."

"Different, but similar enough to mitigate the worst of it, yes." Samantha turned to Kennedy, whose hands had suffered far worse than mine. "And yours are developing well. You'll progress slower than Mr. Matthews, but you'll do."

"Reed, please," I said.

"You're not going to make me run extra miles?"

"You did as told, so no. I don't punish those who give their best effort, and you have. I may be unyielding, but despite being an elf, I'm not unnecessarily cruel. I expect your best. You gave it. You learned that lesson already."

"I probably deserve the extra miles." Admitting my faults didn't bother me, and I shrugged. "I tried to juggle everything, but I recognize I fell short."

"If I were to compare you to Kennedy without considering other factors, I would agree. You act like I'm not aware of what you've been doing for the past two weeks. Silly human. The only running you will do is when I chase you with a sword because you do not learn what I wish to teach you fast enough. Pain is an excellent teacher when time is short, and I suspect you do not have as much time as you wish you did to learn what I must teach you." Samantha circled me, and if I were to assign her a lethality rating, I'd rather swim with sharks while covered head to toe in paper cuts. "Within five months, I will make you capable of standing up against even an angel."

Kennedy sucked in a breath. "That's going to take a miracle."

"Don't look so alarmed, Kennedy. He's part angel, part demon, and enough human to counter most of his elven heritage. Demons and angels alone take to the sword. The elf in him will take care of the rest."

I frowned. "While I've asked for a genetic testing to find out what my unknown percentages were, wouldn't elf have already been easily identified?"

"Not exactly. There are various branches of elves. You're from an extinct line. In short, there are no more full elves of your heritage left. They died out long ago. Frankly spoken, anyone with any sense is grateful they're gone."

Curiosity got the better of me, forcing me to ask, "Why?"

"They'd eat anything that moved in- cluding each other. They had no grasp of morality, no sense of honor, nothing beyond a desperate need to satisfy their relentless hunger. Their breeding practices were, at best, abhorrent. Had you been more elf and less angel, I expect you would have been killed shortly after birth. Elves of your type are born dangerous and hungry. But while you're expressing genes from your heritage and your percentage is higher than it should be indicating your elven heritage has over-written other genes in its effort to regain dominance, you are expressing the safer genes."

My eyes widened. "The *safer* genes?"

"Well, you didn't attempt to eat your mother's placenta, which is excellent evidence the more dangerous genes weren't expressed. You also didn't attempt to eat your mother. Show me your teeth," she ordered.

As I had no doubt she'd hold me down and peel my lips away from my teeth, I obeyed.

She pointed at my canines. "They're slightly more pronounced than a regular human's but within acceptable standards; unless someone was aware of your ancestry, no one would suspect your teeth are more pointed because of your elven heritage. Should your teeth be examined, I expect they'll be harder than standard humans. You've probably never had a cavity in your life; elves don't get them.

You won't experience any tooth decay, either. Should your teeth get knocked out or weaken, you'll grow new ones, one of the advantages of being an elf. That's also why, unlike Kennedy here, you're unafraid of me. I had suspected elven heritage, but the specific breed surprised me. I have high hopes for you, but I'm afraid you'll be very busy for the next few months. When you are not dealing with human matters, I will be transforming you into a living weapon. You aren't an elf, not in full, but your breed will make up for your shortcomings, as will your angelic and demonic heritages. It's not often I get to work with such strong base material."

Kennedy sighed, her shoulders slumping. "I'm going to be the weak link, aren't I?"

"You'll never compare to an elf. That's true. But you have a more important role."

That caught Kennedy's attention. "I do?"

"You do. You will learn to use your Japanese death scythe and your katana, but those weapons are not your true strength. Really, I'm very pleased with how this arrangement worked out. And I will enjoy scalping that angel for extra money under the guise of ensuring your wellbeing. No, you don't need my assurances of your survival. You have something better."

I suspected elves lived to confuse humans. "What are you talking about?"

"You'll find out soon enough. Some secrets are best left discovered naturally. But don't worry. It won't hurt you—or her. Here are my expectations for you until we have completed training. Every day, rain or shine, you will come here when you aren't working or sleeping. On weekends, we will go to your property in Gypsum Creek. You are expected to work as normal, both of you. Should you have to travel, Kennedy, you will do exercises as ordered. I will prepare your meals, as I require you both to be healthy and humans tend to be frailer than elves. No whining. Should you become ill, I will call for a doctor —and don't worry about telling me if you're sick. I'll be able to smell it on you. Likely, I will know before you will. You will trust my judgment in these matters. Understood?"

"Understood," we chorused.

"Good. Before you can wield a weapon, you must understand how it is made. For this, we will spend half of our time at Hamhock's forge so you can learn from her. To truly become one with a blade, you must understand and embrace everything about it. From raw ore to polished steel, when I am finished with you, your blades will be a part of your soul. You will miss it when it isn't in your hand. You will long for the feel of it cutting through the air. It will become another part of you. Everything from every breath you draw to how you stand will be retaught to you. Everything you know is wrong for wielding a blade of any sort. But most of all, remember this truth: the only failure in this is not giving me your very best. Give me your very best, even when your sweat pours from you in a flood and you bleed, and you will transform yourself from nothing into something. Of that I have no doubt. Are you ready?"

Kennedy gulped but nodded.

"I'll have to be," I said, expecting the worst but daring to hope I'd survive five months of training with an elf determined to make me something more—and possibly less—than human.

Then again, I'd never really believed myself truly human anyway.

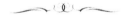

HAD I known what was in store for me, I would've taken a page out of Kennedy's book and run. Samantha would've chased, but the slim chance of escape tempted me. Learning from Hamhock involved working the billows to build our muscle strength; I had an easier time of it than Kennedy. Kennedy struggled, but she'd changed since we'd been in college and discovering the world wasn't as friendly a place as we'd hoped.

Quit was no longer part of her personal dictionary.

I wanted it to be a part of mine, but reality insisted on screwing with me, my damned cat *liked* the sadistic elf and whined if I even considered running for the hills, and Lucavier Buioni insisted on making my work life complicated. The deeper I dove into his activities, the less I liked having anything to do with him. The extended contract negotiations were already giving me a headache. At his insistence, I'd agreed to meet him to finalize negotiations at a charity event—a bloody gala —set to take place shortly after I was scheduled to complete training with Samantha.

He reminded me of a complex puzzle, one I needed to solve without any idea of the final picture and no edges to work with. As I thought, all of the contracts connected, but beyond the obvious potential for a monopoly, I couldn't figure out his end game. What was the point of throwing millions of dollars at my company for a chance to work with me on even one of them?

In a way, I was grateful that Samantha kept Kennedy busy during work hours; it made using practitioner magic easier, and I'd relied too heavily on tricks to hear truth in another's words.

It'd started creeping in on my life without the intact runes fueling the magic. The CDC called it an imprint, a consequence of using the same magic too often.

I figured I'd accidentally woken part of my angelic heritage.

Until I'd started hearing the echoes of truth and lies in my day-to-day life, I hadn't realized how often people lied. Kennedy didn't lie often, and it was always the little white lies meant to make someone else feel better. Sometimes she lied to make herself feel better, sometimes she lied to convince Samantha she wasn't ready to crawl in a hole and quit.

She never lied to me.

Too busy to stop and breathe, I juggled work and torture sessions with Samantha. When I thought of using a sword, I thought of duels and directly battling an opponent. In practice, I spent very little time battling anyone but myself. Most of the time, I repeated the same motion over and over until my body remembered it better than I did. Samantha watched like a hawk on the prowl for dinner, and if I did anything wrong, she showed me why the motions were critical.

Pain taught me the most lessons, and not a day went by without new bruises. When I wasn't working, I held a sword. Despite my ax callouses, I bled doing my best to meet Samantha's standards. Kennedy bled, too, which bothered me more than anything else.

While she worked, too, often spending three to five days out of town doing the FBI's bidding, she always returned with torn hands.

Every cut and bruise woke something in me. At the beginning, I suppressed my irritation; my hands fared no better, and I refused to belittle Kennedy's efforts no matter how much I disliked her being in pain. The days faded into months, but while my hands healed and hardened, Samantha found some way to push Kennedy to new limits, bruising and toughening her hands beyond what I endured.

Somewhere around the four to five month mark, something changed. Kennedy's hands blistered still, although not as often as when we'd first begun the horror show thinly disguised as training.

Samantha watched Kennedy. I watched the elf, and the thousands of repetitious movements clicked, crystalizing into something I could turn into lethal force.

I forgot the names of most of the moves; Samantha didn't care much for naming things, instead doing a single demonstration of what she wanted, slowed down so I could follow, and demanding I mimic it until she was satisfied I could do it a hundred times without error.

Then another hundred.

One of those moves would put my sword

in the perfect position to strike along her ribs, a narrow window beneath her elbow she might not be able to defend. The steps she'd taught me, too, subtle motions meant to put me in the best position to resume any one of the countless exercises she'd pushed me through each day.

"It's about fucking time," the elf muttered, straightening her posture.

The opening vanished, and I tensed as her attention turned to me. "What's about fucking time?"

"You finally looked at me like I was the main dish of your dinner. And don't even try to deny it. I see it every time I look in the mirror. I was wondering how many times I'd have to have a damned mage fix Kennedy's hands so I could beat them up again waiting for you to tire of me smacking your woman around."

"You did that to her on purpose?"

Killing my instructor would land me in prison, deserved, although I doubted I'd survive facing off against her. It'd be worth it, however.

Kitten, Destroyer of Worlds climbed up my legs and sank her claws into my shoulder. I howled at the unexpected feline assault, although I somehow prevented myself from flinging her off. "Kitten!" As cats were above reproach, my feline overlady purred and nuzzled my cheek. Torn between fury and melting over her affection, I surrendered and pet her. "Not cool, cat. You're supposed to play with the damned dog and watch, not use me as your personal scratching post."

"She's smarter than you give her credit for," Samantha announced. "Of course, she has no way of understanding I'm goading you into attacking me so we can have our first proper spar. It's pointless to teach you so many wonderful moves without giving you a chance to experience what it's like to face your death. And when you cross swords with me, I promise you'll be fighting for your life, Reed."

I hated elves. I'd only met one, but if other elves shared even a single similarity with Samantha, I'd do my best to avoid them. Elves meant nothing but trouble. Sighing, I returned to the cat and dog bed set out in the front of Samantha's cabin and tied her leash to the post by the door. To ensure Puppy, Savior of Worlds hadn't learned a habit from his feline sister, I tied his leash to the post as well.

I returned to my spot, fighting to keep my expression neutral. "Let me see if I understand this. Unless I fight you, you're going to willfully continue tearing up Kennedy's hands?"

"If you don't, tomorrow, she'll have

shredded strips of skin over bloodied ruins of muscle and bone. Not only will I make you watch, I'll give her a few licks. Fresh blood's delicious."

"I hate you," I announced, and had I been anything other than tired, achy, and ready to sleep for the remaining time until I had to attend a damned charity gala event at a museum, I might've had the life in me to sharpen my tone.

I wouldn't waste my breath. I'd need it to do my best to land even one hit on the damned elf.

"On one hand, I'd love if I could be left out of this. On the other, I want to grab a beer and watch her kick your ass for implying I'm too weak to handle her." Kennedy shook out her hand, which bled and oozed in several places. "First, while it hurts like hell, she and her goon of a mage patch it up as good as new before bed. Second, I haven't given up, so kindly do not give up for me."

"I'm not asking you to give up! I'm asking her to not lick your blood off your hand. And don't you even start, Kennedy Young. She scared you so much you wanted to run for the border and kill me for having the balls to hire an elf. We get to share the same bed most nights, but that devil with pointy ears has you so worn out you're asleep before I can even join you."

"That's true. Neither of us have gotten any for months. How have we not imploded already?" Kennedy clucked her tongue and shook her head. "That is a crime. I bet if you give her a good sport, she'll let us go to bed early without sending us straight to the end of our ropes. Honestly, after the first month of this bullshit, I got numb to it. Another day, more hell. It ends in a month, right? Then you have that meeting with that devil and we're both free of the elf, devil, and angel. Honestly, I spend most days looking to the bright side of things."

"Riddle me this, Sammy. Why isn't Kennedy terrified of you anymore?"

"Exposure therapy. She's become numb to it. She might have even adapted to it. I haven't eaten her yet, and she's bled around me every day for weeks. If I was going to snap and eat her, I would've the first time a blister bled."

"That's good to know," I admitted. "That's still not an excuse to hurt her to piss me off."

"You need to be willing to hurt me to fight me, and the only way you're going to be willing to hurt me is if I hurt her or your cat. Honestly, while cats are delicious, yours is unfortunately too cute to kill."

"Unfortunately?"

"For my digestion."

"You disgust me."

"If I wasn't disgusting you, I wouldn't be

doing our species any justice. I am an elf, after all. It's one of our few joys in life. Lighten up. One day, you might grow up to be just like me."

I stared at Samantha in horror. Kennedy laughed, adding to my dismay. "Kennedy!"

"What? It's funny. You look like she just kicked your kitten."

"If she even thinks about kicking my kitten, I'll make it my life mission to kill her."

"If I did that, I'd start a cataclysm," Samantha chirped in her sweetest voice. "Tempting, though."

"Reed, if you don't fight her like you mean it, it might be another six months until we get to finally do something together in a bed other than pass out from general exhaustion."

I twitched. "I don't suppose you'll be willing to go into the cabin with our pets while I have a talk with Samantha?"

"Will it be a violent talk?"

"If it means I might get a chance to do something other than pass out from general exhaustion whenever I get near a bed, quite possibly."

"Shout for me when you're done beating a new set of bruises into him, Sammy. I'm going to get these fixed and take a nap. I think I've earned it. You think I've earned it, too, haven't you, Sammy?" Kennedy looked the elf in the eyes and growled, "Haven't you, Sammy?"

Holy hell, I had no idea what had gotten into Kennedy, but I'd never seen anything more glorious in my life. I watched her, holding my breath so I wouldn't interrupt the moment.

The damned elf would probably find some way to quench Kennedy's fire.

"Eat dinner before you sleep or you'll be useless to me after. If I don't disembowel him tonight, I'll even let you two duke it out with the wooden swords. If you both survive tonight, I'll be pleased. A month isn't enough to bring you both up to par, but you'll be close. Playtime's over, children. Off you go, and make sure you do your regular stretches before you sleep. You'll regret it if you don't."

Kennedy huffed, pivoted on a heel, and marched to Kitten and Puppy, scooping both animals up and carrying them into the house. Hooking the door with her foot, she slammed it behind her.

"In case you were unable to translate that, that woman needs to get some action, wants that action with you, and was ready to start making a run at me last month but waited because you're less inclined to indulge in violence than she is. Okay, to be fair, I specifically requested she restrain her bloodthirsty ways until you snapped and attempted to fight me like you mean it."

"I'll cut you a deal," I muttered under my breath, eyeing the cabin in case Kennedy was lurking at one of the windows. To make sure she couldn't read my lips, I turned my back and glared at the elf. "I'll fight you on a single condition."

"This is going to be so good. What do you think you're going to win from me, little boy?"

"An engagement ring. You have to pick it so I won't humiliate myself if I happen to survive attacking an elf. Because honestly, I fully expect to be killed and eaten for attacking an elf."

"A wager it is, then. If you land a single blow on me, I will acquire the engagement ring on your behalf and deliver it to you within the next forty-eight hours."

"And if I don't?"

"You will take off the next two weeks of work to be brutally educated on your failings. I will be merciful and acquire the ring, as you simply won't have time to yourself, but you will pay for it in chopping wood when you otherwise would've been doing your human work."

I feared that while Samantha made no mention of killing and eating me, she'd find a way to put me six feet under within two weeks. "And you won't humiliate me with the ring?"

"The better you fight, the better the ring. You draw blood, and that ring will be a jewel even among elves."

I hated being torn between striving to get in a few hits on my damned instructor for hurting Kennedy and wanting to draw blood so I could make a fool out of myself repeating history.

I didn't even know if Kennedy wanted to give marriage a second shot.

"If you kill me, you're responsible for my funeral expenses and will be required to protect Kennedy for the rest of your lifespan. And you're not allowed to kill her to get out of it, either."

Samantha tossed her head back and cackled. "You're the strangest man I've met in my life, and I've been alive a long time. Very well. I agree to your terms. Do your best, little human. No, do better than your best, because that's what it's going to take to face me in battle."

I NEEDED to ask Kennedy to beat sense into me the next time I invited myself to a trouncing. The wooden swords we used would likely keep my injuries to broken bones and bruises rather than dismemberment, but Samantha wasted no time launching the offensive. Her first hit caught me across the ribs, and had she wanted to kill me, she would've. The blow knocked my breath out, and to make sure I understood she'd win our fight, she knocked my feet out from under me and sat on my chest.

"This is what your ultimate goal is, Mr. Matthews." The elf polished her nails on her shirt. "You're going to have to last longer than a few seconds if you don't want to have your ass handed to you by an angel."

"Why do you think I'm going to get into a fight with an angel?"

"Angels only want fair fights. Why else buy you a sword and lessons? She'd violate their conceptions of fairness if she killed you when you couldn't try to defend yourself. Angels are among the crueler beings. They're honest. If they aren't, they fall. But nothing in their twisted code of ethics state they can't build someone up for the ultimate purpose of tearing them down."

"Then why would she look into the future to keep me from a premature death?"

"It's that whole fair fight bullshit. Or maybe she just hates you so much she wants to kill you herself. But you spared that angel from falling. No. Frankly, I believe she hired someone to inconvenience you. Kidnapping you and dumping you in the state you fear and hate the most would count. As long as she didn't tell them people she hired how to get rid of you, she wasn't technically lying. She's meddling, though. I've been thinking about it. If she's falling, some of the odder events in your life could be a consequence of it. An angel could spawn a tornado in hopes of terrorizing—or killing—a couple of annoying mortals. A flock of pigeons would be nothing to her and inconvenience you, as it did. I'll think about other possibilities later. Anyway, most angels hate our ilk. Consider this: she promised you only the best. I am the best, and angels do *not* ask *me* for help. Never forget that."

"I haven't. My grandparents loathe my existence. Ever since I was a little, they would leave whenever I came around."

Samantha patted my cheek. "Don't be so quick to judge them. They probably didn't want to know what they'd see in your eyes. That's the same problem you have, is it not? You haven't actually looked me in the eyes once since we've met. You won't look into your love's eyes, either."

"Habit," I admitted. "I try not to use my sight."

"That won't allow you to ever control it, you know. It's a part of you. Until you accept everything that it is, you'll never be able to control it rather than it controlling you. That's much like what it is to be an elf. Will you control your hunger, or will your hunger control you? Your breed? They never learned control. They embraced their hunger, and they never went beyond embracing it and doing their best to devour the world. Who do you want to be?"

"I thought we were supposed to be fighting."

"Oh, we will. I'm merely giving you something to consider in the days leading up to your conflict with a devil and an angel, neither of which want the best for you. While angels and devils may fall in love with an individual human, they do not love all humans. Humans are just the pawns of their eternal struggle between law and chaos, good and evil, or whatever you wish to call the forces dividing them."

"You must hate knowing you've wasted months on someone who will probably die within the next month and a half," I muttered, and tired of her using me as a chair, I rolled and dumped her off. "And I meant what I said. If I get my sorry ass killed, you get to take care of Kennedy *and* my cat."

"I see we've moved straight to the acceptance of inevitable death phase of things. Do at least try to provide me with some sport." Samantha scooped up her practice sword, kicked mine to me, and set her stance. "This time, you come at me, and come at me like you mean it."

The only way I'd hit her was if I swung at her, so I obeyed. I recognized the move she used to block me as one she'd beaten into me. I hopped out of her reach, my eyes narrowing while I watched her move. When she didn't retaliate, I tried again, swiping my sword at her knee.

She stepped away, light on her feet, moving only enough to evade my blow. Once again, with one of the moves she'd forced into me through repetition, she deflected my weapon.

I tilted my head to the side. "If you swung at me like that, what would happen?"

She chuckled and swiped at me, and while her motion shocked me, my arm moved, my body remembering what she'd taught me. "That," she replied. "It's clicking. I'm only using what I've taught you, Reed. Every move I used to take you down like you were a rabbit with three legs? I've already taught it to you. None of the time I spent on you was wasted. You just don't know how to use what I've taught you. I prefer to teach through ex-perience. Well, now is your time to experi-ence it. And remember, your goal is to hit me. Again, and do it like you mean it."

AFTER TWO HOURS of trying to hit Samantha only to be blocked by the moves she'd taught me over and over again, I wanted to take my sword and shove it so far up her ass she could retrieve it through her nose. Worse, I bored her. I bored her so much she stifled yawns, paid no attention to me, and beat off my advances with one hand while checking beneath her nails for dirt.

I could deal with failure. Honestly, I hadn't understood what failure truly was until meeting Samantha.

A gentle breeze had nothing on her, I suspected tornadoes feared her and made way, and I wondered if a force on Earth existed capable of tearing her down from her mountain of superiority. She'd tried to teach me a shadow of how she could move.

Compared to her, I flailed. The few times I'd gotten close, she'd graced me with her attention, not that her attention meant anything in the grand scheme of things. Unless I hit her, I'd be her slave for two weeks, and I was certain Kennedy would somehow join forces with the elf to make my life as miserable as possible until I met the elf's ever-lowering standards.

Kennedy would be doing it out of general frustration, frustration I shared. By the time I made it to the gala, I figured the only people happy with life would be my cat and her dog, who lived like royalty as the damned elf refused to accept anything other than the best for our furry charges.

I was convinced they ate better than we did.

I caught my breath. "I don't know what is more frustrating: that you're not putting any effort into dodging me or that I have no hope in hell of hitting you."

"It's because you have a foundation without anything built on it. Do your best to block me," she ordered. Samantha slowed her motions, striking at my ribs. I lifted my sword to deflect her, and the wooden blades met with a clack. "You didn't think about that. At all. You moved because that's how I taught your body to move. Now it's time for me to teach you to be more than a braindead male who waves his sword around expecting it to do something."

I twitched. "Do elves even know how to count past one?"

"Your smart mouth just earned you extra bruises."

"But where will you put them? I don't think I have any space available for new bruises, and we have a no face rule. We do not bruise the face."

"I'm sure I can find a spot or two I haven't

yet bruised." Samantha lunged for me, aiming her sword at my ribs again. Mid-swing, she redirected her strike towards my wrist. I twisted out of her way, slashing at her upper legs in retaliation. As always, she hopped out of my range. "Your neck isn't your face, and I haven't bruised there yet."

"If you hit me in the neck, I'll probably die."

"Damned, fragile humans. Grow another set of arms or something. I need more places to bruise." To make it clear she'd find some way to beat me, she feinted at me before unleashing one of her harder hits to the back of my calf. I went down with a yelp.

To teach me the disadvantages of being on the ground, Samantha slapped my back with the flat of her wooden sword.

From my prone position at her feet, I got a good look at her bare ankles; her lack of socks startled me, but then she gave me the best leverage and took a step closer, putting her in range of my teeth. While our bargain implied using a sword, she liked to claim we needed to use every weapon in our arsenal.

Teeth counted as weapons, especially to an elf. With nothing left to lose, I bit her ankle as hard as I could.

I MADE SAMANTHA BLEED, and she abandoned her patience and laid into me with her wooden sword like she meant it. Something changed in her, and I recognized the moment I shifted from student to prey.

In the future, assuming I had much of one, I needed to remember to think my plans through before implementing them. With only a piece of wood with a hilt coming between me and a quick death, I clutched the sword and hoped it would be enough. I doubted it.

Only a fool provoked an elf. It was right in the CDC's entry on elves. Running from elves stirred their desire to hunt. Challenging an elf needed to be classified as suicide. Biting one?

Biting one needed to be put on the 'never do again' list.

Samantha chased me around the yard, through the trees, and ultimately pinned me against the cabin after demonstrating she was faster and more agile than me.

"You. Bit. Me."

Yep, I'd infuriated the elf, and I thought I'd done well fending off her attempts to end my life. "You wanted me to attack you. I did!"

"I meant with your sword."

"But your ankle was near my teeth."

"I'm going to offer you a reward for being audacious enough to actually bite me. But, as you were incapable of landing a legitimate hit on me with your sword, you belong to me for two weeks starting tomorrow. Get cleaned up and get some sleep. I will think about ways to suitably punish you."

After having witnessed the fury in her eyes, I decided against testing my luck and her patience, retreating to the safety of the cabin to keep Kennedy company.

TWENTY-THREE

Kitten, Destroyer of Worlds found my
suffering entertaining.

HELL CAME IN MANY FORMS, and chopping
wood wasn't sufficient penance for biting an
elf. When awake, only the bathroom provided
any sanctuary from Samantha's quest for revenge. She found delight in launching sneak
attacks, and she only offered rewards—such
as they were—when I put up an acceptable
fight.

Everything went tolerably well until
Kennedy joined forces with Samantha with
her wooden Japanese death scythe.

A wise man hauled ass when two women
were out for his blood, although I had some
faith Kennedy wanted me alive. I ran, they
chased, I fought off their attempts to beat me
black and blue, and I plotted how to escape
their efforts to beat self-defense into me.

To add insult to injury, I was fairly certain
Kitten, Destroyer of Worlds found my suf-

fering entertaining, and the poorly named Puppy, Savior of Worlds didn't care a single iota. Kennedy gave the spoiled rotten corgi a chew toy each morning, and I couldn't compete with his chew toy, not even when I evaded two of the world's most dangerous beings.

Proposing to Kennedy took a temporary second place to an uninterrupted night of sleep, as nothing spoiled my night more than an elf doing her best to rid the Earth of me. If her goal was to teach me how to survive potential assassination attempts, I thought I did rather well.

It didn't help me land a legitimate hit on her, but I never forgot I'd bitten her once. If I could catch her off guard and bite her, striking her with my sword wasn't outside of the realm of possibility. How could I hit her when she danced around me with one eye closed and yawning? Adding Kennedy to the mix hadn't improved my odds any.

"Reed, you can't run forever," Kennedy complained.

"Maybe if you hadn't joined forces with the elf, I wouldn't be running," I countered, making certain I kept track of both women. If I could get Kennedy away from Samantha, I'd be tempted to blurt a terrible proposal so she'd know I wanted to marry her before they managed to kill me. "And don't you even try to look innocent. You could at least try to stop her from ambushing me in bed."

"She leaves me alone. Why lose sleep? Maybe if you'd beat on her like you mean it already, you could get uninterrupted sleep. I'm sleeping just fine."

"They should put your photograph besides cruel in the dictionary."

"I think that honor belongs to Sammy."

"No, she already has dibs on terrifying, relentless, and asshole."

The elf chuckled and stalked closer. "You're only terrified of how much it'll hurt when I get a hold of you."

"That's because I'm a rational sentient with a strong dislike of pain."

"You could just fight her like you mean it, Reed."

"What makes you think I'm not?"

Kennedy halted, put her hands on her hips, and leveled her worst glare at me. "Because I'm not an idiot and am well aware you're terrified you'll accidentally hurt her. No, worse. You're afraid you'll kill her. She's taught me enough to see you're pulling every single hit you try, *especially* if it's aimed at me. I get it. You're not going to overcome that obstacle overnight, but you need to. If that angel wants you dead like Sammy thinks, she's not going to hesitate. The same goes with that devil with those damned delayed contracts you keep fretting over. The only good thing about that devil is he probably won't do anything to you directly unless cornered. The angel will. Right, Sammy?"

"Right. If you stop pulling your blows, you'll do just fine. You've gotten close a few times, but you need to accept someone might get hurt. Someone might even get killed. That angel? The whole point of doing this is if that angel tries to kill you, you kill her first. That's what all this is for. It's either you or her. I'd rather it be you. I hate angels who think it's perfectly acceptable to build someone up to crush them so they appease their twisted sense of guilt. If you hurt me, you've done your job. If you kill me, there is no better end for a teacher to have finally taught a student capable of the deed. I am an elf, Reed. If I were easy to kill, I'd already be dead. You're fighting centuries of experience. Look at you now."

I frowned. "What?"

"You haven't hit me, but you're able to fight me. I come for you, you deflect my blows. Did you think I still hold back?"

"Actually, yes." My eyes widened. "You're not holding back?"

"Only enough to avoid killing you when I'm beating a new set of bruises into you. That's the relationship between a teacher and student among elves. I do my best not to kill you. You do your best to kill me. Should you succeed, you have done well for yourself. It's a badge of honor among elves. You have nothing to fear from my death. My death would become your pride. Perhaps my approach is wrong." Samantha sighed. "It is not the nature of elves to mend minds. We break bodies—and we heal bodies so we can break them again. But consider this: would you have changed anything when you'd saved that girl at the cost of another's life?"

"No, I wouldn't have."

"Everything you learn here serves one purpose."

"What purpose?"

"To kill only those you mean to kill. Your sight didn't lead you astray. You did many a favor ridding the world of that filth. Had he been an elf, he would've screamed even as we stripped the flesh from his bones—and we wouldn't have eaten him despite the effort we'd spend butchering him."

That there were elves who wouldn't eat their prey startled me. "What would you have done with him?"

"Hung his bones as an example to others and left his meat for the fish. It wouldn't do to poison the cats and dogs. I've learned fish will eat things even elves reject."

"And what would a student do if they killed their teacher?"

"Wear their teacher's skull with pride unless the teacher was partnered, in which case the student would take a different bone and leave the skull for their lover. As I do not have a lover, you would inherit my skull. As you are not a full elf, or even half, you would keep my skull but perhaps place it on your mantle to remember me by. That is how we grieve. We carry the vessel of our beloved's soul with us when they go until we are ready to move on. Then we keep it in a place of honor until our dying day."

I found it interesting elves believed the soul resided in the mind. "The mind and not the heart?"

"What we do with the heart would not be palatable for your delicate sensibilities. Humans have a difficult enough time accepting we keep the skulls of our beloved."

"I think he was asking why you believe the soul is in your skull," Kennedy said, her tone amused.

"Ah. Yes, I suppose that would confuse you humans, too. It's simple. Your heart feels, but it isn't what makes you you. Your memories, your actions, your words, all of those things that make you who you are reside in your head. Your heart is there to feel, but your mind is who defines you. There's a reason you fear to look into my eyes. Had my soul resided in my heart, you would not fear my eyes. The eyes are the gateway to the soul. You know this better than most. You have reason to be afraid. I understand this. But I don't do this just for you. It is for her, as well. She would feel the pain of your loss like any elf despite her fragile humanity. She has been broken and reforged. You'd see that if you overcame your fear and looked into her eyes already."

Samantha's grin reminded me of a very hungry shark.

Some secrets were best revealed piece by piece. "I plan to."

"Reed?" Kennedy squeaked.

"Even elves never stop learning, and progress is a daily battle, one we fight with pride should we wish to see tomorrow. I know what you want to ask of me. There is no greater honor for an elf to die at the hands of their student, no greater pride than quenching the steel of a newly forged weapon. Should you succeed where others fail, I would have you take my skull with pride so it might become one of your greatest treasures. No, Reed. You have nothing to fear of my death beyond the grief of a student losing a teacher. Should you hold the blade that takes my life, you've nothing left to learn from me."

Truth. The certainty of her words sank in,

as pure as the chiming of a bell at dawn. I was no angel, but I embraced her truth.

I needed to embrace my truths, too—even the dark ones that kept me awake at night when I remembered a past I wouldn't change even if I could. Changing the past would've changed the future, and my future had somehow become a place I wanted to be.

"I might be the one to die, of shock, should I even hit you," I confessed.

"I'm sure Kennedy would love to give you CPR as needed, albeit I'll have to remind her CPR doesn't involve the use of her tongue until after resuscitation has occurred."

I hadn't tried feigning death as a way to land some affection from the red-haired woman, and I considered if I could act well enough to trick an elf.

"It'd be easier to hit me and earn your evening with her."

"You read minds, don't you?" I accused, glaring at the elf.

"You're part incubus and succubus. I don't have to read minds to understand what you're thinking. Frankly, I'm torn between pride and disgust over your restraint. I don't know which angels resulted in your birth, but I fear they control too many virtues for their own good—and yours."

My eyes widened. "Is it possible to identify my grandparents through my behaviors?"

"Silly boy. You may be your father's son, and you might be the grandson of two angels, but you're your own man. Never allow anyone to forge you based only on who came before you. Except that part of you that is pure elf. That part's important. The rest? Pft. Cast them aside and make your own destiny. Judge yourself without the crimes and aspirations of those who came before you casting you in a different light. I judge only you."

LIKELY TIRED OF pussyfooting around with me and wanting more entertaining prey, Samantha went after Kennedy like a wolf on a lamb. Her first strike got through Kennedy's guard and cracked into her ribs, and the thud of impact woke the anger I'd boxed away since the moment I'd pulled a rapist off his victim and had become a killer.

I abandoned the niceties; if Samantha wanted me to warn her, she wouldn't have turned on Kennedy without warning. My wooden blade caught on the guard of her weapon, and I discarded everything she'd tried to teach me for the one advantage I possessed but had been unwilling to use. My physical strength alone wouldn't defeat an elf in battle—or anyone else, for that matter—

but it gave me an edge in one thing. My arm could overpower her wrist and hand.

I grabbed her blade, uncaring if the carved edge bit into my hand or if I spent hours picking out splinters. I twisted, ripped it out of her hold, and went for her throat.

I wasn't sure which one of us was more surprised when my fingers dug into her neck hard enough her pulse beat against my skin.

"Strangulation is a valid method of killing someone," the elf wheezed.

I eased my hold enough she could breathe but didn't release her.

"Reed," Kennedy chided. "She hit me. She does that every day."

"Not where he can see me do it." Utterly uncaring I could strangle her, Samantha chuckled. "At least not that hard and without warning. Did you see the change in his eyes?"

"He wanted to kill you."

The lack of doubt in Kennedy's tone reined me in far better than anything else, and I forced myself to take deep breaths. I wanted to growl—and squeeze my hand around the damned elf's throat a little tighter as a warning. I forced myself to let her go and back away, sitting back on my heels while I caught my breath.

"Of course he did. He's an elf. I infringed on his territory and hit his woman. That's what elves do. That girl woke part of his elven instinct, and his angelic sight sealed that filth's fate. Without his sight, he might've carried more guilt, but the elf in him wouldn't have let that man walk away so easily. This was a lesson as much for you as it was for him." Samantha smirked at me. "When he faces off against an angel and a devil, stay near him. That's truly the only weapon he'll need, but the one I mean to give him will make his work easier."

"Damn it, Samantha," I muttered through clenched teeth.

"You're only resentful I found your weakness, exploited it, and forced you to hit me. Stop whining. You actually succeeded at something for a change. Get your ass up and follow me." Hopping to her feet, she scooped up her weapon and twirled it in a hand. "Today, children. I have new ways to terrorize you both, and I can't wait to see your expressions. I'll enjoy it much more than you will."

Kennedy crouched beside me and patted my shoulder. "I'm really all right. She smacked me with the flat. It's loud, it stings, but it's harmless. At worse, I'll have a new bruise. I'm all right. Now, if anyone other than Samantha goes after me like that, kill them with extreme prejudice because I don't want to die, and if someone is going after me like that, they mean to kill me. Sound good?"

"I'm not sure you're supposed to be encouraging me to kill someone. Aren't you in law enforcement? FBI-CDC liaisons technically count as law enforcement."

"In defense of another is a legitimate claim in court and is remarkably easy to prove when you tell the complete truth to an angel. Even if the angels don't like you, they're bound to tell the truth or they fall. Never forget that."

I wondered what would happen if I lied. I decided I didn't want to know. With a little help from Kennedy, I got to my feet. "I won't," I promised.

SAMANTHA LED us back to the cabin, went to her truck, and tossed down the tailgate. It still amused me that a little elf drove a big truck, but all the jokes about compensation remained safely in my head where they belonged as she had absolutely nothing to compensate for. If anything, she drove it as a warning to the idiots on the road she'd run them over and then use their bones as toothpicks.

I'd pay to watch someone challenge Samantha in her big, manly truck.

"Have I ever told you I want your truck?" I asked, leaning against Kennedy's rental car, adding another layer of dirt to what I already wore.

"You can't have my truck. It is mine. If you want a truck, buy one yourself. The benefit to trucks? Should you spawn any children, you can eventually toss them in the back."

"That's illegal," Kennedy stated.

"I knew there was something I hated about the modern era. Toss the brats in a cage and let them fight over dinner."

"Now you're assuming there'll be children."

"You are part succubus and part incubus. She's going to geld you after the first ten."

I winced. "Please don't geld me, Kennedy."

"You're useless to me gelded... for the moment."

Ouch. "I don't know what I did, but I'm sorry."

"I haven't gotten laid in months. It's what you didn't do."

I pointed at Samantha. "Blame her. It's her fault. She beat my ability to perform at your leisure out of me."

"You should be grateful I beat the modesty out of him, else you'd still be dealing with his insecurities and other issues," the elf muttered, leaning forward and retrieving a Japanese battle scythe from the bed. "This is a ko-nagi-nata, the woman's variant of the naginata. I

taught you with the ō-naginata, the one meant
for men. You will find this is lighter in your
hand, thus easier for you to kill with. It weighs
more than the traditional ko-naginata, as I
warned its maker you would be trained as a
man to give you the best strength possible. You
will never match a man's brute ferocity, but
you should do well enough. Few know how to
defend themselves from a Japanese death
scythe. In that, your man has done you well."

Kennedy took the weapon from Saman-
tha, her eyes wide as she stared at the rippled
pattern on the curved blade. "It's beautiful."

I wondered when Kennedy would notice
the shaft, decorated with hundreds of angels
and devils in eternal conflict. Black and gold
lacquer filled the lines and brought the raised
images to life.

"This is really for me?"

"You've earned it, and I enjoyed coercing
an angel for the money to pay its maker. I
told the angel she had promised only the best
for Reed, and to bring out his strengths, I
needed to bring out yours. Only in your light
does he shine. Typical human. Perhaps one
day he'll shine without any help from you.
We're not done. There's the matter of your
katana. These two were forged together from
the same metal, and they are meant to stay
together. Treat them well and they will treat
you well."

The ko-naginata's beauty stole my breath, but it lived in the shadow of the katana. Something about the blade sang from the moment Samantha freed it from its sheath, which was decorated in the same fashion as its sister weapon. Most would view the black leather wrapping the hilt as plain, but between the gaps in the grips, the fire of opal burned in the sunlight.

The colors and the play of light over the stones matched what I'd loved about Kennedy's first engagement ring.

"She has been named Evening Star, a common name for a rare blade. She is not yet quenched, so tread with caution, Kennedy Young. The sword she will become is bound to the first blood she drinks and the first life she steals. Some blades develop a mind of their own, and it would not surprise me if she becomes one of them one day. She was created to serve a purpose, and that purpose is to safeguard you—and him. Above all, she best serves raised in defense of another. But should she have to fight, she will know no mercy for the cruel deserve no mercy."

Kennedy leaned the ko-naginata against her car and took the katana, tilting the blade so the sun shined from the polished steel. "I feel like I'm wasted on this sword," she confessed.

"That's because you're learning. Understanding you must grow into that blade is the first step to doing it justice. You have a lot of growing into that ko-naginata, too, but you'll find it is a more forgiving weapon."

I had a hard time believing the Japanese battle scythe was more forgiving than the katana, but I kept my mouth shut to keep Samantha from being tempted to quench my sword in my gut.

"If you want to get a feel for it, do so away from anything you want intact. That sword can—and will—cut through just about anything, and it's a jealous blade. I recommend you start taking it to work with you and introduce it to your gun. Otherwise, I wouldn't be surprised if your gun has an accident."

Perhaps talking to a sword would turn me into a lunatic, but I had agreed to months of training with an elf so I might survive a meeting with a devil. "The only guns I want having accidents around Kennedy are the ones pointed at her, Evening Star. Please make those have accidents. The one she has is for when assholes with guns can't shoot her first. She'll totally use you for the ones dumb enough to get near her. Right, Kennedy?"

"Sounds like a plan," she replied. "The sword won't break my ko-naginata, will she?"

"Only if you love her more. The ko-naginata is far more tolerant, just care for her daily and she'll be fine. Evening Star will need more attention. You'll be fine."

"Reed?" Kennedy's tone warned me I'd done something to earn her ire again. Between her stunned face and the brief moments I risked a glance at her eyes, I determined she was stuck between shocked and ready to pounce me. I couldn't tell if she wanted to take me to bed or beat me for putting her in an awkward position.

Either way, I won.

I couldn't stop my smile. "I'm not sorry I coerced an angel into paying for a possibly sentient sword out to save your life. I am sorry you weren't warned first, but I have to admit, your expression is pretty magnificent."

"He's smitten. Ignore him," Samantha ordered. "Attention to me, Reed. First, I am pleased to announce the price tag of this sword was sufficient to make the angel you call Luna weep. I could hear it in her voice. She'll have a lot of explaining to do to her Almighty, but a debt is a debt, and He would not intentionally turn one of His angels into a liar and trigger her downfall without good reason. Of course, after this, he might not prevent her from falling into a devil's trap, but should a devil be gunning for the angel, he'll face disappointment."

"What?"

Samantha snorted, retrieving a black-wrapped bundle from the bed of her truck. "For someone so smart, you're sometimes quite dense. Do you really think a devil would have any actual interest in *you*, a human? No. He only has interest in the consequences of his games with you. His target is probably one of the angels you associate with, and my bets are on the one who paid for this weapon. Her ego is worse than mine, and it's been over a hundred years since I've had a chance to say that. Angels fall, their portfolios dissipate, and a new angel is born who picks up their mantle. It's the same thing that happens to devils when they cross their maker. The devil takes the seed and makes a new, better devil out of it. Demons are different, but that's no big deal. They die and a new demon is born. The rules of that game never change. And they won't until the End of Days."

I wrinkled my nose at the thought of the world ending due to the battle between good and evil, law and chaos, and everything else that encompassed the Christian religion's apocalypse. I still wasn't sure why the Christian religion's doomsday scenario trumped the others, though I expected when shit went down, everything would end and all religions and their pantheons would find some way to make a mess of Earth. "Are you trying to tell me so much happened because a devil with ambition wants to knock Luna down a few pegs?"

"Essentially, yes."

I clacked my teeth. "Is there a reason I can't kill that devil?"

"Enjoy yourself. Trust me on this one, don't eat devils or angels. They taste bad and would give you indigestion. I expect, if that devil's plan is to make the angel fall to attempt to trigger the End of Days, you will be forced to kill the fallen angel first. Do not hesitate. Once fallen, an angel will attempt to regain its lost divinity. Humans all contain a hint of divinity. Innocents would be slaughtered for their essence. The being you knew will be utterly destroyed upon falling. Until the fallen angel is slain, their seed of life will remain rogue, unable to be replanted. That would, technically, unbalance the heavens and the devil's many hells. It wouldn't do so in a way capable of triggering the End of Days, but the imbalance would exist until the angel's seed can be reclaimed by the Almighty."

My mouth dropped open. "Let me see if I understand this correctly. Luna probably wants to build me up so she can console herself having a fair fight when she kills me. I still don't understand why she wants me dead."

"You're part elf. You're part angel. You're

part demon. You're part human. You're the
embodiment of all things good and evil.
You're also the embodiment of law and order.
But you're also a wild card—something a
little more and less than any one of these
things. Had you been a different breed of elf,
everything would be different."

"But why?"

"Your kind lived to devour the world.
That's why. Most cultures have some form of
monster who is destined to devour the world.
Perhaps she thought you one of those. You
did name your feline Kitten, Destroyer of
Worlds."

"Leave Kitten, Destroyer of Worlds out of
this. Also, when I go to the charity gala that
damned devil insists I attend to 'finalize negotiations' with him, would you watch our
pets?"

"While I will watch them for you, they will
go with us."

Had I possessed a single scrap of sense, I
would've run for the hills. Instead, my
stomach took up residence in my feet and I
sighed. "You got a ticket to the gala, didn't
you?"

"Of course. It will be my honor and pleasure to watch the world meet my student for
the first time. I will keep your animals out of
trouble while you two wage your war, but it
is best they come. Think of it this way. No

one would dare tell *me* I can't bring a cat and a dog into a charity event. Elves have long memories and deeper pockets."

"You're going to bribe the charity to let them in."

"That does make things easier on me. The charity will be most appreciative, and no one will look twice at the number or type of animals once you show off your permit. Enough play. This is your sword, and I think you'll find him eager for any task you give him. He'll be a more forgiving blade than Evening Star, but I think you'll find his determination unmatched. Like you, I expect he'll have a sense of humor."

"When should we expect the swords to start giving us orders?"

Samantha laughed. "You'll be bones long before they learn to speak, alas. It's a pity you mortal types are, well, mortal. In time, they'll find their voices."

Truth.

I found it humbling to own a blade whose consciousness would endure long after my death. I sat on the tailgate, took the cloth-wrapped weapon from Samantha, and unwrapped it.

If I were to judge the weapon from its sheath, my blade loitered among the lowest of the low. The sheath existed for one purpose: function. A dark stone decorated the blade's pommel. "What is this stone?" I touched it, marveling at its smoothness and wondering how it remained affixed to the rest of the hilt.

"It's a diamond. When you quench the blade, it will gain its true color. That is elven magic at work. Everything you are, everything you have been, and everything you will be will color the stone. The sword will understand your heart better than even you, and when the deed is done, so will the diamond."

"It looks like it will fall off," I admitted.

"It can. Cup it in your hand and pull. Don't worry, you won't break it. It's best if it gets to know you."

While puzzled, I obeyed. The stone popped off and landed in my palm, and its warmth startled me even more than the faint gleam in its center. I rolled it between my hands, and its smooth surface glinted in the sunlight. "This counts as one of the stranger things I've done in my life."

"I find that somewhat sad and rather amusing. Have you forgotten you rescued a cat and named her Kitten, Destroyer of Worlds?"

"That's what cats do. They take over worlds so they can destroy them at their leisure. If they weren't more interested in taking naps and enslaving innocent humans like me, they'd probably do it."

"You have more problems than I can help you with."

"Did it really take you half a year to figure that out?" I stared at the hilt and then at the stone. "How do I put it back?"

"Think of it like a very strong magnet that'll only deactivate when you use it."

"Only me?"

"Only you. Did you think those ambushes were because I *enjoy* seeing you naked? No, Reed. The times you didn't bolt upright, I was attuning the stone to you. In good news, you got harder and harder to catch asleep."

"Kennedy," I complained.

"Don't you Kennedy me! Most of the time, I had no idea she'd snuck into bed with us, either. The first time she did it, she held a dagger to my throat and told me to keep quiet. I learned to just let the psychotic elf do what she wants."

"I was hoping he'd wake up, notice, and snap like a little twig while I was attuning the stone to him. The stone would've noticed his determination to protect you and acted accordingly. I think it still figured it out, though. I had a difficult time coaxing him into letting you go long enough to start the attuning process."

"This entire conversation is confusing me," I admitted.

"You're just not sure what to think about

having an ancient woman crawling into your
bed without you knowing about it so you can
be magically bound to a rock."

As I had a feeling I wasn't equipped or
ready for the conversation to continue any
further, I placed the orb to the sword, and it
snapped back into place with a click. "So,
Kennedy should sleep near Evening Star, and
I should probably tuck this under my pillow.
Is that where we're standing right now?"

"I love it when the humans figure things
out on their own. Unsheathe your blade and
stop your whining. I swear, you're worse than
a child today."

I did as told. Like Kennedy's weapons, a
faint rippling in the metal patterned the
blade, and while the same length as the one
I'd used with Kennedy, it was lighter than I
expected. "I see you used the same trick on
me with the weight."

"Not exactly. This one has been forged in
a unique way. Don't ask where I got the diamond; some secrets are best left undisturbed.
I will tell you this much: he is relieved to see
the sun and be wielded by someone with in-
tegrity. The metal is an alloy created from a
meteorite and forged in the hottest fires hell
has to offer, a perfect pairing for a mixed
breed like yourself. To round things out, we
even borrowed a few human techniques to go
into the elven craftsmanship. This weapon

will serve you well, and it'll serve your children well, and it'll serve *their* children well, too. When it comes to a sword, I'm not often wrong, but I think this one will see this world to the end of its days, a true pride of my people—and yours, for all you're an echo of what they once were."

When I'd made a bargain with an angel, I hadn't thought it would come with the weight of expectations, but as far as Samantha's hopes for me went, they were far better than Luna's.

She wanted me to win.

"What is his name?"

"Redemption. However cliché that may be, if the shoe fits, wear it. You'll wear it well, and that's all that matters. Fight well, both of you. Tomorrow, I will teach you everything you need to know about fighting angels and devils while your bodies rest and recover. Training is over. Congratulations. You survived."

TWENTY-FOUR

I did that on purpose.

THE RINGS SAMANTHA had selected burned a
hole in my pocket; she'd slipped them to me
after bequeathing me with Redemption. I
wondered about that.

I thought the rings deserved the name as
much as the sword did.

Both rings sparkled, and as I'd hoped, they
had a low profile without sacrificing the
presence of gems, which caught in the light
and released a cascade of rainbows. Clear
stones took center stage, but they were
flanked with red and gold stones. Tiny braids
of silvery metal weaved around a band of
gold. Something about the design led me to
believe hidden meanings lurked in the pat-
terns, but I couldn't guess what they were.

Like Kennedy, I believed the rings to be
perfectly complicated.

The only thing separating the marriage
and engagement band was size; the wedding

band nestled against the engagement band, and they were meant to be together.

I liked to think Kennedy and I were meant to be together, too.

I just needed to give it to her, and since the elf had left for the day, I knew I wouldn't have any other respite before the charity event where I'd face a devil—and probably an angel, too. I regretted my inability to identify the connections between Luna and Lucavier, but I'd do what I could to protect the future I wanted.

I waited for Samantha to leave in her truck while Kennedy and I watched.

Kennedy's eyes widened. "She really left."

"So it seems." I worried Samantha would return to torment us and hoped the elf had gotten the right size. "Kennedy?"

"What is it?"

After dealing with me and my cursed sight for so long, she didn't turn to face me although I caught her glancing out of the corner of her eye. It gave me the opening I needed. With one hand, I palmed the ring box, keeping it open so the snap wouldn't draw her attention to it too early. With my other hand, I cupped her chin and turned her head to face me.

I wasn't sure which one of us was more surprised: her for looking me in the eyes, or me for seeing nothing when I looked into hers. It wasn't the blank slate I expected, but rather the lack of desire for anything beyond what she already had.

Kennedy clapped her hands over her eyes. "Reed!"

"I did that on purpose, in case it wasn't obvious."

She peeked between her fingers. "But what if you see something you don't like?"

"If I wasn't ready to accept whatever I saw, I wouldn't have looked." As I'd already made a mess of it anyway, I took hold of her hand, pulled it down until I could dump the ring box into her palm, and closed her fingers around it. "I let an elf beat me daily to get you this."

Kennedy lowered her hand so she could stare at the ring box. "You cut a deal with Samantha to get me a ring?"

Was it too late to run into the cabin and hide with my therapy cat, who was likely enjoying a nap with her canine companion? "Of the engagement variety." I hesitated, joining her in a staring contest with a band of metals decorated with gemstones. "Samantha would've literally killed me if I tried to sneak off to get you a ring so I told her I'd cooperate but she had to get the ring, and she said something about hitting her to get the ring, but since I couldn't hit her, I bit her instead, and I'm really not sure how I didn't die, but here we are."

I recognized I babbled, and my face flushed.

"You bit her because you couldn't hit her, but you were trying to hit her because you wanted to get me an engagement ring?"

"When phrased like that, I sound like a lunatic."

"You bit an elf to get me an engagement ring."

The first time I'd asked her to marry me, I'd opened with the big question, and my detour from the expected left me wondering if I'd made yet another mistake. "That wasn't my smartest move. I'm still not sure how I survived."

"Reed, what did you see in my eyes?"

I flinched at her question but forced myself to take a deep breath. I'd never blame her for wanting to know, and to move on, I needed to accept everything I had seen because I hadn't seen anything at all. "I didn't see anything. You already have everything you want."

Her smile robbed me of breath. "That's right. I have everything I want. You, me, this ridiculous cabin in the woods I can't wait to escape from, and a psychotic elf of a teacher fighting to keep you alive so we can grow old together with our equally psychotic pets."

"Kitten and Puppy aren't psychotic."

"They like the elf. They're definitely psychotic. But they're our furry psychos. They're also two rescues for two people who needed to be rescued in more ways than one. As long as I have you, I don't need a ring." She snapped the box and held it close to her chest. "But I will cut you if you try to take it back, I'm just saying."

As she had more weapons than I did, I had no doubt she'd live up to her threat. "So, is that a yes?"

"Conditional on one thing."

I tensed, and my chest burned from the need for air. Waiting in expectant silence took all my will. What could she want from me? Could I give it to her? I'd find some way to, no matter what.

Kennedy held her ring box in her mouth, stuffed her hand into her jean pocket, and pulled out a plastic baggie. She retrieved a suspiciously familiar ring from it. She removed the ring box from her mouth with her other hand. "I told her she could beat me as many times as she wanted trying to get you to go for her throat in exchange for a ring. For you."

My held breath escaped along with a laugh. "I think we've been played, Kennedy."

"I think you're right. So I guess you're not going to go running for the woods screaming? Honestly, I was worried you'd run for the woods screaming if I popped any questions like this without warning. So, if you accept this ring I accepted as payment for enduring daily beatings, I'll accept your ring, which you accepted in payment for… I'm not even sure what you accepted payment for, but you bit an elf to get it, and honestly, I have a difficult time topping that."

I needed to thank Samantha for not killing me for biting her. "There's two rings, technically. If I'd done it right, I would've only given you the engagement band, but I didn't know if she'd come back, and I wanted to give it to you before I got killed either by her or some devil."

"I'm rather hopeful you'll survive. She's going to teach you everything you need to know about fighting a devil. I'll help you, too."

Her helping worried me, but considering I'd gone after an elf for hurting her, I suspected Kennedy would be the ace up my sleeve. No matter how terrifying the idea was, I'd take on the entirety of heaven to protect her, and I didn't care how much blood I'd shed to secure her safety.

But I wouldn't tell her that. She'd worked as hard as I had to earn her place, not behind me hiding, but at my side. "I expected nothing less."

"Technically, you're supposed to wear this one when we get married, but I was planning to propose as soon as the elf left us alone for more than ten minutes, whereas I suspect you were planning to the instant she was out of sight."

"That sounds about right," I confessed. "Although she gave me the rings when you weren't looking earlier."

"I've had this one for about a month. She thought I'd get to it first because you're insufferably stubborn and exist to vex her."

"I can't tell if I'm being complimented or not."

"She didn't kill you, so it's a compliment."

"But I paid her not to kill either one of us."

"Do you think money would really stop her from killing and eating either one of us if she really wanted?"

"That's a good point." I eyed Kennedy's car. "If we pack Kitten and Puppy and leave now, I bet we could find somewhere to put those rings to good use."

"While I'm agreeing to marry you, you're agreeing to a proper ceremony even if it's a small one. Kick that angel's and devil's ass for making a mess of our lives, and I'll rethink this base requirement."

While I had plenty of motivation to remove the angel and devil from my life, her bribe ensured I'd try to put a quick end to any interferences. "Deal."

"I think now is the time to inform you that should a devil or angel lift a weapon against you or another mortal, you're at liberty to kill them without punishment. The CDC has determined your humanity is sufficient to treat you like a standard human, whereas angels and devils do not enjoy such protections."

"Who knew it'd be useful loving someone involved with law enforcement?"

"I'm useful for many things. Come into the cabin with me and I'll show them all to you. Intimately."

With almost half a year of frustration under the belt, I wasn't taking any chances. I grabbed Redemption, swiped my ring out of her hand, and beelined for the cabin. Her laughter followed me.

AN UNINTERRUPTED NIGHT with Kennedy did me a world of good, and she even let me wear my ring without needing to marry her first. She considered it a formality. I wasn't going to argue with her, and for the first time I could remember in years, I slept without my doubts creeping in and eating away at my peace of mind.

Samantha returned at dawn to wake us as always, although she opted for a somewhat pleasant approach. Instead of her stereotypical attack, she yelled at us until we rolled out of bed to get dressed.

Kitten, Destroyer of Worlds claimed the elf's lap the instant she sat at the table, and Puppy, Savior of Worlds showered Kennedy with his affections, leaving me to roll a diamond sphere on the table and amuse myself with the reflections of color and light through its pristine surface.

"Just because your cat likes me more than you isn't a reason to sulk," Samantha scolded. "I'll be giving you plenty of reasons to sulk today, and all of them deal with this Lucavier fellow. I brought you two that disgusting greasy human breakfast food from one of those abominable chain places. I'm not responsible if you offend your stomach attempting to eat that garbage."

After months of eating elf-approved meals, Kennedy and I fell on the paper bags like starved beasts. While I didn't mind eating healthy food, nothing matched the forbidden fruit of devouring a sausage, egg, and cheese sandwich—or three of them.

Maybe four. With hash browns.

"You both realize I didn't starve you, right?" Samantha huffed. "You don't have to eat them like they're going to escape."

I joined Kennedy at staring at the elf, unable to mask my doubt.

She scowled. "I see you also wasted no time exchanging rings. Had I made it out of the driveway before one of you pounced the other?"

I choked down a bite of my sandwich. "Barely." The next bite disappeared with equal enthusiasm.

"And which one of you went for the kill?"

Kennedy pointed at me without wasting any of her time on words. I eyed one of her sandwiches, wondering if I could get away with stealing it. She loved me enough to want to marry me. A sandwich wouldn't test too much, would it?

"Go ahead, Reed. Touch my sandwich. I dare you."

As she could still love me when I had only one hand, I scooted away from her, shuffled my bag of food out of her reach, and double-checked to make certain none of my hash browns had fallen prey to her.

"If you two start fighting over breakfast, I'll take it away," the elf warned. "Pay attention. What do you know about devils, their congregations, and their lord?"

"Little to nothing," I confessed with a shrug. "I'm part demon, yes, but I never felt any need to look into it beyond an expectation of what might happen if I developed any of their abilities. I was warned from an early age I might suffer from an overactive sex drive. There were also concerns I might become a shapeshifter of some sort. Beyond that, it just wasn't relevant."

"Well, it's relevant now. There are two differences between devils and demons. Demons are born on Earth whereas devils are born in hell. Devils have a miasma that demons lack. Some devils have teleportation; the stronger ones always do. Considering I suspect this devil wants to bring about an angel's downfall to unbalance the heavens and hell, I expect he has teleportation abilities. He's got enough of an ego he's borrowed from his maker's name, so I expect he's a higher ranked devil. However, this isn't the devil's style; I doubt it's a sanctioned attempt, so it's probable this devil is a rogue."

"A rogue? What do you mean?"

"It's simple. Devils under the devil's direct control don't attempt schemes like this without approval. It's absurd, really. There are those who fight to trigger the End of Days not understanding that when it begins, everything ends—even them. I suppose it is the nature of devils to attempt to circumvent the impossible. Only two seeds survive for this Earth. Call it what you will, but it's what makes the first divines. This Earth was decreed by the powers that be to be born of law

and chaos, good and evil. Assign whatever
name for it you wish. But I believe I understand why he picked *you*."

"I'm glad someone understands this mess,"
I muttered.

Samantha grabbed an empty wrapper and
tore it into four pieces, arranging them in a
square in front of her. She pointed at one
square. "This is your elven heritage. Consider
it a wild card." She slid it away from the others. "Many like to think humans are to angels
as demons are to devils—angels born on the
mortal coil. That's bullshit. If humans were
the manifestation of angelic divinity, well,
there'd be a lot fewer monsters in the world."

I winced at the thought of an elf considering humans to be monsters—and how she
wasn't wrong to do so. "I follow."

"Humans are much more complex than
being the manifestation of any one thing. In
reality, I believe it's more they're a manifestation of *all* things. Devils. Demons. Angels.
The divine. You mix all of these things together, and you get a plain, boring, normal
human. That's why when you mix the magical, you get a human. Humans are living potential. They can be anything. But one thing
separates them above all: free will. Humans
pick their destiny. They always have. They're
the Earth's natural wild card in a game of the
divine. Devils and angels do not have that

luxury. Devils have more flexibility as they're the representation of chaos—or evil. It depends on your view. It's rare for the children of angels to find each other and marry. It's rarer still for their grandchild to have an equal mix of incubus and succubus. I suspect angels view you as a threat, devils view you as a tool, and well, humans don't know what to make of you because you're everything they're not."

The still, quiet voice deep inside confirmed the truth of Samantha's words, and I wasn't sure what I thought about that. "I wish I could say that makes sense to me, but it doesn't. What do I need to know to get through this charity event alive?"

"Angels view combat as ceremonial to the point they'll take turns exchanging blows. Don't fall into this trap. Whenever you see an opening, take it. By nature, she'll hesitate if she's struck at you already without fair retaliation. Even should she fall, that part of her will remain—for a while. Fallen angels are dangerous. They hunger worse than any elf, and you'll be her first real meal. The longer I think about it, the more I believe the dead pigeons were the first victims of her fall. After falling, she'd seek any way to sustain herself. Even birds have a seed of life, and I believe she stole theirs despite the little good it would do her. In time, she will become a husk of her former glory. In all likelihood, her portfolio will abandon her should she have one within a few weeks. The named angels do. The lesser angels don't. The lesser angels just fall to the Earth and decay, devouring as much divinity as they can along the way. With so much angelic blood in your veins, a fallen angel will try to devour you first."

"Wait, *what*? If she falls, she'll do *what*?"

"Eat you. Falling rips the divinity out of them and they hunger for what they've lost. Think of her as a very intelligent and hungry zombie. In good news, you'll be like a beacon in the darkness to her, so she won't attack anyone else first. You're too big of a source. There's also the risk of her portfolio jumping to you when she falls. Becoming a vessel, even a temporary one, would complicate matters."

"Probability of this happening?"

"I'm prepared to beat you into submission non-lethally should you inherit her portfolio until an archangel shows up and retrieves it. You've enough angel in you that the influx of divinity won't kill you. While you possess the portfolio, it is critical you obey the tenets of her divinity. Lies are the easiest way for an angel to fall. I don't think you'll have a problem. I couldn't force you into aggression until you came in defense of another. That is very angelic behavior. Your nature is ideal for this.

I don't expect you'll hold her divinity for long should it jump to you. *He* might interfere and reclaim the seed of her existence before it has a chance to touch you. We'll see."

"The more you tell me about this, the less I like it."

"That is because you're wise."

Kennedy set her sandwich down and drummed her fingers on the table. "What does this mean for him in the future?"

"Oh, it won't hurt him for long. If anything, it'll do him a world of good. Should he inherit the portfolio, he should also inherit the knowledge of how to control his sight. That knowledge should stick around. It's hard to take away something like that once it's been given. I expect he'll change somewhat, but he's strong for a frail human—and he has enough elf in him to be resilient. I think you'll find him equal to the challenge. That's where the next complication comes into play."

"There are even *more* complications? Don't have I have enough complications?"

"Should you fight this Lucavier fellow, and should he have a portfolio of his own, you might inherit it, too."

I groaned and slumped over the table. "You have got to be kidding me."

"You'd have a pretty unhappy day if you inherited both at once. Actually, you'd be a downright mess. Who knows what sort of devilish powers you'd waken or inherit. Imagine if he developed shapeshifting to an incubus form, Kennedy."

"Yes, please."

I lifted my head enough to glower at my wife-to-be. "You have got to be kidding."

"I would never joke about having my very own incubus I don't have to share with anyone."

"I admire a woman with priorities," Samantha announced. "It's settled. You inheriting a devilish portfolio would likely result in you developing incubi shapeshifting talents, and should Kennedy be lucky, she'll have her very own on-demand incubus, one with appropriate elven loyalty. You'll be a true unicorn of the male species."

I recognized when the women ganged up on me, and I saluted the pair. "I'm so glad you're finding this amusing."

"There's nothing funny about having my very own incubus I don't have to share with anyone. I literally just went over this." Kennedy lifted her hand and wiggled her left ring finger. "This says so."

"I do look forward to the ceremony. Per elven tradition, you will have it exactly one year from now, and as the granter of the rings, *I* get to plan it." Samantha smirked.

"And no one denies an elf her way when it comes to a wedding ceremony."

I opened my mouth to protest, realized I had no idea if she was yanking my leg or if there was such an elven tradition, and snapped my teeth together.

"I think you're right, Reed. We've been played."

When elves smiled, they displayed all their sharp, pointy teeth. "Indeed. Now, onto fighting strategy. Angels fight fair. Devils don't. Both will kill you if you give them the chance, so kill them first. Trust nothing either says or does. That will be fatal. They will try to kill you. That is their nature. But your nature is angel, demon, *and* elf. You are a killer by nature for all you suppress that part of yourself. That is what it means to be an elf. But always remember this: whether you kill is always your choice. You hold life and death in your hands. You control it with your sword. Until it's time for the meeting, I will teach you everything I know of the way they fight. You will use Redemption. I expect to lose many wooden swords to its edge. For your peace of mind, I will teach you the defense. You're on your own with the offense, as I know futility when I see it. You both have two miles to run. When you're back, we'll begin."

TWENTY-FIVE

Everything converged onto one night
at a museum.

SAMANTHA KEPT HER WORD; beyond basic exercising and repetitious sparring meant to acclimate me to fighting with Redemption, she let us rest and gave our bodies a chance to recover from her training. Without the constant work, I found myself easily bored and prone to pacing. Kennedy had her ways of dealing with my excess energy, but even her allure couldn't totally conquer my misgivings of the upcoming charity event.

No matter what happened, I expected my days at my work were numbered; the contract posed more trouble than anyone wanted to admit, and the best thing I could do for the business was to find some way to ruin negotiations. I knew it, my boss knew it, my boss's bosses knew it, but with so much money on the table, failing to secure a signed contract would ruin me.

Everything converged onto one night at a museum.

"Why do these things always happen at a museum?" I complained, adjusting my tie for the hundredth time. "And what sort of idiot allows weapons right on the ticket? It's literally on the ticket, Kennedy. We're allowed to bring sharp, pointy objects into this damned charity event. It's like they want a bloodbath. That's what's going to happen, too. Someone —me—will be bathing in blood."

She laughed. "There will be an angel or two in attendance. I believe they expect the angel to keep everyone in line."

"Is it actually confirmed Luna is coming?"

"Several angels are confirmed to be in attendance. The one you call Luna will be there," Kennedy confirmed. "I told you I got the guest list through work. I still think it's ridiculous you felt the need to notify the CDC you'd be out for an angel *and* a devil if they crossed the wrong lines. I've been assigned as your babysitter. Your *babysitter.*"

"You're my wife-to-be. Doesn't that automatically make you my babysitter? Women are always saying us men are children. They're just paying you to do what you already have to do."

"That's ridiculous. You're going to wear holes through your tie if you keep fiddling with it. Go get your sword and put it on properly, and thank Samantha nicely for getting you an event-appropriate sheath for it."

The event-appropriate sheath pissed me off; diamonds encrusted the damned thing, and I didn't want to know how much it cost, but I remembered Samantha's threat.

The sheath would, no matter what, survive until my wedding. If I wanted to tear it to pieces and decorate my marriage bed with its diamonds, that was my business, but the sheath survived until I tied the knot.

Why, why, why had I allowed Samantha to so thoroughly trick me?

Oh, right. I wanted to marry Kennedy. Damn it. I grunted, stopped fiddling with my tie, and retrieved my sword, which waited for me by the door. "This is ridiculous. This thing is covered in diamonds, Kennedy. Actual diamonds. Do you know how I know this? I bought a machine that told me so. Every damned one of these stones is a diamond."

"I'm still impressed you tested every single one of them."

"I did the math, Kennedy."

"What math?"

I pointed at the offensive sheath. "If these are low-grade diamonds, the synthetic kind *snobbish elves hate*, this sheath cost ten thousand dollars just in accent diamonds. Ten. Thousands. Dollars. There are hundreds of them."

"I did not just hear you claim I'd get a lab diamond," Samantha howled from the cabin's living room.

"You're worse than the devil!" I shouted back, waving Redemption in the air despite knowing she couldn't see my defiance.

"You're such a sweet talker."

Kennedy laughed and patted my arm. "Do I want to know how much the yellow, black, and red ones cost? They're bigger. The pattern is really pretty, though. It matches our wedding rings."

"It's the symbol for eternity in a very old version of elven," Samantha replied. "I've told you this several times already. I know you're edgy, Reed, but really. Relax already. Just put your damned sword on and be happy I gave you the sheath early rather than whining about having to keep an eye on it for one charity event. For the record, every stone in there is natural, and they're all very slightly included or flawless. As if I'd allow anything other than the best to be used. And I only allowed a few of the very slightly included stones to be used because they're special."

I wasn't brave enough to ask an elf what she thought was special. I often didn't like the answers to my questions. I grunted again and belted Redemption into place. "You need any help with Evening Star, Kennedy?"

"I'm good to go. I love this dress. It looks

so nice with my sword. I still think I should get to bring my Japanese death scythe and my sword."

Her dress, sleek and black with a slit from ankle to hip, made me want to abandon attending the event altogether. I'd need a lot of time to properly take her out of the dress, and I'd make no promises it would survive the experience. Until I could get her alone, I needed to avoid making eye contact of any sort. "If you bring both, you'll terrify everyone."

"Bah. That's what Sammy said. Isn't my dress pretty, Reed?"

The question was a trap, and I determined I needed to escape before she caught me and the elf killed us both. "You're an evil seductress," I replied, marching into the living room. "Absolutely evil."

Her laughter did wonderful but terrible things to me.

Like Kennedy, Samantha wore a dress intended to remove a man's base ability to function, although after having been beat into the dirt so many times by the lithe woman, I worried for anyone she ensnared as a result of the evening's activities. To make it clear she was an elf, she'd braided her hair and woven it on top of her head, and someone had pinned an obscene number of jewels into her hair crown to transfer her into a living work of art.

"Well, no one will be looking at Redemption's sheath with you in the room." I wondered how my life had become so damned strange.

Even Kitten, Destroyer of Worlds had a jeweled collar and harness, and she waited by the door with an equally decked out Puppy, Savior of Worlds.

"It seemed appropriate to take some of the attention off you. It wouldn't do if you were mortified by receiving too much attention. Try to contain your demonic nature until after the festivities, no matter how tempting Kennedy is."

"I don't understand why everyone keeps expecting miracles from *me*."

"We should've expected whining," Samantha muttered. "The limo is here, so stop dragging your heels and get your prissy ass outside. The rest of this evening is a no-whine zone. Kennedy, you better not be adjusting anything. Do not make me go in there. Humans! You're such children. It's a charity event that will end with someone else's execution. Don't turn this into a big deal."

Damned elves. I sighed, gathered the leashes of both cat and dog, and headed outside, and as I liked to pretend I was a gentlemen, I held the door for the ladies before acknowledging I'd accepted an invitation to a murder. The only question was who would be committing the murders.

ONCE UPON A TIME, before magic had erupted in the world, the museum had been a Catholic church. I thought it should've counted as a cathedral. Born in a time of grand arches, elegant spires, and copper roofs, I found it appropriate it housed a fortune of art. I wondered what had led to its downfall as a place of worship.

Maybe I'd ask Luna before we tried to kill each other.

In my quest to be a gentleman, I held the door for Kennedy and Samantha. The greeters gaped at the elf, and I appreciated falling a distant third to the ladies.

Soon enough I'd hog the spotlight in the worst ways possible.

I almost hoped our tickets—and our animals—would be rejected, but within five minutes, we were inside in a chattering crowd of the well-dressed waiting to spend their money for charity. My boss had gotten a ticket, and as soon as he noticed me staring at him, he flicked a salute.

Kitten, Destroyer of Worlds pawed at my leg in a demand to be picked up, and I acquiesced, setting her on my shoulder so she could look over her new domain.

Turning to Kennedy, I whispered, "I hope you make enough to support both of us, because my boss is here and I expect to be fired tonight."

"Ah, yes. I saw him with your company's CEO. Don't worry. I'm sure I can take care of both of us without issue. Consider tonight a job interview with the CDC or FBI. Both of my bosses will be here tonight to monitor the situation. They tend to get really interested when the forces of the heavens and hell clash in a public space. I think they're wondering how a disaster on two feet is going to prevent more disaster."

"They're going to be so disappointed."

"We need to work on your self-esteem, Reed."

"You're probably right." I spotted Luna across the room, not far from my boss, and I grimaced. "Well, Luna is here."

"What a poor choice of name. Luna, for an angel? Disgraceful."

While I'd never met either of my angelic grandparents in person before, I'd heard them speak enough times to recognize my grandfather's voice. I tensed, and thanks to months of surviving Samantha, my hand went for Redemption's hilt.

"Ugh. Angels," Samantha muttered.

"Elves," my grandfather replied with identical disdain in his voice. "Did you *really* have to teach him bad habits?"

"If you hadn't wanted me to teach him bad habits, you should've taught him yourself." Samantha huffed and rested her hands on her hips. "The heavens really picked *you* to witness? How droll."

"I wouldn't call it picked. I'd call it issued an invitation. Your grandmother's also here. I thought you'd appreciate the warning."

Kennedy turned to face my angelic grandparent, and her expression turned colder than ice. "You're one of those asshole angels who convinced him he was scum the entirety of his life because you'd flee like a little feathered coward?"

I expected there'd be a fight between Kennedy and my grandfather. I wasn't even sure if he was my maternal or paternal grandfather. Every time I'd seen him, my grandmother had accompanied them, and my parents wisely referred to them as equal parents, resulting in my general confusion.

"Paternal," my grandfather informed me. "And I wouldn't call it fleeing. I'd call it allowing him to grow without him being adversely influenced by our divinity at a young age. It also bothered his mother, who did not inherit a sufficient angelic nature when it comes to the raising of her offspring. That is not his fault. That is not my fault."

Truth.

I really needed to figure out a way to get that quiet voice to shut the hell up.

"Really, Reed? Really?" Samantha pointed her perfectly painted nail at my grandfather. "You're spawned from *him*?"

I echoed my grandfather's sigh, questioning how an angel could even sigh. "Well, no. Not from him directly. Do you think if I keep my back towards him, he'll stab me? He's probably got a sword hidden on him somewhere."

"He's naked, Reed. Angels usually are."

Kennedy stepped to my side, and I moved my arm so she could tuck herself against my side. The entire time, she kept her glare locked on my grandfather.

"I can summon my sword at will, and I've no intention of stabbing you with it. I'm here to witness you stab other beings. Your grandmother is also here, and she's not speaking to me right now. She's easily offended today, but that's natural for the situation. Honestly, most are here for the fight rather than the charity, but they'll pay the charity well in exchange for a good fight. Humans are odd, fickle creatures that way."

"Just how many people know about this? We were just guessing there'd be a fight."

Bracing for the inevitable, I turned to face my grandfather. As always, I could only tell it was him by his voice and the green and gold barring on his feathers. My grandmother had green and red barring.

"She's already begun to fall. The wheels began turning months ago, although you had no way of knowing." My grandfather sighed. "All tonight will do is finish the process."

"What? What happened?"

"She lied to you."

I scowled. "Great. Do you happen to know how she lied to me?"

"Nothing would've happened to you if you hadn't gone home that night. Nothing would've happened to your feline, either. You gave her a most interesting name."

Puppy, Savior of Worlds sat on my grandfather's foot and decided to thoroughly wash himself with his tongue. "I recommend against letting him lick your face anytime soon."

"Thank you for the advice. You gave him an interesting name, too."

"Actually, Kennedy named him, but I've been accused of having a sense of humor on occasion. So, Luna knew I'd be taken in that car accident?"

"Of course. She arranged it in the hopes of fulfilling a promise to a devil she decided to consort with. I've done my fair share of consorting with demons, a requirement to have your father, of course, but there are limits. I limit it to necessity."

Somewhere in the crowd, a woman cackled.

"Are all my grandparents here?" I wondered what sort of mayhem would happen with all six of my grandparents in attendance. I still wasn't sure how my human grandparents had lived for so long, but I suspected it had something to do with their special blend of genetics.

"As a matter of fact, yes. We are. Your mother opted against joining us, but your father is around somewhere. He's rather terrified of your woman, so you may have to find which corner he's in and coax him out later."

My brows shot up. "My father's here? Without my mother?"

"They had a delightful argument over it. So, this is your Kennedy?"

"I would hesitate to claim ownership of any sort over her. She has more weapons than I do and probably knows how to use them better."

My grandfather chuckled. "Her thoughts are very colorful. You'd be pleased if you could hear the profanities she's flinging in my general direction. She's also interested in introducing me to her Japanese death scythe, I'm not invited to the wedding, and I'm concerned about how she wants to use Evening Star."

"You should invite him to the wedding," Samantha said, and when the elf snickered, I worried. "Angels love weddings and will make it far more entertaining for everyone. In the case of angels with children and grand-children under foot, they'll inevitably bring their associated demons. The demons in-evitably embrace their chaotic nature because the laws of the universe dictate an equal amount of order and chaos. If anything, chaos wins when angels attend weddings, and they just can't resist attending them. Having two angels in attendance? It'll be a wonder to behold."

"Don't we have more important things to worry about? Like Luna snapping and trying to eat me?"

My grandfather reached out and patted my shoulder. "It'll come in time. Just be aware she already falls. She made her choice. I thought you'd like to know she'd picked this path for herself long before you were even a thought in your father's mind."

As my mother would've rather I hadn't been born, I appreciated his phrasing. "You angels need to work on the whole dire conse-quences to everyone else thing."

"If she hadn't chosen as she had, there'd be no consequences to anyone. She could've accomplished her goals without lying to you."

"Perhaps, but you're not the one who got beaten by an elf for months."

"It takes an elf to teach an elf, albeit had I considered your grandmother's heritage more closely, I would've had two children instead of only one."

"But why?" I pointed at myself. The move backfired, as kitten, Destroyer of Worlds translated my movement as an invitation to play, resulting in her sprawled on the top of my head and reaching for my fingers. "One of me is bad enough. I don't think the world needs two of me."

"You're unique, and it's best you remain so. No, a second child would've seen my line continued in a more traditional fashion."

"And what do you mean by that?"

"My son won't have another child, and I suspect any children you have will be horrendously elven. Once wakened, some things refuse to return to sleep. Your heritage is one of them, and it will leech away at the humanity of your children, their children, and their children. And should the world be as unlucky as I fear, you may give birth to a new race of elf."

Samantha giggled. "That would be glorious. With his mixed heritage? It's anyone's guess what sort of elf would emerge. Do have many children to maximize the odds of a new elf race developing."

Kennedy wrapped her arm around my waist and squeezed. "Samantha's just trying to agitate you as usual. I don't know what the angel's up to."

"My name is Jegudiel, but most call me Henry."

I had a hard time processing an angel having a name like Henry. "And I thought Luna was a weird name for an angel."

Samantha bowed her head and sighed. "I hate when I'm right sometimes. Do I even want to know who his grandmother is?"

"Pravuil, but she's currently going by Levata."

Samantha looked my grandfather over with narrowed eyes. "Well, I'm not going to have to worry about Luna's divinity erasing my student from existence, then. I was rather concerned about that. That said, is there a reason to believe he won't catch Luna's seed once she's fallen completely?"

"Yes."

We waited, and when the angel didn't elaborate, Samantha spewed curses. "Do you know why elves try to kill angels whenever possible? It's because of this shit. You meddle, leave your offspring to stir trouble, then you take advantage of your offspring's offspring because they're useful and you're limited. You hear me? You're limited."

Had my grandfather possessed a head, he would've been grinning. Something about his posture screamed his amusement at Samantha's annoyance. "You've surrounded yourself with interesting individuals, Reed. An elf with a grudge not even the Grand Canyon can contain, a woman who'll keep you busy for at least one lifetime, and a most interesting feline."

Puppy, Savior of Worlds whined.

"I haven't forgotten you, little one. You're just least likely to shred me with your claws if not properly acknowledged. You're of equal importance."

The corgi huffed and sat on Kennedy's shoe.

I suspected my subservience to the furry beasts came from at least one of my angelic grandparents. "Explain why you can't deal with Luna yourself, please."

"You're the one she wronged, and you're capable of securing your own justice. Divine intervention comes at a price you don't want to pay. Trust me on this one. I can offer you this much: I can't help you, but I *am* allowed to scrape you off the floor and put you back together again if absolutely necessary."

"*He* just doesn't want to deal with your whining if your offspring's offspring died because of some inferior angel," Samantha muttered. "Isn't that right, Mr. Archangel?"

Wait. *Archangel? My* grandfather was an *archangel?*

"Why haven't I killed you yet, elf?"

"I'm paying for his wedding, I trained him because I could kick your scrawny angelic ass with a hand tied behind my back, and you can't handle even the thought of having to cheat to defeat me. Therefore, you tolerate my existence, and when you're angel enough to admit it, you're grateful *I'm* the one teaching your grandson how to survive."

Truth.

I wasn't sure who scared me more: the elf or my grandfather.

I freed myself from Kennedy's hold, dropped a kiss on her lips in the case I needed to be scraped off the floor and pieced back together again, and went to find Luna to put an end to the insanity. The fallen angel seemed a safer option than sticking around for an argument between an archangel and an elf.

TWENTY-SIX

I see we're beyond being civil.

LUNA CONVERSED WITH A DARK-HAIRED MAN; his pristine suit, bronzed complex, and persistent smile, which should have been charming but rang alarm bells instead, all pointed to the same thing. After months of dancing with him on the phone, I'd finally get to meet Lucavier Buioni in person.

I dislodged Kitten, Destroyer of Worlds from my head, relocated her to my shoulder, and strolled towards the pair.

When I'd last seen Luna, she'd been white perfection with barred feathers, the splash of blue and gold, and her voice the only things separating her from her brethren. Gray stained her skin, a faint marring I might not have noticed had I not just seen my grandfather.

Luna turned to me. "So, you did decide to attend." After Samantha glowering at me, I barely noticed—or cared—about the angel's scrutiny. "I question why I wasted so much money on you and that sword."

"Well, I see we're beyond being civil today. Lucavier," I greeted, keeping an eye on the falling angel. "I see you're keeping strange company."

"I find myself intrigued over how she's grown to dislike you so much. Why would a mere human offend an angel? She could wipe you from this Earth without much effort."

"I've heard the story. She'd spent a fortune so she could equip me with a blade capable of waking her greed and appeasing her sense of guilt for killing a human." I shrugged, which stirred the ire of my cantankerous cat, who hissed at the mismatched pair. "While that seems foolish to me, lying to me was just stupid, Luna."

Both angel and devil jerked at my accusation.

"She lied to you?" Lucavier's eagerness confirmed Samantha's suspicions—and her belief I'd have to fight an angel and a devil in short succession.

"You've lied to me, too, but I don't hold that against you. I don't hold it against her, either." My forgiveness wouldn't change anything for the pair, but it eased something within me. "I'm sure you both had your reasons. Of course, one of you is a devil, so you don't need much of a reason to lie to someone, as long as it serves your interests. Isn't that right, Mr. Buioni?"

I needed to have a long talk with both of my angelic grandparents, scolding them both for their influence on my life.

"I didn't lie to you."

Lie. The gray staining Luna's skin darkened, and Lucavier's gaze flicked to her. A smarter devil wouldn't have smiled; his expression spoke more truths about him than I cared to think about. One by one, the cards Samantha believed would be played were laid out on the table, guiding the game to the same place: death.

"I'd just like to know why you trusted a devil with anything. He's a devil. You're an angel. Did you really think he would honestly ally himself with you? He wanted your downfall."

"You think too highly of yourself, *human*," Luna spat.

"No, I think that you tried to hire me an inferior instructor so you could have an easier time trying to kill me. I mean, I never had a great opinion about angels in the first place, but you're the worst of the lot. I'd rather hang out with the headless wonder over there and figure out how to share a beer with the jerk than deal with your meddling. Which, I'd like to remind you, you continued to do after we bargained you wouldn't.

You're here, and you're here because you wanted to work with your ally here. Am I wrong?"

Luna grunted.

"She promised to stop meddling in your affairs?" Glee lit Lucavier's eyes. The scent of brimstone assaulted my nose. "She's been meddling in your affairs since you left Mississippi. Even now, she's meddling in your affairs. She's here because you're here."

"I'd argue that isn't meddling. That's stalking," I countered. "I can assure you, angels are talented stalkers. When they aren't popping in whenever they want, they're listening in on your every thought. I've had a trio of them ghosting me since I was released from prison."

"For a crime you didn't even commit." Lucavier chuckled. "If *you'd* told the truth, you wouldn't have seen any prison time."

"I told the truth. I told nothing but the truth. I just didn't tell the complete truth. But my imprisonment served your cause well, didn't it, Mr. Buioni?"

"A lot of things serve my cause. Your imprisonment did nothing for my goals."

Lie.

"As long as you didn't have anything to do with that filth, I really don't care."

"Why would I have anything to do with the affairs of some uncouth human? That's nonsense. I had nothing to do with the likes of him."

Lie.

Knowledge changed everything, and while my sword had been named Redemption for more than one reason, I wondered if the blade would mind being used for a second cause: justice. It wouldn't change his victims' suffering, it wouldn't change what I'd endured, but I'd sleep a little easier, assuming I survived, after ensuring Lucavier's machinations wouldn't hurt someone else.

Luna's death would be a tragedy.

Lucavier's death would be justice.

If I had to work to redeem myself for the rest of my life after, I'd be content with that. My sword would be a reminder of everything that had happened, all leading to a moment in a crowded museum where an angel, a devil, and a mere mortal clashed.

Luna turned to Lucavier, and while dark stains still marred the angel's flesh, her feathers remained white, blue, and gold, as though she clung to the divinity she'd lost, concentrated in each feather. "You lie. You were involved. You're the reason those women were raped."

"I knew it was a possibility. I merely suggested he might find his type of woman in the area, that's all."

Somewhere amid the truths Lucavier told,

he also lied. I considered his words. "You were certain he'd act, and you're hiding behind the slim possibility he *wouldn't* to pretend like you're not lying when you are. You were hoping something would happen so I'd become involved with angels, which played to your plan. Am I correct?"

"Nonsense."

Lie.

"You lie," Luna hissed, and she held out her marred hand. A crackling, gray blade manifested in her hand, longer and broader than mine, and she held it as though it weighed nothing.

Kitten, Destroyer of Worlds hissed, dug her claws into my shoulder, and spat curses at the angel.

"Silence!" she boomed.

Only the mad would attack a cat, but Luna went for Kitten, Destroyer of Worlds, sword lifted high. I released her leash and drew Redemption in the time it took me to suck in a breath. Our swords crossed. Her blade crackled. Mine chimed with the strong, clarion call of a struck bell. She hit softer than Samantha, and I held my ground, wondering why the angel had held back.

Kitten, Destroyer of Worlds swatted a paw at our crossed blades, her claws unsheathed. Her paw struck the angel's sword.

The sword shattered.

My blade swept down and sliced into Luna's shoulder near where her neck would've been if she'd had one. Black blood sprayed. She screamed, her voice piercing through my skull. My body moved as Samantha had beaten into me; the follow-through carved a deep line across her chest, the tip of Redemption digging across her breastbone.

"Fall!" Lucavier crowed. Like Luna, he conjured a sword of his own, and his swallowed the light and created a black cloud obscuring my view of him. The devil cackled and lunged towards me.

I hopped back, but he went for his true target: Luna.

A better man—or an angel—would've ignored the devil's back, the target Samantha had promised no sane being would ever present to anyone with even a smidgeon of elf in his blood. The devil who sought the angel's fall attacked her when she couldn't defend herself.

A better man would've hesitated, but I wasn't that man.

I tossed Redemption so I could reverse my grip on the hilt, wrapped my left hand around the diamond sphere of its pommel, and drove it through Lucavier's back. The tip slid through with little resistance until it hit the devil's chest. The bone cracked, and Redemption continued its lethal journey until its hilt collided with the devil's spine. Golden light flashed from beneath my left hand and washed over my victim.

Luna's scream cut off.

Lucavier went limp and his body slumped to the floor, and Luna fell with him. Their bodies twitched, their life bleeding out of them. In what I'd always consider a freak accident, a hole the match of Lucavier's bore through Luna's chest.

Kitten, Destroyer of Worlds jumped off my shoulder, hissed and clawed at the devil's face. From my position, I couldn't see his expression, but the way my cat tore at him, he wouldn't have much of an expression left when she was finished. I cursed and reached for her leash.

A black seed the shape and size of an almond rose from the back of the devil's head, and tendrils of smoke spread from it like roots seeking a place to take root. Cold dread cramped my chest, and the sense of being watched settled over my shoulders.

"I am, I was, and I always will be Kimaris," a deep voice thundered through my head, triggering a skull-splitting headache. *"I am he who forges warriors in my likeness as you have been forged. You think you have killed me, but I will never die. None of us ever truly die."*

Shit. I'd known devils had names although

most knew of Satan and his many names. While unfamiliar with Kimaris, I recognized when I faced bad news. I remembered Samantha warning about the seeds of life angels and devils possessed, but she'd neglected to warn me they were sentient—and capable of speaking their opinions.

Kitten, Destroyer of Worlds eyed the dark seed.

I snatched for her leash to stop her from playing with it. Like she did at night when hunting anything that moved, my cat pounced and swallowed her prey.

Horror froze me in place, leaving Kitten, Destroyer of Worlds free to resume slashing the deceased devil's face with her claws, adding to the blood spilling onto the floor.

While in life, Luna's fall had left her gray, her seed of life glowed with a golden light. As though afraid it would be devoured by my cat, too, it flitted away, leaving streamers of white and gold in its wake. The excited yips of a puppy gave me enough warning to jolt me out of my shock and dive for the dog's leash.

I slipped, hit the floor with a yelp, and missed the leash.

Puppy, Savior of Worlds seemed to enjoy his snack of angel, then he washed my face with his tongue, his entire body swaying in his excitement.

My cat and Kennedy's dog eating the seeds of an angel and devil hadn't been a part of the plan. When honest with myself, there hadn't been much of a plan to begin with. I groaned rolled onto my back, and lurched upright. Streams of golden light coiled around Redemption's blade, and the blood that fell into its radiance shimmered and transitioned from black to the bright crimson of human blood.

I felt a lot how the crowd around me sounded: shocked into silence. My grandfather's laughter chimed in my head. "Had you planned on quenching your blade in the heart of a devil and an angel at the same time?"

"I had a plan? If I had a plan, I would've made sure both pets were securely leashed before executing it."

For someone lacking a head, my grandfather had mastered glaring. "Yes, you were supposed to make a plan."

I grunted at his disapproval, got to my knees, and used Lucavier's suit to clean Redemption's edge. The body crumbled away beneath the sword's golden glow. Luna's body followed, deteriorating to ash. Even their blood dissolved into wisps of pale smoke. "Well, that simplifies cleanup."

"You're handling this a lot better than I thought you would."

"He attacked her while she was defense-

less. Only seemed fair I repay him the favor."
Unless asked, I wouldn't mention the truth I'd
learned about Lucavier's plotting, leading to
the day I'd killed another man. "I hadn't
meant to hit Luna."

"She was already dying. Consider it a
mercy. That devil would've taken his time
finishing her, and that would've haunted you
far worse than a quick end. No, it's better this
way. Not how I would've done it, but it's
better this way."

"Why is everyone so quiet?" I glanced at
the crowd, which still stared as though frozen
in time.

"We're in the space between seconds. For
us, time has stopped. For them, we will seem
to have moved in the blink of an eye. It won't
last long. It is her doing mostly." My grandfather pointed at Kitten, Destroyer of Worlds.
"The puppy played an equal part, but his role
is easier. How aptly they were named, although it's not worlds they both destroy and
save. It's always a delight to live in a time
where myths become reality."

"Myths? What myths?" I eyed my cat, who
continued to express her opinion about Lucavier through the use of her claws on his
abandoned suit. "I think I've had enough
myths for one lifetime."

"Learning you are a myth is hard on a
soul, but I think yours is robust enough to

endure it. As for your beasts, you aptly named them."

"I only named Kitten," I protested.

"Still. They're aptly named. I'm surprised they weren't born at the same time. That's usually how it goes. But perhaps strange times call for stranger measures."

"Cryptic angelic nonsense is inappropriate for this situation. Spit it out, please. Without dancing around the subject."

"It's hard to explain how one being can split and become two beings for a lifetime and ultimately become one being again. Your beasts are not individuals. They are halves of a whole, always connected. And she usually eats her own tail rather than seeds of life, but I suppose the eclectic relationship of a cat and a dog sharing living space might count as equal chasing of tails. But I suppose this works best. You didn't inherit the seeds of life, so you can live out the rest of your days as normal of a human as you can get rather than forever touched by powers you'd be unable to control. And they? They won't notice a thing. That is who they are."

"Who are they?"

"Which version would you like? They're Egyptian. They're Greek. They're even Norse. There's a little bit of the whole world in them, but that makes sense. That *is* what they are.

You might call them special pieces of the Universe, if you will."

"That's still cryptic," I complained.

"Ouroboros. The World-Serpent. The unification of Ra-Osiris. She's even more complex that, but view her as the encompassing of all things in this world and a promise of the eternal cycle. Even the End of Days is the beginning of a new world. Consider her a caretaker of the balance. Dumah fell, but Kimaris fell with her as well. Their seeds will be returned to their rightful places, and they will be born again."

Dumah? I was afraid to ask, so I didn't. When I asked about identities, I found I disliked the answer. "Kimaris spoke to me as a seed. Does that make me crazy?"

"No. Being unforgivably elven is what makes you crazy. He said something that bothers you. What did he tell you? Perhaps I can lay that to rest."

"He told me his name, and he told me he forged warriors in his likeness as I had been forged. Then he said none of us ever truly die."

"It is the way of devils to speak the truth while planting the seeds of a lie, but he's not entirely wrong. You were forged. In part by him, in part by Dumah, in part by me, in part by your grandmother—in part by a lot of people. But no matter how many people took

part in your forging, everything of importance was made by your hand. And as for the
seed of a lie amongst his truths, he's correct.
None of us ever truly die, but when the seeds
of our life are replanted, we are not who we
once were, even among angels and devils. We
change—or the Universe changes us. So in
that regard, we can only live one life."

A headache developed behind my eyes,
and I wasn't sure if my grandfather, the fight,
or stress were responsible. "So they'll be all
right?"

"I suppose it isn't cheating to tell you how
history has repeated itself. Your life is tied
with that human woman's, and their lives are
bounded to yours. When you and she perish,
they will reclaim your life seeds and return
them to the Universe. Consider it their grati-
tude for what you have suffered to bring you
to this moment where you kept things in balance. While an accident in your eyes, you did
it exactly right. And that is why it takes a
mortal man to do an angel's work. *I* could
never stab a devil in the back. That's not our
way."

"Any other pearls of wisdom?"

"Don't be alarmed should you dream of
two dragons devouring their own tails while
entwined. It's their nature, and like it or not,
you're part of them now. Enjoy the rest of
your evening. We'll see you at your wedding,

invited or not. If you don't invite us, you'll get to watch that elf snap, and it will bring much entertainment to your festivities. I highly recommend it." My grandfather vanished in a flash of silver light.

I stared where he'd been standing before turning my attention to my cat. Kitten, Destroyer of Worlds paused in her mutilation of Lucavier's clothes, looked me in the eyes, and winked.

Elves needed to get over their
gemstone fetish.

ONE YEAR LATER

ACCORDING TO ELVEN TRADITION, I spent
the week before my wedding revisiting life
training with my sword. Redemption's typical
golden glow had taken on a gray hue, which
I'd learned to associate with its annoyance. I
understood annoyance. I wanted to take Redemption and shove it up Samantha's ass.

Unfortunately for me, Samantha wasn't
anywhere to be seen, and she'd assigned two
elves to keep me contained in some damned
mountains in North Carolina while she 'prepared poor Kennedy' for a lifetime of marriage to me. I wondered if the two men
prepared me for life with Kennedy. I supposed it was possible; male or female, elves
were dangerous and as likely to eat me as
help me.

The pair ran me through my paces, gifted me with a collection of bruises for my wedding day, and ensured I had no hope of escaping, crawling into bed with Kennedy, and hiding under the covers. I thought I'd done well enough; I'd managed to make both of the smug bastards bleed at least once.

Redemption had helped with that, although I doubted I'd ever get used to the sword having the ability to nudge me in the right direction when I wasn't strong or fast enough.

At dawn on my wedding day, they wrangled me into a black suit, cleaned Redemption until he shined, polished his sheath until every stone glittered, and treated me like a doll for their amusement. Kitten, Destroyer of Worlds got the same treatment, except instead of a suit, she got to wear chainmail and a diamond-encrusted collar. Since 'the skins of her enemies' wasn't a possibility, they made her a little black cloak hemmed with even more diamonds.

Elves needed to get over their gemstone fetish. Fortunately, I was wise enough not to say that to their faces.

It took them almost two hours to dress me to their satisfaction, and I considered myself lucky I'd escaped without additional jewelry. Both of them eyed my tie like they wanted to rip it off and replace it with something as gaudy as Kitten's cloak and collar.

It was a good thing they hadn't told me their names; I would've spent the whole time cursing them both to eternal damnation.

"I just have one question." I glared at each of the picture-perfect elves in suits that made me look like a reaper of death out for souls compared to their blue-green peacocks. Add in their elven features and pointy ears, and no woman would look twice at me with them present.

I'd forgive Kennedy if her jaw dropped in their presence; they oozed natural appeal out of their pores, which woke the more demonic side of my nature. I supposed territorial disputes were part of elven culture in some fashion, as the more I'd bristled over the week, the happier they'd been about it.

Damned annoying elves.

They stared at me, and their perfect brows rose in unison in silent questioning.

"Are you a test of temptation for her? Because seriously? No sane woman is going to look twice at me with you two standing around."

They chuckled, and the one I'd dubbed the leader of the duo shook his head. "We're the ones Samantha deemed most likely to survive a week training you with minimal injury to you and to us. It is our honor to present ourselves accordingly for your ceremony."

"If Kennedy uses her Japanese death scythe on you for covering me in bruises, it's not my fault. And don't ask about Evening Star."

The elves only seemed amused. "I think we'll be fine."

"I'm not carrying your skull around if you get yourself killed underestimating her," I warned.

"You concern is appreciated. Our families would take care of our skulls, so don't worry. The only skull you need to worry about is hers should you outlive her, and yours should she outlive you."

Kitten, Destroyer of Worlds regarded me, and if she had eyebrows, I was positive she would've hiked one up. Ever since she'd devoured Kimaris's seed, she'd abandoned her purely feline ways for something a little more cunning, a little more intellectual, and a lot more troublesome.

She'd developed a taste for human food, as had Puppy, and with the understanding they were more than just a cat and a dog, I'd gone along with it, planning meals for four instead of two. Kennedy accepted my insistence they live the high life for one reason alone: Kitten, Destroyer of Worlds no longer inflicted biological warfare on us for feeding her cat food.

Nowadays, she reserved her most potent weapon in her arsenal for when we withheld milk or catnip, both of which transformed her into a menace.

"Where *is* the wedding taking place?"

"A short drive from here. Part of the ceremony is simple. You will walk a path lined by members of her family and associates. They've been encouraged to add to your bruises to prove your dedication to your bride. You're invited to return blows as you see fit. The only rules are any who challenge you must do so with handheld weapons; no guns." The elf turned his nose up at that. "As we've been warned you will not fight in earnest, we've taken the liberty of coaxing Redemption into dulling his edge and using only the flat for your challenge to reach your bride. Once you have met in the middle, you will walk to the altar. This represents you completing your journey to becoming a partnership together. At that point, you will take your traditional human vows."

"What would elves do?"

"Fight, of course. We've determined that you two have weathered enough conflict and do not need to participate in the marital brawl."

Marital brawl? "Elves fight each other before they're wed?"

"First they fight each other to the first

blood, then they fight a mutual enemy. Alas, the enemy typically doesn't survive, as two elves attacking the same target usually doesn't end well for someone. Samantha thought it would be wise if we skipped that phase of the ceremony. It seems there will be those law enforcement types on your bride's side." Both elves rolled their eyes. "And there have been rumors of angels joining in, so you may get your marital brawl after all."

"You know what? I don't want to know. Just point where I'm supposed to go."

Next time an elf volunteered to coordinate anything for me, I'd make sure I respectfully declined. Then I'd pack my bags and leave for a place so remote they wouldn't be able to find me and carve out my heart for the insult of refusing their help.

I UNDERSTOOD why I wore a plain suit around the time I saw the gauntlet waiting for me, and at the front of the line was my grinning boss, who held a wooden baseball bat in his hand. "It's not every day I get to send off an employee to the rest of his life with a baseball bat. I absolutely couldn't refuse that invitation. I can't believe you're leaving me for a woman who drove you into hiding beneath my desk with your cat."

Kitten, Destroyer of Worlds purred and rubbed against the legs of the elves holding her leash so I could wade through the mayhem to reach my bride. I wondered if my side of the family was giving Kennedy issues.

Kennedy's side had at least a hundred men and women, all armed with some form of weapon, eager and willing to add to my bruises. I drew Redemption, and the golden diamond flared before encasing the blade in its glow. "So you joined her team? How is that fair?"

"You resigned. Her team got me a baseball bat with your name on it."

I pointed Redemption at him. "I resigned because she's convincing about career changes."

"I'm sure your future co-workers are going to enjoy discovering if you're even remotely up to par," he taunted.

I turned to my elven escorts. "Just for clarification, this is a non-lethal beating, right?"

"They've been asked to limit your beating to survival levels. We've a few people, including a pair of unwanted angels, who can help with the injuries afterwards."

"Am I attending my own wedding or my murder?" I sighed and rolled my shoulders. "All right. If you folks insist on being in the way, then I'll just have to go through you."

My newly former boss laughed. "Who are

you trying to fool, Reed? You're an angel in disguise. You wouldn't hurt a fly without a damned good reason."

"Coming between me and my bride is a damned good reason." When it came to winning a fight, I'd given up on the idea of being the better man. I'd leave him only a little battered and bruised, but I'd leave no doubt in anyone's mind I meant to make it to the altar no matter how many people I had to beat to do it.

EVERYTHING WENT to plan until an entire quartet of elves, Samantha included, decided I hadn't earned Kennedy. I thought I'd done a good job; I'd beaten bruises into every last one of my contesters without drawing a drop of blood. Maybe the lack of blood annoyed them, although I suspected Samantha had joined Team Kennedy to make certain I was worthy of my bride.

In either case, if the elf wanted a fight, I'd give her one.

Had she wanted to kill me, she would've, but as she didn't, Samantha beat me with a stick, one she'd wrapped in padding. It still hurt when she thwacked me with it. Her trio of accomplices, all women, went for me like I was their favorite dessert.

Any other man might've liked the idea of four women out for him, but I knew better. Alone, one of them could pound me into the ground. Four of them? I was a dead man walking, and I'd need a miracle to make it to the altar.

"I don't fucking think so!" Kennedy howled and waded into the fray.

A miracle or Kennedy on a rampage would work. Like Redemption, golden light enveloped Evening Star's blade, transforming the lethal weapon into the equivalent of a club. Her war cry alerted the quartet of elves, not that I held much faith the changed odds would work in our favor. As Kennedy wanted to fight with the elves, too, I'd join her.

And I'd also marvel how the hell she fought in a white, frilly dress with a fortune in pearls covering it. It had a slit up the side that convinced me my new goal in life was to get her somewhere private so I could take my time admiring—and removing—her clothes, especially the taunting little garter hugging her leg.

Despite the dress adhering to modern standards of decency, the top clung to her chest and left no doubt she was a woman in her prime, the slit drove me crazy, and even her shoes, spiked weapons attached to her feet and encrusted with pearls, existed only to make me want her more.

"More fighting, less drooling!" Kennedy barked.

The elves laughed and engaged with my bride, leaving me to enjoy the view. A year ago, I never would've imagined Kennedy holding her own against four elves, but she'd lost all her hesitancies around Samantha and her pointy-eared cohorts. My bride wanted their blood, and she meant to get it. I relaxed my grip on Redemption, torn between watching her go for them, one of the sexiest things I'd seen in my life, or wading in to help her.

Did she need my help? Despite the odds, I thought she held her own, which made the whole thing even sexier.

"I think you're supposed to go in and help her," my father said, and he had the evidence of a black eye forming. "Though I'm not sure she needs it. Your woman hits hard."

"What did you do to deserve it?"

"I didn't get out of her way fast enough."

"Sounds about right." I rolled my shoulders. "Did Mother decide to attend?"

"With minimal protest, much to the surprise of that elf, who swore vengeance on the entire family line, save for you, if we breathed wrong and ruined your wedding."

Elves liked it when their students hit them. I could repay her with a few good hits.

"Excuse me for a moment. I have an elf to thank."

"Just how to do you plan on thanking her?"

"I'll hit her a few times."

My father sighed. "Damned elves."

"This won't take long," I promised. It wouldn't take long because I'd turn murderous at unnecessary delays between marrying Kennedy and escaping everyone. Firming my grip on Redemption's hilt, I wielded it like a baseball bat and waded into the fray.

Smacking the blade into the back of Samantha's knees counted as cheating. The elf yelped, whirled, and spat curses at me. "Why the hell did I teach you to cheat?"

"Poor foresight," I replied, unable to hide my grin. Since giving her a single chance to retaliate would either hurt or knock me out of the fight, I joined Kennedy in beating back the quartet preventing us from getting to the happily married portion of our day. "Why are we fighting you?"

"We were fresh out of enemies for you two to fight together, so we're standing in as evidence of your willingness to fight together." Samantha hopped back and lifted her hand. The rest of the elves backed away. "I forgot to account for your maleness."

"My maleness?"

"You saw her and you lost your ability to string two words together."

"Samantha, any man with functional eyes is going to have trouble stringing words together when she's looking like that."

She'd been a marvel to behold while diving into the fray to battle with elves, but her smile stole my breath. "You're not too bad yourself in that pretty suit, although I have to admit, there was something rather satisfying watching you spank my co-workers and boss."

Well, shit. "One of them was your boss?"

"Your boss starting in a month," she confirmed.

"Should I be worried?"

Kennedy stepped closer and returned Evening Star to her gem-encrusted sheath hidden among the skirts of her dress. I followed her example, and as soon as I'd sheathed Redemption, she linked her arm with mine. "You have nothing to worry about. He's never gotten to meet an elf before. There are twenty-two here today for the festivities."

"Why so many?" I whispered.

"Friends of Sammy's. They wanted to witness her students marrying each other."

"I don't suppose they told you how this was actually supposed to work, did they?"

"Sammy assumed you'd see me in this dress after being worked up in a fight and be incapable of remembering your own name, so she coached me on what we needed to do."

Considering my common sense had dribbled right out of my ears, I couldn't blame the elf. "Please tell me we go to the altar and then get to run away."

"Sammy was also concerned after a week of seclusion, you would be rather eager to get to our evening activities."

"With you in that dress? Only a fool would assume otherwise."

"I'm glad you like the dress."

"Please tell me you get to keep the dress."

Laughing, she nodded before checking over her shoulder. I checked, too. The guests gathered behind us, a mix of my family, hers, too many elves for anyone's comfort, and more of Kennedy's friends and co-workers than mine. They must have been coached on what to do, as there seemed to be order to the chaos.

Both of my angelic grandparents stood with their demonic counterparts and my human grandparents, and as my father had promised, my mother stood with them. She didn't smile, but I refused to worry about it. She'd bothered to come, which exceeded my expectations and hopes. I doubted we'd ever become anything more than a wary mother and a wayward son, but I could live with the memory of her coming despite failing her expectations.

I would make it enough.

Samantha strode to us, and a tall, golden-skinned man with ivory wings and a laurel wreath encircling his curled hair followed her. I'd heard of divines who walked among men and choose to meddle in their affairs, much like angels, but I'd never met one before. I could make a guess at who joined Samantha in standing before us: some called him Cupid, others called him Eros, but I couldn't think of any other divine who fit the mold.

The divine flashed a smile at me. *I do enjoy when the mortals recognize me for who I am without thinking my mother's the better choice. How refreshing.*

If anyone dared to question my union with Kennedy, I'd laugh myself sick. I should've known better than to expect a normal marriage with an elf at the helm.

Samantha clasped her hands in front of her. "The altar's a metaphorical one today, but I don't think you'll mind. The results are the same. Forces beyond mortal under-standing brought you here. Some may say it began with The Almighty, as two of his angels found love within their hearts pure and strong enough for them to leave their mark on this Earth in the form of their mortal children. Their children, touched by the heaven's angels and the hell's demons with the spark of human life led to you."

I supposed I was living evidence of the Christian faith in more ways than I cared to admit.

"If we were to judge you by those who came before you, we'd be mistaken to ignore the presence of elven blood in your heritage, strong enough we welcome you among us. But it's not your blood that defines you, it's your deeds. You're much like the still surface of a lake. We think we understand it peering through the water, but in truth, your depths hide a complexity that's been a joy to watch grow. The road you've walked here was a long one, and for much of the journey, you were hidden from the light. Those days are done. You have surpassed them."

Kennedy tightened her hold on my arm, and I placed my hand over hers.

Samantha's attention shifted to Kennedy. "Your journey has been a much different one, and your haunting regrets transformed you from a girl to a woman, one with an understanding of truth, consequence, and loyalty. Some will judge you for your choices. Let them judge. They have not walked in your shoes. They have not endured the darkness like you have. You have earned your place at his side as much as he has earned his place at your side. When they judge you, remind yourself of one thing: *they* did not endure the tender, loving care of an elf for so long and live to tell the tale. Like him, your journey here was long, and you, too, were hidden from the light. Those days are done. You have surpassed them."

The crowd behind us broke into titters, which they did their best to quell. The elven men who'd kept me busy brought Kitten, Destroyer of Worlds forward while two elven women brought Puppy, Savior of Worlds over. I released my hold on Kennedy's hand so I could take my cat's leash.

She climbed up my leg, dug her claws into my back, and settled on my shoulder.

Kennedy regarded her corgi with an arched brow. "Don't even think about trying that stunt, pup."

Puppy, Savior of Worlds sat down and panted, the image of canine contentment.

"We would be amiss if we didn't welcome the two lives that made so much of a difference in binding you both together until your dying day. Throughout my long life, there have been few beings quite capable of healing broken hearts quite like a pet. For you, Reed, it took a little kitten who found her way to the hood of your car in the wee hours of the morning. For you, Kennedy, it took the help of an abandoned puppy you found on the side of the road. They taught you both many lessons, and I expect they'll teach you many more throughout the years. They've earned their spot here as much as you have, although I refuse to wed a cat and a dog."

I pressed my lips together so I wouldn't snicker, and Kennedy bumped my foot with her weaponized shoe. Our family and friends laughed behind us.

"Elves do not speak vows, not in the way humans do. We prove our devotion through the deeds of our life. The exchange of rings become a visible symbol of deeds already done. You have done this. In elven eyes, you were wed the instant you dedicated your-selves to each other the day you exchanged rings and confirmed your determination to see your journey to its end together. All this does is satisfy human laws for tax purposes, so I'll leave that nonsense to Eros."

The laugh I'd been attempting to smother escaped, and Kennedy elbowed me in the ribs. I wasn't the only one to laugh, and my father's chuckles rang out loudest of all.

"Humans," Samantha muttered.

"Taxes are a critical factor," I whispered, careful to keep my voice down. "She's worth good credits."

"Reed," Kennedy complained. "You're im-possible."

I smiled at her, and since we'd already

abandoned our traditional wedding, I leaned towards her and kissed her cheek. Not to be undone, Kitten, Destroyer of Worlds crawled over my head and batted at Kennedy's hair. We both laughed, and I retrieved my cat and returned her to my shoulder.

Eros cleared his throat. "Love comes in many forms. For some, it is blind. For others, it is found in an unusual clarity of vision. It can be easily won but also lost, such as a mother's love for her child."

I resisted the urge to glance in the direction of my mother, the target of Eros's jab.

"Your journey is just beginning, but your love is old and tested, proven true beyond expectation." Eros held out his hand and several sheets of paper popped into existence along with a white quill. "In the eyes of men, I declare you husband and wife, and may those who find themselves displeased with this cross swords with an elf. You may kiss your bride, but please restrain yourself from any further activities in public." Eros scowled. "The elf made me say that."

I laughed, lifted Kennedy's hand to my lips, and gave her a gentle kiss. "You're worth the wait."

She always had been.

Fowl Play is the next book in the Magical Romantic Comedy (with a body count) series. These stories, with the exception of Burn, Baby, Burn (sequel to Playing with Fire,) can be read in any order.

About R.J. Blain

Want to hear from the author when a new book releases? You can sign up at her website (thesneakykittycritic.com). Please note this newsletter is operated by the Furred & Frond Management. Expect to be sassed by a cat. (With guest features of other animals, including dogs.)

A complete list of books written by RJ and her various pen names is available at https://books2read.com/rl/The-Fantasy-Worlds-of-RJ-Blain.

RJ BLAIN suffers from a Moleskine journal obsession, a pen fixation, and a terrible tendency to pun without warning.

When she isn't playing pretend, she likes to think she's a cartographer and a sumi-e painter.

In her spare time, she daydreams about being

a spy. Should that fail, her contingency plan involves tying her best of enemies to spinning wheels and quoting James Bond villains until she is satisfied.

RJ also writes as Susan Copperfield and Bernadette Franklin. Visit RJ and her pets (the Management) at thesneakykittycritic.com.